Zara Cox writes cont... She lives in the Garde... with her hubby and tw... travel. In 2017 she managed to visit her number one bucket list destination—Hawaii—and is now actively pleading with her husband to live there! She loves to hear from her readers and you can get in touch with her via Twitter (@zcoxbooks), on Instagram (zaracoxwriter) or Facebook (zaracoxwriter).

Ever since **Lisa Childs** read her first romance novel at the age of eleven—a Mills & Boon story, of course—all she wanted was to be a romance writer. With over forty novels published with Mills & Boon, Lisa is living her dream. She is an award-winning, bestselling romance author. Lisa loves to hear from readers, who can contact her on Facebook, through her website, lisachilds.com, or at her snail-mail address, PO Box 139, Marne, MI 49435, USA.

If you liked *Worth the Risk* and *Legal Desire*
why not try
Wild Child by Christy McKellen
Getting Even by Avril Tremayne

WORTH THE RISK

ZARA COX

LEGAL DESIRE

LISA CHILDS

MILLS & BOON

First Published in Great Britain 2018
by Mills & Boon, an imprint of HarperCollins*Publishers*
1 London Bridge Street, London, SE1 9GF

Worth the Risk © 2018 Zara Cox

Legal Desire © 2018 Lisa Childs

ISBN: 978-0-263-26655-9

MIX
Paper from
responsible sources
FSC® C007454

This book is produced from independently certified FSC™ paper
to ensure responsible forest management.
For more information visit www.harpercollins.co.uk/green.

Printed and bound in Spain
by CPI, Barcelona

WORTH THE RISK

ZARA COX

MILLS & BOON

PROLOGUE

Gideon

GREAT-AUNT FLO WAS pacing my office.

Seventy-five-year-olds, regardless of how sprightly they still were, had no business pacing three months after double hip-replacement operations.

Normally I welcomed her out-of-the-blue visits, because out of all my blood relatives, she was the only one I could tolerate for more than five minutes. Which was great, because I adored every wrinkled inch of her.

Normally that adoration was returned.

Today, however, every look she speared at me from her light blue eyes sparked an unsettling amount of disappointment.

My nape tightened.

I ran through the list of possible unsavoury things I'd done since I last saw her—bloody hell, there were a lot—and tuned back in just as she gave a melodramatic sigh.

'The last straw was when they called you a reckless playboy.'

I resisted the urge to roll my eyes. 'That's absurd, Aunt Flo. For starters, I'm most definitely not a boy. If we weren't related, I'd drop my trousers and prove it to you right now.'

Nelly, Aunt Flo's trusted assistant, choked, spilling the tea she was pouring.

Aunt Flo clicked her tongue. 'Gideon Alexander Mortimer, this is serious. And no, you can't charm your way out of it.'

I straightened from where I was perched on the corner of my desk and pulled out a chair. 'Please sit down, Flo. You're making me dizzy.'

'Because you're hung-over again?' she sniped.

I wasn't, and I was more than a little disconcerted by her sharp tone. Usually Florence Jane Mortimer, known as Flo to her nearest and dearest, was soft-spoken, endlessly indulgent and thoroughly enjoyed my brand of wicked humour. Apparently not today.

'No, I'm not hung-over,' I stated truthfully. But I could've done with more than the two snatched hours of sleep after ending a call with Vadim Ilyev, the Russian businessman whose delay tactics on my multi-billion-pound deal had made my life hell for the past few months.

Note to self: never start a conversation with an intransigent Russian after midnight.

'The senior board members are at their wits' end.'

I snapped into full focus. 'What?' She was talking business. I never tuned out anything to do with the company.

Her lips pursed as she accepted the tea from Nelly

and took a delicate sip. 'The Mortimer Group has a long, untarnished history of excellence.'

'Yes, one whose final chapter would've been written without a happy ending six years ago if I hadn't stepped in,' I muttered under my breath.

'Don't be a braggart, Gideon. You know how much I despise conceited men.'

My frown deepened. 'What's going on, Flo? Usually you're the first to laud my achievements to anyone who'll listen.'

She took another dainty sip, her gaze firmly avoiding mine. 'The board has grown tired of your extra-curricular antics.'

'Doesn't the very definition of *extracurricular* mean that it's *my* business alone?' I asked as reasonably as I could manage.

'Not when you're the head of a multibillion-pound corporation, no.'

Now it was my turn to pace.

There'd been growing rumblings about my work hard, party harder lifestyle recently, most likely because it was a healthy, fully fuelled juggernaut I had no intention of parking any time soon. But in light of the fact that I'd single-handedly dragged TMG from the dark ages and made it insanely profitable meant those rumblings had been behind my back. No one dared to question Gideon Mortimer about what he got up to when he wasn't expertly manning the helm of the most profitable construction company in the western hemisphere.

Besides, Aunt Flo had been my bulwark against all that nonsense. A five-time divorcee, she was used

to scandal and gossip, and at seventy-five still enter-
tained the occasional gentleman caller in her Fitzro-
via house. She supported me, too, because she liked
to give her various stick-up-their-arses nieces and
nephews a moderately arthritic middle finger.

On top of that, she was the only one who knew
what had really happened with Damian that night
three years ago. She was also there when Penny
dropped the final soul-destroying bombshell.

She alone understood why I went off the rails for a
solid six months after my life had crashed and burned.
Without her intervention, I'd probably be in jail for
murdering my cousin. She'd kept my secret, used her
connections to keep the most salacious morsels of my
breakdown and the reason behind it out of the press.

If I hadn't been in awe of her before then, I certainly was by the time the red haze cleared and I discovered I had a semblance of a life left.

The raw double betrayal still haunted me. The
one that followed haunted me even more, I wasn't
ashamed to admit. The only time the demons grew
quieter was when I deliberately drowned them out
with a willing woman and single malt whisky. Apparently that was unacceptable to a few sanctimonious
members of my family. I hid a grim smile, wondered
whether they would be so hypocritical if they knew
the reason behind my behaviour.

'Especially since you turn thirty-three in four
months—'

Bloody hell, I really needed to focus. 'What's my
age got to do with anything?'

'You're no longer a boy. They want to see a marked change, a more grounded outlook on life—'

'Or what? They'll vote to chop my bonus in half?' Who cared? I was already wealthier than I would ever be able to spend in two lifetimes. Plus, with a twenty-three per cent share in a company worth thirty-one billion, I had more clout than every individual shareholder.

'Or they'll consider putting Harry in charge for a while.'

I stopped midpace. 'Harry?' Derisive laughter spilled out unchecked. 'Are they out of their damned minds? I taught that little pissant everything he knows—'

'Which means he'll do a stellar job. Especially if he conscripts one of your other cousins to assist him. The board are confident they can elect someone else to head the company without the accompanying Page Three snippets of the CEO's X-rated lifestyle shoved in their faces every time they open their newspapers.'

That neat little nugget was a bullet to the chest. One I couldn't argue with. I felt it penetrate deeper, causing as much damage as possible.

My cousin Harry was duller than a puddle in winter, with zero personality and even less of a life. I wouldn't be surprised if he went to bed fully dressed in his staid brown suits, his brown hair neatly combed, tie in place, ready to spring to work like a robot.

The last family member who'd been thrust into the demanding CEO position had lasted just six months before succumbing to a nervous breakdown and a long stint in rehab.

I'd been considered too young when I presented them with a three-year projection of where the company would be without radical changes—which was basically bankruptcy—and offered to save The Mortimer Group, on condition I was made CEO.

In the six years since I took over, I made the company wildly successful, and unfortunately pissed off more than a few members of my own family along the way.

'Page Three no longer exists,' I murmured abstractedly while my mind raced to tackle what could possibly be a real threat to my position.

Despite his shortcomings, Harry was a hard-working and intelligent subordinate, but he was no-where near ready to take the helm of the company I'd shaped into running like a Swiss watch. Nor was he in any way equipped to be trusted with the biggest deal TMG was within a whisker of bagging. The deal that had demanded ninety-nine per cent of my working life for the last eight months.

'It's not going to fucking happen,' I snarled under my breath.

The clink of her teacup against the saucer preceded Aunt Flo rising to her five-foot-two-inch height. In her Chanel suit, flawless make-up and contemporarily styled hair, she looked a decade younger. 'No, it's not. Because the last thing I need is your uncle Joseph giving me one of his damn I-told-you-so lectures.'

I'd spent most of my life wondering when the permanent stick Uncle Joseph had up his arse would turn into a tree. At sixty-eight, he was one of the oldest of the remaining Mortimer clan and probably the one who hated my guts the most, although he had no problem cashing the huge cheques my hard work brought him while not so secretly keeping the lynch mob at the ready in case I fucked up royally.

'If you don't want that to happen, then you'll keep your antics down. At least until this Russian deal is done. That's what we agreed.'

'Wait, that's what *who* agreed?'

'An informal family meeting was called this morning.'

I raised an eyebrow. 'To which I wasn't invited?'

'It was agreed it would be best if you weren't involved. Besides, you were tagged on social media with the caption that read "Just Done Being Banged." I thought you needed your sleep before this meeting.'

'I was on the phone to an intractable Russian oligarch until three a.m. this morning. Trust me, I had no energy after that to bang anyone.'

'But you realise there's a pattern that supports these allegations, don't you?' she insisted.

For the first time in for ever I couldn't hold the gaze of the only person who meant a damn to me. Spiking my fingers through my hair, I paced to the window.

I was pretty sure I knew who'd posted the fake news, and if I hadn't dumped Mischa last week over her many flaws, I'd do it all over again, just for her insane Instagram obsession.

With a sigh, I faced Aunt Flo. 'So you had the meeting. And you all agreed to this…rancid little attempt at blackmail?'

Her lips pursed. 'I'm your greatest ally, Gideon. You know that. But even I've noticed that you've… regressed a little lately.'

My teeth ground together and I forced myself to remain silent. It was true I'd made full and frequent use of the handful of exclusive gentlemen's clubs I patronised. And so what if I didn't date the same woman for more than a handful of weeks and that each sexual encounter left me a little more jaded than the last? Didn't someone marginally profound suggest that the best way to get over mediocre sex was to fuck someone else?

I grimaced inwardly at the hollow echo of the reminder, ruthlessly suppressing the voice that suggested the bandage I'd slapped over the gashing wound of betrayal was in serious risk of failing.

'So they elected you to be the bearer of this momentous news?'

She cracked her first smile since entering my office. 'I was tempted to send one of your uncles just to see what colourful name you'd come up with this time. I believe last time it was a giraffe's arse?'

I shrugged. 'Uncle Conrad shouldn't have walked into my office without knocking. He embarrassed the hell out of the Aston Martin saleswoman. It wasn't my fault she chose to make her presentation minus a substantial amount of her clothes.'

Aunt Flo shook her head as we shared a grin. After a moment she sobered up. 'I love you, dear boy. Enough to let you know things are serious this time. There are whispers of board members band-ing together to gain enough shares to form a majority. I'll happily throw in my six per cent behind you but if this becomes a reality, it still won't be enough.'

'I can't believe this tripe. I've made them all more money than they'll ever be able to spend.'

She nodded a little sadly. 'They're ungrateful bastards. Every last one of them. But they're still part of this family. And they're powerful enough to pack a collective punch if it comes to it. I don't want to see that happen to you.'

'So they're holding my sex life prisoner?'

'Not your sex life. They just don't want any unsavoury publicity or social media posts like the one from this morning risking this deal. Get one of those sex-bot things that seem to be the rage nowadays.'

I snorted. 'No, thanks. If that's my only choice, I'd rather stay celibate.'

Flo's carefully plucked eyebrows shot up before she laughed. 'Be careful what you wish for or the lawyers will put that in the contract.'

I froze. 'What contract?'

She made a face. 'They want something binding so you take this seriously. They think thirty days of no adverse publicity ought to do it.'

Sweet Lord, this just got better and better. 'They've got the bloody lawyers involved without even discussing it with me first?' The realisation shouldn't have hurt. But it did. Same way what Damian had done continued to drill a gaping hole inside me.

Not for the first time, I wondered why I'd bothered returning home to London. Why I didn't stay in Singapore, co-managing the hotel construction company I started with my brother, Bryce, eight years ago, instead of merging it with TMG. Everything outside the glass walls of this giant skyscraper that housed The Mortimer Group had gone to shit the moment I took the CEO position.

'Nelly, wait for me outside,' I heard Flo murmur. She waited until her assistant left the room before she approached. 'I'm the last one to be indelicate but I'm going to come right out and say it. You're in danger of being permanently scarred from what happened three years ago. It's time to take firmer control of your life, Gideon.'

My fist balled and that tight band of rage around my chest I kept especially for such reminders threatened to suffocate me. 'I was betrayed by my own flesh and blood, Flo. By the person I trusted the most,' I gritted out.

She laid a gentle hand on my arm. 'I know. And while this may sound like an atrocious idea to you right now, taking a step back from the…excess may provide a little clarity.'

She meant well, and yet I couldn't stop the rancid bitterness that ploughed through me. Nor did I particularly welcome the unspoken accusation. The one that suggested I was repeating past mistakes of parents I barely knew.

'I'm not like my mother, Flo,' I bit out tersely. 'If I suffered from any form of addiction, I wouldn't turn up at six a.m. every morning and work my bloody arse off for this family.' I knew my mother's addiction to the heroin that eventually caused her to drive her Maserati off a cliff in Switzerland ten years ago was another invisible stain on my character. 'There's nothing to remedy. But I'll sign their damn paper if that's what they want. And when I pull this deal off without hint of a scandal, I expect every last one of them to come crawling to me on their hands and knees to beg my forgiveness.'

'And I'll sit by your side and we'll sip cognac and laugh as they do.'

I couldn't summon the smile she expected so I just nodded.

'I'll tell the lawyers to have the papers ready for you to sign this afternoon. Now, I'd better be on my way. I don't want to be late for my next appointment.'

Alone in my office, I stood at the window and stared, unseeing, at the view.

What the bloody hell did I just do?

You just agreed to behave for thirty days. Ergo, no partying. No gentlemen's clubs. No sex.

No finding an avenue—no matter how futile—for the demons that crawled out of the woodwork at night and taunted me with might-have-beens. No distraction from the hell of losing the person I'd once believed was my best friend to an act of betrayal that still hollowed me out in the dead of night. My fist clenched as memories raked raw pain over me.

I hoped to God my impending suffering was worth it or someone's head would roll.

CHAPTER ONE

Leonie. Two weeks later

NO MAN WAS worth it.

I slammed the phone down, and then got even more annoyed that I'd lost my cool. For three days I'd jumped through every hoop imaginable and some I'd never thought even invented.

Granted, if I succeeded, this would be the sale of a lifetime. My fifteen per cent stake in this deal would double my already-impressive bank account but, more important, put me squarely on the map in a place where arrogant billionaires with egos the size of small countries lounged on every corner.

Hell, I could even relocate to another sun-drenched locale. One that didn't hold the ravaging memories this place did.

I glanced out of my office window and was greeted by the stunning marina a good percentage of the world's population believed was the gateway to paradise. Most people would give a piece of their souls for this.

Not me.

To me, this would always be ground zero of the worst moment of my life. The most humiliating, too. Definitely the most heartbreaking—

I wasn't ashamed to admit part of my reason for wanting this deal over and done with was the shattered heart bit. I'd used my work to patch myself together and lately I'd become aware that I might have missed a few vital pieces in my repair job, like a broken leg that hadn't been set properly.

It supported you by keeping you alive, breathing, reasoning, but toss in more challenging things like trust and emotional investment and, heaven forbid, taking another chance on happiness, and it withered and shrank, its acute flaws lighting with the dire warnings of its impending malfunction.

It was too late to salvage the pieces of my heart that betrayal had rotted away, but it wasn't too late to hit the reset button on the rest of my life.

If only this damn client would play ball.

I sighed and let my gaze drift over the horizon.

The Côte d'Azur in June was living up to its hype where the cloudless blue sky, dazzling sunlight, sparkling ocean and blinding bling were concerned, at least. In the marina, multimillion-pound yachts bobbed smugly in the midmorning heat.

With almost undeniable compulsion, my gaze shifted left beyond the marina wall to the superyacht moored a quarter of a mile away in deeper waters.

La Sirène.

My biggest and riskiest investment to date.

Larger than all of the other boats currently moored, it was a sight to behold. Every client who'd attended the boat show a week ago had rhapsodised over it.

Fresh off the tram lines of the shipping yard in Greece, it was truly breathtaking. The most innovative vessel of its kind with unimaginable luxury to please even the most jaded appetite.

The day I'd received the call that my investment had been accepted, that I was part owner of one of the most breathtaking vessels ever built, was the proudest moment of my life.

But I'd learned to detach myself from falling in love with it. I didn't get attached to things any more, especially things I was actively attempting to sell.

One by one the stragglers had fallen away until only one remained.

Gideon Mortimer.

A potential client who could be the answer to my achieving next-level status. A client with demands so absurd—

I jumped as the phone rang. I took a beat to calm my pulse before picking up the handset.

'Branson Sales and Leasing, Leonora Branson speak—'

'You hung up. I wasn't done talking, Miss Branson,' interrupted the deeply masculine, very arrogant voice.

Despite my irritation, the sheer sexiness of his voice sent a decadent shiver over my skin. I turned my back on the view and tried to ignore the sensation.

'I got tired of being on hold after ten minutes.'

He made a sound as if he was grinding his teeth. 'It was for less than five minutes and I believe my assistant told you I might have to take a call I'd been waiting for all day. Maybe you need a refresher course on the basics of customer service?'

Maybe you need a refresher course on how to be a human being.

In the six years since I defiantly started my own business on the southern French coast, I'd dealt with clients with egos of all shapes and sizes and heard enough outrageous demands to last a lifetime. Gideon Mortimer's requests came within the top five per cent.

'The yacht has a crew of twenty-five. That's more than adequate to provide the service you need. As for your other requests, the captain also has a helicopter licence, twenty years' flying experience under his belt and can fly you anywhere you need to go from the vessel.'

'I'm bringing my most important client on board to finalise a business deal I've been trying to close for the best part of a year. Absolutely nothing can go wrong.'

'And nothing, within my purview and the terms and conditions I sent to your assistant, will. All your demands…within reason, will be met.'

'"We provide a three-sixty-degree service of excellence, one hundred per cent of the time." Isn't that your slogan?'

'Yes, and the crew you need are ready to be allocated to you should you wish to lease the yacht. That includes three extra staff from my Monte Carlo office. Any more and I'll have to shut that office down for the summer.'

'Then do it.'

'No, I won't. You're a potential valued client, but you're not my only client. As a businessman you'll understand that I can't place my eggs in one basket. And frankly, the staffing ratio you're asking for is excessive so if you're not willing to budge on that, then we've come full circle.'

'As a businesswoman, you should know that sometimes success hinges on making that one bold decision that could turn a crucial tide in your favour.'

I allowed myself a small smile at the irony. Gideon Mortimer had no idea how much I'd risked to be a part of the consortium that had built the yacht. How much he himself was crucial to achieving my next goal. 'Trust me, I do. But from where I'm standing, I'm not sure you're that tide bringer.' Right now, he was more like a pain in my ass, albeit a very sexy-sounding one.

Silence greeted my response.

Had I been too bold? I might not be the biggest dog in the yard but I hadn't let that stop me from barking long and loud when I needed to.

I mentally shrugged. If Gideon Mortimer wanted to take his business elsewhere, it'd be a blow, but it wouldn't kill my plans for the future. It'd just delay it a little.

That stony ache beneath my breastbone rubbed hard, as if reminding me of its existence. I breathed through it.

'A bold move, insulting a potential client,' he said, but there was a hint of amusement in his voice.

'I believe in playing a straight bat. If that's too offensive for you, I've given your assistant the names of much larger firms who could cater to what you want.' Those firms believed in landing their business no matter what it took. I didn't.

'It's not my assistant's job to sell the yacht to me. It's yours. Shouldn't you be bending over backwards to please me? Or are you inflexible?'

'I'm flexible in every way that counts. I was a junior athletics gymnast before I went to university and I have three medals to show for it, two of which are gold.'

'And how long ago was that?' he mused. 'Thirty? Forty years? You've obviously grown rusty.'

My fingers tightened around the handset as I counted to ten. I'd let a personal detail slip. My number-one rule of business was to keep my emotions out of it. That included not letting clients rile me.

'I can fly in the special smoked salmon you requested so it's ready for you each morning. Same goes for the caviar from Iceland and the tuna from Norway. Any other culinary requests will be catered for, you have my word. And… I can stretch the crew to twenty-seven if you really need it. It would involve taking more members of staff from Monaco but with some clever balancing, I could make it work.'

'My client is bringing a large entourage, possibly his extended family. So might I. That's why we're hiring a twenty-cabin vessel. Three weeks is a long time on a boat. We'll all require various forms of entertainment. A crew of twenty-seven at full capacity would be a stretch. On top of that, I believe you told my assistant the captain is the only one who knows the vessel inside and out. I'll need an experienced member of crew who is not the captain—since I believe he'll be otherwise occupied *actually* piloting the boat—to answer any questions my client will have about the yacht. This is your golden opportunity to turn a lease into a sale. I may be in the market for the right yacht. My client has two and is looking for a third. Does that register at all?'

'Of course,' I said through gritted teeth. 'Every crew member is given a tutorial on the boat.'

'Really? And how long was this tutorial?'

I felt heat rise up my neck. 'Sixty minutes.'

He didn't respond for a long time. 'For a five-hundred-foot, five-deck yacht?' Disbelief rang through his voice. 'Do you want this commission, Miss Branson?'

I bit the inside of my cheek until my eyes watered. With every atom of my being I wanted to say no. I'd sunk all my capital into this vessel in the hope of making a once-in-a-lifetime sale that would be an answer to all my dreams. But the rental Gideon Mortimer was dangling in front of me, with the possibility of an extension, would also bring in a considerable injection of cash, enough for me to expand my business.

To do that, I needed men like Gideon Mortimer. 'I want your business.'

'Then find a way for us to both get what we want.'

I took a breath. 'Fine. You'll hear from me by five p.m. today.'

'Wonderful. And please bear in mind that if you *don't* call me back, I'll remember it for a very long time.' The line went dead.

This time I resisted the urge to slam my phone. After replacing the handset, I went to the kitchenette attached to the open-plan office, boiled the kettle and dropped a teabag into my favourite mug.

I stirred slowly while counting to a hundred. Then I threw the whole thing down the drain. Normally, I loved my job, loved turning a dream into reality for the average Joe like my grandfather, who'd made my childhood a little bearable by passing his love of sailing to me.

He'd take me out on the water when my mother's mood swings veered into bitterness and depression, or when my father made one of his transient, illicit visits to the woman who'd never managed to free herself from a man unworthy of her love.

The freedom of being out on the open sea had helped me to forget the man who'd never been interested in fatherhood.

It'd been a natural transition to turn that hobby into a business with Adam, the man I'd thought I'd marry.

Until he'd nearly derailed my life with his betrayal.

But there was a reason Grandma Agnes had claimed my middle name was *stubborn*. Letting treachery get the better part of me hadn't been an option.

Maybe in the beginning, with my name over the

door and gleaming on my stationery, I'd hoped Adam would crawl back and beg forgiveness for the shitty move he'd pulled.

Or maybe I'd wanted to rub my success in the faces of those who found it so easy to snatch my happiness from me. I wanted to show them that I could exist in their world, hell, even rub shoulders with them.

Whatever. Freud would have a field day with me.

But those sensations had passed quickly and left a burning need to succeed for *me* and me alone.

But not the memory of Adam's betrayal.

I rinsed the cup and walked over to the large corkboard where I'd pinned the itinerary for the next three months. I had the same schedule on my laptop but it pleased me to see my hard work laid out in pretty stationery.

May to August was the height of boating season. Most of my full-time staff were all on board leased vessels.

Monaco was especially busy. But a quick calculation confirmed what I'd told Gideon Mortimer. I could spare one member of staff, two at a stretch, which left Andrea, my second in command, and our part-time secretary. At seven and a half months pregnant and seasick even when on land, Andrea was going nowhere.

As if conjured by my thoughts, she waddled in a second later and stopped in surprise when she saw me. 'Oh, I thought you'd have left for the day.'

'No, I've been on the phone with Mr Mortimer.'

She rolled her eyes and fanned herself with a paper

napkin. 'Oh, jeez, is he still going on about the extra crew?'

Among other things. 'Yep.'

'And?' She shuffled over and dropped heavily into the nearest chair.

'I'm going to see if any of the other leasing companies can spare any crew members.'

Andrea grimaced. 'Not to be a pessimist but you don't have a hope in hell of that happening. They were super pissed when Giannopolous Boats chose you to join in the investment consortium on this yacht deal. They won't be in a hurry to help you out.'

Just what I'd feared. I forced a shrug. 'Then come five p.m. I'll be calling Mortimer back to tell him to look elsewhere.'

Andrea rubbed one hand over her belly and continued to fan herself with the other. I was about to offer to crank up the AC when she looked up. 'What's the most important thing he's asking for that we haven't been able to provide him, apart from the unnecessary crew?'

'From the sounds of it, he's looking to buy a boat, and this client he's expecting to wow the pants off of is a boat fanatic. He wants someone on hand 24/7 to spout statistics should he need it.'

She stared at me as her eyes brightened. 'Pregnancy brain might be affecting me but aren't I looking at the person who learned every nook and cranny of Giannopolous's business so you could land a spot on the consortium?'

I shook my head. 'Yeah, but it's not going to work—'

Andrea started to lean forward, winced and sat back again. Her hand shifted to rub the side of her stomach. 'Okay, no need to kick me quite so hard, *mon petit coeur*,' she murmured to her baby. After a moment, she looked up. 'Leonie, think about it. You're exactly what this client needs. Are you really going to lose this commission or sale over one extra person?'

I frowned. 'He hasn't even stepped aboard yet and he's already a giant pain in my arse.'

'So what? You've dealt with worse and come out smiling.'

'Not like him, Andrea.' Not with that voice and that take-charge manner that had always been a weakness for me. They said opposites attracted. But I wasn't shy and retiring one little bit. Besides stubborn, Grandma Agnes had also referred to me as a charging heifer once or twice. Unattractive but accurate. So Gideon Mortimer should be the last person to make my lady parts quiver. But quiver they did. I'd ignored my reaction but its effect lingered for a little longer than I wanted it to.

'Well, I looked him up on the internet on my break. He's effing loaded, Leonie. And not just him. His family are seriously influential. Like, related-to-royalty-from-the-year-dot type of influential. He's a mathematical genius or something. His IQ is through the roof. Don't ask me what it is, I don't remember. Did I mention he's loaded?'

My mouth twitched in a reluctant smile. 'Yes, you did. Still doesn't change the fact that I can't conjure up crew I don't have.'

'No, but you can offer yourself.'

'What?'

'For the service he needs,' she stressed.

I pulled my overactive brain from images of me servicing Gideon Mortimer in the most basic of ways to a much more professional arena. 'It's not just that. I can't leave you to man the office for three weeks.'

'Sure you can. Laurent loses a little more of his mind every time I walk out the door. I thought I was bad, but he's been getting progressively worse as the birth gets closer. He finishes with the market at midday. He'd love nothing more than to spend the rest of the afternoon here keeping me company. Plus, if you do get the rental commission or—please, God— the sale, that would solve a few money issues for us.'

I mulled it over for a minute. If I sold the boat I would be able to do much more than that. I could make Andrea a partner, a plan I'd been mulling over as part of my expansion. 'Are you sure?'

She nodded eagerly. 'Absolutely.' She struggled to her feet and headed towards the back of the office. 'I need to pee. Don't overthink it, Leonie. Just call him back and say yes.'

Don't overthink it.

I took a deep breath and reached for the phone. 'Hello, can I speak to Gideon Mortimer, please?'

He answered immediately, 'You're calling me with a yes, I hope?'

I ground my teeth for a single second. Any more and I risked a cracked molar. 'Yes. On the crew front, you'll have the additional staff you need. On one condition.'

'I hate conditions.'

'And I detest games, Mr Mortimer.'

'All games or just specific ones?' he drawled, amused.

'For the sake of our *potential* business relationship, let's stick to *all* games,' I responded tightly.

'Shame,' he murmured. 'What's this condition?'

'That you let me have full control of the crew and rotate them the way I see fit without any interference.' The last thing I needed was any unreasonable demands on my crew.

'I accept your condition. But before we move forward I also need your reassurance that you will be as flexible as you claim you can be.'

For some absurd reason my breath caught, my imagination latching on to sexual positions and breathless fucking. Exhaling slowly, I reined myself in. 'Yes. Fine.'

'No, I need a little more than that,' he insisted, his tone half amused, half irritated, if such a thing was possible. 'So say the words, Miss Branson. Tell me you can accommodate my wishes.'

I crossed my fingers and prayed my response would hold true a day, or even a week from now. That I wouldn't be tempted to throw Gideon Mortimer overboard before he'd bought my boat. 'I can accommodate your reasonable wishes.'

'Good. I arrive at seven tomorrow morning.'
The line went dead.

I stepped into my shower two hours later with a sigh
of relief. My apartment on the Rue Jean Jaurès in
Cannes was large and spacious and beautifully dec-
orated. It was a little on the extravagant side, but I
was determined to make a statement straight off the
bat. I meant business and I wanted anyone who paid
attention to know it. The sea view alone was worth
the five figures I paid in monthly rent.

But if I had to pick my favourite thing about my
apartment, it was the luxurious power shower and
sauna. With multiple jets and settings that delivered
everything from rainforest mist to candlelit steam,
it'd been love at first viewing.

For the first four months after I started Branson
Sales & Leasing I'd lived on bread and cheese just so I
could pay the rent. I could afford a more well-rounded
meal in the best Michelin-starred establishment these
days, but, while I thoroughly enjoyed those solo treats
or client-wooing power lunches, my apartment was
my sanctuary.

A place to forget men like Gideon Mortimer, with
their endless bank accounts and lofty demands and
pussy-tingling voices.

I braced my hands on the tiles and willed my irritation away. Two seconds after I'd hung up, I'd realised he hadn't told me which airport he'd be flying
into. His assistant had informed me when I called

back that Gideon had left for the day and she had no idea what his plans were since he hadn't informed her.

So now I had two limos heading to two private airports. It wasn't a big deal—my business could easily absorb the costs—it didn't augur well for ignoring the temptation to throw him overboard at the first opportunity.

Just a little longer.

By this time next month, the yacht would either be sold or the rental commission would be a huge boost to my firm's profile and hopefully attract more clients like Gideon Mortimer.

Then I could be rid of the lingering sense of unworthiness I'd never been truly able to shake since Adam—

Dammit, why was I thinking about Adam again when he hadn't crossed my mind in weeks? I hated that he'd compounded feelings my father had engendered within me by his blatant dismissal of me as a child.

But then, your fiancé running off with a rich heiress weeks before your wedding had a way of totally sideswiping you. And as much as I tried I couldn't rid myself of the hollow sensation inside me.

Enough!

I was probably thinking about the past because Gideon's air of entitlement triggered traits I'd seen in my father before I'd cut off all contact with the man.

As for Adam…it'd been a relief that six months ago he'd finally stopped opening dummy accounts in the hopes of friending me on Facebook. Not so much the hang-ups I'd been getting on my mobile phone lately, forcing me to change my phone number.

Whatever he was selling, I wasn't buying.

Being rejected once by your own flesh and blood was bad enough. A repeat by the man you'd thought you'd spend the rest of your life with had a way of sharpening your perspective on men and relationships.

These days I was much more discerning of men to the point where the occasional one night was more than enough for me. The rest of the time, my battery-operated boyfriends sufficed just fine.

I turned off the shower, dried off and sprawled out on my bed. Unbidden, the conversation with Gideon Mortimer replayed in my mind, especially the naughty bits, uttered in that unbelievably sexy voice of his.

Find a way to get us both what we want. Tell me you can accommodate my wishes.

Did he use suggestive words like that in the bedroom? Or was he an outright dirty talker?

What the hell did that matter to me?

I flipped over, my body growing hot and clammy as his deep voice continued to echo through my head. Clamping my eyes shut, I growled in frustration and tugged open the drawer of my bedside table. I hadn't touched my vibrator in a while, not since the preparation for the busy season had kicked in. Usually I was too tired from a hard day's work and crashed the moment my head touched the pillow.

Today I knew I wouldn't be able to sleep without a little carnal therapy.

With an anticipatory shiver, I turned on the device. I slid it over my belly and between my legs, my breath catching at how wet I was already. At the first touch of the vibrator against my clit, my nipples pebbled, pleasure radiating from my groin. As a resident of a place that boasted more beautiful people per square metre than anywhere else on earth, I never lacked visual fodder for my sexual fantasies.

A French count with a hot accent.

An Australian bodybuilder here for the summer.

A Californian surfer crewing on a catamaran while learning French.

They were a dime a dozen along the coast.

But of course, the moment I found my groove and my hips began to move in pleasurable rhythm, the deep, sinfully cultured tones of a minor British aristocrat invaded my brain.

Miss Branson...

I need a little more than that...

Accommodate my wishes...

Say the words, Miss Branson...

With a broken gasp, my orgasm tore through me. My back arched off the bed and my whole body shook as I came harder than I had in a long time. I dropped the vibrator and boldly cupped myself, eager to hold on to the release for a little longer as my body continued to convulse, my gasps growing louder as I teased out of the last of my climax.

The descent was slow and languid, my body humming contentedly as I regained my breath.

And then with a groan, I buried my face in the pillow.

Hell.

Gideon Mortimer hadn't made an appearance yet and he was already more than a pain in my arse. He'd just elevated himself to an ache in my pussy.

CHAPTER TWO

Leonie

AT A QUARTER to seven I stood by the limo in the private airstrip that serviced Nice airport. A few more phone calls this morning had finally furnished me with the info of at which airport Gideon would be landing.

As his private jet landed and taxied closer, I eyed the gleaming silver Aston Martin DB11 parked next to the limo.

Although currently driverless, it still evoked irritation. There were no other planes scheduled to land for another hour—I checked with VIP staff. Which most likely meant one thing.

The client I'd risen at the crack of dawn to pick up had arranged his own ride.

Deep breaths…

I despised the careless waste of money his unreasonableness triggered. Which was a little ironic considering the line of business I was in but still… I shrugged away my ire and watched the sleek private jet come to a standstill.

Two minutes later, the jet's engines powered down and short steps dropped onto the tarmac.

And from fifty feet away I caught my first glimpse of Gideon Mortimer.

Holy God.

I'd thought his sex-stroking voice was sinfully aggravating. But the man's face, lean hips and long-limbed body...*everything* about him was captivating enough to make my jaw sag in wonder for three embarrassing seconds before I caught myself.

Still I couldn't look away.

Dark brown wavy hair, glossy beneath the resplendent sunshine, tossed about in the morning breeze. As I watched him approach in a slow saunter, I could've sworn every movement he made was precisely choreographed by the director of a perfume ad.

Aviator shades perched on a patrician nose stopped me from seeing his eyes, but that didn't even matter. I was already preoccupied with the square jaw that held an I-didn't-bother-to-shave-deal-with-it stubble that prompted fingers—not mine—to test its roughness.

As he drew nearer, my gaze dropped to his mouth.

Dear heaven. Every millimetre of that mouth was built for filthy, decadent sin. For making fast and furious friends with a woman's lady business, and not disengaging until someone was clawing at silk sheets, screaming for mercy.

Thank God I took the edge off last night, otherwise I'd have a hard time functioning right now. Gideon Mortimer was the epitome of everything I'd thought him to be—sinfully handsome and very much aware of his power over women.

Just like the man whose blood unfortunately ran through my veins; the man I'd never called Dad because he didn't deserve the title. A no-good son of a bitch I'd never forgiven for what he did to my mother. To me.

Those reminders helped shore up my foundations as I briskly tugged on my bespoke Armani jacket and pinned a cool professional smile on my face. 'Mr Mortimer?'

He ignored me, peering first into the limo and then, frowning, at his immediate surroundings before his jaw clenched. 'Jesus, she didn't even bother to turn up,' he muttered. 'Fucking unbelievable.'

I took a deep breath and stepped forward. 'Mr Mortimer?' I waited for him to pluck his sunglasses off his face before I thrust out my hand. 'Welcome to Nice. I'm—'

'Not who I'm expecting. As much as I appreciate a pretty smile and saucy little chauffeur's uniform, your boss should've come here herself, like she promised. I should've guessed that promise of flexibility was too good to be true. Probably that bragging about her gold medals, too,' he muttered under his breath as he turned towards the Aston Martin.

'First of all, this isn't a chauffeur's uniform. It's bespoke Armani. Second, I don't believe she promised she would be here. If you would just—'

'What are you? Her assistant? Her driver? Are you even old enough to drive this thing?'

'Mr Mortimer—'

Again he cut me off. 'Fucking typical. Forget it.'
He pointed his electronic key at the sports car. The
boot popped open and he threw his weekend bag into
it and slammed it with repressed force. 'When someone gives their word I expect them to abide by it.' The
set to his jaw suggested he wasn't talking about the
wrong he believed I'd committed. 'Tell her she just
lost my business.'

'Did she even have it in the first place?' I snapped.
'Or were you just toying with her in between playing
with your millions?'

He froze with one hand on the door. 'Excuse me?'

'Are you sure you want to be excused? Only you
seem to enjoy riding roughshod over anyone who so
much as throws the tiniest protest your way.'

He slowly leaned his rangy body against the car,
crossed his ankles and folded his arms. It was really
hard to know which part of his body to look at. Or to
avoid looking to prevent sensory overload. He moved
like the gears of a well-oiled machine, with impressive fluidity and contained power. I tried not to think
of what all that power could do if concentrated between a woman's legs.

Because the potential to unleash mayhem was
there. Barely restrained. Waiting to explode. Something about his unshaven face and the beaten leather
jacket draping his body spelled unbridled danger I
had every intention of avoiding.

'You have something to say to me?' he asked in
a tone saturated with English boarding-school arrogance.

I steeled myself to hold his gaze. 'Funnily enough, yes. Question is, are you going to listen or keep talking over me?'

Dark grey eyes flecked with gold and hazel, surrounded by the most lush lashes I'd ever seen on a man, raked me slowly from head to toe, and back again. He lingered on my legs, my hips, paused the longest on my breasts. Gideon Mortimer was a breasts man. And my breasts were tightening, tingling, in preparation to savour that revelation.

Oh, hell, no.

I clenched my fist over the car key until faint pain in my palm distracted my body from the thick, drugging sensation swirling through me. I couldn't be attracted to Gideon Mortimer. I just couldn't.

Before he could respond, I held out my hand once more. 'Good to meet you, Mr Mortimer. I'm Ms Branson.'

His arms dropped and he looked from my outstretched hand to my face. 'You're Leonora Branson?'

'Yes.'

His eyes narrowed. 'Shit. I thought she…you fobbed me off with an assistant.'

'I know. You made your feelings very clear on the matter.'

He had the grace to grimace. 'Apologies. I've had a testy few weeks.'

A little mollified, I attempted another smile. 'Apology accepted.'

He took my hand as his gaze made another subtle pass over my body. 'How old are you, Leonora Branson?'

Nope, not going near that one. 'Old enough to have run a successful company for six years with a portfolio of satisfied customers.'

'Doesn't really answer my question, does it?' he said.

'No, it doesn't. Besides not playing games I also don't give out personal information. Is that going to be a problem?'

'Only if you have a problem with me being impressed that someone so young would be in the position you're in.'

The unexpected compliment blew a hole through my irritation, just as the pressure of his hand on mine was eroding my intention not to be seriously seduced by his drop-dead gorgeousness.

I knew I was younger than I looked, a fact that had surprised a few people who thought at twenty-six I had no business running a multimillion-pound company. 'I...' God, what had he said? Something about being impressed? 'Thanks.'

'You're welcome,' he said in a deep, gravel-rough voice that reminded me of what I did to myself last night.

I tugged at my hand. He kept a hold of it for another long second, a frown flicking over his face as his jaw clenched and unclenched.

The depth of his examination began to grate. Then the grating turned into something else. Something darker, saucier. Something that emphatically reminded my pussy that a vibrator wasn't enough any more and what it truly yearned for was a hard, experienced cock.

Please. Not now.

I exhaled in relief as he dropped my hand and then relief morphed to irritation as he turned·to the sports car.

'Are you leaving in that?'

'I should hope so, since I asked for it to be delivered for that very purpose.'

It took monumental effort not to grit my teeth. 'You should've informed me you would be driving yourself. As you can see, I came to pick you up.'

He tossed a mocking glance at the Rolls Royce and his mouth quirked. 'It's a gorgeous ride, but I'm in the mood for a little more horsepower this morning.'

Calm. Be calm. 'Very well. Shall we arrange a time to meet later?'

'I have meetings scheduled all day. Then a hot date with the sexy roulette table at the Casino de Monte-Carlo later. She's always a tease, but an enjoyable one.'

In anticipation of a hectic Monday getting the crew ready to sail, I'd given myself the day off tomorrow. I watched it disappear in a puff of smoke. 'Why did you ask me to come here this morning if you can't meet with me?'

'I asked you to come because it's a half-hour drive to my hotel. And I believe in time efficiency.' With that, he opened the passenger door and raised an eyebrow at me. 'So are you coming, Miss Branson?' The suggestive decadence in his tone should've made me madder. But my traitorous pussy grew damper.

'I can't just leave the car here.'

'There you go again, throwing obstacles in the way of our fledgling…liaison.'

I cast a look towards the hired driver of the limo and nodded, dismissing him and the waste of money Gideon had just cost me.

I grabbed my small purse and the folder I'd brought with me before heading over to the Aston Martin, where Gideon Mortimer stood holding the door open for me.

That small act of chivalry was still unravelling a tiny wave of shock through me as he slid behind the wheel. The throaty engine roared to life the same time I was hit with a lungful of whatever delicious aftershave he was wearing. It was like a shot to the chest from a double-barrelled gun. Compounded by the power of the car when he accelerated out of the airport and the play of his thighs when he aggressively changed gears, I was struck dumb for several minutes.

The busy streets of Nice were filled with tourists at this time of year but Gideon seemed to know how to avoid getting caught up in traffic. At the first set of red lights, he slanted a glance at me. 'Is the crew issue resolved?'

Shit, he had to give me the tough question straight off the bat. I took a moment to savour my freedom for one last time. 'If you go ahead and lease the boat, I'll resolve the crew issue but I won't act on it until we have an agreement. If and when we do it'll bring the manpower total to twenty-seven. Trust me, I can make that work.'

A cloud drifted over his face. 'Trust isn't a commodity I find very easy to part with.'

The little rush of affinity warmed me before I killed it dead. If the Devil didn't trust, there was a good reason for it. 'The other company you're thinking of going with, have you used them before?'

He cracked a hard smile. 'Don't come at me with that angle, Leonora.'

It was the second time he'd used my given name. When had we even agreed to that? And why did each enunciation make me wildly hot?

'Why not? Why would you decide to go with them and not me?'

'Because they're weren't as…intransigent.'

My fingers tightened around the folder. 'I can guarantee you a better service.'

He remained silent for a short mile. 'That remains to be seen. Now, run me through your list,' he said briskly.

A little more settled now we were on a business footing, I went through the extensive list of everything, from how often the sheets were changed on board the yacht to the ingredients used on the most elaborate meal. I'd found out early in my career not to leave any detail unmentioned.

By the time I was done, he was pulling up in front of the Riviera One hotel in Nice. The cheapest room in the six-star hotel was upward of fifteen hundred euros a night with a stay in the presidential suite extending to the tens of thousands. It was number one on my client recommendation list.

I wasn't even a little bit surprised that Gideon was greeted by name by the doorman when he stepped out of the Aston Martin.

'*Bienvenue*, Monsieur Mortimer.'

'Thanks, Pierre, it's good to be back. How are the wife and kids?' he asked after he tossed his keys to the valet.

'Very well, *monsieur*. I must thank you again for that letter of recommendation.'

Gideon clapped the man on the shoulder. 'If you must, but that's the last time. Thank me again and I'll have you fired.'

Pierre looked startled for a moment, before he chuckled. 'Understood, *monsieur*. I'll make sure your bag is delivered right away.'

'Good man.'

He sauntered into the stunning atrium of the art deco hotel as if he owned the place, striding over to the VIP concierge desk. 'Everything is ready for you, Mr Mortimer. If there is anything else you need, please do not hesitate to ask and I will personally see to it,' the chief concierge said.

'I know you will. I might even start by asking you to teach true customer service to a few people I'm thinking of doing business with,' Gideon replied, sending me a speaking glance as he pocketed his black key card and headed to the lift.

'If that comment was aimed at me, I'll have you know I haven't had a single complaint since I started my business. In fact, I have several glowing testimonials I'm happy to show you if you want.'

He had the audacity to grin. And, oh, what a spectacular sight it was. It transformed his face from devilishly handsome to downright sacrilegious, stopping my breath dead two seconds after the brilliance of it hit me square in the chest.

Sweet God.

I entered the lift and clung to the railing, desperately willing myself to avoid looking at him, and failing, as he lounged against the wall, arms crossed.

'I have a feeling you're not very happy with me, Leonora,' he mused. 'Is it because you find me too demanding?'

God, why was he saying my name like that? 'Wasn't that the impression you wished to create?'

His shrug was shamelessly unapologetic. 'My mum used to call me her greedy little bastard, among other things. The way I see it, why ask for the moon and stars when the sun is just begging to be tossed in, as well?'

The use of the past tense triggered curiosity I wrestled down. 'And you don't care if your greed earns you a certain reputation?'

'I'm a big boy. I can take care of anyone who pays me a less-than-stellar compliment to my face. What they say behind my back—' he shrugged again '—I care very little about.'

The realisation that he meant it, that power and privilege had insulated him against the barbs of ordinary men, grated. It was the same entitlement that my father fed on, using it to prey on defenceless people like my mother until she was a husk before throwing her away. The same entitlement with which another woman had looked at my fiancé, decided she wanted him and had taken him without compunction, Adam's own collusion aside.

Dammit, there I went thinking about him again. Something about Gideon Mortimer triggered unwanted memories. The sooner I got our business squared away, the better.

Except, if he signed on the dotted line, I'd be stuck with him for the next few weeks.

'You should learn to school your expressions better, Leonora.'

I refocused on him but didn't bother to hide my derision. 'Pray tell, what do you think you see?'

'There's a lot about me you don't like. But you're swallowing your pride for the sake of our business relationship. Bravo on that, by the way. But there's something you do like and you're desperate to keep that under wraps.'

My heart rate spiked just a little north of uncomfortable. 'Wow, you can tell all of that just by looking at my face?'

'I can tell that by the way you're gripping that railing as if your life depends on it, and the way you're plastering yourself so hard against the wall. Oh, and the way you haven't stopped looking at my mouth since we entered the lift.'

I opened my mouth but the lift doors parted just then, possibly saving me from voicing a response that would've killed this deal once and for all. With a cocky smile, he stepped into the corridor and waved me out.

When I was two feet from him, he braced his hand on the door frame to his suite, stopping my progress.

'It's okay, Leonora, you can tell me what you really think of me. One of my many assets is a thick skin.'

I took a breath, got hit with that sinful aftershave again and clenched my gut against all the decadent sensations buffeting me. He was just a man. His type was a dime a dozen in this part of the world.

Except it wasn't true.

Gideon Mortimer was exceptional in many ways. Magnetic. Charismatic. Electrifying. And extremely easy on the eyes.

'I was going to advise you not to get high on your own supply but I realised I'd be wasting my breath. What I'd like to know, though, is why have you brought me to the penthouse suite?' I was too busy being dazzled by his smile to check what button he'd pressed. Foolishly, I'd assumed we were going to the tenth-floor brasserie, where I usually met with clients.

He dropped his hand and turned towards the imposing double doors that led into the impressive luxury suite. 'We haven't finished our discussion, and I need a shower before my next appointment in twenty minutes. Two birds and all that. You don't object, do you?'

I didn't answer because his question sounded annoyingly rhetorical.

Swiping the key card, he shoved the doors open, leaving me trailing after him with a reel of indecent images of a naked, shower-soaked Gideon cascading through my heated brain.

When I eventually made it inside, he was standing

before the floor-to-ceiling glass windows staring at the stunning Côte d'Azur view. I'd been in this suite a few times. The magnificent blend of art deco and modern furnishings, the deep blue of the sky outside and the sparkling ocean never failed to leave me breathless. Today that image, framed around Gideon Mortimer like a specially commissioned painting, was threatening to stop my breath altogether.

He really was too much.

Even as the thought deepened in my mind, he was shrugging off his leather jacket, all fluid grace and masculine beauty, carelessly tossing it away to leave a Black Sabbath T-shirt that moulded to his divine V-shaped torso. My gaze dropped lower to lean hips and powerful thighs. And his tight, masculine arse encased perfectly in his jeans.

Thoughts of sinking my nails into that prime piece of flesh as he penetrated me topped my dirty thoughts with even filthier images. Images that should've shamed me but instead just escalated my craving.

For the first time in years, I truly acknowledged my woefully neglected libido and admitted that I needed to get laid.

Pretty. Damned. Soon.

He started to turn. I swallowed before I did something unseemly like drool, and fixed my gaze somewhere over his right shoulder as he approached.

'What else did you want to discuss?' I prompted, hoping to get back on an even keel.

He stopped a foot in front of me, stared down at me with narrow-eyed intent, then jerked his head behind him. 'That window is fantastically reflective. I think it's only fair that if you're going to ogle me like that, I should return the favour?' His voice had grown thick and raspy and, oh, so sinfully delicious.

The punch of heat to my pelvis triggered liquid warmth in my pussy. But I raised my chin in challenge, even as I pressed my thighs together in a useless effort to hide my arousal. 'I meant business, Mr Mortimer. Let's talk *business*.'

'There's nothing wrong with admitting you like what you see. I'll happily supply you with a list of things I like about you, too, if you like.'

I didn't want to know. I truly, truly *didn't*. 'What makes you think I want to hear such a list?' Hell, even my voice was a husky mess.

'I'm taking a leaf out of your book and playing a straight bat, too, Leonora.' His wicked tongue stroked all over my name. 'But speaking of business, I meant what I said earlier. What you've achieved is impressive. Even more so in such a cut-throat world.'

I didn't want to be affected by the sincere respect in his eyes and tone but a different sort of warmth licked through my veins. 'I'm not scared to go after what I want.'

The heat in his eyes receded. 'I know one or two people who share those views.'

I had the distinct idea we weren't talking business any more. 'But not you?'

A hard gleam lit his eyes. 'Oh, I believe in going after what I want. It's in my blood, after all.'

'Oh?'

'My grandfather was a little like you. He started everything in his life much earlier than strict norms dictated he could,' he said. 'He opened his first shop when he was fifteen. Had three more by the time he was seventeen. By twenty-one he was married with two kids and two mistresses stashed on opposite ends of London. He tried to instil that ambitious ideology in his children and grandchildren. Some hit the mark, others didn't.'

I was aware we'd strayed from the professional but I couldn't curb my curiosity. 'And you're one of those who overachieved before their eighteenth birthday, I'm guessing?'

'I borrowed ten thousand pounds from the family trust fund after my first term at university. While everyone was obsessed with becoming the next dot-com millionaire, I started an on-campus three-square-meals food delivery service long before it became a thing. I had five universities under my belt and was turning over half a million by the time I was twenty. I had zero interest in food production, but I left university with enough capital to start my own company.'

'So if you're following his footsteps, why aren't you married with a clutch of kids like your grandfather?' I wasn't going to ask about extramarital bits on the side. That was beneath me.

Like a storm cloud blotting out the brightest sunshine, his face closed up completely. With a graceful swivel that wouldn't have been remiss on a male ballet dancer, Gideon turned and started walking away.

'Where are you going?'

'Shower,' he tossed over his shoulder.

'We still have fifteen minutes.'

'I'll be back in five. Or…' He paused on the threshold of a door I guessed led into a bedroom.

I held my breath. 'Or?'

'Killing two birds is still an option. Your choice entirely, though.' With a mocking grin that didn't quite reach his eyes, he disappeared into the bedroom.

I couldn't.

I *shouldn't*.

Everything about what I was contemplating was wrong. Unprofessional. And yet my feet moved a second later, drawing me inexorably to the open doorway of Gideon's bedroom.

He stood next to a four-poster bed, reefing his T-shirt over his head. Once my gaze locked I couldn't take my eyes off the ripped muscles of his broad, strokeable back displayed in all its indecent glory. My brain was struggling to track when his hand went to the buttons on his jeans.

I must have made a sound because he turned.

Stormy grey eyes drifted over me before he flicked open the first button. 'Are you sure you want to step over that threshold, Leonora?' There was something dark, dangerous and a touch apprehensive in his voice. As if he was fighting his own demon.

Absurdly, it was that note that made me a little bit reckless. 'I'm a big girl, Gideon. A big girl who wants to be done with this meeting.'

His jaw clenched and he turned away. A second later, I imagined I heard him mutter, 'Shit,' under his breath but when he turned back around, that expression of sexy male confidence was back. 'Fine, it's your funeral,' he bit out. With that, he coolly stepped out of his jeans, leaving on a pair of boxers that didn't hide the impressive, mouth-watering bulge behind the thin layer of clinging cotton.

Oh. Sweet. Lord.

The man was *really* well endowed, and from his swagger as he headed for the bathroom, he knew it.

I was replaying every ripple of sleek muscle when I heard the loud hiss of the shower ten seconds later.

I should leave. Retreat to the living room like a sensible professional before it was too late. But again my feet moved of their own accord, crossing the room to yet another, even more dangerous doorway, my pulse racing like a wild thing.

Was this really happening? Was I really doing this? I met the man less than an hour ago, for heaven's sake.

A cloud of steam greeted me as I entered. My fingers tightened around my folder as I stared at the parts of Gideon's body I could see through the gaps in the fog.

One hand was braced on the tiles beneath the shower, while the other sluiced water through his hair. And, holy shit, the reality was way more potent than the fantasy. I wanted to be that water licking over his skin, dipping and sliding over the hard, sleek muscles framing his arse. I wanted to be the gel he grabbed off the shelf and glided lazily over his massive chest, under his arms and lower to his fog-shrouded stomach.

My pussy tingled, my clit plumping and screaming for attention.

'We can continue this discussion or you can leave. What you can't do is stare at me like that unless you want to give me specific ideas.'

Heat that had nothing to do with the shower temperature singed my face. Resolutely, I cleared my throat and reopened my folder. 'I'd like to know about your guests. There's a confidentiality clause that every crew member signs so their privacy will be protected.'

'First things first, did you take my advice and relocate your crew members from Monaco?'

'Not exactly.'

He turned and speared me with piercing grey eyes. 'One thing you should know about me, Leonora, I despise the nebulous. After you explain what *not exactly* means, I never want to hear those two words or anything resembling them again.'

'Has anyone ever told you you're an unpleasant boor?'

He flashed that grin again but again his eyes remained flat. Clearly, my question about having a wife and kids had struck a nerve that still rankled. I curbed my curiosity as he answered, 'All the damn time.'

'And let me guess, you wear it as a badge of honour?'

'You're changing the subject. Explain yourself. And if you're staying in here, come closer. I can barely hear you over the sound of the shower.'

With every cell in my body I wanted to withhold

the information. Or miraculously find a different way of sealing the deal that didn't involve spending almost a month on a boat with this man.

Because my stupid body seemed bent on betraying me, craving him in all the specific ways he'd just suggested.

'Leonora?'

With a deep breath, I did what I came here to do. Offered myself up on a silver platter. Professionally, of course.

My starving libido and needy pussy could take a running jump.

Directing my gaze to his face and nowhere near his spectacular body, I answered, 'I'm the extra staff member. I'll be joining the crew on Monday.'

Several expressions flitted across his face in vivid real time. Anticipation. Hunger. Triumph. Black fury. That last one stayed for a few seconds too long. Then he veered away from me as if he couldn't stand to look at me. He jerkily sluiced back his wet hair and his shoulders heaved as if he was reining himself in.

It was beyond fascinating to watch.

'Fuck.'

The word was delivered with such venom I would've taken a step back had I not felt more than a little powerful at eliciting such a charged response.

'Problem?' The question was a shameless taunt.

He didn't answer. He continued to stand, head bent beneath the spray.

It prompted me to speak just to defuse the thick tension. 'Or if you've changed your mind and no longer need extra crew, I assure you you'll still be well catered to.'

Another few beats went by. Then he lifted his head and looked at me, and my stomach dipped as a lethally gorgeous smile spread across his face. 'I haven't changed my mind, Leonora. I still want what I want, for good or ill.'

'What's that supposed to mean?'

That darkness descended on his face again. 'It means my every instinct suggests it's a bad idea to take you up on your offer. But I'm going to anyway.'

My mouth dried as he twisted the shower tap off. Steam and silence shrouded us as he stared at me.

'Why is it a bad idea?'

He speared me with a telling look. 'Don't play games, Leonora. You know,' he said, his voice softly accusing. 'It's why you're in here when you should be safely in the living room. It's why I'm going to stay put right here while you hand me a towel and leave. Because if I step outside, all bets are off.'

Leave, that voice prompted, a little more insistently. My feet refused to comply.

'So what? You plan on using me as some sort of litmus test of your control?' I asked, my voice a husky mess even to my own ears.

'Yes,' he answered honestly. 'I've been accused of not having enough…restraint lately.' Eyes on me, he licked a drop of water that dripped onto his upper lip. 'So I'd be ever so bloody grateful if you'd hand me the towel, Leonora, and leave.'

I sucked my own lower lip, crazy sensations careening through me as he continued to hold my gaze in the sultry bathroom. 'Say *please*,' I commanded.

His sinful lips slowly parted as he reached out and swiped a slow hand across the glass, clearing a swathe of condensation. His gaze bore deeper into mine, before dropping down my body, and I watched him suck in a pained breath. His eyes were twin pools of turbulent hunger when they met mine again. 'Please,' he gritted out.

My hands were nowhere near steady as I plucked a towel off the heated rail and took a step towards the stall door.

The steam was fast dissipating, revealing more of Gideon's mouth-watering body. In another minute he'd be fully exposed to me.

For another tense few seconds, we stared at each other.

Then those sleek fingers pushed the glass door open and, eyes still holding mine, he held out his hand.

My arm extended but I didn't let go. Couldn't. We stayed connected, our breathing turning more frantic as seconds ticked by.

When he snapped the towel from my fingers it was like a gunshot in the heated room.

I didn't linger to watch him wrap the towel around his lean hips, or step out of the stall. But as I walked away, I knew I'd never been more turned on in my life. Never wanted to fuck another man the way I wanted to fuck Gideon Mortimer.

CHAPTER THREE

Gideon

AFTER TWO LONG weeks of self-enforced celibacy—maddening, unrealistic and utterly fucked-up celibacy I'd imposed on myself because I'd never been a half-measures kind of guy—the delicious challenge of Leonora Branson was like a shot of morphine in my bloodstream.

Hell, she'd nearly made me blow my load with that 'say please' shit.

I'd never begged for anything in my life.

She'd made me *want* to beg. For the damned towel and a whole lot more besides. It was that combination of sexy stubbornness and pure defiance that did it. Not to mention that unfettered boldness.

But if I was honest, she'd floored me back at the airport by being the polar opposite of what I'd expected. Her stiff intransigence over the phone had reminded me of a schoolmistress, and instead she'd turned out to be a nineteen fifties pin-up bombshell.

Simply put, Leonora Branson—even her name was

cruelly deceptive—was too bloody gorgeous for her own good. Coupled with the intelligence that shone from her eyes and her impressive achievements with such a new business success, it was enough to throw me seriously off guard.

It was almost amusing that she was doing her damnedest to wrestle all that brain power and fist-biting perfection into a military-like Armani suit. Leonora would command attention adorned in a sack and still have sex-starved fuckers like me at her mercy.

Or seconds away from stroking their cocks in the shower in full view of her.

Bloody hell.

I sucked in a shaky breath, knew that if I didn't shut off the image of those wide, delicious ocean-blue eyes, I'd come all over the bathroom tiles.

Her expression was cool and collected when I stepped into the living room five minutes later, save for the telltale pulse beat at her throat. I barely managed to resist the urge to test her resolve.

To test mine.

Maybe Aunt Flo was right and I'd developed a self-destructive streak somewhere along the jagged path to oblivion these past three years. It was that niggling suspicion that had made me go the whole hog and throw in full celibacy on the thirty-day no-scandal stipulation. I could only stay on the edge for so long before something gave.

Regardless of whatever state I was in, I couldn't very well blame Leonora for asking the one question that triggered all sorts of shit for me, particularly since for most people the subject of children was a run-of-the-mill question, usually with an easy enough answer.

Not for me.

Not since Damian and Penny betrayed me and I was denied a chance at fatherhood I hadn't even known I wanted until it was snatched from me.

I clenched my teeth and smashed away the memory. But like always, it lingered, acid hot, burning its corrosive poison bone deep. I breathed through it, centring on the more immediate, less volatile picture.

I needed my focus fixed firmly in the present to finalise this deal with Vadim Ilyev, not in the past, where betrayal and back-stabbers lurked.

Since the word had spread that I'd agreed to sign the blasted agreement, a few more brazen family members were openly sharpening their tools in anticipation of my failure.

The Russian deal couldn't fail.

I crossed the living room to where a carafe of coffee sat on a silver tray. Leonora stood next to the sofa, her leather folder braced before her like a Viking shield.

'Coffee?'

'No, thank you.'

I poured a cup, letting the addictive scent of roasted beans suffuse my senses.

She cleared her throat. 'Before we go any further, I think we need to clear up a few things.'

Cup in hand, I strolled over to her. 'You *think*?'

Her chin lifted in a way that made me want to kiss the hell out of her. Then beg her for more. Shit, there was that begging thing again. Curious thing, that.

'I don't usually conduct business meetings like that,' she said.

'So I'm special? I'm pleased to hear it.'

Her lips pursed, then she took the high road. 'I'm willing to forget that…that happened if you are?' A faint blush kissed her cheeks.

I bit back a grin, knowing she wouldn't appreciate it if I said exactly what was on my mind right then. 'Your generosity is much appreciated, Leonora.'

Her eyes widened a touch at my use of her full name. 'It's Leonie.'

'I prefer Leonora. For all sorts of reasons.'

She opened her mouth, no doubt to berate me again, but then changed her mind. I hid my disappointment and gulped my coffee, hoping the caffeine would shock my brain into full efficiency.

'Do you have the leasing agreement?'

She gave a brisk nod and plucked it from the folder. I'd read an electronic copy of it on the plane so I signed it and handed it back.

The breath she released was tinged with relief I was a little envious of because I had a feeling the coming weeks weren't going to be a piece of cake for me.

Damn Vadim and his feet dragging. Damn my blasted family…

'You were going to give me a list of your guests earlier.'

I paced the window and turned around, again find-

ing her gaze on me. This time she was quicker to neu-
tralise her expression.

'By order of importance, my client, Vadim Ilyev,
four or five of his cronies and various hangers-on.
They'll be aboard from anywhere between a few days
to a couple of weeks, depending on how our negotiations go, although I bloody well hope it won't be that
long.' I ignored her startled glance and continued, 'At
some point, some of my family members may drop
by.' Again she sent me a wary glance, no doubt at my
less-than-enthusiastic tone. 'Florence Mortimer is to
be given priority above everyone else if she makes
an appearance.'

Leonora paused her furious scribbling. 'Is that
your mother?'

'In all the ways that count except by birth,' I replied.

She stared. Attempted to read between the lines.
Then she went back to making her notes. 'And you?
Will you be entertaining any special guests?'

'Is that your way of asking me if I'm bringing my
lover aboard?'

She shrugged, her gaze fixed on her notes. 'I'm
simply gathering as much information as possible.'

'Leonora…' I waited till she looked my way. 'It
wounds me that you consider me a man who enter-
tains a beautiful woman in his bathroom when he's
involved with someone else.'

Her gaze didn't waver. 'Technically, I invited myself,' she rebutted firmly.

That brazen way of stating the unvarnished truth
impressed the hell out of me. Penny had been eco-

nomical and manipulative with the truth, right up until her ultimate, unforgivable betrayal.

'But I also think you're the kind of man who enjoys getting under people's skin.'

My grin came away a little stiff. 'Do you think I'm spoilt, Leonora?'

'I think you're impatient and opinionated and domineering and a little entitled. But not spoilt.'

'Why not?'

A triumphant smile played around her luscious lips. 'I know how spoilt, rich people behave. For starters, they don't write letters of recommendation for doormen. It's clear that you can be generous and accommodating when you want to be.'

Bloody hell, she was fucking adorable. And sexy and intelligent in a way that pressed all the buttons that had grown a little rusty in my bid to use superficial pleasure to dull my pain.

Ignoring the resurgent twitch in my groin, I strolled over to perch on the arm of the sofa. She angled her head towards me, her delicate jaw tilted in open defiance that turned me on even more.

'And do you want to know why, Leonora, you in particular—with your charming little suit, your prissily knotted hair and your ballpoint pen—have brought out the worst in me this morning?' I demanded softly, finally giving in to the urge to stroke my finger down her jaw.

She sucked in a sharp breath through slightly parted lips. Her eyes widened but she didn't move away. She stayed exactly where she was, taunting me with her warm, silky skin. Taunting me with what I couldn't have.

When my thumb brushed the corner of her mouth, her lips parted wider. 'What—'

The knock on the door made her jump. I gave an inner groan, dropped my hand and downed the rest of my coffee.

'That would be my next appointment.'

She blinked, then frowned. 'We're not done, Gideon. I need more information.'

'I can fit you in tonight,' I said as I walked to the door. 'We'll meet back here, but be prepared to go out. We'll do dinner first, then… Who knows?'

'I thought you had plans with a roulette table,' she snipped as she slammed the folder shut and rose.

I shrugged. 'She's a cruel mistress when she wants to be. But she's also very patient.' I looked over my shoulder, paused with one hand on the doorknob. 'And, Leonora, wear something that's…not that suit you're wearing.'

Her eyes narrowed. 'There's absolutely nothing wrong with this suit.'

'No, there isn't. And that's exactly my problem.' I didn't think I could handle being in the same room with her without ripping that single, naughty little button holding in her assets.

I pulled the door open before I changed my mind about ending our meeting. On the threshold stood a tall, leggy brunette in a very short dress.

'*Bonjour*, I'm Monique. I'm here as requested, Monsieur Mortimer,' she said with a toothpaste smile.

Behind me, I heard Leonora choke before she covered it with an unnecessary throat-clearing.

I hid a smile. 'And right on time, too. You'll do, sweetheart. Come in.' I pointed down the hall. 'First door on your right.'

'*Merci.*' She sailed into the suite with a wide smile, which faltered when she spotted Leonora.

The two women eyed each other before Leonora tugged on her sleeve and fixed me with a baleful stare. 'Would it be better if I deal with your assistant back in London? That way I can save us both time?'

'No, Leonora. You deal with me and only me.'

I walked to the lift and held it open for her. She slid past me, trailing an evocative scent of lushness I wanted to inhale long and deep from all her pleasure points.

When she reached the back of the lift she executed a sexy little turn, her gaze fixed on my chin for a moment before she flicked it up to mine. 'Thank you for your business, Mr Mortimer. I aim to do everything I can to make your time on board *La Sirène* exceptional.'

I held the door open as it went to shut. 'I'm sure it will be one way or the other. And it's been an interesting experience meeting you, too, Leonora. Expect my call tonight.'

The lift doors shut on her warily speculative gaze.

I gave in to my grin for as long as it took to re-enter the suite and head down the hall to the study.

Monique was already stationed at the spare desk, her laptop opened and the files I'd brought with me set out beside her. She looked up as I entered, a professional smile fixed on her face.

I returned it with a nod and moved to my desk. 'How's your Russian, Monique?'

'Still fluent, Monsieur Mortimer.'

'Excellent. Start with translating the report that I printed off last night. Then we'll make amendments to a few subcontracts.'

'Right away, *monsieur*.'

I slid open my own laptop, answered a few emails and made a couple of urgent phone calls. Then my mind began to drift to a certain curvy blonde.

The bold challenge in her eyes as she'd demanded I say *please*.

The touch of vulnerability she'd tried so hard to hide that made me want to dig until all her secrets were exposed to me.

The business savvy that had seen her land the sort of deal that was usually reserved for much larger outfits than hers.

That pretty pink mouth.

How the hell was I going to survive weeks with her on board a yacht without going insane, breaking my promise to Aunt Flo and acting on the growing list of every fucking filthy thing I wanted to do to the prim and proper Miss Leonora Branson?

Leonie

Stop staring at your bloody phone!

I glared at the mobile in my hand as if it carried the

blame for remaining stone-cold silent. Then I went one better and tossed it on the sofa as I passed it in another fit of restless pacing. It was my own fault for coming up with the brilliant idea to get dressed a whole hour before Gideon was supposed to call. *If* he called.

More than likely he had his hands full with the brunette who'd showed up on his doorstep. Of course, he'd never bothered to introduce her. Nor had he got around to answering my question about whatever special guest he intended to bring aboard the yacht.

So yes, I'd wanted to know for reasons other than my list. Were they even now rolling around on his king-sized bed? Or was he delivering the filthy promises his stormy eyes had promised *me* in the shower?

The memory of my last moments in his bathroom rose like a 3D image—big, thrillingly sinful before my eyes. Gideon might be a cocky bastard, but he had the equipment to back it up, and then some. I hadn't lost my virginity to Adam, but he was my only long-term, meaningful relationship before it all went to hell. Since his betrayal, I'd indulged in two meaningless one-night stands, enjoyable at the time but regretted soon afterwards.

None of the men in my past came close to the heat Gideon was packing. Since leaving his hotel, I'd been struck at the oddest, most inconvenient times during the day with an insane craving to uncover what the steam had hidden from me, watch his beautiful face go slack with lust and arousal as I pumped him. In those dreadful and wicked moments, he'd reduced me to needy ravenous hormones that yearned for one more orgasm with a man who knew how to wring the last ounce of pleasure from a woman.

From the moment I met him, every look, word and deed pointed to the fact that Gideon Mortimer knew the road map to a woman's every pleasure point or would make it his mission to discover even more.

I stared down at my favourite little black dress, picked out with a curiously compulsive need to look my best. My ears and wrists were adorned with my favourite tasteful diamonds and I'd washed and curled my hair.

I grimaced.

My actions whiffed of desperation, which sparked irritation and another round of pacing that took me to the window.

Meeting Gideon had escalated the turbulent emotions he'd evoked over the phone yesterday.

Since my father's atrocious treatment of my mother and Adam's cutting betrayal, I'd sworn never to tolerate bad boys in any shape or form. I didn't need a crystal ball to know I'd be letting myself in for that special brand of male arrogance the moment I stepped aboard the yacht.

Stubbornness attempted to kick in but I resisted. I was used to being shoved out of my comfort zone. Hell, I'd started my business with little more than my meagre savings, a polished business plan and a driving will to succeed, and I'd triumphed.

My hormonal teenager days were behind me, and yet within hours of meeting him all my senses seemed to be poised on some insane precipice that beckoned a recklessness I hadn't felt in a long time, if ever.

The excuse that getting ready early was simple efficiency was bullshit. Truth was, I wanted to see him again. And the anticipation bubbling in my veins had very little to do with business.

A deeper agitation drove me from the window. This was dangerous. Probably because I recognised this burgeoning madness for what it was.

I'd seen a variation of it on my mother's face time and again, even after she'd claimed to have got over my father. The mere mention of his name would bring a rabid anticipation to her eyes that used to embarrass me. Over time, I'd grown to pity that look. That in turn had morphed into helpless bewilderment and anger, which still lingered.

I was nowhere near experiencing that same emotion, but I was cognisant of the fact that it had a starting point. If what I was feeling now was even a fraction of what my mother had lived with for years, then I was better off staying away from Gideon Mortimer.

And yet…

A part of me wanted to wipe that arrogant smugness from his face. I was in complete control. Besides, he had his brunette to occupy him. He could play his wicked little tricks on her.

The annoying twinge in my breastbone mocked my throwaway thoughts. I wanted to laugh at myself for the jealousy spiking through my blood. Instead, I retrieved my phone and placed the call I needed to

Monaco. Five minutes later I'd officially taken my-self off the roster for *La Sirène*'s crew.

Because I'd be foolish to stare at the ashen evidence of my childhood and what Adam had done to me and not learn from my mistakes.

I ended the call, contemplated placing another one to Gideon to tell him of the replacement but stopped myself. It would be better to tell him in person, draw a line underneath that dangerous attraction.

I walked out onto my balcony.

The sunset on the balmy evening attracted the great and beautiful onto the streets below. I people-watched, until my gaze inexorably drifted over to the soaring turrets of the Riviera One hotel.

To Gideon Mortimer and all the dirty things he could be doing with the brunette. Impatient with the direction of my one-track thoughts, I walked back into the living room just as my phone buzzed.

Change of plan. Need to reschedule dinner but meeting is still on. My driver will pick you up at seven thirty.

Irritation flicked to disappointment then back to anger with myself for being disappointed. I was a grown woman draped in diamonds and my best Louboutin heels. Hell if I was going to let that go to waste. My fingers flew over the screen as I tapped out a reply.

Where is he taking me?

The dialogue cloud bubbled and I realised I was holding my breath. I released it impatiently.

Casino de Monte-Carlo.

Cancel the driver. I'll drive myself.

The cloud rippled again.

Very well. But you won't always have things your way, Leonora.

For some stupid reason I gave in to the urge to smile, then I closed my eyes and imagined him saying that last line to me, that edgy hunger on his face.

God, I was losing it.

And yet, despite my admonishment to myself, two minutes later, I grabbed my clutch and leather jacket, and headed down to the private garage of my apartment building. I slipped behind the wheel of my silver Porsche Roadster, my heart thumping as I secured the seat belt and gunned the throaty engine.

The Côte d'Azur was always meant to be where I returned to make one definitive point before moving on. It was where I would rise like a phoenix from the ashes of my relationship and walk away whole again.

And are you whole?

My smile dimmed a little as the question shot alarm through me, bruising a little bit as it slammed into my heart. After a minute, I let it drift away unanswered, relieved when I saw signs for Monaco.

In Casino Square, I handed the valet my keys and, settling my jacket over my shoulder, I entered Casino de Monte-Carlo. Membership of the iconic establishment had been a necessity for my business. Almost every client who visited the South of France craved the singular thrill of throwing a die in the famous casino. I knew the staff by name and I greeted a few as I made my way into the main gambling salon.

Wine spritzer in hand, I drifted through the crowd, the excitement I'd been trying to ignore resurging through my blood as I entered the inner sanctum, where staggering amounts of money were won and lost on the gambling tables. This was where Gideon was likely to be.

When a quick look failed to reveal him, my excitement dimmed a little. I attempted to shrug it off, smiling as a waiter approached with a single glass of vintage champagne.

'Courtesy of *monsieur*,' he said with a thick French accent. I accepted but before I could enquire as to exactly who *monsieur* was, he'd discreetly melted away. When another surreptitious look around the room didn't produce an insanely sexy Englishman with luscious face and panty-melting body, I approached a blackjack table.

I wasn't going to look for Gideon. I intended to deny this crazy craving, for ever if I could. On a reckless whim, I played the next hand of blackjack. And the next. When five in a row tripled my thousand euros, I decided to quit while I was ahead.

Or it might have been that alarming tingle between my shoulders blades that suggested I was being watched. Breath catching, I looked around again, but none of the male eyes checking me out were Gideon Mortimer's. Irritation ratcheted up.

'Buy you another?'

I glanced to my left and the owner of the American accent. He was pleasant-looking enough, and had my treacherous interest not been rooted in a certain businessman I probably would've been flattered.

'Thank you, but no,' I replied.

He tried to cover his crestfallen look with a smile. 'My loss.'

I turned away, suffered through another five minutes before giving in and digging my phone out of my clutch. We hadn't set a definite time for our meeting, and my fingers trembled lightly as I toyed with the temptation to text Gideon.

But again, that smacked of desperation.

'Are you sure I can't tempt you?' the American coaxed again, nodding at my glass.

I smiled. 'I'm still halfway through this one. Let's see how I feel when I'm done, okay?'

His smile broadened. 'Sounds like a plan.' He held out his hand. 'I'm Andy, by the way.'

'Leonie,' I replied, my stomach dipping with chagrin as I placed my hand in his and watched him kiss the back of it.

I didn't want to encourage him, so I quickly retrieved my hand, took another sip of my champagne and noticed a light buzzing in my head. I hadn't drunk enough to be tipsy.

So maybe I was imagining that crazy tingling moving inexorably down my back, intensifying and leaving my whole body gripped in little tremors.

Or maybe it was my need to be fucked, specifically by Gideon Mortimer since those intense minutes in his bathroom, that was driving me insane.

I fished my phone out and typed out a short message.

I'm here.

His reply was equally short and immediate.

Are you? You seem otherwise engaged.

Excuse me?

No, you're not excused, Leonora.

Even via the stark typeface, I could tell he was disgruntled. I was staring at my phone when the next message popped up.

Turn around.

I spun around.

He stood five feet away, piercing grey eyes locked on me. The man was pissed, even as he stared at me as if he owned me.

Those eyes shifted a second later to Andy, dismissed him before returning his stormy gaze to me. 'Leonora.'

It wasn't exactly a greeting. His voice throbbed with something savage and visceral that raced fresh skitters of awareness over my skin.

I stared at him, let his gaze rake me from head to toe, let that barely disguised hunger in his eyes wash over me. I indulged in it for a stolen moment, let it sting my nipples and saturate between my thighs so possessively that it felt as if he were stroking my clit without lifting a finger.

I was still absorbing the effect of his presence when he closed the gap between us.

Andy shifted towards us. 'Hey, how about that drink?' he asked.

Gideon's face tightened. 'That's not going to happen. She's here for me,' he said through stiff lips, his gaze not once leaving my face. 'Aren't you, Leonora?'

Something in his demeanour sent a different set of tingles racing down my spine. A warning that something else was going on here.

I was so caught up in figuring it out, I barely saw Andy leave.

'Shall we go somewhere a little more private?' Gideon asked with that escalating edge in his voice.

'Let's get something straight first. I'm here for a *meeting* with you. Nothing else.'

'I never suggested otherwise. But since we're casting insinuations about, is that how you use your pre-meeting time? Having men slobber all over you?'

A blush surged into my face. 'Excuse me?'

'Again, no,' he rasped.

I took a breath, and bit back my hot response when I noticed we were attracting attention.

Confidentiality rated very high on my list. I never discussed client business in public. Even if this particular client seemed determined to burrow his way under my skin.

'The request still holds,' he extended after half a minute.

I swallowed my irritation. Come Monday he would be my client. I had to maintain a degree of professionalism.

'Fine, lead the way.'

Gideon took hold of my arm but instead of heading to the stunning balcony a few dozen feet away, he steered me to another blackjack table.

'I thought we were going to talk.'

'We were, but I don't think it's a great idea for us to be alone right now.'

My pulse tripped wildly. 'Why not?'

'For one thing, your little flirtation disrupted my lucky streak. I fancy one more roll of the dice before we get down to business.'

Exhaling was a shaky, rushed mess. He nudged me into an empty spot at the table where an indecently high pile of neatly stacked chips stood and fenced me in, his hands braced on either side of me.

When it became clear he wasn't going to continue, I glanced over my shoulder. 'And for another?'

He paused, stormy grey eyes weighing me. 'I believe in brutal honesty, Leonora.'

'That works for me, too.'

'Good. Then you won't be surprised to hear I'm attracted to you. Insanely so.'

Heat licked my skin, inside and out. 'Gideon—'

'So watching some tosser kiss your skin doesn't exactly put me in a good mood.'

'That would explain your rudeness, then.'

'I wanted him out of the way,' he breathed into my ear.

The heavy thudding in my chest went against every instinct to remain objective. As did the sudden craving to lean back against the heated column of hard body. 'But that wasn't just simple jealousy,' I said. I'd seen something more in his eyes.

Again, he hesitated for an uncomfortable stretch. 'No, it wasn't. Someone I trusted took what belonged to me. More than one someone, actually. Between them they destroyed something precious. And I've discovered that a double betrayal has wrecked my ability to be rational in certain situations.'

The raw admission in the middle of the crowded casino staggered me. Enough for me to drop my guard, to let in a kinship I'd never felt before. 'I know what that feels like,' I found myself replying.

His expression shifted, a little of that edge dissipating to leave that sizzling sex appeal threatening to drown me.

'Then you'll forgive any future transgressions.'

God, how was it that even that wry self-condemnation was beyond sexy?

'I don't belong to you, Gideon,' I stressed, perhaps more for me than for him.

He shifted to stand beside me, a wicked smile curving his sensuous lips as his gaze swept over me. He stared at my mouth for an interminable age, prompting a yearning to slick my tongue over my tingling flesh. 'Point taken.' His voice was thicker, deeper, his eyelashes sweeping low and seductive. 'But don't forget the warning, all the same.'

'Place your bets, please.'

The croupier's accented request shattered our strange little cocoon. I yanked my gaze from Gideon's but he continued to stare at me.

'What?' I asked after charged seconds.

'Let's make a wager.'

I shook my head. 'I'm all gambled out for the night.'

'Scared?'

I shrugged. 'I'm not a huge fan of sharks but I swim in the ocean. And I also know when to get out.'

'Take a last dip with me,' he coaxed. 'One small bet.' Contrary to his words, the pile of chips he pushed towards the croupier amounted to tens of thousands of euros.

'Why?'

He sent me a cryptic glance. 'I like to keep things…interesting.'

An alien need to throw caution to the wind seized me and this time I couldn't even blame the champagne swiftly fading from my system. 'What happens if you win?'

'We discuss business…and you spend the rest of the evening with me.'

A steady pulsing between my legs joined the strumming in my chest. 'And if you lose?'

'You get to call the shots on how the evening goes. You can stay or you can leave.'

I hesitated, common sense warning that I was playing with fire.

His eyes gleamed, made another hot pass over my mouth. 'Make up your mind, Leonora. The crowd is growing impatient.'

A quick glance testified to that. 'Okay, we have a deal.'

The words were barely out of my mouth before he nodded to the croupier. As was the norm when staggering sums were at stake, the table went quiet, all eyes on the cards that were doled out and then sequentially revealed.

His arrogant smile said he'd expected to win.

He lost.

While I winced inwardly at the small fortune being scooped up by the croupier, Gideon barely glanced at it, his attention again fixed on me.

I wetted suddenly dry lips, attempted to tell myself I hadn't won any special prize. All I wanted was to finalise our business, tell him I was taking myself off the crew and leave.

The electricity zapping through my system told me differently. For one thing, he was leaning close, way too close, his gaze on my face. 'I'm in your hands now, Leonora. Your wish is my command.'

'Talk,' I blurted. 'Let's find somewhere to talk. Like we intended to…before.'

A smile whispered over his lips as he held out his arm. 'Of course. I know just the place.'

The private salon he led me to was opulent, decadent and empty.

The fireworks detonating beneath my skin grew bolder. Wilder. I attempted to mitigate the sensation by taking several steps away from him. But not once did Gideon's eyes stray from me. I was very much aware he was tracking me as I pretended to inspect every inch of the room.

'How many private gaming rooms did you rent out for the night?' I asked, turning away from that hypnotic gaze to drift my fingers over the velvet blackjack table.

'Three, but Vadim and his entourage seem to prefer the roulette room.'

I stopped, surprised. 'Your client's already here?'

He nodded, prowling slowly towards me. 'That's why I cancelled our dinner. Vadim likes to play games. I suspected he'd pull something like this so I came prepared.'

So he hadn't been delayed by the brunette. The strong relief that washed over me made me frown. 'Do I need to be prepared to sail early, too? I might need to make a few calls to the crew members if—'

Gideon's head shake stopped me. 'He's a heavy gambler. He won't be ready to leave the casino until Sunday night at the earliest.'

My relief evaporated a moment later when Gideon arrived in front of me. 'I don't like to encroach on another man's property, Leonora, so tell me there isn't some guy climbing the walls somewhere while you're here meeting with me.'

'Is that your trust issue rearing its head again?'

Cold, brutal anger shifted through his eyes before it evaporated. Strangely, I wasn't terrified because I knew it wasn't directed at me. 'Very much so.'

'There's no guy,' I replied.

'Good,' he said, but just when I thought he'd move closer, he straightened and put the width of the table between us. 'You wanted to talk business. Let's hear it, Leonora.'

The long, shaky breath I took was filled with him. Hell, his scent invaded me everywhere, including places I desperately wanted him. 'No one calls me Leonora.'

'Then I'm honoured that you grant me that privilege.'

Oh, God.

Right. Business. 'I wanted to know more about your client. His needs.'

'Anything with a fast engine to get Vadim from the yacht to a casino or nightclub when we dock will suffice. And several bucketloads of caviar—he consumes the stuff like it's oxygen. Any other form of entertainment he will provide for himself.'

'Is there anything else—'

'Enough about Vadim, I want to talk about me.'

'What about you?'

He leaned closer, his mouth hovering tantalisingly close. 'I lost a huge sum of money five minutes ago.'

Heat billowed through my body. 'You knew what you were letting yourself in for.'

He winced. 'Ouch. Have a little mercy, Leonora,' he whispered.

God, the way he said my name. Where was the mercy there? 'Fine, I'm sorry you lost a shitload of money. Now, can we get back to—'

'Who was he?'

'Pardon?'

'You said you knew what it felt like. So who let you down?' he demanded, that edge back in his voice.

I swallowed the boulder wedged in my throat. 'I'm not in the habit of divulging my personal details to my clients, Mr Mortimer.'

His mouth twisted. 'Don't give me that Mr Mortimer bullshit. We're past that. Just as we're past all that surface stuff, regardless of how much you want to cling to it. You watched me almost lose control in the shower this morning because you're so fucking sexy I can't think straight around you. Then the next time I see you, some idiot with wandering hands and busy lips is all over you. I lost our little bet, which means you can walk out that door any minute. But before you do, I want to know you a little better, and not just as a damned client. So let's have a simple conversation, shall we?'

It was too much. *He* was too bloody much.

'Simple? You think prying into a painful subject like that is *simple*?' I said through numb lips.

He stared at me for a charged second, then he grimaced. 'Fuck. Any chance that little shitty outburst can be slotted under a misdemeanour?'

I wanted to hold on to the pain and anger mixing inside me but hell…the way he was looking at me…

I dragged my eyes from his, although I felt the steady pressure of his gaze as I walked over to the bespoke bar equipped with a stunning array of liquor. 'Drink?'

He gave an abrupt nod.

I poured a shot of whisky, added two cubes of ice, then fixed a rum and Coke I didn't really want for myself. If he was surprised I knew his choice of drink—courtesy of a little internet research this afternoon—he chose not to comment.

I held out the glass, trying not to ogle his sexy body as he came towards me. He took the drink from me, and I clinked my glass against his. He sipped his Macallan without taking his eyes from me. I followed suit, licked a drop of Coke that lingered on my bottom lip.

Then a fiercely important question burst from my lips. 'Who was the brunette from this morning?'

His throat moved as he swallowed. 'A Russian translator I hired to do some work while I'm here. Are you going to leave, Leonora?'

I didn't answer immediately. I let him wait while I took another sip. Then I set my glass down and stepped up to him. He stilled, his eyes watchful as I reached out and toyed with the top button of his shirt. 'Maybe. I haven't made up my mind yet. But I know that I don't want to talk about my ex-fiancé, who ran off with another woman two weeks before our wedding.'

He inhaled sharply. 'Jesus. I'm—'

I surged onto my tiptoes and silenced him with my mouth. In the last twenty-four hours I'd let things slip to Gideon about myself I hadn't told anyone in years. This man was unravelling me in ways I didn't like, even while he reeled me in with his insane magnetism.

One kiss. That was all I wanted. One kiss and I'd remove myself from his orbit before he delved deeper into places I didn't want him to go.

Except, the moment the gap closed between us and I felt the bold imprint of his cock against my belly, I knew I was sunk.

CHAPTER FOUR

Leonie

TIME STRETCHED ON a taut elastic string, steeping each moment in vivid colour. The hot brush of his firm, smooth lips as I tasted him. The sharp explosions of our breaths mingling when I flicked my tongue over the seam of his lower lip. The springy luxury of his hair between my fingers as I clutched him closer, opened my mouth and boldly attempted to devour him.

The faint aroma of whisky on his breath as he leaned into my touch, imprinted his lower body deeper, harder into mine.

My hips undulated independently of my brain's direction, the bold thrust of his cock firing lustful craving throughout my body.

I wanted this man.

Desperately.

As if he'd heard that unguarded confession, a rough sound rumbled through his chest.

I drew back, a proud, desperate need to know

I wasn't alone in this scything through me. 'You want me.'

Stormy eyes met mine. 'After this morning in the bathroom, you need further proof?' he growled.

I shrugged. 'Maybe.'

His eyes grew watchful, a little wary. My gaze dropped to the drink he still clutched. My fingers wrapped around his wrist, felt the powerful flex of muscle as I nudged it upward. Eyes reconnecting with his, I pressed my lower lip against the glass and tilted it.

Gideon's breath expelled in a heated puff. 'Leonora…'

Despite the fever in his eyes, there was a reticence in his voice that rubbed me the wrong way. Just like this morning, something drove me to test his control, gain the upper hand before he snatched it from me.

With a step back, I perched my bottom on the edge of the blackjack table, and braced my hands behind me.

Gratifyingly, his gaze dragged down my body, lingering on my breasts, my hips, to stare brazenly at my legs as I slowly crossed them.

'Let's finish this meeting, shall we? What else do I need to know about your client?'

He visibly gathered himself, his Adam's apple bobbing as he swallowed again. Draining his glass, he discarded it, then stepped closer. Our bodies didn't touch but his heat drew me like a seductive fire, inviting me to lose myself in his warmth.

Or burn in his dangerous flames.

'He's been dragging his feet on this deal for weeks. I've just about reached the end of my rope with him.'

I uncrossed and recrossed my legs. 'So this is a last-chance schmooze to get him to sign on the dotted line?'

Gideon hauled his gaze up my body. 'Something like that. Although I can't promise I won't throw him overboard if he refuses to play ball.'

'I have insurance for that sort of thing but I wouldn't recommend it.'

A strained smile lifted one corner of his sexy mouth. 'What would you recommend for an intransigent Russian?'

'You're already doing it. You're bringing him on board my boat.'

One eyebrow lifted. 'You're claiming magical powers,' he stated drolly.

'You doubt me?'

He sucked in a slow breath. 'Right this minute, I'd doubt nothing you told me,' he replied, his voice slurring sexily.

The evidence of his fractured control made me wetter. I knew I didn't want to leave this room without at least tasting him again.

Slowly, I let my thighs fall apart. 'Come here, Gideon.'

His eyes grew a shade darker. 'You enjoy calling the shots, Leonora?'

'Does that bother you?' I parried.

His jaw clenched hard, as if fighting his response. I spread my legs wider, my pulse accelerating when his gaze dropped to where my dress had ridden up to reveal more of me.

He resisted for ten long, excruciating seconds. Then he lurched forward. Gideon's hands arrived on my arse, his movements rough as he jerked me forward.

The bold column of his erection slotted perfectly against my damp, silk-covered sex and we both groaned. For a full minute we did nothing but grind against each other, our breaths growing choppy at the delicious friction.

'Fuck, Leonora,' he rasped when I rocked harder against him.

The look on his face was a cross between savage hunger and pained bewilderment, then, with a rough groan, he swooped down and slammed his lips against mine.

Gideon kissed with a ruthless edge that fanned the raging fire inside me.

Our tongues glided together in a bold getting-to-know-you tasting that made me see stars. God, why was I even surprised that he was such a skilled kisser? That I was almost on the brink of orgasm when he dragged the full length of his cock against my needy pussy?

'Jesus,' he muttered against my lips, 'you have an amazing arse.'

'You have an amazing…something,' I muttered back.

He laughed under his breath, raising his head once again to look into my eyes. Bewilderment had receded a little to be replaced by starker hunger. His fingers hooked into my panties and he hesitated, a clear question in his eyes.

Belatedly, I remembered I was supposed to be calling the shots. 'Take them off, Gideon.'

His fingers tightened on my hips for a moment, then he drew my panties down my legs.

God, I was really doing this.

'I've wanted to do this since the moment I saw you,' he muttered against my lips.

'Drag my panties off at a blackjack table?'

'The location wasn't a priority in that particular fantasy, but yes, it involved ripping your panties off at some point and finding out if your pussy tasted us phenomenal as your eyes promised me it would.'

'My eyes said all of that?' My voice was a desire-soaked mess as he planted a firm hand on my midriff and gently pushed me back.

'Oh, yes. Don't attempt to play poker at any point in your life. You'd be shit at it.'

'Thanks for that rousing endorsement.'

'It's not a bad thing, baby. You have the most expressive eyes I've ever seen.'

'What are they telling you right now?'

'That you love sex, that you love being seen to. And that's exactly what you want me to do right now.'

'Guess what, Gideon?'

Gleaming eyes met mine. 'What?'

'You're right.'

I lay flat on my back on the blackjack table and watched him push my dress higher until it was bun-

dled around my waist. I dragged back enough sense
to flick my gaze enquiringly to the door.

'It's locked.' He patted his jacket pocket. 'I have
the key right here.' He reached for my knees, pulled
them up, parted me wider with his gaze still fixed
on my face.

Then, as if he couldn't help himself, his gaze
dropped to my core.

'Fuck, you're beautiful. Pretty, pink and damn
wet.' His fingers tightened fractionally and a muscle
ticced in his jaw. 'Leonora, are you sure about this?'

The cautionary question softened something inside me, even as the thought of him stopping made
me want to sink my claws into him so he couldn't go
anywhere. Again my contradictory feelings towards
this man made no sense. So I pushed them away, concentrated on what I wanted in the moment.

'Yes. Do it, Gideon. Give me what I want.'

Again he seemed to debate with himself.

Then all doubt cleared from his face. His cocky
smile should've put me off but I was long past car-
ing. The way his lips parted hungrily as his bold gaze
stroked my pussy fanned the flames of my lust. The
masterful way he planted my feet on the edge of the
table and drew his fingers down my inner thighs
threatened to make me come there and then.

Slowly, he leaned over me, his goal blatant as his
gaze dropped to my mouth. I stopped him with a finger on his lips.

'I need to say something.'

His eyes narrowed. 'Yes?'

'This is a one-time thing. I'd be disappointed if this ends up affecting our business relationship.' Even as the words spilled out, I knew that when it came right down to it I'd take tonight and let the chips fall where they might. Even if this deal fell through, I would survive.

A hard little smile curved his lips, visceral hunger etched on his face as he stared down at me. 'I'm a big boy, Leonora. I can handle your neat little lanes of business and pleasure without turning into a blithering idiot, if that's what you're worried about.'

His answer wasn't wholly satisfactory but I chose to let it be. After tonight, once this bout of madness passed, I intended for it to be all business.

So I let him close the gap between us, kiss me senseless again while his hands roamed all over my body. At some point, firm fingers hooked beneath the straps of my dress and pulled them down. Between one breath and the next, he had me down to my bra, and his lips were leaving mine to trace hot kisses along my jaw, down my neck to the valley between my breasts.

I didn't need much prompting to lift my torso off the table and let him unhook my bra. I watched Gideon's face as my breasts were exposed to his avid gaze. I didn't like to brag, but my breasts were one of my best features and, from the look in his eyes, he appreciated them.

'Bloody hell,' he muttered thickly, 'you really are incredible from head to toe, aren't you?'

'I can't answer that without seeming horribly egotistical, now, can I?'

He laughed, a deep and sexy sound that washed the tops of my breasts with warm air. 'With a body like yours, sweetheart, you can say whatever the fuck you want.'

'Then what I want is for you to stop talking, Gideon. Right now.'

He delivered another heart-stopping smile as he cupped my breasts in both hands. 'I take it you want my mouth to be busy doing other things?'

I nodded, a little too eagerly and then watched, breath held, as his head slowly descended until his lips hovered over one puckered nipple. He paused for an interminable age, dragging needy pants from me as he teased out the moment. Then he was sucking my nipple into his mouth, his eyes devouring my expression as he teased and tormented the tight peak.

'Oh, God,' I gasped when he dragged his teeth over me. With his other hand he tormented the twin, raining shudders of pleasure down my body.

My fingers sank into his hair, holding him tight to his task as he alternated his attention between one peak and the other. It was a testament to his expertise that I was on the brink of coming just from his nipple action alone when he finally moved lower down my body, trailing kisses on my belly.

'Gideon…'

'I'm not supposed to speak, remember?' he teased, planting kisses on my inner thigh.

I didn't want him to speak either, not really. I preferred his lips exactly where they were, driving me out of my mind. Teeth nipped teasingly at my sensitive flesh, and my hips jerked off the table.

He growled and repeated the action, a little rougher this time. My needy moan seemed to trigger him and this time when his lips trailed down to my pussy, he didn't stop.

He blew softly on my clit, drawing a harsh cry from me right before he slowly licked me from taint to hood.

'Oh, yes.' I loved the way he savoured me with the patience and expertise of the connoisseur.

'Sweet, sexy Leonora.' Hard hands gripped my thighs, holding me wide open as he went back for a deeper taste, his lips and tongue and teeth devouring me as if I were the only tangible thing in his universe.

My hips began to undulate, the whole body hooked into his savouring with an undeniable rhythm born of my hunger.

'Fucking hell, woman, you had to be so damned responsive, didn't you?'

My answer was an incoherent groan. His thumbs parted me wider, held me firmly apart as he zeroed in on my clit, his tongue working me with fevered flicks designed to incite pure insanity.

From behind closed lids, I felt my orgasm approach, bearing down on me like a freight train. Just before it crashed on me, he withdrew, dropped kisses lower, then shamelessly lapped at the wanton wetness he'd drawn from me.

'Gideon, please.' My fingers locked in his hair, attempting to redirect him to where I needed him most.

He didn't answer, nor did he comply with my request.

I dragged myself onto one elbow, watched him lazily lapping me up, then brazenly French kiss my pussy.

'Please. I need it.'

His nostrils flared, as if he'd been waiting for that desperate admission. 'Not yet,' he replied, his voice thick with arousal. 'I want this to last just a little bit longer.'

There was an odd edge to his voice that drew an inner frown. I was too far gone to decipher it, so I resigned myself to letting him use and torment me, my cries growing louder the closer he pushed me to the pinnacle.

When it all got too much to bear, I collapsed back onto the table, threw my legs even wider open and I shamelessly rubbed my pussy against his kiss.

Whether he chose in that moment to grant me mercy or he was also at the breaking point, I would never know. Two fingers slid deep inside me, mouth latched on to my clit, and the dual pleasures quickly tossed me over the edge.

A breath-stealing climax crashed over me, bringing every forgotten erogenous zone in my body into vivid life and reminding me of how badly I'd neglected my needs. And even as I was coming harder than I'd ever come in my life, I still wanted more, wanted it to last for ever.

'Don't stop, Gideon. Please don't stop!'

His groan was a harsh rumble, sending my feminine senses singing at the thought that he was also enjoying himself despite being the one delivering all the pleasure.

Eventually the pressure became too much, my body oversensitised beyond imagination. When I whimpered, Gideon relented, softening his touch and kisses, letting me slowly drift back down.

His fingers were still buried inside me, his breaths washing over my heated core when I dragged myself up onto my elbows. The sight of him, fully dressed in his tux complete with bow tie while I was virtually naked, should've embarrassed me. All I could think of was how incredible he'd made me feel. How soon I wanted to experience it all over again.

My gaze dropped to the impressive bulge between his legs, my body snapping desperate signals. My craving intensified, dragging me up to the edge of the table again, my hands travelling up to circle his neck.

He let me pull him down, let my hungry lips seal his in a kiss aimed to project my renewed hunger. Maybe it was tasting myself on his lips that made me bolder or the fact that he just couldn't seem to keep his hands off me.

I trailed a hand down his six-pack to grip his cock. At his tortured groan, I drew back a fraction.

'Fuck me, Gideon,' I whispered against his mouth.

He tensed, then muttered a curse against my lips.

I stroked him harder.

Dear God, he was big. I went to town, testing his girth, dreaming of everything that awaited me.

Gideon pumped once within my hold, setting my blood alight once more.

'I need you.' I wasn't ashamed to beg.

But I was ashamed when he froze. Then cursed again.

Okay. Not what I'd expected. Maybe I hadn't been clear. 'I want you to fuck me, Gideon. Right here.'

'No. Leonora, dammit. Stop.' It was a command. Ravaged and harsh and reluctant. But an order none-theless. With a pulse of self-loathing anger behind the words that threw cold water over me.

Had I read him wrong? Was this insane hunger only one-sided? Hell, no, it wasn't. I literally had the evidence in my hand.

But he wrenched himself from my grasp, and with quick strides, he put the width of the room between us.

I watched, stunned, as he dragged his fingers through his hair, shoulders rigid as he stared out of the window. Tense minutes passed. We remained locked in place, my senses crackling like fireworks as I tried to understand what had just happened.

Like waves crashing against rocks, it hit me that our little fooling around was over. Hastily, I righted my dress before snatching up my panties. The last thing I wanted was for him to turn around and see me skip hopping into my knickers so I stuffed them in my clutch.

When he faced me, his features were drawn tight, his jaw locked in tight control.

Before he could speak, I raised my chin. 'I'm not sure exactly what's going on here but I'm not going to apologise for anything.'

'Nor do I want you to.' His tone was terse.

'Good, because I could've sworn we were both into it,' I blurted before I could stop myself.

Again he dragged his fingers through his hair, then shoved both fists in his pockets. He rocked back and forth on his heels, his gaze dropping to his feet for a moment before he started towards the door. 'I gave you what you wanted, Leonora. But I can't give you more.'

Can't or won't? The question trembled on my lips, all the reasons why he was denying me flying like crazed bats around my head. I'd sensed his reluctance all along but being rejected still hurt. Not on the scale of my fiancé running off with another woman, but still…

'Come on, I'll take you home.'

'No, you won't. I came here on my own and am perfectly capable of seeing myself home.'

'You've had more than a couple of drinks.'

'What's it to you?' The bewilderment I'd caught in his face moments ago now pulsed through my own voice and I was more than a little irritated with myself for it. This was supposed to be a one-time hookup. The fact that he was calling a halt to it should've pleased me. Yet I couldn't contain my sense of loss.

'It's simple, Leonora,' he drawled. 'I'm not letting you get behind the wheel of a car when you've had a drink.'

'I wasn't planning to. I've got a perfectly good car service on speed dial.'

Impatience twitched across his face. 'Since we're both heading in the same direction, why bother?'

'Don't you have a client to entertain?'

'Vadim can take care of himself. I'm not his babysitter.'

'That still doesn't mean I'm willing to go anywhere with you.' Especially not after that rejection.

'Not even after seeing to that incredible pussy of yours and making you scream my name?'

I couldn't stop from blushing like a hormonal teenager, but I could glare at him and I used the full force of my befuddled anger. 'That was enjoyable enough, sure. What's happening right now isn't, though. Is playing hot and cold your thing, then?'

He muttered something under his breath I didn't quite catch, then he advanced towards me, his eyes roving up and down my body as if he couldn't get enough of watching me. Which was even more puzzling.

When he reached me, he slowly drew his hand from his pocket and rubbed a knuckle down my cheek. 'Do you really think I don't want to fuck you? That every cell in my body isn't yearning to lay you back down on that table and pound us both into next bloody Wednesday?'

I opened my mouth to ask him why the hell wasn't he doing exactly that but I'd already begged him to fuck me, *twice*, and he'd responded by turning his back on me. I wasn't going for thirds.

Right then, another terrible thought hit me, drenching me with ice water. 'Please don't tell me you performed oral sex on me but finally grew a conscience and stopped because of another woman. Because no matter how much you justify it to yourself, what we did already crossed the line the moment you laid a finger on me.'

His face turned to stone. 'One thing you should know about me, Leonora, is that loyalty and fidelity are paramount in my book. I don't forgive easily and I never forgive the smallest betrayal. Remember that.'

Relief crashed over me, as did the unsettling question of why he'd stopped himself from doing what we clearly both wanted. I wasn't going to ask, though. With my orgasm now a hazy memory, my brain was circling back to the initial reason for coming to this room. I hadn't told Gideon about my decision not to join the crew Monday.

I opened my mouth to speak but he was striding towards the door. 'Hang on a second.'

He didn't stop. 'No, sweetheart, I can't.' Again there was that painful throb in his voice. 'I bloody well can't stay in this room much longer, smelling you, remembering how you taste, how you screamed my name when you came, the way you roll your body when you're lost deep in pleasure. You've damned well pushed my control to the limits twice already. I don't want to test it a third time. So I'm taking you home right now.' He yanked open the door and stepped out into the hallway.

The forceful delivery of his words and the renewed fireworks erupting through my body struck me dumb for several seconds, the questions that bubbled to the tip of my tongue forgotten.

When he raised his eyebrow, I forced myself to move.

In silence we left the casino. At the front entrance, a limo pulled up. He held the door open for me. I slid inside, stowing myself at the far corner.

His admission that he wanted me affected me in ways I couldn't describe.

I'd never once taken advantage of my feminine power but, watching Gideon's masculine body slide in after me, I was tempted to push his buttons, tempt him into taking things further.

The door slamming yanked me back into my senses. Was it only yesterday that I'd condemned him for being just like my father in his brazen playboy attitude? And here I was, contemplating playing the siren.

Shame dragged through me, rendering me silent as Gideon pulled his bow tie free and flung it away. It landed on the adjacent seat. Then he tugged on a few buttons before reaching for a decanter of cognac.

When I shook my head at his raised eyebrow, he poured himself a shot and knocked it back.

He was clearly wound tight, and, fresh from examining my own questionable feelings, I chose the safer subject of business. 'There's something I need to tell you.'

'Is there?' Clipped words, as if he was barely holding himself together.

'I won't be joining the crew on Monday.'

Grey eyes snapped to my face. 'Why the hell not?'

'I redid the ratios and I'm confident you'll be fine without me. I also spoke to the captain and his assistant. Between them they can tell you everything you need to know about the vessel.'

'You knew all of this when you came to meet me. You knew this when I signed the agreement. So you deliberately misled me?' Anger throbbed in his voice as he disposed of his glass.

'I thought I could make it work but I can't.'

'Bullshit. You waited until I signed on the dotted line before attempting to renegotiate the terms. Well, too bloody bad for you, Leonora. I'm holding you to what we agreed.'

'Your guest list isn't so extensive that it needs the extra staff member, so it all works out—'

'It doesn't work out if you're not part of the crew. The vessel is your baby. You're supposed to be a good businesswoman. Are you really going to trust someone else to sell it for you?'

'Are you really in the market for a new yacht?' I countered.

One eyebrow lifted. 'If you don't turn up on Monday like you said you would, you'll never find out. And should you not turn up, I'll do you one better and pull the commission altogether. Is that plain enough for you?'

'Gideon—'

'Remember what I said about loyalty?'

I bristled but he had me cornered. 'Yes,' I snapped.

'Good, then this discussion is over. Attempt to pull

something like that with me again and both of us will be very unhappy.'

'Is that a threat?'

'It's whatever the fuck you want it to be. But here's an interesting statistic for you. I had my assistant ring round yesterday to speak to a few of your other clients. They speak highly of you. You've never pulled anything like this before. So I'm thinking this sudden change of heart is related directly to me and not with any crew problems you're having. Am I right?'

I knew backing down would be a sign of weakness. 'It makes business sense to recognise that we're not compatible and to ensure you have a smoother sail without me on board.'

He laughed, deep, but that edge still lingered in his voice. 'You think we're not compatible? You didn't think so when you were begging me not to stop. When you were fucking my face into that screaming orgasm I can still hear echoing in my head.'

'I didn't mean that and you know it.'

'Do I?'

'You're making this unnecessarily difficult.'

'Not at all. You'll sleep on it and know that I'm right. And come Monday morning, you'll be on board along with your crew. Simple as that.'

'You always this intractable?'

'No, Leonora. Anyone else would've been fired on the spot.'

'Why?'

'Because you asked me not to let business interfere with what we did in the blackjack room. This is me not letting it interfere. Shame you can't get out of your own way to make this business opportunity happen for you, too.'

His censure smarted but I knew I'd left myself wide open for that.

'Was there anything else you want to discuss?'

I shook my head, my thoughts scattered and irritated.

'Good,' he replied before dropping back against the headrest and closing his eyes.

I would've thought he'd gone to sleep had it not been for the muscle ticcing in this jaw, and the rod of his erection, still very visible behind his fly. The thickness of it, the memory of it in my hand wouldn't go away.

Again I puzzled over why he'd called a stop. The thought that even now he could've been buried deep inside me, riding us both to bliss, wouldn't let me go.

My pussy pulsed hard and fast back to life, my blood firing up as my clit reawakened to clamour for another experience of what Gideon had given me.

'Please do us both a favour and stop staring at me, darling,' Gideon growled with his eyes still shut. 'I'm hanging on by the barest fucking thread.'

I jerked my gaze away from his cock, but not before I saw his hands bunch on top of his thighs.

'If it's this hard for you, why did you stop? And why the hell did you offer to take me home?'

For tense moments I thought he wouldn't answer.

Then his fists slowly unfurled and he lowered his head to spear me with an intense gaze.

'Because I'm lucky enough to have been born into a family who think it's great fun to stab me in the back just when I'm about to pull off the biggest deal in the company's history. And I—' he gave a self-deprecating laugh '—not only agreed to play by their idiotic rules, I went one better and swore I'd remain squeaky clean for thirty days.'

I was aware my jaw had dropped, that questions were darting all over my face. Questions he could read and half amused him if that tilt of his lips was an indication.

'*Squeaky clean* means what, exactly?'

'It means being a good boy and not begging you to let me fuck you this morning in my bathroom. It means resisting the urge to bury myself in that tight pussy on top of that blackjack table when you asked me to. It means not punching that asshole in the face when he slobbered all over you in the casino. Do you want me to go on?' he demanded tightly.

'So…you can't have sex for thirty days?'

'No, I can't. But when we fuck—and trust me, we will—it'll be filthy and noisy and without a deal I've worked on for over a year hanging over my head. It'll be messy in a way that'll probably make my family ashamed of me all over again, and I won't even care. I have another two weeks on the clock for those damned thirty days and I intend to close the deal in that time. Guaranteed it'll probably be the longest two weeks of my life but what the hell, no pain, no gain, right?'

I wasn't even aware the car had stopped until he leaned close, bringing that hard, hot, delicious body into stinging proximity once again. 'As for why I'm taking you home, damned if I was going to leave you in that casino for another bloody bastard to salivate over, especially with that just-come look lingering in your beautiful eyes.'

'You do realise that with everything you've just told me, I have you in the palm of my hand, don't you?'

He smiled. 'Your integrity won't make you use it against me. Hell, I'm even willing to bet you'll help me bring this deal home.'

'Are you?'

'Oh, yes. If for nothing else, because you want to wield that power you have over me. You want to hear me beg to be inside you as badly as I want to feel your pussy milking my cock as you come.'

The very thought of it made me want to climb into his lap right now, tease him until he gave in. But that brutal honesty he'd laid bare to me was impossible not to respond to. And, dammit, calling me out on my integrity made me yearn to prove him right.

But he was stepping out, coming round to open my door. 'Get out of my car, Leonora. Before both our good intentions turn to shit.'

I stepped out and watched him steel himself against the temptation to touch me. 'You really think you're a special snowflake, don't you?'

He smirked. 'Yes, but you'll relish the chance to teach me otherwise, I'm sure.'

'Are you sure it's a lesson you want to learn?'

'Probably not but I look forward to it all the same.'

I shook my head but before I could walk away, he captured my elbow. 'Please don't disappoint me by not turning up on Monday, Leonora.'

I knew I'd be there. Over and above the tantalising promise of sexual fulfilment, something inside me wanted to discover if Gideon Mortimer was different from the man I'd initially judged him to be.

'I'll be there,' I murmured.

'Excellent,' he breathed.

'Goodnight, Gideon.'

'Before you go…' He casually reached for my clutch. With a deft flick of his fingers, he pulled out my panties. 'I'm keeping these. I think I've earned them.'

I'd never be sure what prompted my response when he released me. 'You can keep them if you want, but next time I'm taking a souvenir of my own. I'll let you decide which form it comes in.'

His smile widened, respect gleaming in his eyes alongside a whole load of anticipation.

'I look forward to our journey together, Leonora,' he echoed my thoughts, then, lowering his gaze to my panties, he twisted them between his fingers for several seconds before tucking them into his pocket.

I walked into my apartment building on unsteady legs. Inside the lift, I turned and saw that his limo still idled on the kerb, the window wound down as he stared at me from across the space between us.

As the lift doors slid shut, I accepted, with more than a little trepidation, that I might end up surrendering a lot more than a pair of silk panties.

CHAPTER FIVE

Gideon

I STARED AT the overweight middle-aged Russian sitting across the table from me, wondering if I'd get away with punching him in the face before his goons wrestled me to the floor.

Probably not. But I was sorely tempted. Four excruciating days after setting off from the Côte d'Azur, we were nowhere near agreeing on the final terms of the construction deal. The only thing Vadim seemed interested in while we sailed past Portofino and the Amalfi Coast was making a dent in my caviar and vodka supplies. Many times I'd come close to calling it and walking away.

But I'd put too much blood and sweat into this four-billion-pound deal to walk away. Besides, I knew my impatience to seal this deal stemmed from another source.

Leonora Branson.

What I'd tasted in the casino back in Monaco had only stimulated my appetite for more. What I hadn't taken into account was that the need would intensify to insane proportions.

It didn't help my frustration that Leonora and her yacht had lived up to their reputation and delivered everything I'd hoped for and more.

Hell, it'd probably worked a little too well where Vadim was concerned. The man seemed determined to take partying to a whole new level. But I was done with his stalling bullshit.

As for Leonora herself…

I wanted her to be mine without the yoke of the idiotic terms I'd agreed to weighing me down. Put bluntly, I'd never felt anything like this in my life. Not even with Penny in those wild days before she'd shown her true colours.

And yet within hours of meeting Leonora I'd referenced the double betrayal that'd nearly sent me tumbling down a self-destructive rabbit hole.

Even in retrospect I didn't regret showing a little bit of myself to Leonora and telling her about the family that was the bane of my existence. And while the little witch tortured me with her tight uniform and sultry looks whenever she was in my presence, Leonora had otherwise remained supremely professional.

Which of course meant I couldn't go five minutes without thinking about her, without silently offering up my left bollock to be done with this deal just so I could hear that breathless *'Fuck me, Gideon'* again.

Frankly, my insane need for her was disconcerting the shit out of me. That pathetic leaping in my chest when I'd spotted her on the marina on Monday hadn't happened since those foolish days back at Oxford when Penny Winston-Jones had strategically placed herself in my orbit and I'd been daft enough to believe it was a fucking cosmic event.

Despite all the warning signs, I'd carried on believing that nonsense, right until I'd found her flat on her back, freely giving away what I'd possessively believed to be mine to another man.

And not just another man. My cousin. My best friend.

The man whose name was in the subject line of the unopened email currently sitting in my inbox. I had no intention of acknowledging the email or having anything to do with Damian. Now or ever.

So I refocused on the beefy Russian. 'There's no getting around this issue, Vadim. This is what we agreed to four months ago. It's still the only deal on the table where the subcontractors are concerned.'

Vadim shook his head. 'It's an insult that they will not deal with me directly.'

I exhaled. 'Let me be blunt. The contractors won't deal with you because you've missed more than a few payments.' I raised my hand when he spluttered a protest in his mother tongue. 'These things happen, we all know that. But your interior ministry won't proceed unless a third party oversees the subcontractors. This is where my company comes in. You still get paid and save yourself the time and energy of having to deal with subcontractors.'

'For an extra fee for you, of course.'

'The Mortimer Group isn't a charity. And I think, for a three-billion-pound profit, you can withstand a small insult, correct? Just think, two years from now, when we've built the most impressive stadium-and-hotel complex the world has ever seen, you get the last laugh.' I gritted my teeth and shamelessly stroked his ego, knowing the subject of money and prestige never failed to win him over. 'So how about we get this deal done?'

He lifted his shot glass, his movements slower, expression circumspect.

I decided to play my ace in the hole. 'One more thing. I have it on good authority that if this deal isn't completed by the end of this week, you'll receive a notice officially withdrawing the tender on Monday.'

He jackknifed upright, the complacency gone. 'What the hell are you talking about?'

'Feel free to look into it. I'm just trying to save us both time, but my company will be happy to wait and deal with the next person who wins the tender.'

His smile evaporated. 'They dare to give me an ultimatum?'

I shrugged. 'I'm just giving you the facts, plain and simple. Five of your companies are fitting out the hotels and leisure attractions attached to the stadium once they're built, with a further two running them for the first ten years. That was our deal.'

'Okay, I'll think about it. Now, it's time for lunch. Your chef has promised me a feast of the best lobster. You will join me for caviar and champagne while we wait for him to delight us, *da*?'

I hid a grimace and followed him out of my office, grateful for the state-of-the-art gym on the lower deck I used twice a day to keep fit. 'Sure, why not?'

His gregarious smile reappeared. 'Wonderful. Leonie will join us, too. I want to hear more about this beautiful boat.'

The skin of my nape tightened. 'Do you now?'

'*Da.* I really like it. I'm hoping to soften her up a little bit so she will renegotiate the price. If we can reach a suitable agreement, I will take her home with me.'

Acrid bile boiled in my stomach. 'I'm assuming you're talking about the yacht?' I bit out.

Vadim paused, a look of surprise on his face. 'Of course. Wait, you think I mean Leonie?' His head tilted, then his smile grew. 'I'm not stupid, my friend. I know when to keep my hands off what doesn't belong to me,' he said, reconfirming the integrity that had stayed me each time I'd been tempted to walk away from this deal.

The acid receded. 'I'm glad we're agreed on that at least.'

Vadim clasped my shoulder. 'You worry too much, my friend. Relax. We will agree on other things, too.'

I stopped myself from demanding his agreement now, just so I could move on to other pressing matters.

Leonora would be worth the wait.

We exited the lift to sun-splashed splendour. As usual, Vadim's right-hand men were present. Although he partied with his entourage, Vadim only dined with his cousins and their wives, none of whom spoke English. It'd turned out to be advantageous since I'd learned one or two things about Vadim's business.

Despite his billions, he was leveraged up to his eyeballs and in urgent need of a fresh cash injection. Which meant his stalling tactics were just for show. And frustrating as hell.

A different set of unsettling emotions whistled through me when I spotted Leonora leaning against the railing, her eyes on the Croatian coast that had come into sight early that morning. I took a moment to run my gaze over her, reacquainting myself with her gorgeous body.

The tailored crew uniform she'd chosen to wear since we came on board did nothing to hide her killer curves and spectacular legs. If anything, like that Armani suit, it stoked my hunger, a hitherto unknown proclivity for a woman in uniform taking me by surprise.

I lingered on the heart-shaped arse cradled in the black knee-length pencil skirt, the memory of caressing those firm globes redirecting my blood south. The neat little waist I'd pictured my hands gripping as I thrust over and over into her from behind was cinched with a utilitarian black belt while a short-sleeved white shirt hugged her top half.

Knowing I risked broadcasting my filthy thoughts to the Russians, I paused at the bar and poured myself a glass of wine.

Leonora executed a perfect pirouette, reminding me that she'd also been a gymnast. Bloody hell, my fantasies grew dirtier. I schooled my features as she approached, that cool, professional smile pinned in place.

'Good afternoon, Gideon.'

'Hello, Leonora.'

Her gaze met mine, paused for a brief, saucy second, then flicked past me to Vadim. 'How are negotiations going, Vadim?'

Vadim shrugged. 'A little give, a little take.'

'And a whole lot of stalling,' I grated.

Vadim smirked. 'He's impatient, this one,' he said to Leonora.

Ocean-blue eyes reconnected with mine as she tilted her head. 'I don't know, Vadim. He strikes me as being infinitely patient if he really wants something. But if you want my opinion, I'd say don't wait too long. There's a fine line between playing hard to get and batting yourself out of contention. It'd be a shame for the latter to happen. Especially since, according to the *Financial Times*, this is considered to be the deal of the year.'

Vadim shrugged again, but I caught a flicker of uncertainty in his eyes as he pulled out his chair.

'If you'll take your seat, your servers will be here momentarily with the first course. I hope everything is satisfactory so far?'

'*Da*, everything's fine,' Vadim said.

I was struggling to wrap my head around what had just happened. With a few clever words she'd placed enough doubt in Vadim's mind to make the Russian ponder the real possibility of losing this deal.

In the past few days, I'd caught several glimpses

of why she was a success at such a young age. She worked hard. But beyond that, she worked intelligently and with a sharp insight to what her clients needed without being a pushover. Even when she said a firm no to the most outrageous demands from Vadim's entourage, they still walked away with a smile.

When Vadim turned to rattle off a stream of Russian to his cousin, I approached her. 'You clever, clever girl,' I breathed softly in her ear.

She rewarded me with the faintest blush and a little pleased shiver without losing the professional smile. 'I'm sure I don't know what you're talking about, Mr Mortimer.'

'Of course you don't.' I poured another glass of wine and offered it to her. 'Here, have a drink.'

She grimaced. 'No, thanks, I don't drink when I'm on duty.'

'There's a difference between having a glass of wine at a business lunch and getting pissed, Leonora.'

The look she gave me told me she was remembering how our last business meeting had ended. All the same she nodded and accepted the glass. 'Thank you,' she said, her voice a shade huskier than before.

My gut clenched against its erotic effect. 'Not at all.'

The arrival of waiters bearing ice buckets of champagne put an end to my wayward thoughts.

Once we were seated, she turned to Vadim. 'We should be docking in Montenegro by sunset. Are you planning on going ashore? If you need recommendations for restaurants or nightclubs, I have a list for you.'

Vadim swigged a mouthful of champagne before

answering, '*Spacibo*, Leonie. Maybe you will like to come out with us this evening?'

'Thanks, but no. It's my day off tomorrow, but I have a ton of work to do so I'm clearing the deck so I'm free to enjoy it.'

'Ah, you work too hard.'

Leonora's smile thinned a fraction. 'I'm ambitious. I make no apologies for that.'

Vadim nodded. '*Da.* But what about other things in life? Look at me. I have my family. Gideon, too, *da*? What about your family, Leonie?'

She tensed. I would've been irritated by Vadim's prying had I not been keenly interested in her answer. 'My mother lives in England with my grandmother. My granddad passed away two years ago. I don't have any sisters or brothers.'

'And your papa? He's dead also?'

Her long lashes swept down, veiling her expression, but I still caught the flicker of distress in her face. 'Not quite.'

The Russian frowned, like me, pondering that she'd left unsaid. 'Being far from them is hard, no?' Vadim pressed.

She shrugged a little stiffly. 'I see them a few times a year. I fly home every few months and they come and see me.'

Vadim opened his mouth again. I stepped in. 'You wanted to ask a question about the boat?'

'*Da, da.* Your boat. It's beautiful. But the price is too high for my blood. I think perhaps we can come to some agreement.'

Leonora sent a stiff smile Vadim's way. 'You're not bartering for a piece of meat, Mr Ilyev. This is a superyacht with a fixed price tag. You've taken the tour and you know no expense has been spared. I'll make you a promise, though. If you make a serious offer, I'll take it back to my consortium and we'll seriously consider it.'

'Or you can let this one go altogether and consider a less expensive toy?' I threw in.

He smiled a little philosophically. 'Maybe...maybe.'

He grilled Leonora about the boat through the rest of the meal. A meal she picked at, while her wine went untouched.

By the coffee stage, I'd had enough. 'Ilyev. You've had three tours of the yacht. The stats aren't going to change. If you need specific workings of the yacht, speak to the captain.'

Beside me, Leonora let out a sharp breath. 'What the hell are you doing?' she demanded fiercely under her breath.

'Saving you from bullshit,' I muttered.

'I don't need you to run interference—'

The hand I placed on her thigh halted her words. She masked her tiny jump by shifting sideways, attempting to dislodge my touch. I grasped her tighter, slid my hand under her skirt to grip her bare flesh.

Tense seconds passed in silence. She met me stare for stare as her hand dropped to grip my wrist. Heat spiked through me as her nails dug into my skin.

'Go on, then,' I urged, noting that she wasn't actively trying to displace my touch. Taking the chance,

I slid my hand higher, encountering warm, supple flesh that I wanted to glide my tongue over again. I drew slow circles on her skin, then went another inch higher.

She drew in a sharp breath, clamped her thighs together and cleared her throat. 'Did you need anything else, Vadim?'

His eyes swung from Leonora to me. Then he sighed and rose from the table. 'Gideon is right. The time is not right. Maybe in future we can do business.' With that he snapped his fingers at his entourage and one by one they staggered off the deck.

'What the hell was that about?' Leonora hissed at me.

'A reminder of what I told you in Monaco,' I rasped.

I was pleased that her breath shook when she exhaled. 'You assume that I'll forgive your caveman tendencies.'

I shrugged. 'I live in hope?'

One sexy eyebrow lifted. 'Is that a question?'

'Will it get me out of the doghouse?'

'Please remove your hand and I'll think about it.'

'I have an idea. How about my hand stays exactly where it is and I can reward you for what you did with Vadim earlier?'

Her breathing altered again. I shifted in my seat as my cock reacted to her.

'I prefer to choose my own reward, thanks.'

She didn't ask me to remove my hand. I took that as progress. 'Very well. Drink your wine while you think about it, though. It's a good vintage. It'd be a shame to waste it.'

She toyed with the stem of the glass for several seconds, her eyes slowly lifting to meet mine. I felt my hackles rise. I probably wouldn't like whatever she was scheming but I didn't want to stop touching her so I stayed put. 'Tell me more about your family,' she said after taking a sip of her wine.

'Bloody hell,' I snarled.

'Gideon…'

'Do you have any idea what it does to me to hear you say my name like that?'

She blinked. 'Like what?'

'It starts off prissy but ends in a sigh. It's really quite extraordinary.'

'I'm not… I don't… You're changing the subject.'

'Yes, I am.'

'Would it help if I said I'd looked you up on the internet, in the name of research?'

My thumb glided over her silky smooth flesh. 'No. Because whatever you read is probably not true or just the tip of a colossal iceberg.'

'Give me just the tip, then,' she said, then blushed.

I laughed at the unfortunate double entendre. 'In this instance, okay. What do you want to know?'

She drank another sip, her tongue gliding over her bottom lip when she set the glass down. 'You started a separate business with your brother after university. Why isn't he working with you on this deal? Did you two fall out?'

I felt my spine stiffen. 'Not exactly. Bryce enjoys

building hotels. The market for that is bigger than ever in the Far East. When we merged our company with the family business, he chose to stay in Singapore, build a few more hotels for The Mortimer Group there.'

She regarded me steadily. 'And...?'

Dammit, she was a little too perceptive. 'Things have got a little...strained between us since I returned to London.'

'Because you left Singapore?'

'Because he sided with the enemy,' I replied with more than a little snap in my voice.

'How?' she asked softly.

Tension throbbed at my temple. 'You haven't earned the details, Leonora.'

She remained silent for several seconds, then her hand slipped beneath the table. Eyes on me, she trailed her fingers over mine before pressing my touch deeper into her warm inner thigh. 'Haven't I?' she breathed.

Bloody hell.

I cleared the lump of arousal in my throat. 'He went against my express wishes and did business with the person who betrayed me.'

She gasped softly. 'Did he know he was doing that?'

My teeth ground together as I shrugged. 'Remember that streak of irrationality that plagues me sometimes?'

'You didn't tell him why?'

'He didn't need to know why. He needed to be loyal to me.'

Her smile both condemned and absolved me. 'Okay.'

I nudged her legs wider apart, my fingers seeking further warmth. 'Enough about Bryce. Graciela, my sister, I see a little too much of in the tabloids, which you'd think would be a problem for my stuck-up family considering she works in PR for TMG, but apparently they're more forgiving when it comes to her. As for my parents...' I took a breath. 'They're dead—my father from a heart attack brought on by too much drink and my mother from a heroin addiction that caused her to drive off a cliff at high speed.'

Sympathy darkened her eyes. 'Gideon, I'm so sorry.'

'At the risk of sounding heartless, I don't feel their loss that much. They were strangers for most of my life.'

'But if you've wished for a moment that they weren't then you've felt something,' she said, again in that gentle voice I wanted to wrap myself in.

I pulled myself back from that temptation. Trust had got me nothing but pain and betrayal. Whatever was happening between Leonora and me didn't need that elusive ingredient to make it work.

I lifted her leg and draped it over mine. 'We're done talking about my family now, Leonora. But I feel like I owe you.'

She reached for her glass and took a slow sip of wine before her gaze swept up to meet mine. 'So?'

My gaze dropped to where my fingers caressed her, and got momentarily lost in the beauty of her skin. Her small hitched breaths weren't helping me stay coherent either.

I leaned in close, brushed my lips over her earlobe and thrilled in her small shiver. 'So for helping to push this deal along and for possibly stopping me from tossing Vadim overboard, I'd be honoured if you'd let me watch you come again.'

Heat surged into her face, her jaw slackening as lust filled her eyes. Then she pressed her lips together. 'Gideon…'

'You want me to beg, Leonora? I will. I'm going out of my damned mind imagining what it'd feel like to be buried deep inside you. Give me the second-best thing.'

She took another shaky breath. 'Aren't…aren't you risking your deal by pursuing this?'

I grimaced. 'Well, if I ever get round to pulling it off, it'll be the biggest in my company's history. There are a lot of people rubbing their hands in anticipation of me getting the job done.'

Her eyes widened. 'What exactly are you negotiating?'

The deal had been in the financial papers for months so I wasn't breaching confidentiality. 'I'm building a stadium, five sports centres and fifteen hotels. Once completed it'll be the largest such complex in Europe. *Once completed* being the operative words.'

'Wow,' she murmured.

'Can I say that impressing you turns me on even more?'

Her sexy smile only heightened her beauty. 'You can say it, sure.'

My gaze dropped to her lips, and I was struck with the need to kiss her again. Instead I slid my hand higher until my fingers brushed the edge of her panties.

'Gideon, wait.'

I forced my fingers to halt their exploring.

She exhaled a little shakily, a wariness creeping across her face. 'That look on your face at the marina on Monday? What was that all about?'

Unease punched me in the gut. 'I wasn't absolutely certain you'd turn up. In fact, I was surprised to see you there.'

Her gaze probed mine. 'That wasn't surprise I saw, Gideon.'

My unease grew. What did she see when she looked at me? The tatters left behind after a double betrayal? 'What did you see?' I dared.

Her eyes grew a shade darker. 'It was…the way you looked at me. As if you were pleased to see me and hated yourself for it.'

Brutal honesty demanded I come clean. 'I was. I did.'

'Exactly how am I supposed to react to that?'

'We're talking without games or artifice.'

'Are we? Then tell me what you're hiding.'

'Leonora.' My voice pulsed with warning she couldn't miss.

But her gaze boldly held mine. 'You didn't hate me for turning up, you hated me because I don't fit into some perfect mould in your life and you don't know how to handle it.'

'If we're speaking plainly, then yes. You intrigue me, Leonora. Very much. And I'm not sure if I'm ready for this level of intrigue. But I do know I've been dying to touch you for four bloody days. And here you are. But you're hiding something, too, aren't you?'

Her gaze dropped from mine.

I renewed my caress, my fingers brushing her silk-covered pussy. 'But while I'm greedy to know you inside out, I'm willing to let you keep your secrets. For now.'

She made a little sound in her throat.

'Do you want me to stop?' I asked.

Her eyelids fluttered. 'Would you believe me if I said yes?'

'I'd believe you.'

Her lips parted but no words emerged.

'Say it, Leonora. Be honest with me.'

'Okay. You intrigue me, too.'

'And?' I pressed, that alien need clawing at me.

She shook her head. 'Gideon, this is crazy.'

'You're saying a lot of words but I'm not hearing a no.' My fingers slid beneath her panties, grazed her clit.

She jerked in her seat and her thighs fell open just a fraction wider, enough to grant me further access.

'This thing between us is driving you as insane as it's driven me,' I muttered, the scent of her washing over me, fracturing my concentration.

'This *thing*?' she slurred slightly. 'You mean the *almost* sex you're *not* supposed to be having?'

I couldn't help laughing. 'Is that what this is?' I pressed my middle finger over her clit, applying increasing pressure to the bundle of nerves.

She gasped, her fingers gripped tight on the edges of her seat.

With my free hand, I dragged her chair closer. I wanted to absorb her every expression. 'Leonora?'

'Yes?' she moaned the word.

I made another pass over her plumping flesh. She shuddered and pushed herself against me.

'Open your shirt for me, darling. I've been dreaming about your gorgeous tits for days.'

We were at full sail towards Montenegro with no one around to witness our activities on the top deck. Her crew were well-trained not to interrupt unless they were summoned.

With hands that weren't quite steady, she undid the first three buttons of her shirt, exposing a lacy bra with a front fastening. A quick snap and her full, ripe breasts spilled out, drawing a groan I couldn't stem.

'Jesus, you have magnificent tits. Do you know that?'

Her very feminine smile was my answer. Hell, the woman confidently owned her assets and celebrated them.

I slid my finger through her wet heat, delighting in her small pleasured cry as I repeated the action.

After several passes, I buried two fingers fully inside her. 'Do you like that?'

She inhaled sharply and nodded.

I cupped one heavy breast, glorying in the immediate tightening of her nipple. Unable to resist, I lowered my head and drew the puckered bud into my mouth.

God, she tasted like heaven. Her head tilted back as she attempted to ride my fingers.

Her unfettered responses were the stuff of carnal dreams. Leonora was the only woman in a long time that I'd craved seeing after our first sexual encounter, one-sided though that had been.

I wasn't selfish in the sack by any means, but in the past my goal had been to achieve mutual satisfaction as many times as possible in an allotted time frame.

The fact that I was gifting her another one-sided trip to ecstasy should've irked the selfish bastard in me, but damned if I didn't want to keep hearing those mindless little cries and feel the sensation of her wet pussy tightening around my fingers with every thrust inside her.

What the fuck was going on? It was almost as if I was addicted to the way she rolled her hips while in the throes of pleasure. I sucked her harder, and was rewarded with a deeper moan.

'Good?' I asked.

Her eager nod proceeded a gasped 'Yes!' that wrapped itself tight around my cock.

And still I couldn't get enough. 'Are you going to come for me, sweet Leonora?'

'Yes!' She raised her whole body off the chair, undulating with abandon as she met my piston-fast fingers. 'It's so good, Gideon. Don't stop. Please,' she begged mindlessly.

Wasn't it just beyond ironic that the moment I

agreed to behave myself for the sake of my unde-
serving family, a unique woman like Leonora would
land on my lap? I was pretty sure Lady Karma was
laughing herself stupid for fucking me over like this.

Every second of the remaining days of my self-
imposed celibacy would be hell, but if this was a
fraction of what awaited me at the end, it would be
worth it. Her soft cries grew sharper, her skin flushed
deep pink.

'Are you close, baby?'

'So close,' she gasped. Her whole body shook as
the first wave of her orgasm hit hard. I drew back a
touch, not wanting to miss a single frame of the incredible scene unfolding before me.

A blush suffused her whole body, her parted lips
temptation itself as her breasts lightly bounced to my
thrusts. When her convulsions intensified, I reached
for her nape, holding her in place as she shuddered
wildly around my fingers. Her sweet pussy clenched
and unclenched, so beautifully tight, it was all I could
do not to drop my trousers and ram my throbbing cock
inside her. When the urge grew too hard to resist, I
dragged her closer and fused my mouth over hers.

I kissed her down from her high, waited until her
breathing quieted, before I withdrew my fingers.
Eager for a taste of her, I licked my fingers. Lust-
drugged eyes widened as she watched me.

'I wish we were somewhere more private so I could
taste straight from the source.'

Her blush deepened. 'Oh, my God, you're unbelievable.'

I laughed and the sound was a gruff mess even to my own ears. '*Now* you're embarrassed?'

'I'm not used to a guy who's so unapologetically vocal about everything.'

That grated more than it should, probably because of all the secrets I'd exposed to the light of day. 'What kind are you used to?'

She fastened her bra and began rebuttoning her shirt. I wanted to bat her hands away, command her to leave it so I could continue feasting my eyes on her. But there was the credible threat of tossing anyone who saw her like this overboard.

'I thought you were going to let me keep my secrets for now?'

Her reluctance chaffed even more. 'Maybe I've changed my mind.'

'You think you have rights just because you've given me two orgasms?'

'Two *incredible* orgasms. I'm keeping tally, Leonora. Zero for two isn't really my ideal score.'

Her gaze dropped to the crotch and the full tent in my trousers. 'Abstention is meant to be good for the soul, isn't it?' she teased.

'My soul would be no bloody use to me if I die of blue balls, would it? Tell me I can have you any damn way I want when the time comes and I may just survive.'

She tilted her head. 'I'll think about it.'

Her features settled into a different expression as she stared at me for several long seconds.

'What?' I asked when I couldn't stand the silence.

'You may not be the total bastard I took you for when we first met, after all.'

The oddest sensation tightened on my nape. 'Don't be in a hurry to change your mind about me, Leonora.'

Her eyes darkened. 'You're warning me off?'

'I'm dying to feel your tight pussy around my cock. I'm dying to see the rapture on your face when I make you come with more than just my fingers. I may let you into a few personal details along the way. But don't hold out hope for more beyond that.'

She tensed and pulled away. 'How conceited of you to think that just because I find you remotely redeemable, it automatically means I'm catching feelings. Let me be clear. It just means that *if* at some point in the future I let you have me, you not being an arsehole means I can live with myself afterwards. If that's too much for you to handle—'

'I can handle that,' I slid in, that unnerving sensation that I was losing the plot intensifying.

'That's good to know.'

'And I prefer *when*, not *if*.'

'We'll see about that.' She rose and straightened her clothes. 'I have work to do. I'll see you later.'

CHAPTER SIX

Gideon

I WATCHED HER leave the deck, my cock on fire and my insides all twisted up once again. What was supposed to be an enjoyable interlude had turned into something else.

She reached the stairs and glanced back at me, a contemplative look in her eyes that unsettled me further. It said she saw beneath my surface, perhaps saw something even I wasn't aware of. I wanted to race after her, demand she tell me.

I stayed put and let the moment pass until she left the deck.

Maybe I was overthinking things. I blamed that email sitting in my inbox and the flurry of emails from Aunt Flo that had followed it.

As if conjured up by my thoughts, my phone buzzed, displaying a picture of Aunt Flo.

With more than a little trepidation, I snatched it up. 'Calling to check up on me?'

'You haven't answered any of my emails. Do you need checking up on?'

'Probably.'

'Should I be worried?' Aunt Flo asked.

My irritation dissolved and I smiled. 'No.'

'Good. Now, tell me how the business with the Russian is going.'

I filled her in, welcoming the chance to dwell on something other than Leonora. Or Damian. Or Bryce. Or, dammit…my *feelings*.

'Hmm, I've dealt with a troublesome Russian once or twice in my time.'

I laughed. 'I feel a bout of sage advice coming on.'

'The trick is to drink them under the table first. Once you show your stamina they'll be yours for life.'

'I need him sober to sign on the dotted line.'

Aunt Flo snorted. 'Well, that's unfortunate. But you're clever. That's why you're my favourite.'

The peculiar note in her voice drew me up short. 'Is everything okay?'

'I'm fine. You know I always get a little low just before my birthday. Besides, I didn't call to talk about me.'

Her voice had grown soft, a sure sign that I wouldn't like what was coming. 'Whatever you called to tell me, let's have it.'

She sighed. 'I know you haven't opened the email. But there's no other way to say this, my dear. Your cousin is back.'

The sunshine beating down on my shoulders turned arctic. 'Say that again.'

'Damian is back in London.'

'Did we or did we not agree I wouldn't kill him

on condition he stayed away for a bloody long time? And by a bloody long time I mean *indefinitely*. The last I checked indefinitely wasn't *three fucking years*.'

'Things were said in the heat of the moment that night, Gideon. I had to get you out of there before you two killed each other. I'm hoping cooler heads will prevail now—'

'I wouldn't hold your breath. You give me too much credit if you think I'm anywhere near as calm as you want me to be.'

'You can't avoid each other for ever,' she snapped, her voice brusque once again. 'And, like it or not, he's still a member of this family.'

'That's where you're wrong. He means less than nothing to me.'

Aunt Flo gasped. 'You don't mean that.'

Unfortunately, the pain-filled rage rippling through my chest cemented my certainty. 'Don't I? He betrayed me.'

'I know. And I know how much loyalty means to you. But you must find a way around your feelings. He's retaking his seat on the board at the end of the month.'

My jaw ached from being clenched so tight. 'The last I heard there needed to be a vote before that happened.'

'There will be. I'm just telling you what the outcome will be.'

I didn't soften my curse.

Aunt Flo sighed again. 'Haven't you both suffered enough?'

'No, I don't think he suffered nearly enough. In fact, the whole of his lifetime sounds just about the right amount of suffering.'

She didn't reply for a handful of seconds. 'I hear you're thinking of buying a boat.'

I breathed deep, accepted the change of subject. 'It's a superyacht. It's beautiful. You'll love it.' For a moment I wondered whether Aunt Flo would like Leonora, too. Then I realised what I was thinking and stepped back from the thought.

'Hmm. Maybe I'll come and see it myself.'

'Aunt Florence—'

'You leased a floating palace for the better part of a month and issued an open invitation to your family. That includes me, doesn't it?'

'You know it does,' I murmured, trying to think what her angle was.

'Wonderful. I'll let you know when to send the plane for me.' She hung up abruptly.

I stared down at my phone, knowing I should've seen this coming. Aunt Flo wouldn't have sent the email if she hadn't wanted to prepare me.

Damian had balls to show his face, I had to give him that.

My lips twisted. Wasn't his ruthless audacity the reason we'd been so close once upon a time?

I slid the phone into my pocket, my gaze bouncing over the horizon. Any enjoyment of the stunning blue waters or the way the sleek yacht cut through them was gone.

With the distance of the Atlantic between us, the

ashes of my relationship with Damian had been truly out of sight, out of mind. But I admitted there were times when the consequences of his actions reared its ugly head.

I thought about him and his betrayal every time I glimpsed a deepening interest in a woman's eyes and questioned its authenticity. Hell, I'd done that at the marina with Leonora, and repeated it less than ten minutes ago.

Each time I left a lover's bed with that hollowed-out feeling deep inside, I cursed him.

Granted, with the kind of parents I'd been cursed with, trust had already been a dicey issue for me. Damian's actions had shattered that beyond repair. Penny's contribution had cemented that destruction and, between the two of them, they'd fucked me over well and good.

So no, I was nowhere near ready to bury the hatchet. Unless I was burying it in the back of my cousin's skull.

Fresh anger riding me, I headed for my office on the lower deck but, once there, the mountain of work I'd intended to bury myself in lost its pull. Instead I found myself thinking about Leonora. The look in her eyes when I'd talked about my brother. The one that now had guilt tightening my nape.

Bloody hell.

She was screwing with my head, evoking emotions I'd thought had turned to dust in my broken soul.

At least one advantage of Aunt Flo's call was that the pressure below my waist was no longer a problem.

That would change the moment Leonora came within touching distance. Hell, she turned me on as no woman had in a long time. Even without the benefit of the complete picture, the look in her eyes when I'd told her about my agreement lingered in my head.

With startling clarity, I realised I wanted more of that look, wanted a change from the shallow sex and mindless pleasure-seeking.

Sure, it had *potential emotional landmine*—the kind I avoided like the bloody plague—written all over it. But had I really left the landmine behind after Damian's betrayal or had I simply been too numb to feel the detonations? I rose, prowled to the window and stared unseeing outside the porthole.

What the hell was she doing to me?

I should be concentrating on finding a way for Vadim to fall in line. Instead I returned to my desk, pulled up the programme that listed all The Mortimer Group's work in progress around the world, specifically the Far East file.

After a quick perusal, I fired off a text.

I received a response within minutes.

WTF? I don't hear from you in over a year and you get in touch to criticise my work?

I grinned at Bryce's belligerent tone.

The Diamond Bay's rooftop pool should've been twenty metres longer. At least.

It still won the award for the largest suspended pool in the world. And shouldn't you be concentrating on a certain Russian who I hear is drinking our coffers dry?

I wasn't surprised Bryce was up to date with my stalled deal.

It'll be in the bag before the week's out.

Big talk. Want to back it up with a bet?

A case of Macallan 1926 *when* I bag the deal?

Make it more interesting. A bottle of Macallan M hand delivered by the loser.

My fingers paused above the keyboard, a curious sensation I recognised as elation expanding in my chest. I placed the blame squarely at Leonora's feet.

You're on.

I look forward to enjoying it with the view from *my* rooftop pool.

I was chuckling when the next message arrived.

It's good to hear from you, Gideon.

Part of me wanted to stay pissed that Bryce had consulted with Damian on a few projects against my express wishes after Damian had relocated to New York. But then I'd never told him why I suddenly detested Damian. Bryce hadn't taken that well.

I sighed and typed. It's good to be heard.

I sat back in my chair, feeling lighter than I'd felt in a very long time.

And when the urge struck me to find Leonora and tell her about my exchange with Bryce, I killed it dead.

I couldn't deny that whatever it was that pulled me towards Leonora, she had me hooked. Nor could I deny that I was looking forward to riding the storm. But that was all.

And right now, I had a bet to win.

I tackled my paperwork for the next two hours, then fired up my laptop. My assistant had done a good job of streamlining my inbox, which meant *that* email was at the top of the queue, highlighted and screaming for attention.

The lightness faded. Everything blurred away until only a single image remained, one I'd been trying to forget for the better part of three years.

Damian and Penny.

Their double betrayal had derailed me for a long time. Enough for me to keep tabs on Damian for almost a year, the need for vengeance burning harsh and bright.

He'd more than succeeded with his business ventures in the States. Hell, he'd *thrived*, the addition of his name to a popular venture capitalist TV show elevating not just him, but The Mortimer Group by association.

For the better part of the year, the desire to destroy him the way he'd destroyed me had occupied vast amounts of my waking moments. That need for vengeance no longer burned bright.

Granted, I'd redirected it when the true depth of betrayal had been revealed much later. The final blow Penny had struck by getting rid of my child was not only unforgivable. It'd been unforgettable.

Unlike with Damian, I hadn't throttled back my vengeance when it came to her. Especially when I found out she was using my name to bolster the event-planning career that was so precious to her.

I'd derived immense satisfaction from watching her twist in the wind after losing one client after the other.

That satisfaction eased my fury now.

If Damian was intent on bringing himself back into my orbit, then I'd deal with him when the time came.

Till then, I had an empire to run.

Leonie

I watched the speedboat depart with the last of Vadim's guests for the bright light of Budva, a quarter of a mile away.

At just past eight p.m. I was officially off the clock, but my inner boss lady hadn't relaxed until the guests were off the boat.

I was dressed to go out, too. Montenegro in general and Budva in particular were two of my favourite places. While researching places to bring my clients, I'd fallen in love with the place. From my balcony, I spotted the smaller water taxi I'd organised for myself approach. Purse in hand, I left my cabin and headed for the first-floor deck.

I hadn't seen Gideon with Vadim, and, finding myself watching out for him, I'd grimaced with self-disgust. The hours I'd spent convincing myself I was better off staying clear of him frittered away to nothing as I caught a glimpse of his tall, breathtaking body, leaning against the railing.

I still couldn't believe what had happened at the lunch table, and not just that mind-blowing orgasm he'd given me. There was something about hearing the man admit his flaws while clinging to his vows that had kicked something into life inside me. I'd walked away from the deck craving him even more.

But as he'd pointed out himself, I'd be a fool to let any newly discovered attributes sway me from the fact that the man could reduce me to a blithering mass of sexual emotion while barely exerting himself.

Our business together was transient at best. And now I knew the true nature of what was going on with him, I didn't intend to become the toy he amused himself with while he waited for his self-imposed sentence to be over.

Gideon spotted me and approached as I reached the exit ramp. 'Going somewhere?'

'Yes, I'm heading into town. I'm officially off the

clock. If you need a ride off the yacht, I can make a call for you.'

One corner of his mouth quirked in that sexy way of his and I struggled not to let his heated gaze affect me as it moved from the top of my head to my feet.

'Or I can catch a lift with you.' His eyes performed a return journey up my body.

My olive-green dress wasn't as sexy as the black number I'd worn to the casino, but it showed enough bare legs, arms and shoulders to make a statement.

The bareback design also negated the need for a bra and I watched his gaze blatantly linger on my breasts for five flame-inducing seconds before moving up to my face.

'Do you mind?' he asked.

When I shook my head, he held out his hand.

I took it, let him help me into the taxi, and when his fingers lingered on my skin I tried not to hyperventilate. He followed me to the bench seat at the rear of the boat, sat down next to me and spread his arms along the top of the cushioned seat. The action brought his body sizzlingly close to mine, his aftershave tantalising my nostrils.

When the movement of the boat nudged his body against mine, I clenched my thighs to keep from making full body contact with him.

'Aren't you joining your guests?' I asked as the small speedboat raced us towards shore.

'No. A tactical withdrawal is in order tonight.'

I took in his attire, the way the tailored black trousers clung to his powerful thighs and his dark purple shirt emphasised the lean, hard masculinity of his upper body. He'd showered recently if the damp strands neatly styled were any indication. Thoughts of showers reminded me of what had happened in his hotel suite on our first meeting. Imploring myself not blush, I met his gaze.

'Are you headed anywhere in particular? The taxi can take you if you like.'

He didn't immediately answer, granting me the excuse to study his face as we stepped onto the pier. Something wasn't quite right. There was a stiffness to his jaw, tension riding his shoulders. 'Is everything okay?'

Piercing grey eyes locked on me. 'Nothing a few drinks won't take care of. And since I don't have a destination in mind, mind if I join you?'

'Join me?' I parroted, fighting the throb of excitement suffusing me.

He nodded. 'Unless you object? Where are you headed?'

'For an appointment five minutes away. I don't want to be late.'

His eyes narrowed. 'Take me with you.'

There it was again, that odd note in his voice that tugged at something inside me. Still, I bit my lip in hesitation.

He closed the gap between us, wrapping me in his heat as he stared down at me. 'I'm feeling...out of sorts. Not the kind that makes me want to drink alone and not the kind that wants Vadim's sort of company.

That leaves you. Also if I remember correctly we're currently zero for two in the IOU stakes.'

'And taking you with me goes a step towards evening our odds?'

A darkly wicked light gleamed in his eyes. 'I'd prefer to even it out in like-for-like terms but if an evening with you is what's on offer, then I'll take it. Unless whatever you're doing involves another man. In that case I'd strongly advise you to get rid of him. I'd hate for him to be an unwanted third wheel.'

I couldn't help myself. I laughed. 'Okay, you can come with me.'

He inclined his head in that almost-regal way that emphasised his upper-class upbringing and fell into step beside me. But even though we walked in companionable silence, there was an edge in the air, a swelling of angst and anticipation that shortened my breath.

Whatever he was feeling out of sorts about was huge, and I couldn't help wondering if he regretted telling me about his family this afternoon.

Despite the dysfunction he claimed, every member of his family was supremely talented, with a sickeningly accomplished Gideon topping the bill. And while his playboy status was notable, it hadn't disturbed me as much as I'd thought it would. I'd indulged in my first one-night stand as a means to numb my pain after Adam's betrayal.

Gideon had admitted he'd gone off the rails after the double betrayal he'd suffered. His refusal to give in with me despite his blatant need turned me on more than I cared to admit.

'Where are we going exactly?' he asked in that deep sexy voice I wanted to hear up close and very personal.

I pointed to the street up ahead. 'The restaurant's a little more than a hole in the wall, but the food is good and the owner is great.'

'As long as he has barrels of good wine on tap, I'm sold.'

I glanced at his clenched jaw and wondered if I was doing the right thing by letting him tag along.

Maximo, the Balkan Italian whose restaurant bore his name, greeted me with a smile. '*Bellissima*, it's good to see you again. Welcome!'

He glanced at Gideon but didn't address him as he showed us to a secluded table in the small restaurant.

Gideon pulled out my chair, then sat across from me.

'You'll have your usual, Leonie, yes?' Maximo said.

'Yes, thanks.'

'And I'll have a bottle of your best red, unless you have a Macallan stashed away in the back?' Gideon asked.

Maximo smiled. 'I'll rustle up the perfect red for you, *signor*.'

When Maximo hurried away, Gideon glanced at me. 'Your usual? How many times have you been here?'

'I come every time I'm in town, which is about once every couple of months for the last three years.'

He looked around, and to his credit managed to keep his expression neutral.

'Don't judge before you try the food.'

His mouth twisted. 'Food isn't my number-one priority right now.'

'What is?'

His gaze lingered on my face, my mouth. 'Something else.'

'I hope you don't expect me to sit here and watch you get blind drunk to forget whatever's bothering you. Because that wasn't how I anticipated spending my evening.'

He regarded me for a long spell. 'I got in touch with Bryce this afternoon.'

My breath caught. 'Really? And...how was he?'

He shrugged. 'We reconnected. There's a strong possibility I'll see him sooner rather than later.'

There was a throb of emotion in his voice. Fondness remembered.

'I'm glad.'

'You should be. It's your fault,' he said with a wry, fleeting smile.

I laughed. 'I accept full responsibility, then.'

His gaze dropped to my mouth, charging the air with relentless lust as time ticked by.

'What about your cousin? Damian? The one with the TV show—'

'*Him* I most definitely do not want to talk about.'

The thick bitterness behind his words robbed me of breath. 'He's behind the betrayal you talked about, isn't he?'

His eyes turned almost black and then his lashes swept down. 'Yes.' It was a cold, bleak word.

'And is he why you're feeling out of sorts tonight?'

When he raised his gaze again, his expression was chillingly neutral. 'Enough, Leonora. It's your turn to balance the soul-baring deficit.'

Tension clenched my belly. 'I wasn't aware it would be due so soon.'

He shrugged. 'You'll agree that a few things have taken us both by surprise since we met. This just happens to be one of them. So who was he, Leonora? Is he the reason you're in a hurry to sell the yacht?' he asked, his voice tight.

'What makes you think I'm in a hurry?'

'I've done my homework, too, Leonora.'

The arrival of our drinks stopped me from replying. By the time Maximo took our food orders and departed, I had myself under better composure. 'I thought I was done with the South of France.'

'*Was?* Why?'

'Because this was never meant to be a long-term thing.'

Intelligent eyes rested on my face. 'You've grown a multimillion-euro business, which you were just going to pack in and walk away from?'

I attempted to shrug away the unnerving sensation that I'd nearly made another mistake. Let betrayal get the better of me. 'Yes.'

'What was the plan?'

I watched him raise his glass and take a long sip

of wine before I answered, 'I wanted to prove a point to myself.'

'To yourself or to him?' His keen intuition threw me. At my gasp, his mouth twisted. 'It's written all over your face, Leonora.'

My fingers circled the rim of my glass as I debated my answer. In the end I went with opening up to him because what I'd achieved was nothing to be ashamed of. Adam's betrayal had cut deep but I'd triumphed over it. I was a financial success, with a business I was damn proud of.

'It was supposed to be a five-day semibusiness trip before our wedding. We were both into sailing and planned to open a boating company after we got married.'

His nostrils flared but he didn't speak.

'We were supposed to attend a three-day course on a superyacht to learn the ropes together but we couldn't afford it in the end so he went and I stayed at a hostel in town. He called at the end of the first day to say the owner had extended his stay for the full five days at no extra charge. I was a little pissed but Adam was excited and I couldn't say no. Turned out the owner of the superyacht was a shipping heiress with more money than she knew what to do with. I'm assuming at some point one of them seduced the other or maybe it was a simultaneous seducing. Who the hell cares? Bottom line is I got a call on the last day of the trip from Adam to say he wasn't coming back. He'd already called his parents to tell them the wedding was off.'

'Fucking bastard. So you stayed?'

'No, I flew back home and licked my wounds for two months.'

Something flickered his gaze but he remained silent.

'Then I took my share of our savings and came back here.'

'You wanted to succeed where you'd lost before.' It wasn't a question. I liked that he got my determination and my ambition.

'Yes. And I did.'

'Good for you. Success is the best way to fuck your enemies over.'

His praise warmed me and when he raised his glass to me, I let myself get lost in that hard, edgy hunger in his eyes.

I sipped my wine, watching him over the rim as he returned my stare with an unwavering one of his own.

'Are you speaking from experience?' I eventually asked, unable to curb my curiosity.

'Of course I am,' he replied. 'I didn't get to where I am without knowing a thing or two about being fucked over.'

The arrival of our food didn't save me from the intensity of his unblinking stare. To be honest, I wasn't sure I wanted to be saved any more.

'Are you going to elaborate or shall we talk about the weather now?' I asked as he spooned stuffed peppers and *cufte* onto my plate. Although he served himself, he made no move to eat. I took a bite of the delicious food, chewed and swallowed.

His smile evaporated far too quickly. Long, elegant

fingers toyed with the stem of his glass, his pensive gaze raking my face to rest on my mouth for a long moment before rising to spear mine again.

'I was betrayed by my fiancée, too.'

Shock squeezed my insides tight. 'You were engaged?'

His phone buzzed. He slid it out of his pocket, read the message and tucked it back. 'Yes. Eat up, Leonora.'

I stared blindly down at my plate, then back at him. 'Are we in a hurry?'

'I sure as fuck hope so. Vadim has agreed to the final terms of the deal. His lawyers have just sent the signed papers to me.'

My heart lurched wildly, then proceeded to bash itself crazily against my ribcage. 'And that means…?'

Gideon sat forward, trailed his forefinger over my lower lip. 'It means I've been a good boy long enough. Now I intend to be very, very bad.'

I had very little memory of finishing my meal. But I must have because by the time Maximo appeared to clear the table, my plate was empty.

'Are you ready to go?' Gideon's demand was rough, barely coherent.

At my nod, he rose, tossed down a handful of crisp notes and meshed his fingers through mine. Whatever he muttered to Maximo on the way out made the other man smile. I added a quick smile of my own before we burst out into the quiet street. Lightning forked from where our hands connected and radiated through my body. Anticipation rippled through me, dragging a jagged little sound from my throat.

Gideon froze, his grey eyes spearing mine on the shadowed street. 'Fuck, I'm not even touching you properly and you're already turned on, aren't you? I can't wait to experience all this sexiness.'

Was it possible to both love and hate that level of arrogance? I remained in place when he started to move again.

He dropped my hand and planted himself in front of me. 'What are you up to, Leonora?'

'Are we headed back to the yacht?'

That edgy look in his eyes increased a hundred-fold. 'Yes. Any objection?'

I laid a hand flat on his chest, felt the hard thump of his heartbeat beneath my palm. 'No, but I'd like to start with a clean slate so let's even out the odds right now.'

The look on his face was a reward of its own. He laid his hand over mine, trapping it against his chest. 'I'm up for that. What do you have in mind?'

We were on a quiet street, with many dark shadows at this time of night. I curled my fingers around his and tugged him towards a darkened doorway. We risked discovery but I didn't really care in that moment. I'd wanted him for way too long and I was going to have him, self-preservation be damned.

'Leonora.'

I ran my fingers down his hard torso. 'Are you ever going to call me Leonie? I bet I can make you,' I teased.

His mouth twisted in a half-smile, the heat blazing in his eyes adding a layer of lethal attraction to the dynamism that was Gideon Mortimer. 'Sweetheart,

I'm learning that you can probably make me do a hell of a lot of things,' he rasped gravely.

I took three steps up into the sheltered doorway. Lust and darkness saturated the air as I pushed him against the wall.

The flash of surprise on his face was immediately masked by fevered anticipation. Without giving him a chance to speak, I dropped my clutch, curled my fingers into his collar and pulled him down to me.

His lips met mine, allowed me entry with an eagerness that matched my own. Hot and urgent hands wrapped tight around my waist, yanking me to him a second later.

We kissed like ravenous beasts, everything that had gone before a mere foretaste of what was coming. I flicked my tongue against his and then boldly licked my way into his mouth. He tasted of wine, agitation and barely leashed hunger, and I wanted him badly.

When the need for oxygen pulled us apart, I trailed my hand down his chest again, releasing a few buttons as I planted open-mouthed kisses along his jaw and down his throat. The sensation of his five o'clock shadow against my bruised lips sent flames arrowing to my core. I was supposed to be turning him inside out and yet I was the one growing wilder by the moment. The need to up the ante firing through me, I nipped at the taut skin beneath his jaw and felt him shudder.

'Fuck.'

His skin was warm, a touch rough and, oh, so sexy. I could've spent all night exploring him but a different need powered through me. I drew my tongue over his Adam's apple as I freed a few more buttons.

'Whatever the fuck it is you're doing, know that if we end up getting arrested, it'll be totally worth it,' he grated.

I smiled and dragged my nails down his abs to his belt. A couple of quick movements and I released it and tugged down his zip. My eyes locked on his, I slipped my hand inside his boxers and boldly captured his cock.

A fevered hiss tore from his throat before his head dropped back to thump against the wall. An instant later, he was back to watching me, his greedy eyes following my eager stroking.

The beauty of his cock overwhelmed me. 'God, you're so hot.'

He gave a husky chuckle. 'Keep stroking my ego like that, and this will be over much quicker than you want it to be.'

'No, it won't. You'll come exactly when I want you to.'

One eyebrow lifted but I sensed a change in him. Perhaps he was used to taking control with his previous lovers. I intended to meet him on equal footing or not at all. 'Do what I say and I'll give you a choice.'

'A choice of what?' His voice was gruffer.

I glided my clenched fist from the root of his cock to the tip where a cheeky drop of precome glistened. 'I'll give you a choice whether to come down my throat or on my tits. I know how much you love them.'

His head jerked back against the wall, and he groaned deep. 'Bloody hell, Leonora.'

'Is that a yes?'

'It's a hell fucking yes.'

The taut admission drew a smile from me. 'Good. Kiss me again, Gideon,' I instructed.

Large hands cupped my face and he dragged me into another mind-blowing kiss. It was rough and hard and almost bruising but I loved every second of it. When I wrenched my lips from his, we were both panting. Gideon stared at me with that bewildered look in his eyes again. 'Jesus, you're beautiful,' he muttered.

Propped against a wall with his shirt undone and savage hunger on his face, he was the most incredible thing I'd ever seen.

'So are you,' I blurted with unfettered honesty.

A blush stained his cheekbones as I slowly dropped to my knees. A shudder rolled through Gideon as he watched me from beneath hooded lids. Eyes on him, I leaned forward and flicked my tongue over the tip of his cock.

His breath hissed out.

'Do you like that, Gideon?'

He exhaled audibly. 'You know I bloody well do, you witch,' he growled.

'A witch, am I?'

Without giving him the chance to answer, I wrapped my lips around him and sucked him deep. His fingers convulsed in my hair, his stance widening as he jerked forward.

'Leonora…'

Something tugged in my chest at hearing him say my name with that gruff helplessness. His use of my full name might have irritated me when we first met but something about the way it fell off his tongue had grown on me.

God, the list of things I liked about him was growing by the minute.

With a soft moan, I slid my tongue down the underside of his beautifully veined length, then drew him into my mouth, intensifying my suction as I took more of him.

I established a rhythm, learning what made him grit his teeth, what made him groan and tremble in my hold. He loved it most when I drew him all the way to the back of my throat and hummed against his sensitive head. It made him bump helplessly into my mouth, drip more precome.

The taste of him was heady, musky. Need turning me bolder, I tugged at his trousers until his balls fell hot and heavy into my palm. On my next downward glide, I drew one into my mouth, rolling it over my tongue before repeating the action with the other.

'Shit!' The tendons in his neck stood out as he panted.

It was addictive to see him so lost in pleasure.

His head lowered a moment later, and I watched him watch me as I played with his balls for another minute. Then I drew his cock into my mouth again.

'Damn, Leonora, you look sensational sucking me off like that.'

For some unknown reason, his ragged words tugged at my heartstrings. The need to pleasure him grew stronger than the need to have him inside me.

When his breathing turned harsher, I knew he was close. Stormy eyes begged me to keep going, the fingers locked in my hair holding me to my task.

Positively sinful, I released him. 'Do you want me, Gideon?'

Voices drifted nearby, reminding me that we were in public. I continued to pump him, waiting for an answer.

A feral growl rumbled from his throat. 'In every way. I'm fucking you thirty ways to Sunday the moment we get back.'

'Where do you want me now?' I asked.

'If I only have one choice, baby, then I choose your throat. I want to watch you swallow every drop of my come.'

The thought of doing just that ramped up the screaming emotions inside me as I sucked him deeper than before.

With a hoarse shout, Gideon exploded in my mouth, drenching me with his liquid essence. I swallowed hungrily, overwhelmed by the filthy decadence of it and the uncontrollable shudders washing over him.

'God… Leonora,' he groaned. He was still caught in the tail end of his helpless convulsions when he dragged me upright and captured my jaw in his hand. Intense grey eyes hooked deep into mine in silence for a handful of seconds. 'That was fucking incredible,' he finally breathed.

He dragged me close and he sealed his mouth over mine, ruthlessly tasting me as if he couldn't get enough of me.

I wasn't sure how much time passed, but eventually we parted and Gideon righted his clothes. My hand back firmly in his, he picked up my clutch and handed it to me.

The walk back to the pier was hurried, charged with sizzling anticipation.

As before, he sat next to me in the speedboat but this time with one arm draped possessively over my shoulders, and the other splayed on my thigh. And I leaned into him as the boat sped us back to the yacht, shamelessly tucking my face into his neck, inhaling his heady scent.

CHAPTER SEVEN

Leonie

WITH THE CREW in their cabins and Gideon's guests still ashore, our hasty flight to the master suite on the third deck didn't attract witnesses.

The moment the door shut behind us, Gideon grabbed my waist and pinned me against the polished wood. His fingers attacked my hair, tugged out the pins and tossed them away.

'I want you naked,' he said thickly. 'Peel that sexy dress off and show me your glorious body.'

'Only if you show me yours, too.'

He hadn't got round to doing up all his buttons, so he made short work of shrugging his shirt off without taking his eyes off me. The sight of his bare chest dried my mouth and I watched, slack jawed, as he toed off his shoes. Trousers and boxers followed, and between one breath and the next, Gideon's vibrantly male body was exposed, mine to shamelessly ogle.

He'd called me beautiful, but he was magnificent. His time on board the yacht had graced him with a golden tan, highlighting every virile square inch of him.

'You're only allowed to devour me like that with your eyes if you're naked, too,' he growled.

I tossed away my clutch, then reached behind me and tugged on the ties that secured the upper half of my dress. Although loosened, the spaghetti straps held the dress in place.

To tease him, I faced the door and then pulled down the short zip. A small shimmy and the straps fell down my arms. With a hand over my breasts holding the material in place, I glanced over my shoulder at Gideon.

His eyes were hot, heavy, his face a taut mask of hunger as he returned my stare. 'You want to make me beg, Leonora?'

'You've waited this long. You can wait just a little bit longer, can't you?'

Next to his muscular thighs, his fists clenched and unclenched.

'Or is it too much for you?'

At his harsh exhalation, I smiled.

That smile evaporated a second later when he delivered a wicked smile of his own, then wrapped one hand around his cock.

God above, he was hard again, his erection boldly jutting from his groin. 'Torture me all you like, sweetheart, but you're only prolonging the moment when you get all of this inside you.'

The memory of him in my mouth drenched me

with liquid heat. I let go of the dress. It glided over my skin to pool around my ankles.

Gideon froze, his gaze locked on my body. 'Jesus,' he muttered under his breath.

I hooked my thumbs into my panties. 'Want me to take these off?'

'Please,' he begged gruffly.

The sight of his stroking hand, his magnificent body planted solidly three short steps away, almost brought me undone. Struggling to hang on to the last of my composure, I slowly dragged my panties down my thighs and over my knees, the former gymnast in me adopting the perfect pose to drive him out of his mind.

Above the rush of blood in my ears, I heard him curse again. 'You have a very filthy mouth, Gideon.'

'And you have a fucking indecent body.' He released his hard-on and bridged the gap between us. Firm hands recaptured my waist and then he was curling his body over mine, his head lowering until his lips brushed my ear. 'I'm going to kiss every inch of this magnificent body later. But first I want you to repeat what you said to me in the blackjack room.'

His naked body caging mine robbed me of the ability to think. 'I said a lot of things, Gideon.'

Calloused hands glided around my waist to my front, caressed my belly before rising to capture both breasts. Mercilessly, he teased the sensitised tips. 'You know very well what I want to hear. Say it again.' He nipped at the skin beneath my ear, dragging a wild shudder from me. 'Tell me what you want me to do to you.'

Need overcame any further urge to tease him. 'Fuck me, Gideon.'

'And how do you want it, Leonora?'

'Hard. Fast.'

'Your wish is my command.' He released me, strode to his bedside table. By the time he returned, he was gliding a condom over his cock.

Anticipation rose to fever pitch as he stepped closer.

'Open your legs wider for me, baby.'

I altered my stance, angled my bottom towards him. 'Hurry.'

He positioned himself at my entrance, cupped my bottom in a rough squeeze, and then he surged upward into me with his thick cock.

My haggard scream mingled with his tight groan as he filled me up, burying himself to the hilt. 'Fuck, you feel as exquisite as I imagined you would. So tight and wet and hot.'

'Move, Gideon. Fuck me.'

He shuddered at my demand, sliding his delicious length completely out before cramming back inside me again. My vision blurred, my lungs forgetting to refill as he executed a series of thrusts that rocked me to the tips of my toes. Every thought evaporated from my head, my only focus the glorious sensations climbing through my body as Gideon turned me inside out with pleasure.

Over and over he dragged me to the edge only to

leave me hanging as he changed angles, introducing me to a whole new world of sensation I never knew existed. He lifted me clean off my feet. Easily supporting my weight, he continued to fuck me, rasping deliciously filthy words in my ear with every penetration until I couldn't take it any more.

'Dying to come, aren't you?'

'Yes!' I groaned.

'Go on, then. Milk me with that tight little pussy the way you sucked me off in that alley,' he urged hotly.

Like floodgates opening, I succumbed to the wild rush, letting go as sensation completely engulfed me.

With a tight groan, Gideon peeled me off the door, invading me even deeper as he shackled both arms around me.

'God, yes,' he groaned. 'I can feel your every convulsion. Feel you attempting to wring me dry. I'm not going to let you yet. You sucked me off so beautifully and now I can go all fucking night.'

With that promise, he stalked to the bed and lowered me onto it without disengaging. I was lost in bliss; the touch of the cool sheets on my skin felt like heaven. And even as I climbed down from one peak, Gideon started fucking me again.

Toes curled, my fingers dug into the sheets, and I lost my mind all over again as he thrust in and out of me with a languorous rhythm that melted my very bones.

'Do you have any idea how many times I've dreamed of having you like this in my bed?'

I squeezed my eyes shut. God, he was just too much. 'Gideon…'

'Shh, don't speak. Just let me pleasure you.'

I wasn't prepared for him to pull out and roll me over. I squealed as he buried his face between my legs, inhaling me long and deep before he licked me with bold sweeps of his tongue.

I tunnelled my fingers through his hair, mild shock giving way to pleasure. My hips rolled mindlessly, already straining for more as I ground myself closer.

He raised his head a fraction, speared me with those intense grey eyes. 'I love it when you fuck my face. I love it even more when you come all over my mouth.'

Like a Pavlovian response to his words, flames engulfed me. Within minutes, another climax barrelled through me. I came hard, the power of it arching my torso clean off the bed.

With eager sucking sounds, Gideon lapped me up. Then, barely waiting for me to descend from my high, he kissed his way up my body, gently cupping my breasts as he slid inside me again.

Sensitised inner tissues welcomed him, the sensation even more acute after two powerful orgasms.

'I can't get enough of how phenomenal you feel.'

I groaned into the decadent kiss he initiated. This time the rhythm was slow and steady until sweat slicked his body and glistened on mine.

When harsh colour tinged his face, he braced himself on his elbows. 'Cup these glorious breasts for me, sweetheart. I want to watch you playing with them when I come.'

Capturing my tits, I squeezed them for a moment before catching the tight peaks between my fingers. At the absorbed look in his eyes, I went one better, sucking one forefinger and then the other before rolling them over my nipples.

Gideon's eyes turned almost black, and his thrusts grew frenzied as his need overtook him. I repeated the action, until the tips of my breasts glistened.

'Fuck,' he groaned, then he gave a guttural roar, his mouth-watering body straining as he came. The sheer pleasure of watching him lose control tipped me over the edge again.

Unbelievably, another climax slammed into me. My legs locked around his waist and he dropped on top of me, burying his face in my neck as shudders rolled through him. Long lazy minutes passed. When we'd caught our breath, he rolled off me, trailed kisses on my cheek before rising from the bed.

'Stay right there,' he instructed.

I couldn't have moved if the world were on fire, so I contented myself with watching him head into the bathroom. He joined me beneath the sheets when he returned and pulled me close. Gentle fingers cupped my jaw, angling my face up to his. 'Spend your day off tomorrow with me?'

My heart gave a little lurch even as I attempted to dampen down the excitement. 'What about your guests?'

'The moment my lawyers approve the deal, I'm tossing Vadim and his gang off the boat,' he replied without an ounce of regret. 'Until then, they can en-

.tertain themselves. My plan is to stay here with you for the next twenty-four hours.'

My brain attempted to skip ahead to what happened after tomorrow but I reined my thoughts in. What happened tonight had been unbelievable, so much more than I'd imagined. But it was still just sex.

Sex I wanted to experience a whole lot more of, sure. But—

'Leonora.'

I blinked to find Gideon staring at me, incisive eyes attempting to burrow into my thoughts. Within the grey depths were deeper, turbulent waters I didn't want to navigate.

It was just sex. Nothing more. 'Sure, I'll spend tomorrow with you.'

Sunlight was slanting through the shutters when I next opened my eyes. The space beside me was empty, but there was a note propped up against the pillow. I unfolded it and read Gideon's impatient scrawl.

Gone to toss some Russians overboard. Stay where you are. I'll bring breakfast.

Smiling, I traced my fingers over the black ink. Even the way he wrote indicated an arrogance that endeared and grated at the same time. He'd brought those qualities to bear with wicked results last night. The reminder heated me inside and out and I rolled over and buried my face in his pillow. He'd promised me an all-night fucking and he'd more than delivered.

The force of his possession lingered between my thighs, muscles I'd forgotten existed twitching with each movement. We'd eventually tumbled into sleep around dawn, my body draped over his in a useless heap of satiation.

The thought of another twenty-four hours experiencing more of the same sent a decadent thrill through me.

But…twenty-four hours and then what?

Acidic unease burned through my anticipation and my smile. Like black crows storming the horizon, unsettling questions flooded in.

The text about Gideon's deal had interrupted our conversation last night but not before he'd dropped the bombshell of his fiancée. Pictures I'd seen online of him and his cousin Damian were over four years old. They'd been as thick as thieves before so it didn't take a genius to surmise the two might be connected.

The burn in my chest intensified, startling me with the possibility that if Gideon's playboy lifestyle was just a front, then it hid something deeper. A carefully guarded pain?

Whatever personal angst rode him last night had been close to the surface. And there'd been sizzling recognition when I retold Adam's betrayal.

Someone I trusted took what belonged to me. More than one someone, actually. Between them they destroyed something precious.

Was I foolish getting involved, even temporarily, with Gideon? My misery didn't want company, especially not if it involved an ex who'd driven Gideon to cultivate that veneer of a dangerous, transient Lothario.

Or was I way off base, overanalysing what should be a simple fling before we went our separate ways?

The sound of a helicopter taking off startled me. Gideon had successfully rid himself of his guests.

As the sound faded, I attempted to distance myself from my disturbing thoughts by flinging aside the sheets and rising from the bed.

My wobbly legs reminded me how thoroughly Gideon had used my body. No matter how today ended this would remain an unforgettable experience. So why did the thought of it ending make me anxious?

What the hell was wrong with me?

Impatiently catching my hair up in a knot, I hurried to the bathroom, eager to wash my thoughts away.

Like every other amenity on the yacht, the bathroom was the last word in luxury. A spacious sunken Jacuzzi took up one corner, while the other housed an ultra-modern shower complete with a wide bench and multiple showerheads. I headed for the shower.

For endless minutes I let the jets wash over me, hoping it'd help blank my mind. When it didn't I reached for the shower gel, then froze when the bathroom door opened.

'You were supposed to wait for me in bed,' Gideon grumbled.

My heart jumped into my throat as I watched him pull on the ties of his dark-coloured lounge pants and kick them off. Naked and shamelessly aroused, he walked into the shower and plucked the bottle of shower gel from my hand.

'I got impatient,' I said. 'And hungry.' Not to mention a whole load of other things I wasn't about to voice.

'I brought breakfast as I promised. But now you don't get it until I'm done with you.'

He squeezed gel into his hands, rubbed them in slow sexy circles before gliding them over my shoulders. I welcomed the hot swell of desire that left no room for thoughts of Gideon's past or the knot of anxiety that came with considering that today would be all I had with him.

Instead, I let myself burn in the carnal promise etched on his face as he cupped my breasts and flicked his thumbs over my nipples.

'I heard the helicopter leave.'

'As of ten minutes ago, my colourful guests have been dispatched,' he replied without taking his eyes off my breasts. 'Do me a favour and give the crew a day off, would you? I want to be alone with you on board today.'

Excitement leapt through me. 'And what will we do with all that time?'

His cocky smile swept into place. 'We'll find something, I'm sure. I can be very inventive when properly motivated.'

'Then I guess we'll have to find ways to keep you fully motivated.'

He chuckled. And then speech became redundant. With mind-boggling attention to detail, Gideon washed every inch of my body. Then, sliding one hand under my knee, he lifted my leg to curl around his waist. He plucked a condom off the shelf, his gaze not leaving mine as he tore it open.

I took it from him, slowing my movements as I slid the rubber over his steel-hard length.

The hand wrapped around my hip tightened as his lips parted on a hoarse pant. 'Who named this boat, Leonora?'

I dragged my gaze up his glorious body to his face. 'What?'

'*La Sirène.* The siren. You named it, didn't you?'

'What if I did?'

'Then this insanity you wreak in me will be totally understandable.' The raw confession shook me to my toes.

'Gideon—'

'I can't go five fucking minutes without thinking about you,' he interrupted harshly. 'Do you know that?'

The wild thrumming in my blood intensified. 'You don't sound too happy about it.'

'If you want to make me happy, put me inside you, let me feel you hot and tight around me again.'

With a helpless moan I dragged him closer, gliding my fingers over him for one stolen moment before guiding him to my entrance.

Hand on my hip and the other hooked under my knee, he thrust hard and deep inside me. I screamed, my nails sinking into his nape as pleasure tore through me.

Gideon slammed inside me over and over, his movements growing frenzied. 'Fuck, Leonora, I can't get enough of you.'

I kept my mouth shut, instinct warning me not to vocalise my own growing addiction to him.

The instantaneous attraction I'd felt from the moment we met had only intensified with each minute I spent with him. Admitting unguarded feelings would be inviting trouble. So I let my moans and my touch and my writhing hips speak for me.

But Gideon wasn't content with that. With a grunt, he pressed me against the wall and dropped his gaze to where we were intimately connected. And then piercing grey eyes reconnected with mine. 'Do you like what I'm doing to you?'

'What do you think?'

'I think I'd love further demonstration.'

'Why, Gideon. You sound almost insecure,' I muttered huskily as he surged inside me.

Bewilderment mingled with arousal. 'Funny thing, that. I've never felt like this with anyone else. You make me want to do things I don't normally do, Leonora,' he gritted out.

Oh, God. I squeezed my eyes shut, the potency of his words threatening to shatter my defences. 'Things like what?'

He leaned close, bit the corner of my lip before gliding his tongue over it. 'You've reduced me to constant begging. I find myself baring my fucking soul like I'm at confession. And I'm not even Catholic.'

He surged deeper, lifting me to the tips of my toes.

'Oh, God!' The tempest brewing in my veins intensified. I dragged my eyes open, met turbulent ones. 'This feels one-sided to you? You want to see what you do to me?'

'Yes,' he encouraged thickly.

I dragged one hand down his body and transferred it to my own. The first brush of my fingers over my swollen clit tightened my internal muscles, nearly sent me over the edge. My whole body shook with the precursor to my impending climax.

'Fuck yes. More, Leonora,' Gideon demanded gruffly.

I touched myself again, this time prepared for the zap of electricity.

Gideon swivelled his hips, aiming his thrust to hit me at an angle that turned me liquid.

'Gideon.' His name was a drawn-out moan. 'I… I don't know if I can take it.'

Teeth clenched, he continued to work me, his eyes growing darker by the minute as we both surged towards completion. 'I have you, sweetheart. Go wild for me.'

I fondled myself again, gliding my fingers on either side of his thrusting cock. Then I brought my fingers to my clit, circling my needy flesh. Once started, I couldn't stop.

'God, you're so beautiful, Leonora.'

Raising my gaze from the intensely erotic sight of our joining, I met Gideon's compulsive gaze. We stayed like that, an intense and hypnotising connection locking us in place.

Then he gave a harsh groan. 'I feel you, baby. You're ready to explode, aren't you?'

Words failed me. A moment later, he fused his mouth to mine just as a tsunami of sensation smashed into me.

Gideon's shout filled the heated space a moment later. I felt him catch me as every ounce of energy rushed out of me and my vision blurred.

When I came to, he was seated on the bench and I was sprawled all over him. Soft kisses trailed down my face as his hands smoothed back damp tendrils. 'This was how I wanted to wake up. Good morning, Leonora.'

I smiled, feeling beyond sensational. 'Good morning, Gideon.'

With a deep chuckle, he rose with me in his arms. At the door he set me down long enough to drape a thick bathrobe over me and one over himself before we returned to the bedroom.

Our breakfast was still warm and I followed him as he pushed the breakfast trolley onto his private balcony. The smell of scrambled eggs and bacon and coffee reminded me that we'd barely made it past starters last night.

We wolfed down a plateful of food in silence. Then he lounged back in his chair, lazily watching me as I devoured a small bowl of strawberries.

'Are you going to give the crew the day off?' he asked, his gaze dropping to linger where my robe gaped to show the curves of my breasts.

I shrugged. 'If you don't need them, they'll be thrilled to have a day off.'

'Good. And let them know that under no circumstances are they to return to the upper decks before midnight.'

I smiled. 'What exactly have you got in mind?'

'For starters, I'm going to watch you sunbathe. Nude. After that—' he shrugged '—you get to pick. Will you do it?' he asked with a gruff plea.

His unique way of disarming me when I needed to keep up my guard unnerved me further. Like last night when he'd asked to join me for dinner. I stared at him, knowing in my heart I wasn't going to refuse this either. I'd already agreed to spend the day with him anyway. What we did during that time didn't really matter.

It should.

I ignored the voice, took a sip of coffee before I answered, 'Yes, I will.'

'And would I be pushing my luck if I said I want a repeat of the same when we dock in Sicily, too?'

So he wasn't leaving for another couple of days.

I cleared my throat and strove to maintain a neutral expression. 'Yes, you would. For all I know spending today with you might prove a huge ball of disappointment.'

His eyes gleamed. 'Is that the challenge, Leonora?'

'Maybe…'

He rose, a wicked smile turning his face even more mouth-wateringly gorgeous as he held out his hand to me. 'Then I guess it's game on.'

He spent an hour videoconferencing with his office, while I video called with Andrea.

'So everything's going well?' she asked, peering into the screen.

I prayed my face didn't give me away as I nodded. 'Yes, no major dramas so far, thank goodness.'

Andrea smiled, then winced as her overexuberant baby kicked inside her. 'And? Is he going to buy the yacht?' she asked eagerly.

I wasn't about to confess I hadn't given it much thought in the last couple of days. Now that I'd decided to remain in the South of France, there wasn't an urgency to make the sale. The consortium had given me a year to find the right buyer, and I was confident I would.

So I shrugged. 'I'm not hard selling. He'll either buy it or he won't. If he doesn't, I'll cast my net wider.'

Andrea nodded. 'Sounds like a plan. Well, don't worry about the office. It's been pretty quiet. I'll email if anything crops up that I can't handle.'

I signed off, went to my cabin to grab my sun protection.

Four hours later I was sprawled on the top deck, glistening from head to toe in the coconut-scented sunscreen Gideon had liberally massaged into my skin. With my only apparel the oversized sunglasses shielding my eyes from the sun, I waited for him to return with the cocktails he'd gone to the bar to make.

I'd dismissed every crew member, including the captain after he'd found us a private cove to moor the yacht a short distance from Budva. We had six hours to ourselves. I wasn't sure whether it was being completely alone with him or the promise of more sex that had me hyperaware.

I heard him approach and, unable to help myself, lifted my head to watch him. Like me, Gideon was completely naked. Unlike me, though, there wasn't an ounce of self-consciousness visible as he set the tray of drinks down next to me.

'You never answered my question.'

'What question?'

'The boat. Did you name it?'

Smiling, I accepted the dirty martini he handed me. 'Yes, I did.'

He chuckled. 'Thought so.'

I sipped my drink and attempted to play it cool beneath his intense scrutiny. But it was no use. The moment his ravenous gaze dropped to my breasts, they began to tingle and tighten. 'Stop that.'

His smile widened. 'I don't plan to. You really are incredibly beautiful.'

There was an odd note in his voice that triggered a series of rapid heartbeats but I played it down.

'You're not so bad on the eyes either.'

He dropped down next to me. Completely ignoring his drink, his gaze slid down my body with growing hunger.

'Will you be visiting England any time soon?' he asked abruptly.

The unexpected question threw me. There was something almost wrong with discussing my future plans with a man I'd probably never see again the moment he stepped off the yacht, never mind doing so while I was completely naked.

'I'd planned to visit my mother and grandmother when the season was over.'

His forefinger drifted down my collarbone. 'Where in England are they?'

I tried to read his face, but I saw nothing but steady interest. Well, that and the ever-present hunger that lurked in his eyes when he looked at me.

A girl could get hopelessly addicted to that full-on intensity.

Then it's a good thing this thing is temporary.

I clenched my gut against the sharp arrow that lodged itself in my chest. 'They live in the Lake District.'

He caught a strand of my hair and teased it through his fingers. 'What about your father, Leonora? Any reason he's *not quite* in the picture?'

I tensed, fiercely glad for the protection of the sunglasses. 'He never wanted to be. But that didn't stop him from selfishly dipping in and out of our lives when it suited him.'

His mouth twisted. 'I'm not sure which is worse, a parent's physical presence and emotional absence, or a deprivation of both,' he mused bitterly.

I caught his hand, a strong urge to connect with him making me mesh my fingers with his. 'In the long run, I preferred the latter because the former fed me with hope that was never fulfilled.'

He brought our joined fingers to his lips and kissed my knuckles. 'Do you still see him?'

Pain spiralled through me. 'Not if I can help it. Unfortunately my mother hasn't abandoned the idea of using me as bait to hook an imagined relationship. We butt heads over the issue more often than I want.'

He remained silent for a long time before grey eyes met mine. 'So this is yet another area where we've both been fucked over. Perhaps we should form a support group.'

The words were throwaway but his eyes held an intensity I desperately wanted to fixate on. 'I prefer not to spend time raking over the past.' Or rabidly dwelling on the many other ways I wished we were connected. 'I'd rather help you celebrate your deal.'

'I'm already celebrating. You're my prize.'

'I'm no one's trophy, Gideon.' That smacked too much of what I'd seen my father do to my mother. When the whim took him, he'd arrive in a blaze of glory, take her down from the shelf he'd placed her on. Play with her until he grew bored. Then he'd toss her back until the next time.

Gideon's face slowly straightened, his eyes darkening. 'Too bloody right, you're not. You're so much more.' Again that peculiar note throbbed in his voice.

Before I could decipher it, he caught a thicker strand of my hair, wrapped it around his hand and pulled me close. He reached into the ice bucket and plucked out an ice cube.

Wild tingles raced through my body. 'What are you doing?'

'Open up,' he said.

He placed the ice on my tongue, then he took my

glass, held it to my lips. He allowed me a small sip before setting the glass down on the tray.

When he brought his fingers to my lips again, I shook my head. 'It's mine now.'

His breathing altered a little. 'What are you going to do with it?'

I let my gaze drift down to his cock, and then up his body. 'Have you ever been fucked with ice, Gideon?'

Fervent excitement leapt in his eyes. 'Are you offering to blow my mind, Leonora?' he asked hoarsely.

'Lie down and let's find out,' I instructed.

He complied with a feline unfurling of his body.

I settled on my knees beside him, the effect of his eager anticipation already making me wet. With languid movements, I lowered my face to his until our lips were an inch apart.

A drop melted onto his lower lip. He licked it off with a lazy swipe of his tongue. I allowed another two drops to drip before closing the gap.

He sucked in a sharp breath as I dragged the ice cube back and forth over his lips. Despite the blazing sun's heat at my back I shivered at his unfettered response.

His eyes darkened dramatically as he watched my nipples pebble, his throat moving in a convulsive swallow.

'Take your shades off, Leonora, I want to see your gorgeous eyes.'

I pushed the ice between his lips, then pulled away before his lips could cling to mine. 'Not yet. You only get what I give you.'

He smirked. 'Yes, boss lady.'

That cocky smile evaporated when I grabbed another cube of ice. By the time I trailed it down between his hard pecs to his left nipple, Gideon was panting. 'Sweet Jesus...'

'Too much?' I asked.

'Too fucking good,' he slurred.

Without warning, I transferred the cube to his right nipple, then lowered my head and grazed his left with my teeth. His back arched off the deck, his teeth clenching until his jaw was rigid with barely leashed control.

Between his thighs, his cock jerked to stiff attention.

'I love the way you show your pleasure,' I murmured.

'I love the way you provide it,' he croaked.

I returned to my task, not stopping till the ice melted.

He was cursing and groaning by the time I grabbed the next one. A slow trail down, I dropped it on his belly button, swung my thighs over his lean hips, then retrieved the ice.

'Watch me, Gideon. Don't move.'

With his eyes locked on mine, and the tip of his cock inches from my heated core, I dropped my head back and trailed the melting ice down my body. Electricity zapped up my spine when the chilled cube touched my nipple. My rough moan made his stomach muscles tighten.

'Jesus... Leonora,' he muttered brokenly.

I felt my pussy dampen shamelessly, the need to fuck him a twisting live wire inside me. Still, I took my time, torturing us both with my slow, excruciating tease.

Gideon groaned when liquid dripped from my body to his. His gaze swung feverishly from my sex to my breasts to my mouth.

When need grew too much to contain, I slid my hand over my belly to my clit. With a sucked in breath, I pushed the die-sized cube into my pussy.

'Bloody hell. Have mercy,' he rasped, his black gaze on the finger I was using to hold the ice inside me.

'Put the condom on, Gideon,' I ordered hoarsely.

His gaze left mine for the mere second it took to snatch up the condom, then he was ripping it open, his movements frantic as he sheathed himself.

My impending orgasm whistled in the distance as I braced myself over him. Then with a twist of my hips, I took him deep inside me.

His shout of pleasure was music to my ears. Muscles straining in his neck as he tried to hold himself under control made my blood sing. With my hands planted on his chest, I went to town.

'Fuck, Leonora. Fuck, fuck, *fuck*.'

I didn't give him a moment to regain control, driving us both towards the edge until Gideon's teeth clenched and he shouted his climax. Only then did I let go and surrender to my own blissful orgasm.

Spent, I collapsed over him, sighing in pleasure when his arms immediately folded around me.

'Bloody hell,' he muttered again.

I smiled against his heated skin. 'I'm guessing that was your first experience with ice, too?'

He chuckled, and then we were both laughing. 'My first but hopefully not my last.'

My laughter slowly died. I averted my face from his even though I had no right to let thoughts of other faceless women in Gideon's future intrude in the moment.

I was still telling myself that when the dart of pain expanded in my chest. When it reached the point when I couldn't quite catch my breath.

Relief washed over me when I heard the steady sound of Gideon's breathing and knew he'd fallen into light sleep.

Only then did I allow myself to glance into his face, knowing that I'd crossed a certain line that would be hard to uncross again.

And that I only had myself to blame.

CHAPTER EIGHT

Leonie

FOR THE NEXT six days, we repeated the routine.

We would find private coves to drop anchor and spend the day. After breakfast I dismissed the crew, who were overjoyed to be given so much time off. The only time Gideon and I stepped off the yacht was to go skinny-dipping or jet-skiing in the turquoise waters of the Adriatic. The rest of the time was filled with new and inventive ways of fucking each other's brains out.

And, boy, were we inventive.

To my delight, and Gideon's, I discovered that deep throating wasn't a myth, after all.

We separated to catch up on work for a couple of hours every day. Mine were oftentimes smooth, but Gideon tended to return to me a little distant each time, tensing each time his phone rang.

He was on another call to his office now while I stood on the balcony of his bedroom suite, basking in the sunset and the approaching lights of St Tropez.

I jumped when my phone rang. Then guilt struck because I'd missed my weekly call to my mother. It wasn't her. I frowned at the unfamiliar number as I slid my finger across the screen. 'Hello.'

'Leonie.' The voice was abrupt. Nasal. Instantly recognisable.

'Adam?' A clammy sensation drifted over me and I couldn't hide my grimace.

Low, cocky laughter. 'Hey, babe, I guess it bodes well that you still recognise my voice, right?'

No, it didn't. At all. 'How did you get this number?'

'It's not exactly a private number, is it? And let's face it, you were never good at playing hard to get, were you, babe?'

My teeth clenched as fury swept through me. 'Was there a specific reason for your call, Adam, or did you just disturb my evening to ask me stupid questions?'

He paused and I felt a pulse of reciprocal anger down the line. He'd never liked it when I spoke back. 'I see some things haven't changed,' he snarled. 'And here I was hoping not to start off on the wrong foot.'

'A lot has changed, including the fact that there's nothing *to* start. Not where you're concerned anyway.'

'Dammit, Leonie. You know I've been trying to reach you. Why are you avoiding me?'

My hand tightened on the phone. 'Do I need to spell it out for you?'

'Didn't you get my emails? It's all over between me and—'

'I don't really care.'

He laughed again, with a nasty edge to it that made my skin crawl. 'Are you sure? According to a few folks back home you cried for weeks when I left. Look, I'm back now. We can go for a coffee—'

'And what? Pretend that what you did never happened?'

'If that's what you want,' he replied smoothly. 'Congrats on making our dream come true with the boating business, by the way.'

'*Our* dream?'

'Don't pretend selective memory. Opening the business together was always our vision.'

'Until you tripped and fell into another woman's bed—why am I even rehashing this?'

'Because you're still hurt. You still care about me. I'm back now. Let me take you to dinner. We can pick up where we left—'

'You're really unbelievable, do you know that?'

'Is that a yes?'

'No, Adam. It most definitely isn't.'

He paused for a second. 'I think you should take time to think about it before you say no, baby.'

I was reminded then how pig-headed Adam could be. I hadn't missed that. 'No time needed. It's a no. It'll *always* be a no, so don't bother trying again. Goodbye.'

I hung up and blocked his number. And as I took my next breath, a knot unravelled inside me. It might have been a little unpleasant but my instincts told me this final call with Adam was just what I'd needed.

I'd come full circle, drawn a line under my past.

As the lights of St Tropez drew closer, I smiled.

Adam's betrayal didn't hurt any more. It hadn't for a long time. Perhaps I'd needed a different perspective to see it.

Or a different person.

Gideon.

I exhaled. Maybe I'd take him up on that support group thing after all, make more trips to England…

As if conjured from my thoughts, I sensed him behind me. Turning away from the view, I found him leaning in the doorway, arms crossed.

His gaze went from my face to the phone and I knew he'd overheard some of my conversation. His eyes were the colour of a churning thunderstorm. 'Who were you talking to?' he asked, his voice silkily dangerous.

'I think you know.'

'Your ex? I thought he was out of your life.' His voice was tight. Edgy.

'He is. He was.'

'So what did he want?'

'To buy me dinner.'

He jerked away from the door, pushed into my space. 'And are you going to let him?'

I lifted my chin. 'I wasn't planning on it, no.'

A little bit of the ice receded from his eyes, but the tension gripping his shoulders didn't dissipate. His fingers meshed with mine and he nudged me into the bedroom. 'That's something, I guess, considering you took his call at all.'

'Is it? Why?' I asked boldly.

He froze halfway across the room. 'You're asking me why I don't want some bastard sniffing around you while you're mine?'

While...

'I must have missed the memo where I agreed to be yours,' I replied.

His hand cupped my jaw, tilting my face to his. 'You really need a memo, Leonora? Don't you know that every time you wrapped that addictive pussy around my cock you possessed me just as I possessed you? Until we walk away from each other, no other fucking guy gets to call you. Or buy you bloody dinner. Is that clear?'

I smiled even though the action felt tight. 'No, Gideon. What's clear is that you're pissed off about something and are taking it out on me. Maybe you didn't hear that I said no to Adam. Even if he was a decent guy and not my cheating ex, I'd still have said no because I'm here for now, with you. Can you say the same?'

He inhaled sharply. 'Excuse me?'

I looked down at the tight hold he had on my hands. 'Tell me you weren't dragging me to bed just now so you could forget whatever it is that's got you so wound up? Tell me you didn't just get off the phone and come here so you don't have to deal with what I'm guessing is a Damian-sized issue?'

His lips thinned. 'Watch it, Leonora.'

I snatched my fingers from his. 'No, Gideon. *You* watch it. If you want my panties to melt with that caveman display, then do it when you've dealt with the shadows of distrust lurking in your eyes. I *might* find you much sexier when you're not trying to use me as another anti-emotional roadblock.'

His jaw slackened, and pure shock blazed in his eyes. 'Jesus, you have a set of balls on you, don't you?'

I shrugged. 'I seem to recall us agreeing to call it like it was. What are you going to do about it?'

He continued to stare at me for another handful of seconds. Then his expression chilled. 'Is this some sort of challenge? What? You've dealt with your issues so I need to deal with mine?'

'It's a simple observation that you're sucking at remaining as emotionally detached as you want to be. It's a recommendation that you deal with it instead of exploding it all over me.' Something inside me cracked at the bleak look that shifted in his eyes. 'It's also an offer to—'

He shook his head in a firm refusal. 'If you're about to put yourself up as my shrink, then no, thanks. I have enough people in my life who think they know what's best for me. Like you said, you're here *for now*. I'm sure neither of us wants to delude ourselves that trust and dependency are part of this deal.' The way he uttered those two words stung. I barely managed to hide my flinch. 'But since I crave the role you've carved out for yourself in my life, *for now*, I'll learn to compartmentalise better so I don't…explode it all over you. Does that work for you, Leonora?'

I curled my hands into fists, knowing in part I'd brought this upon myself by challenging him in one breath, then offering to help heal him in the other. For all I knew he didn't want to get over what had happened.

By pushing him, was I recklessly risking what little time we had?

My heart lurched. 'Fine,' I replied through numb lips.

He stared at me for another fistful of heartbeats. Then he sighed. 'I sense that I've blown my chances of fucking you, for the time being. So shall we go to dinner? Or is that off the table, too?'

I forced myself not to glance at the bed. 'Dinner is fine.'

Dinner wasn't fine. It was stilted and tense. Right up until he set his glass down with a definitive click and speared me with sombre eyes.

'Contrary to what you think, I'm not attempting to avoid my issues. My phone call to my office today was to confirm my attendance at a board meeting I don't particularly want to attend. I was getting stick for not committing to attending in person. Normally, I would've told them where to get off. But the call took longer because I was attempting reason with irrational people. It's the most peculiar thing, this new giving-a-shit business. I'm not sure what the fuck it is you've done to me. And right now, I'm not entirely sure I like it.'

My heart stuttered. 'Are you saying—'

He stopped me with a finger on my mouth. 'I may have attempted to take a leaf out of your book, but regardless that, I've bared myself more to you in the last few days than I've done with anyone else for a long time, I don't deal in blind trust.'

'That's fair enough. Trust is earned in my book, too.'

He exhaled with what sounded like a little relief. 'Okay, and if…if you want me to throttle back in other areas, too, then I'll try to oblige.'

Sex. He meant sex. Did I want him to throttle back? God, no. Our exchange in his cabin had left me with the sensation that I was already losing ground where Gideon was concerned. Ground I didn't even know I wanted. If sex was all I had…

This time my heart stuttered for a different reason. 'What if I don't want you to throttle back? What if I want more?'

For the longest time he stared, unsmiling, at me. Then his gaze turned stormy. 'Then I'll say be very careful what you wish for. You might just get it.'

We went to bed with residual tension still lingering. No matter how much I tried, I couldn't dispel the notion that something between us had changed. Something irrevocable.

When I next opened my eyes, the space beside me was empty. At some point in the night, we'd docked in St Tropez. Half of the crew were on board, the other half on shore, restocking supplies. I knew Gideon's standing privacy directive meant I wouldn't be spotted when I shrugged on his shirt and left the master suite.

The door to his office was ajar and I spotted him

behind his desk. Although he stared at a bunch of papers in his hand, his gaze was off.

I leaned in the doorway, my heart thudding louder as the sheer impact of him hit me sideways. His head snapped up, his gaze locking onto me.

'Gideon…'

'We have company for dinner tonight,' he said.

'We?'

He turned to face me, one eyebrow lifting. 'Yes. We.'

I couldn't bring myself to ask if my inclusion was in the capacity of his lover or merely business-wise so I nodded. 'We should be all stocked by then. How many guests are you expecting?'

'Not guests. My cousin Gemma and her husband. You'll be meeting them as you, Leonora, not as the badass businesswoman you're attempting to hide behind.'

'I'm not hiding,' I replied briskly, 'but if you want me to join you, you should ask me properly.'

His gaze rolled over to me, all deceptively calm and dangerous. 'Do you have a bee in your bonnet about something?'

I left the doorway, crossed the cabin to stand in front of him. 'Don't change the subject. My time is precious, Gideon. I don't like to waste it. If you'd rather be alone…'

He took a deep breath, then slid a finger down my cheek. 'How the hell can I when you're around?' he demanded thickly.

'That sounds like an accusation.'

He dropped his hand, stood and walked to the French doors leading onto his balcony. I wrapped my arms around my middle and waited for him to turn around.

'Do you care about me, Leonora?'

The question shocked me enough to jerk me out of my pretended nonchalance. 'What kind of question is that?'

'A simple one, I think,' he countered.

'I…' I had no way of answering that without baring my soul so I clamped my lips shut.

His face settled in harsh lines.

The ashen hollow inside widened. 'Gideon?'

Bleak, distant eyes found mine. 'I told you I had a fiancée. You've probably guessed the reason she's not my fiancée any more is because she cheated on me. With Damian. How fucking clichéd is that?'

Hearing the intricate details didn't make me hurt less for him. 'I'm sorry.'

Lips compressed, he glanced away, as if he didn't want my sympathy.

'Has something changed? With Damian, I mean?'

He gave a harsh laugh. 'If I had my way, he'd be rotting at the bottom of a ravine somewhere. But no, the fucker's decided to rear his head again.'

'He's coming here?'

'I bloody well hope not, for his own sake. But he's back in London making noises about rejoining the board. Hence my required attendance at the board meeting.'

'And you don't want that to happen.'

'What the hell do you think?'

Like a beam of light cutting through a thunderstorm, I saw through his bravado to the pain lurking beneath. The band around my chest squeezed tighter.

Gideon was still in love with his fiancée.

It explained his edginess at his cousin's reappearance.

Gideon's rabid need for loyalty and fidelity made sense now, too, especially if he still loved a woman who'd betrayed him.

I shoved away all the jagged angst those conclusions threatened to rip through me and focused on him. 'You think your family are coming over to try to talk you into allowing him back into the company?'

'Of course they are. They don't miss a chance to chuck a spanner in the works.'

'Can they do that?'

He shrugged. 'Technically, he never left, merely took a leave of absence. So yes.' Despite his abrasive words, there was a longing in his voice that snagged me. The Mortimer family was large and rambling, and like most dynastic families it was fraught with drama.

Despite my own unsettling emotions, my heart went out to him. 'Why exactly do you want me there tonight, Gideon?'

'Gemma is Damian's sister. She's bound to rabbit on about him at some point.'

I frowned. 'Surely she won't be that insensitive?'

'She doesn't know what he did. Surprisingly, it was one family secret I managed to keep under wraps.'

I gasped. 'No one knows?'

'Aunt Flo does. And that wasn't by choice. She just happened to be there at an...inopportune moment.'

'I see.'

His gaze flickered over my face. 'So now you know another torrid little secret. Will you be there?' he asked tersely.

I wanted to refuse. Withdraw.

My own situation with my mother had made me wary about the emotional entanglements and anguish that family brought. For longer than I could remember, she'd dangled at the end of my father's string, refusing to see his true selfish nature.

'I'm not great with family situations, Gideon.'

'I still want you there. We can muddle through the bullshit together.'

I bit my lip, recalling how it'd felt to return wedding gifts and cancel invitations, to endure the pitying looks when they discovered what Adam had done. Surprisingly, my mother had stood by me through it all and on some level we'd reconnected.

The softening inside me unsettled me further but I pushed the feeling aside. 'If you want me there, I'd love to join you.'

Gideon

Leonora's agreement should've pleased me. I should've been satisfied since as of last night we'd established that trust wasn't a ready commodity for me to offer anyone, especially in a transient sex fling.

We'd drawn clear lines and she'd agreed not to step over them.

It was what I wanted. So why did I lie awake all bloody night, unable to shake the sensation that I'd fucked up somehow?

And why did seeing her this morning only confirm that chilling idea?

Even now, as she smiled at me, I knew something was up. It was right there in her face but I'd spent so long stumbling around in emotional darkness, that clarity I was striving for was damned hard to find.

Was it her ex? From what I'd caught from the phone call, she'd rebuffed him. *For now.* But what about later? Forgiveness was a sneaky thing. Hell, I'd spent a full sixty seconds this morning in my office contemplating forgiving Damian.

And that wasn't even the worst of it.

For another full minute I'd wondered if I should do something about the sensation that something important was slipping through my fingers. Something remotely resembling removing the other so-called anti-emotional roadblocks Leonora had accused me of erecting.

But who the hell was I kidding? There was nothing beyond the roadblocks but a harsh desolate wasteland triggered by betrayal and an emotionally barren childhood. I'd caught glimpses of it over the years, when the veil of partying had dropped for a few terrifying seconds.

It was why those sixty seconds had rattled the fuck out of me with its vivid potency.

No other woman—including Penny—had impacted me like this. I'd gone from thinking about Leonora every five minutes to every five bloody seconds. Even in my arms or when I was deep inside her, I still craved more of her. Somewhere along the line, she'd burrowed under my skin and was digging deep into places I'd clearly marked forbidden.

As with Bryce, I'd woken this morning with a reluctant acceptance that I had to deal with Damian.

The thought of returning to London and picking up my life where I'd left it several short days ago was suddenly deeply unattractive.

As for telling her about Damian and Penny...

'Gideon?'

I stared at her, catching another glimpse of that wary sympathy in her eyes.

'Damian and I are the closest in age of any of my other siblings or cousins. He was closer to me than Bryce. We were inseparable.' The words spilled like an opened tap, pouring free, eroding foundations I'd painstakingly built. It had to stop.

Otherwise...

Otherwise something...*someone* might slip through?

A deep pang caught in my chest as she approached, wide blue eyes locked on mine as she slid her hand onto my waist. 'That's why it hurts so much, isn't it?'

I pressed my lips together. Trust her to get to the heart of it.

'Did you ever let him explain?'

My laughter grated my throat. 'The evidence was pretty damn self-explanatory.'

She drew in a sharp breath. 'Maybe you should hear him out—'

Dark dismay punched me in the gut. 'Are you re-thinking dinner with your ex? Are you going to hear him out, give him a chance to win you back?'

She paled, and her hand dropped from my body. I wanted to catch it back, reverse that unnerving feeling that she was slipping through my fingers.

Yeah. Trust. Betrayal. Forgiveness. Slippery fuck-ers.

'My situation is different.'

'Is it?'

'If you're trying to pick a fight with me, you're wasting your time. I've dealt with what happened to me and I've moved on.'

For a disgraceful second, I envied her strength.

I cupped her jaw, tilting her face up to me before sealing my mouth over hers. Yes, I wanted to shut her up.

I also might have hated her a little for being so bloody self-contained while I was unravelling. I at-tacked her tongue with mine, that fever to see her undone clambering through me.

At her moan, my heart leapt. I wanted her raw, un-fettered and all bloody mine.

Mine. The realisation that I wanted Leonora be-yond today, beyond this time and place, even if I had nothing to offer, struck me hard. Enough to deepen the kiss, grab her by the waist and stride towards the nearest wall.

It took a few confusing seconds to realise she was shoving at my shoulders.

What the fuck? 'Leonora,' I growled under my breath.

'No.'

Her denial took a moment to sink in. 'What?'

'You're doing it again. I won't be used like that.'

Her fierce condemnation staggered me. Shame flamed inside me and I realised she was right. Again.

'Fucking hell.' I turned away from her and attempted to claw back much-needed control. When I could take half a breath without choking on the fumes of my less than stellar reaction, I faced her again.

But she was walking away.

'I've got work to do. I'll send the head steward along to get a menu approval. Be sure to let him know when you want dinner to be served.'

I was being dismissed. And I'd earned this one, too.

More than a little shaken, I headed for the deck where, on the horizon, the picturesque coastline of Sicily baked in the sunlight.

The scene was the exact opposite of my mood. I reached for my phone, toying with the idea of cancelling the dinner.

I abandoned the idea.

Gemma and her husband, Giles, were pleasant enough. I couldn't stomach the thought of disappointing one more person and I was sure Aunt Flo would roast me alive about it when she arrived in a few days.

I hadn't told Leonora yet.

For some reason that triggered a deeper disquiet, which was absurd considering I'd already told her Flo was the most important person in my life. It didn't escape me that all this frustration, trepidation and damn *neediness* would disappear if I called it a day and just left the bloody yacht.

Now the deal was signed, Vadim was chomping at the bit to get moving. A week ago that would've pleased me no end.

Today, not so much.

My phone buzzed, fracturing my thoughts. The London office number dragged me back into business mode.

I took a breath and answered but not before admitting a crucial fact to myself.

If I had nothing to offer Leonora Branson, then the time was drawing near when I had to root her out from under my skin and send her packing, before my life went to shit. Again.

Leonora was late.

I stopped myself from looking at my watch for the umpteenth time.

Seven thirty for predinner drinks was what I'd clearly stated when I gave the head steward instructions about tonight.

This was what I got for my shitty behaviour this morning. Leonora was probably still pissed off with me. And I couldn't blame her.

All the same, she'd promised to be here.

'Something wrong with your Macallan, old boy?'

I looked up at Giles's query. He and Gemma were watching me with that look I'd come to expect from my family. The look that said they were unsure of my mood. I frowned, shifting my gaze to the amber liquid in my glass.

'Not at all.'

'Okay, then, is there a reason you've been eyeing the stairs for the last ten minutes? Are we expecting someone else?' Gemma asked.

I stared at her. Like Damian, we'd been close once upon a time. And like with Bryce, I knew I'd been wrong to cut her off after Damian's betrayal.

No wonder she was wary. She probably wouldn't have come if Giles wasn't obsessed with yachts.

Another wrong to right.

'Matter of fact, I am. She's running late.'

Gemma's eyes widened. 'She? But I thought…' She stopped and pressed her lips together.

'You thought what?' I asked sharply.

'Nothing,' Giles jumped in. 'So…who is she?'

I curbed my unease. 'You'll meet her soon enough.'
If she bloody turns up.

I caught movement from the corner of my eye and turned as Leonora stepped onto the deck.

My breath strangled in my throat.

So far I'd seen her in various forms of dress and undress. The cocktail number in Monaco had been exquisitely eye-catching, the uniform she wore for work evoking an endless stream of filthy fantasies.

Tonight, dressed formally, with diamonds winking at her wrist and throat, she looked phenomenal.

The olive-green sequinned dress shimmered in the deck lights, a form-fitting sleeveless thing that slithered to the floor with high splits that showcased her spectacular legs when she moved.

Dumbstruck, I couldn't take my eyes off her.

Gemma and Giles stared, too, their speculative gazes shifting from me to Leonora, but I was too busy staring at the sensational woman gliding towards me to pay them any attention.

Because in that moment, watching her walk towards me, I knew I wasn't ready to root Leonora out of my life. Not by a fucking long shot.

Giles cleared his throat pointedly.

Unable to stop myself from touching her, I slid my hand around Leonora's waist under the pretext of nudging her forward.

'This is Gemma, and her husband, Giles. Meet Leonora Branson.'

Leonora smiled. Pleasantries were exchanged before I beckoned to the hovering waiter. 'Champagne?'

Half expecting her to refuse, I was pleasantly surprised when she smiled. 'Thank you. I'm sorry for being tardy. An unexpected phone call.'

'No worries. We've been admiring this beautiful boat,' Giles gushed.

'Bloody hell, put your tongue back in your head, Giles,' Gemma teased.

Giles choked. Gemma laughed, and Leonora joined in a moment later.

Something green and slimy slithered inside me. 'It's not that bloody funny,' I grumbled.

Leonora shot me a look, more than a trace of cool detachment lingering in her eyes. Hell, I just couldn't seem to stop digging myself into a hole.

'So, how did the two of you meet?' Gemma asked.

'Leonora owns this yacht with a consortium of investors.'

Giles stared at Leonora with wide-eyed adoration. 'No bloody way.'

Leonora smiled. 'Until I find a buyer.'

'It's for sale?'

'Not to you, my darling, so stop your slobbering. We can't afford it. Not with four children and another one on the way,' Gemma snapped.

Giles gave a wounded groan.

'Perhaps if you stop getting me pregnant every time I blink in your direction, we'll be able to afford a vessel like this when you're sixty.'

The ashen void inside me threatened to choke the life out of me. Over the buzzing in my ears I heard Leonora offer congratulations. I attempted to speak but my words locked in my throat.

Three pairs of eyes swung to me, each holding various degrees of wariness.

'Everything okay?' Leonora murmured.

I forced a nod. 'Yes. Fine.' I glanced pointedly at my watch. 'Dinner should be ready, right?'

Leonora spotted my evasiveness and her eyes shadowed. 'Yes. Shall we go in?'

Giles offered his arm to Leonora. I swallowed my jealousy and offered mine to Gemma.

'Are you sure you're okay?' Gemma asked.

My smile felt tight. 'Frankly? No. But will you consider forgiving past transgressions if I say I'm working on it?'

Her face softened, the wariness receding. 'Of course. Gideon—'

'Congratulations on number five, by the way,' I slotted in before she could dig deeper.

There was only one woman I let that deep. Only one woman I might be too flawed to deserve. The sense of loss sucker-punched me.

Between Giles, Gemma and Leonora, dinner conversation flowed seamlessly, though my less-than-stellar dinner-hosting abilities attracted more than a few pointed looks as the hours dragged on.

When a throat was cleared I realised I was staring at Leonora.

'Do I have something in my teeth?' Her smile was pleasant but barbed questions brimmed in her eyes.

'Even if you did, you'd still be magnificently stunning,' I replied.

Gemma grinned. 'Is this our cue to take our after-dinner drinks elsewhere?'

Colour tinged Leonora's cheeks. 'No, it's not.'

'Shame,' I muttered under my breath.

'It's good to see you like this again, Gideon,' Gemma said.

I stared at her. 'Like what?'

'Like your old self. We've been worried about you since Penny. I'm glad you're moving on.'

Beside me, Leonora stiffened.

'I moved on a long time ago, Gemma.' I attempted to modulate my voice.

'There's moving on and there's relocating to Detachment Town. I, for one, am grateful you're back,' she said, taking another bite of food.

I caught Giles's gaze. He shrugged.

Gemma smiled. 'Did you know Damian's back in London? He's dying to see you.'

A flaming arrow pierced my chest. 'Is he?'

'Well, he tried to play it cool but I know he is. He still won't tell me why the hell he buggered off to America so abruptly, though.' She frowned, then a wide yawn caught her unawares.

'Giles, I think your wife is tired. Perhaps you should see her to bed?'

Leonora flowed to her feet, her movements sensually graceful and her eyes avoiding mine as she stepped away from the table. 'I'll take her if you two want to have your after-dinner drinks upstairs. It's all set up for you.'

Giles smiled. 'Excellent idea.'

I was in danger of letting my shredded control get the better of me, so I stayed seated and watched her escort Gemma off the deck.

Three excruciating hours dragged by before I entered the master suite. As I suspected, Leonora wasn't there.

I arrived at her door a minute later, stopped to take

a breath before I knocked. She took her precious time to answer it.

She'd changed out of her dress into a thigh-length negligee that tripled my heartbeat. My gaze ran feverishly over her before meeting hers.

'Will you let me in, Leonora?'

Her chin lifted. 'Why should I?'

'So I can apologise.'

Her censorious stare pierced awhile longer before she pushed the door open.

I got halfway to the bed before changing course. If I hoped to make a half-decent job of apologising, I needed my faculties intact. 'What I did this morning was less than admirable.'

'You mean trying to use sex to shut me up again?'

'I wanted to fuck you because you're bloody irresistible. I won't apologise for that. And yes, you drive everything else out of my mind when I'm inside you.'

Colour flared up into her cheeks. 'Is that supposed to be an apology?'

I sighed. 'I'm a bastard for trying to take advantage of the situation. The timing was awful and you didn't deserve to take the brunt of my shitty mood.'

'Apology accepted,' she said, but shadows lingered in her eyes. My stomach dropped when she stepped back and reached for the door. 'Was that all?'

The jagged ache cracked inside me. 'You're kicking me out?'

She hesitated, her gaze dropping to where I'd impatiently freed the top buttons of my shirt somewhere between Giles's tenth and fifteenth drinks. She licked her lower lip. 'I should.'

I reached for the next button and casually flicked it open. Her breath puffed out of parted lips. I released the next one.

'You don't play fair, Gideon.'

I continued undressing as I walked towards her. I stopped when we were an inch apart. 'I want you, Leonora. Badly. Enough that I don't want to play fair.'

'Then I should warn you that equity is high on my must-have list.'

I dragged a finger over her lower lip. 'Tonight you hold all the power. Tell me if you want me to go. But I'd much prefer it if you command me to stay.'

She didn't immediately reply. Then, 'Tell me something first.'

Tension knotted my nape. 'What?'

'Why were you so weird when Gemma mentioned she was pregnant?'

I staggered back, my insides turning to ice. 'Leonora…'

'You don't play fair. Neither do I. I'm renegotiating our deal. I want to know more about you. And this one is a take-it-or-leave-it deal.'

I caught a glimpse of that bleak landscape again and I knew I had to refuse. She was stripping me of everything. If she took away my barricades, what would I have left?

What do you have now?

Nothing.

So what did I have to lose?

I swallowed hard, walked to the armchair and sank into it. Elbows on my knees, I braced myself for the hardest thing I'd ever said out loud. 'Penny was pregnant when I tossed her out. I'd be a father by now… if she hadn't got rid of my child.'

She gasped, regret for my pain pooling in her eyes. 'Oh, my God! I'm sorry, Gideon.'

My insides clenched tight, raw pain threatening to overwhelm me. 'It's one of the many things I try not to think about but which ends up fucking up more areas in my life than I want to acknowledge.'

'You wanted to be a father?'

I drew shaky hands down my face, suddenly wishing I hadn't started this harrowing recounting. 'I wanted the chance to give it a bloody good go, not have it thrown in my face as hellish punishment for refusing to give Penny the time of day when she begged me to take her back a month after we broke up.'

'You mean she didn't tell you she was pregnant when… After Damian?'

'No. I refused to see her or take her calls after it happened. I think at some point she knew there was no chance so she got rid of it. We met by accident a month later. She begged me to take her back. When I refused, she tossed it in my face. Then had the nerve to tell me if I really wanted a child, we could try again if I took her back.'

'And did you? Want a child?' Leonora asked.

My shrug felt as if it were weighted with lead. 'As the product of a dysfunctional childhood, thoughts of fatherhood didn't manifest without a little…trepidation and, hell, downright terror. But it was also a challenge I could see myself rising to. A chance to succeed where my parents had failed so abysmally. Penny and I talked about it on and off. But it was always a far-off prospect, not a reality snatched from me before I knew it existed.'

'When…? How old?' she whispered.

A ragged breath whistled out of me. 'My child would've been three by now.'

Silence throbbed between us, then she cleared her throat. 'Are you sure it… That…?'

I knew what she was asking. It was the same question I'd asked myself a million times. 'I've no idea if the child was mine or not. And you know what? It didn't even matter. Not when it comes to that. It deserved more than being a fucking bargaining chip to be discarded when things went wrong. And the funny thing is, if she'd kept the baby, I would've considered…maybe…'

I heard Leonora's breath catch. 'Maybe what?'

I shook my head, my jumbled thoughts churning a million miles per second. 'Whatever. Doesn't matter now.'

Silence throbbed between us. When I raised my head, Leonora's gaze avoided mine for a long minute. 'Does Damian know?' she asked.

The crack inside me widened. 'I have no clue. I might hate him now but we had similar shitty childhoods and once upon a time we had the same dreams of doing better than our parents. If he knows, then he's going through the same hell. If he doesn't know, then…'

Something shifted in her eyes, something I desperately wanted to explore. Cling to. 'If he doesn't, then you want to spare him the agony.'

It wasn't a question.

'It's not a step I can bring myself to take,' I confirmed.

'Oh, Gideon…'

That open-tap sensation intensified, soaking up the dry dirt beneath my feet. The only trouble was that it was now turning my landscape into quicksand. Equally devastating. Equally dangerous.

I was sinking. So when Leonora lifted herself up, slid her body against mine, even though there was a hesitation in her eyes, I clung on tight.

Her surrender was conditional but it didn't stop me from wrapping my arms around her anyway, grateful for any reprieve from my anguish.

'I'm sorry I brought up a painful memory for you,' she murmured.

'You have the power to make it go away, even for a little while. Take it, Leonora.'

'Yes.'

She offered me her lips. I took them. But as I lost myself in her, my question came back to haunt me.

What did I have to lose?

I'd asked her if she cared about me.

She'd never answered.

CHAPTER NINE

Leonie

'STAY WITH ME.'

I desperately clung to the last of my self-preservation even as I melted beneath the glide of Gideon's wickedly hot mouth across my shoulders.

'In case you haven't noticed, I'm already in your bed.'

His smile branded my skin. 'I don't mean this. I mean, take the time off you said you would and spend it with me.'

Tension rippled through me.

It'd been two days since Gemma and Giles left the yacht. Since Gideon revealed the raw, devastating layer of treachery that had shattered his trust. Two days since the revelation that had rocked any notions I'd had that this thing between us had a shelf life after we left the boat.

Regardless of that knowledge, I was falling for him and it scared me shitless enough for me to wish this trip were over while praying it would never end.

'Nope. This is my busiest season.'

He froze against me. I glanced over my shoulder, saw a mutinous look across his face and hardened myself against it. 'Besides, don't you have to get back to London?'

As if on cue, his phone buzzed. The frequency had increased over the last twenty-four hours. The more it rang, the more Gideon ignored it.

'You should really get that.'

'I really shouldn't,' he countered testily. 'I'd much rather talk about this.'

'There's nothing to talk about.'

'I beg to differ.'

One large hand slipped around my waist, a precursor to him pinning me close to mount a concentrated campaign.

Self-preservation kicking in harder, I popped out of his hold. 'I need to check in with my office.' Just as I needed to remind myself that, had it not been for her miscalculation, Gideon might still be with Penny, despite her betrayal. Hearing his confession had brought home to me like nothing else how stuck he was in the past. How I needed to find the strength to distance myself from falling further under his spell. No matter how agonising it was proving to be.

He flipped over and sat up, sexily dishevelled and growing steadily pissed. But underneath the irritation, there was a wary watchfulness.

Slowly another look slid into his eyes. It was the one I'd been fighting against since he walked into my room two nights ago to apologise. That ferocious possessiveness and a yearning that eroded my defences.

'What's going on, Leonora?'

I balled my fists until my nails scored grooves in my palm. Then I let the pain fuel my anger because I knew that would be the only way to protect myself. 'I don't like being pressured.'

Myriad expressions chased through his eyes. I dropped my gaze to the sheet I was mangling between my fingers, too terrified to admit that I wanted the man beneath the crumbled facade of the superficial playboy I'd thought him to be. That I desperately craved this man whose integrity, loyalty and steadfast faithfulness to those he cared about burned through his bravado.

Because the thought of losing all of that when he stepped off this boat and walked away was too much to bear. My heart was already on the line, on a collision course guaranteed to be more devastating.

'Or maybe it's something else?'

'What are you talking about?'

'You've been strange since I told you about Penny two nights ago. You pushed me to tell you and now what? My baggage is too messy for you to deal with?' he asked icily.

'If you're going to answer your own questions, why bother asking?'

'Because you get evasive, and you throw your work in my face, just like you're doing now, right before you disappear. You want me to beg? Is that it?' Underneath his frustration, Gideon's voice throbbed with what sounded eerily like entreaty. Need.

That ball of self-preservation threatened to unravel. 'I don't want you to beg, no.'

'Then give me a straight answer. Will you stay?'

No. Say no. End this now before it's too late.

'How long do you want me to stay?'

A flame seared his eyes, but it was the light of triumph, not the emotion I'd hoped to see. 'How about we don't put a time frame on this? Let it play out the way it feels right?'

No. I was a planner at heart. Nowhere on the list of how I lost my heart included throwing caution to the wind and bungee jumping into the unknown. 'That doesn't work for me.'

Ruthless determination settled on his face. 'Tell me what works and I'll make it happen.'

My needs were simple. And endlessly complicated. 'I'll think about it.'

'Leonora—' He swore as his phone burst to life again.

Seizing the reprieve, I rose from bed, grabbed a bathrobe. 'You really should get that.'

His jaw tightened for a second before he snatched up his phone. 'Aunt Flo, unless this is urgent…' He paused to listen to whatever his aunt was saying but his gaze didn't waver from mine.

I knew our conversation wasn't over but I needed to retreat. To think without the juggernaut of his will bearing down on me. I backed towards the door but Gideon was faster. With lightning speed, he launched himself off the bed and wrapped an arm around my waist, holding me prisoner as he carried on his conversation.

'A little more notice would've been nice,' he said into the phone.

I tensed. His eyes met mine and he grimaced. 'Well, if you're here a day early, then of course you must see the yacht. I'll make sure brunch is ready for you when you arrive.'

He hung up, then pulled me closer. 'You heard that.'

I nodded. 'I'll inform the chef.'

Gideon regarded me steadily, another layer of resolve sliding into place. 'I want you to join us.'

And hasten my heartbreak? I wasn't in the mood for further revelations about Gideon and Penny.

His aunt was special to him, the one who most likely held the key to all the layers of the man I was sure I was falling for. The man I suspected would never be available to me. 'It's not a good idea, Gideon.'

'Why the hell not?' he growled.

'She's the most important person in your life. I'm just the woman passing through. Ships in the night and all that.'

His lips brushed my ear. 'In case you haven't noticed, I'm attempting to anchor you.'

Yes, but for how long?

I was saved from facing my own question when his phone buzzed again. I took advantage, dancing out of his distracted hold. 'I'll see you later.'

'Join us, Leonora. Or I'll come and get you.' He turned away, his finger stabbing the answer button.

I shut the door and hurried to my cabin. Inside, I phoned the chef and relayed instructions for brunch. Then I froze, my gaze moving erratically around the room.

Gideon wanted me to stay. Every cell in my body screamed at me to say *yes*.

But could I afford to *let this play out*? The real world waited. Gideon's world. So did the demons he was choosing to fight alone. I might have pushed him into revealing his past to me, but it'd done nothing to dissipate its bleakness. My sole role on the yacht was to provide an escape. Oblivion.

But at what ultimate cost?

Deathly afraid of the answer, I pushed the question aside and headed for the shower. Once dressed, I placed a scheduled call to the office, frowning when it went to voicemail.

It was after nine and my part-time assistant's day off but Andrea should've answered. A call to her mobile produced the same result. I was leaving a message when the sound of rotor blades pierced the air.

Flutters of trepidation grew into steel butterflies in my stomach as the decision firmed in my mind.

I was going to stay, enjoy this exhilarating ride for as long as it lasted and tend to whatever fallout came later. If that meant meeting Gideon's great-aunt straight off the bat, so be it.

Resolute, if a little anxious, I headed for the fourth-deck helipad.

Gideon was assisting a stylishly dressed diminutive figure off the aircraft. Once at a safe distance, he drew her into a hug.

When they separated, she stared up at him for several heartbeats before placing a gentle hand on his cheek. There was no denying the affection between them as he took her hand in his.

I pinned a smile on my face as they approached. 'Miss Mortimer, it's lovely to meet you. Welcome aboard.'

Florence Mortimer weighed me up for several seconds before taking my hand. 'No wonder he's tied up in knots. It all makes sense now,' she said.

Gideon's gaze locked on mine, but other than the flame of possessive heat, his gaze was carefully neutral.

'What does?' I asked.

'You can call me Flo. And it's nothing to worry about for now, my dear,' she responded. 'Can't promise it'll all be smooth sailing later, though.'

Gideon stiffened. 'Flo, behave yourself.'

'Escort me to a pot of Lady Grey and I'll think about it.'

'Brunch is ready for you downstairs.'

'Wonderful. After brunch I'd love a tour of this beautiful boat I've heard so much about.'

Gideon's hand landed on the small of my back on our way off the deck. When I jumped, he curved his hand around my waist and pulled me closer.

Brunch was an outwardly pleasant affair but beneath the surface, choppy tension resided.

It was a relief to slip into professional mode for the tour, but even then, Gideon sent me heavy, searching looks that multiplied the butterflies in my stomach.

'My dear, do you mind giving my great-nephew and I a few minutes alone?' Flo asked when we returned to the shadier second deck.

Gideon's face turned stony. Before he could raise an objection, I smiled. 'Of course. I need to touch base with my office.' Andrea hadn't returned my call and I was beginning to worry.

Gideon's gaze branded me as I hurried away. I told myself the fact that he wasn't trying to hide our liaison didn't mean a thing. We were both consenting adults.

Back in my office, I redialled Andrea. When it went straight to voicemail again, I dug out Laurent's number. It rang half a dozen times before rapid-fire French instructed me to leave a message. Talking myself down from panic, I left a message and headed for the galley to consult with the chef over lunch.

I was redialling Andrea again on my way back to my cabin when I spotted a sleek speedboat heading for the yacht.

Was Gideon expecting another guest? Surely, he would've notified me. Curious, I went down to the landing deck and waited for the vessel to pull up.

The man who jumped lithely from the speedboat onto the landing deck was pure Mortimer through and through.

His hair was a shade darker than Gideon's and his eyes, when he took off his stylish sunglasses, were a pronounced hazel to Gideon's grey. Beyond those minor differences, the two men could've been brothers.

Perhaps they had been, once upon a time. I had a feeling I knew who this man was. He'd walked onto the boat as if he owned it and was sizing me up with those incisive eyes.

'Hi. May I help you?'

The barest hint of a smile curved his lips. 'I might just need your help later, depending on how things shake out. For now, a simple indication of where I might find my cousin would be appreciated.' He extended his hand. 'Damian Mortimer.' He raised his eyebrow and waited.

'Leonora Branson.'

'Ah…' His gaze grew sharper as he scrutinised my face. 'I heard we may be buying a boat from you.'

Surprise bolted through me. 'Did you?'

'A memo crossed my desk along those lines. But I'm not here to check it out.' His eyes shadowed. 'Not just yet anyway.'

'Then should you be here at all?' I blurted.

All trace of humour left his face. 'I see you're informed. Well, partially anyway.'

'Partially?' I parroted.

'There are many sides to a story, Leonora. Don't organise the plank walk yet until I've had a chance to say my piece, would you?'

'What makes you think I'm interested?'

That unique Mortimer smile made another faint appearance. 'You are. There's nothing wrong with that. In fact I'm happy to see he has you on his side. Maybe it'll make this easier.' His face grew solemn. 'Take me to him, please. I'm done waiting on Aunt Flo to talk him into it. This has gone on too bloody long.' He stepped closer and crooked a finger under my chin. 'And if you're worried about the fallout, you have my word I'll make this as—'

'What the fuck are you doing here?' Gideon's voice was a naked blade slashing through the air.

Damian froze, his gaze growing haunted as it flicked over my left shoulder.

'Gideon—'

'Did you hear me?'

'I heard you. I haven't gone deaf in the last three years.'

'That's a shame,' Gideon responded cruelly.

Damian's wince was barely perceptible but I caught it. 'We need to talk.'

'No. You need to take your fucking hand off her before I break it.'

Damian's hand jerked away from my chin as if I'd burned him, and when his eyes met mine there was a hint of apology in them.

Acrimony, thick and volatile, infused the air, trapping us in place. When it grew too much to bear I stumbled to where Gideon stood frozen in the doorway.

'I'll let you two talk.'

Gideon moved directly in front of me, blocking my path. 'What did he say to you?' he demanded in a voice I barely recognised.

'Nothing important. But he's here for you.'

'No, he's not. He's leaving. Right now.'

Damian merely smiled at the callous dismissal and strolled towards Gideon. 'You plan on throwing me overboard? Because that's the only way you're getting rid of me.'

'Don't tempt me.'

I attempted to slide past Gideon again. He curled his fingers around my wrist.

'Let me go,' I whispered.

'No,' he growled under his breath. 'This is bullshit and I don't have time for it.'

About to ask whether he meant Damian, or me, I swallowed my words when Aunt Flo appeared behind Gideon. 'You two are going to be the death of me.'

Gideon swung an accusing glance her way. 'You knew he was coming.'

'Yes.'

'If I must deal with him, he can wait until I'm back in London.'

'For fuck's sake, ten minutes is all I need,' Damian interjected.

Gideon didn't respond, and the two men eyed each other.

My phone blared to life. Thankful for the reprieve, I tugged my hand from Gideon's.

'Who's that?' he asked.

'It's business,' I replied.

'Ten minutes, then I'm coming to find you. You and I need to talk, too.'

I hurried away, lifting the phone to my ear as I entered my cabin.

It took a couple of seconds for Laurent's heavily accented English to make sense.

'Wait, can you repeat that?'

'*Oui. C'est* Andrea. She had the *bébé* a few hours ago.'

'What? But that's too early.'

'*Oui*, but the *bébé…mon fils…*is okay. Andrea also. She wanted me to tell you.'

'*Merci*, Laurent. And congratulations to you both!'

The moment I hung up, my thoughts immediately zeroed in on Gideon. God, the man's effect on me was all-encompassing.

Was I making a mistake by not walking away now? I squeezed my eyes shut, trying to grapple with the push and pull of my emotions. But even before I opened my eyes again I knew that I couldn't let go. Not yet. Gideon wanted me. I wanted him. I was in for as long as it played out.

But with Andrea officially on maternity leave, I needed to make a quick visit to the office, if only to make arrangements to transfer my office temporarily onto the yacht.

I tossed my overnight case on the bed and started packing. But even the thought of the short absence from Gideon tore at my insides. I dropped to the corner of the bed, fighting tears because I knew it was too late.

I was in love with Gideon.

And he…he was shredded from a double betrayal

he might never recover from and a cruelly thwarted promise of fatherhood. My heart broke all over again thinking of what he'd been put through.

Even if Damian's presence today brought him closure, could he move on, or was this sizzling sexual attraction all we'd ever have?

Questions weighed heavy, but I pushed them aside. Again.

Flowers and a gift for Andrea's newborn sorted with a few phone calls, I touched up my make-up, slipped into my favourite heels and left my cabin.

Gideon had promised to find me in ten minutes. That was twenty minutes ago. Despite the fireworks arching between them, I'd seen the looks on both men's faces. A bond remained between them. One they might be able to salvage.

But as I neared Gideon's office and heard raised voices, that possibility grew bleak.

Gideon's was hoarse with pain. 'What the hell does it matter? I trusted you more than I've ever trusted anyone else. You took that trust and trashed it.'

'She lied, Gideon. About everything. You saw what she wanted you to see because she's a manipulative bitch.'

'Are you saying you didn't sleep with her?'

My breath caught as Damian hesitated. 'I don't fucking know. I was completely out of it. She knew that. She claims we did. Dammit, I don't remember.'

'Let me refresh your memory. I came home to find you both bare-ass naked in my guest bedroom.

And she was damned sober when she told me you fucked her.'

'So what if I did sleep with her? *You* told me it was over. After *she* told me it was over. I was away for two months and you didn't bother to tell me you were back on.'

'That's your bloody excuse?' Gideon railed.

'No excuses. I fucked up. Are you going to spend the rest of your life punishing me? Because if you are, you're going to have to look me in the face every day from now on when the board votes me back in on Monday.'

'What next? You're going to make a bid for my CEO seat? Or are you after something else?'

'What the hell could I possibly— If you're worried about your new woman, don't be.'

Gideon laughed, the sound so harsh, it grated my heart.

My feet propelled me to the doorway. They didn't notice me because both men were facing the view, shoulders tense and bodies bristling. 'I'm not worried. In your own unique way you taught me a lesson. Opened my eyes to a few things. All that emotional bullshit is overrated.'

Damian dragged a hand down his face and shook his head. 'Are you sure your Leonora knows that?'

'She's not my anything. And yeah, she knows it's just sex. It will always be just sex. If she needs a reminder, I'll provide one when the time comes. But this time round if you're that hard up, make sure I'm done with her before you make a move.'

My gasp wrenched both men around.

'Bloody hell,' Damian swore.

Gideon froze for a long second, his face ashen. Then he stumbled towards me. 'Leonora—'

'No.' I held up my hand, backing away from him.

He didn't stop. 'Leonora, please—'

'I said no!' My ankle twisted as my stupid heels caught. The pain barely registered as I raced back to my cabin.

Gideon caught up with me before I could shut the door in his face. The door slammed shut behind him. I whirled to face him. 'Whatever you're going to say, save your breath.'

He jabbed shaky fingers through his hair. 'What you heard sounded bad, I know, but—' He stopped, his eyes darting to the suitcase on the bed. 'What the hell is that?'

'What does it look like?'

Gideon

She was leaving.

My gaze swung back to her; I was dazedly aware that my lungs felt as if they'd been electrocuted. Hell, my whole body felt as if it'd collided head first with a cement truck. 'You were already packing to leave?'

Her blue eyes flicked over me, and for a moment I saw pain and fury. Then she dismissed me as if I was nothing. 'Looks like I've saved us both time.'

I tried to catch my breath. No fucking dice. 'How long have you been planning this?'

'Since I decided this was over for me.'

'When exactly was that?'

'Does any of that really matter now?'

A parade of emotions stampeded through me, the strongest of all the need to reject what she was saying. This wasn't over for me. Not by a long shot. The kind of long shot that had *for ever* shimmering all over it. But…hadn't I seen this coming? She'd been dropping hints over the last few days. Since I told her about Penny. About Damian. About the child I lost.

I swallowed hard. 'Tell me the truth, Leonora. Is this about everything I told you?'

'You mean the information I had to wring out of you? Information you only gave in return for sex? That was what you were doing, wasn't it? Trading the *emotional bullshit* for sex? So again, what does it matter now?'

The barbed wire wrapped around my heart tightened, sinking anguish deeper. 'It fucking matters,' I snarled.

The agony intensified as she lifted her chin. For a moment I wanted to tell her not to say whatever she was about to say.

'Fine. Here's the truth. It's because you're letting what happened colour every corner of your life. I just got rid of my own baggage. I won't be weighed down by yours. Like you said, it was just sex. But as great as it's been, I want more. And don't flatter yourself by thinking I want more with *you*. But I want more out of life. I want love. I want *everything*, Gideon. And you're not the man to give it to me.'

For the first time in my life, I knew what true panic felt like. 'So what? You're going back to Adam?'

She had the audacity to laugh. 'You're really hung up on him, aren't you? Why do you even care?'

Because I want to be the one to give you more.

The words ricocheted in my head, but again, they stuck in my throat. Everything inside me screamed against letting her go.

My gaze shifted to the half-packed suitcase and something cracked inside me. 'Leonora...'

'Service on the yacht will continue as normal. You don't need my professional services and I'm needed back at my office so I hope you won't insist I stay and make things awkward.'

'No problem. I don't plan on being aboard for much longer.' Not without her. Not when I could already feel her absence tunnelling a hole in my chest.

'Good. Then it all works out,' she said coolly.

A frigid wind swept over me. I probed her expression, desperate to see something else other than the icy indifference staring back at me. Perhaps it was wishful thinking when I thought I caught something in her expression. But it was gone a second later. Still it didn't stop me from taking a jerky step towards her, my hands dying to touch her one last time. 'So that's it?' was all I managed.

She stared at me for another elastic second, before she returned to her suitcase. 'Goodbye, Gideon.'

I had no memory of leaving the cabin, only of stumbling onto the first-floor deck, which unfortunately also held Damian.

'What happened?' he snapped.

'Nothing I want to fucking talk about with you.'

I wanted to blame his arrival on the boat for this. But even I wasn't that desperately childish.

When he pushed a drink into my hand, I grimly and gratefully clutched it.

We drank in silence. Until I heard the unwelcome approach of a speedboat. I tossed the drink aside and dashed to the rail. My lungs flattened as I watched Leonora board the boat.

'Fucking hell, are you really letting her leave?' Damian demanded.

'She was already leaving,' I replied. 'She was always going to leave.' Because I had nothing to offer her. Or anyone.

'You're not going to want to hear this, mate, but I'm going to say it anyway. You're going to regret this very quickly. When you do, do yourself a favour and don't wait three fucking years.'

Damian's words were ringing in my ears as I stood frozen, gripping the railing, watching the speedboat make a wide arc. My insides turning to stone, I willed Leonora to turn around.

She did.

And in that moment I knew what true desolation meant.

CHAPTER TEN

Gideon

I TOOK MY seat at the head of the conference table, ignoring the disdainful stares from the usual suspects. So, fuck it, I hadn't bothered to shave. They should be thankful I'd poured myself into a laundered suit and remembered how to tie a decent Windsor. I didn't plan on being here long enough to permanently damage their delicate sensibilities. I was here to vote on Damian rejoining the board and to deliver news of my own.

'Shall we get down to the first item on the agenda?'

'Yes, by all means,' I drawled, drawing a cold glare from Uncle Conrad. I ignored him, drummed my fingers impatiently on the polished wood.

I'd already wasted a week in the pit of my own misery before accepting I'd made a huge mistake. I didn't want to waste another minute.

I was in love with Leonora Branson.

And I'd fucked it up royally by going mute when I should've pleaded for her with every word in my vocabulary. The frantic twenty-four hours I'd spent trying to track her down had so far hit dead ends. I glanced at my watch, wondered if the PI I hired had located her in the last forty-five minutes since we spoke.

He'd better have something new for me, or…

What? This glorious mess is down to you and you alone.

I deserved every second of this agony.

'Gideon?'

I refocused on the faces staring at me. 'Yes?'

'We need a yea or nay on reinstating Damian on the board.'

My gaze travelled down the conference table to where Damian sat. Something shifted inside me at seeing him in this room. It struck me hard how much I'd missed him.

His revelations on the yacht hadn't been all that surprising. Penny was a manipulative bitch, and it didn't take a genius to know she'd played us both. I'd let her come between us and lost my best friend for three years. It was time to let it go.

'I vote yea.'

Damian's gaze remained on mine, then he nodded. I nodded back and the knot I'd carried for years melted away.

Throats cleared, and I shifted my gaze back to Uncle Conrad. 'Now, there's the matter of your broken agreement.'

'Excuse me?' My snarl caused bodies to shift in seats.

'What are you talking about, Conrad?' Aunt Flo

barked from her seat at the opposite end of the table. 'This wasn't on the agenda.'

'A last-minute addition. I have it on good authority that you broke the terms of the agreement before your thirty days were up.'

I bolted upright in my seat, rage boiling in my gut. 'I hope for your sake that *on good authority* doesn't mean you have photographic evidence of whatever the fuck it is you think I've been up to. Because if you do, you'll be in for a world of pain.' If Leonora's privacy had been compromised, heads would roll.

Conrad bristled, his double chin wobbling as he attempted to stare me down. 'There has to be some accountability or all of this means nothing.'

'You talk to me about accountability? I single-handedly brought home a multibillion-pound contract and you're what? Blackmailing me with technicalities?'

'Terms are terms, young man. You signed on for thirty days. You didn't honour it.'

A thick wave of ennui swept over me and I subsided back in my chair. Halfway down the table, Harry all but vibrated with excitement. It was the most animated I'd seen him. Ever.

'Let me save you the trouble. You want me gone? Fine. I'll go.'

Gasps echoed around the table.

Damian jerked upright in his seat. 'What the hell, Gideon?'

I waved him away. 'Don't worry, Damian, I'm not stepping down. I'm stepping *away* for the ninety days my position allows me. I see Harry over there, chomping at the bit for his chance. You're welcome to it, mate. You all need a taste of what it's like to run this company without me.' I stood up and laid my hands flat on the table. 'I give you three months to come to your senses, and I expect a lot of grovelling when you do.'

I walked down the length of the conference table to stunned murmurs. Damian blocked my way. After a long stare, he held out his hand.

I clasped it, renewed emotion moving through me. When he stepped back Aunt Flo took his place, her gaze sombre. With a strained smile, I leaned down and kissed her cheek. 'Give 'em hell while I'm gone.'

'You can count on it.'

As I straightened she grabbed my arms, and, looking deep into my eyes, she smiled. 'Godspeed. Don't come back without her.'

Sucking in a deep breath, I walked out.

Leonie

Vacations in paradise sucked.

Vacations in tropical paradises where couples canoodled *everywhere* sucked even harder.

Purchasing a first-class ticket to Maui to celebrate the sale of *La Sirène* to an anonymous buyer, and my decision to not only remain in the South of France but also open a new office in Montenegro had seemed like a fabulous idea at the time.

But I didn't account for the harrowing misery that tracked me to the Pacific haven.

I fooled myself into thinking that, because I'd managed to put Adam in my past, I'd be able to deal with losing Gideon.

This pain was a million times worse. I couldn't breathe, blink or speak without missing him. And the pain seemed to multiply by the second.

Even my stubbornness had folded under the weight of my agony.

The moment I returned to my hotel room, I was checking out. Maybe returning home, busying myself with opening the new office would take my mind off this never-ending torment.

At least it'd save me from being slapped in the face with the stupid lovey-dovey shit going on around me.

But I was damned if I left the island a complete loser. I'd failed abysmally at love. Again. But I planned to make this surfboard my bitch even if it killed me.

I flattened myself on the board and paddled furiously for the quarter-mile my instructor suggested. When a decent wave came along, I tightened my core, got onto my knees and, with a deep breath, rose to my feet, bending my knees for maximum stability.

My position held for all of five seconds before a stronger wave tossed me into the sea.

I gave up, rubbing helpless tears and salt water out of my eyes.

The sun was rising on another glorious Maui morning. Time to leave paradise.

I staggered onto the shore, dragging my surfboard behind me.

'Giving up already?'

My breath punched out of me as misery knotted itself tighter. I blinked at the apparition. Except ghosts didn't look this virile. This heartbreakingly gorgeous. *This painfully real.*

I greedily devoured his face, his body. His bare feet. His white T-shirt moulded to his body and his hair tossed about in the early-morning breeze.

I wanted to charge him, wrap every inch of my body around him. But he was the same man who'd broken my heart long and savage weeks ago. 'What are you doing here, Gideon?'

'Waiting for you.'

My heart lurched. I managed to bite back the *why* before it spilled out.

His face looked drawn, and a strained smile played at the corners of his lips. 'You shouldn't give a shit about me but I'd really like you to ask me why, Leonora.'

'You're right, I don't want to know.' I picked up my board and started walking away.

He followed. 'Please, Leonora. Hear me out.'

'What makes you think I have time for you? For all you know I could be here with someone else.'

His nostrils flared and his face went a shade paler. 'Are you?' he bit out.

I shrugged. 'That's for me to know and for you to go away and never find out.' I walked faster.

'God, I know I deserve that, but…even if you're here with someone else, I can't stay away. Staying away is killing me.'

That stopped me dead in my tracks. The board

dropped into the soft sand. I pressed it in deeper, desperate for something to lean on.

'Why is it killing you? If you're after more of that *just sex* you wanted, you're out of luck.'

He gave a stern shake of his head. 'I don't have a right to ask, I know. But I'm asking anyway. Don't go. Give me a chance—five minutes—to plead for your forgiveness for fucking up so spectacularly.'

My jaw dropped.

He took a step closer, his gaze devouring my face. 'What I said to Damian was a shitty attempt at self-preservation. I thought he took something from me. What I had with Penny was broken long before Damian. She knew it. That's why she set her sights on him. But you…you were the real deal. When I saw you with him on the yacht, it scared the shit out of me. I got caught in this nightmare loop where I was going to be betrayed again and I overreacted.'

Pain hollowed my legs. 'I would never betray you, Gideon.'

His eyes darkened and his throat moved as he swallowed. 'I know.'

'Do you?' I probed.

He nodded. 'Leonora, you have a pure heart. You drew me into confessing things I'd never told anyone else. My heart knew it could trust you even if my head took its time. Even if I was too blind to realise how precious that was until I'd messed it up.'

'You hurt me, Gideon. A lot.'

A bleak shadow crossed his face and the lines around his mouth deepened. 'I know. And you have no idea how much I wish I could take it back. I didn't mean a single word of it. I should've told you that on the boat, too.' He gave a self-deprecating laugh. 'I've wrestled with corporate giants, fast-talked hard-arsed businessmen into parting with money for multibillion-pound deals, but when it came to the most important deal of my life, I turned into a fucking mute idiot.'

My heart did that stupid flip-flop again. 'The most important deal?' I whispered.

'By far,' he confessed gruffly.

'What are you saying, Gideon?' My voice shook and I didn't even care.

'That I want to be the one to give you more. I'm here to tell you that watching you board that launch to leave me felt like my heart had been ripped out. I'm here to tell you that I love you. You're the love of my life and everything I have, everything you want from me, it's yours.'

I swallowed the rock in my throat but I still couldn't speak. So I stayed silent.

Gideon stepped towards me, his hand hovering next to my cheek before he dropped it. With eyes glistening fiercely, he stared down at me. 'Please tell me you'll consider it, Leonora. I know you're hurting, that you won't forgive me easily. But…'

'But…?' I croaked.

'But my five minutes are up. And you're still here.'

Despite the tectonic shifting inside me, I managed another question. 'What do you think that means?'

He shook his head. 'I'm not fucking this up again by second-guessing. I'm begging for another chance,

Leonora. A chance to worship you. A chance to plan a whole lifetime with you, wherever you want that to be.'

A whirlwind eddied inside me, gathering up the shattered and scattered pieces of my heart. 'I'd be careful if I were you. I'd go to town with carte blanche like that.'

The cocky smile I was expecting didn't appear. 'I would agree to every single stipulation of that plan if that means I get to see your beautiful face every day, touch you every night and fuck us both sense-less in between.'

My fingers tightened on the board. 'Keep going,' I whispered.

He breached the gap between us, bringing his body heat and his intoxicating scent to my starving senses. 'Within a handful of weeks you've helped me repair broken relationships, and given me a glimpse of the sort of husband and father I can be. Please tell me I haven't thrown away the chance to find out?'

My sob caught us both unawares.

Gideon caught me to him when I let go of the surf-board. Gentle fingers stroked my cheek. 'When the time is right, I want a chance to have a family with you. Nothing would please me more than to see you pregnant with my child.'

Tears prickled my eyes. He brushed them away with his thumb.

'I love you, Leonora. These past couple of weeks have been hell. Put me out of my misery.'

'Gideon?'

'Yeah?'

'I love you, too.'

His breath fizzled out of him, his gaze growing stormy as it feverishly searched mine and then raked down my orange surf suit.

'Any chance I can convince you to ditch your imaginary boyfriend and come back with me and let me demonstrate just how much I've missed you?'

I laughed, growing breathless as joy burst through me. 'I should make you work for it.'

Finally, that cocky smile I craved made an appearance. 'I'm sure you'll come up with something.'

He yanked my surfboard out of the ground and held out his free hand. I took it and we raced across the sand. I thought we were returning to my hotel, but he surprised me by steering me to an open-top Jeep. 'Where are we going?'

'I have a surprise for you but first I intend to make you scream long and hard for the next few hours. I don't want to be disturbed by hotel security.'

At my giddy laughter, he spun me around, dragged me close and sealed his lips to mine in a hot, carnal kiss that tunnelled deep into my heart and began to heal the broken pieces. After endless minutes, he lifted his head.

'Damn, I've missed that so much. I never want to be without you again, Leonora.'

'I don't want to be without you either. Can you take me wherever we're going to, Gideon?'

He fired up the ignition. Ten minutes later we pulled up next to a sleek helicopter.

With a nod to the pilot, he shut us in the private compartment and dragged me into his lap. We spent the short flight with Gideon's adoring hands and sexy mouth reacquainting themselves with my body. I whimpered when he reluctantly pulled away. 'We're about to land,' he murmured against my lips.

I looked out of the window and gasped at a familiar vessel sparkling against the backdrop of the Pacific Ocean. 'You're the anonymous buyer who bought *La Sirène*?'

He nodded. 'I didn't want to risk losing it to anyone else. Without that yacht you wouldn't be in my life. It'll always be special to me.'

Blinking back tears, I let Gideon carry me out of the chopper. At the first view of where we were, my jaw dropped.

'We're on a private island?'

He nodded.

'Whose?' The view was breathtaking, the house even more so.

Gideon grinned. 'It's ours. I needed somewhere far away from my annoying family.'

'It's a hell of a way to commute to work.'

'Then it's a good thing I won't be working for a while.'

'What?'

'I'm officially on a sabbatical. I reserve the right to make that permanent. Or take up a new challenge. Come here.'

I went into his arms, let him wrap me tight the way I loved. 'What challenge do you have in mind?'

'My immediate one is to get you back on that yacht. We never got round to fucking on every surface the way I fantasised. But first I'm taking you inside our house and peeling this suit off you. Then I'm going to make you scream.'

I laughed as he swung me into his arms and marched towards the stunning house made of teak and glass. I barely saw the decor, nor did my feet touch the ground.

I was completely lost in the love and magic of Gideon as he skilfully demonstrated how much he'd missed me.

Several hours later, as we stood on the deck of *La Sirène*, I leaned back against him and basked in the glorious Maui sunset.

'I want to sail the world with you,' he murmured. 'See the world through your eyes.'

'We will.'

'I never want to be parted from you. You're the reason I breathe.'

I fought blissful tears as he wrapped his arms around me.

There were no words needed. My heart had healed because of him and I intended to keep it beating just for Gideon.

* * * * *

LEGAL DESIRE

LISA CHILDS

MILLS & BOON

CHAPTER ONE

EXCITEMENT COURSED THROUGH Trevor Sinclair. He'd barely been able to wait out the weekend to tell his friends what he'd figured out. They were all in relationships now, so he'd forced himself to be patient even though it had nearly killed him to keep the news to himself.

Finally, he heard the ding of the elevator as the car arrived at the floor for Street Legal, the law practice he owned with his three best friends—guys with whom he'd survived living on the streets. The rumble of deep voices echoed off the high, open ceiling of the reception area. They were probably complaining about his calling this early Monday morning meeting.

Their usual business meeting was Tuesday morning. But this wasn't business as usual, and it couldn't wait any longer.

Along with the voices, he heard the tap of dress shoes against the hardwood floor: Simon. The heavy strike of boots: Stone. And the soft squeak of tennis shoes: Ronan.

They were all here. And within seconds they trudged into his office. Like Simon, who was the managing partner, Trev had a conference table in his. As a class-action-lawsuit attorney, he always had multiple clients. Sometimes even this voluminous space wasn't big enough for those meetings.

But it was big enough for this one, for the four of them.

Ronan glared at him through narrowed dark eyes. "Why do you look so damn happy?"

"Maybe he finally got some," Stone suggested. He was equally bleary-eyed.

Simon shook his blond head. "Nope. He would look as exhausted as we do if he was getting any."

"You all do look like hell," Trev agreed.

"Jealous?" Ronan said as he dropped onto one of the chairs around the conference table. Then he eagerly reached for the carafe of coffee sitting in the middle of the reclaimed wood table.

Trev felt a pang of something that could have been jealousy. But he dismissed the ridiculous thought. He had no reason—absolutely no reason—to be jealous of these guys. He could have sex any time he wanted. And love? He wanted no part of that mess.

"Disgusted," he corrected Ronan, and he shook his head to emphasize his point. "How the mighty have fallen." He made a tsking sound with his tongue against his teeth. How had it happened when they'd all sworn they would never risk their hearts?

Fools...

He really did pity them. Just pity.

Not envy.

"Yup, he's jealous," Stone said with a deep chuckle.

Trev snorted. "Yeah, right."

"Did you call this meeting for dating advice?" Simon asked. Since Simon was the managing partner, he usually called the business meetings. "Do you want to find out if Bette or Muriel or Hillary have a friend that they can set you up with?"

He felt another pang, but he knew what this one was: his pride was stinging.

"I don't need a setup," he assured his friend. "I am the only one of us thinking with his dick nowadays, which is probably why I'm the one who finally figured out who the hell the mole is."

He had their attention now. Three pairs of eyes widened and focused on him as three jaws fell open in shock.

"You figured it out?" Simon asked. As managing partner, he had considered it his responsibility to find out who the hell the mole was that had been selling information from their case files or passing off forged or real information as coming from their case files.

It wasn't that Trev hadn't trusted Simon to find the mole. But he'd had a vested interest. Since Trev had been the first one the mole had hit—during his biggest class-action lawsuit yet—he'd taken it personally. And because he hadn't been willing to risk the mole compromising his next case, he had put off taking another one until the damn mole was caught.

"Who is it?" Ronan asked.

Trev was surprised the rest of them hadn't figured it out yet. Now that he knew, it seemed obvious. How had they not suspected her sooner?

"Who?" Stone asked.

All of them were impatient to hear the identity. Maybe they wouldn't have minded if he had cut their weekends short for this.

"I don't have proof," he cautioned them. "Yet. But I'll get it." He had already put a plan in motion.

Simon arched a blond brow. "Are you really sure you know who it is? Remember that I once thought Bette was the mole."

And instead, she'd turned out to be the first woman for whom Simon Kramer had ever fallen. That would not be the case for Trevor.

"Who is it?" Stone asked again, his voice gruff with impatience.

Trev shook his head as he had earlier—with pity—that they hadn't figured it out like he had. "Allison McCann."

"No..." Simon shook his head now but in protest. "That's not possible."

"It's not just possible," Trev replied, "it's probable. She's the one thing every one of those cases has in common. She and her public relations firm worked every one of them." He gestured toward his door. "You've even given her an office to use on our floor with access to our computer system that has all our files."

Simon's face paled. He was the one who had set up the office for her—the one who'd hired her firm to ramp up their public image years ago, the one who encouraged them all to use her to help sway the public to their side of their cases. He shook his head again, but it wasn't in protest. It was in self-disgust. He looked sick.

While Simon's face had paled, Ronan's flushed with anger, and he cursed.

But Stone was stubborn. He snorted. "C'mon, Trev. You just want to sleep with her, so you're trying to convince yourself she's the mole."

Simon had tried to seduce Bette into admitting she was the mole. Instead, she had seduced him.

Trev had no intention of seducing anyone let alone being seduced. He had a better plan than risking the frostbite having sex with Allison McCann would give him.

"You were there when she admitted she hates lawyers," Trev reminded him.

And Stone's face paled. He released a ragged breath.

"If she hates us all so much, why the hell does she do our PR?" Ronan asked. He was clearly on board.

Even though they were all lawyers who loved to argue, none of them could belabor the point that it all made perfect sense. It had to be Allison McCann.

She was the one who'd been selling them out and sabotaging them.

"Why?" Simon asked.

"Who cares?" Trev shot back at him.

He didn't give a damn why she'd done it. He just intended to stop her.

That wasn't all he planned to do to the mole. He wasn't going to risk frostbite. But he was intrigued and attracted enough to see if there was any thawing the ice goddess that was Allison McCann.

She had been summoned. She hated that. She had her own business. She was the boss. But if she wanted to keep that business going, she had to have clients. So she worked for them. They were the boss. And she was their bitch.

Allison had learned young how to be a bitch. She'd been taught by the biggest one she'd ever known. But she had no time to think about the past because the elevator bell dinged, announcing her arrival to the floor of Street Legal.

These were her best clients but her least favorite. The things she did for them...

Would have kept her awake had she had a conscience anymore. She'd sold that long ago—along with her soul—in order to have her own business. With a sigh, she stepped off the elevator and headed through the reception area.

The receptionist, a former gang member, watched her approach. She had never understood why they'd chosen his face to be the one clients saw first. No smile curved his lips or warmed his dark eyes. He was not welcoming. At least he had never been welcoming to her.

But then few people—besides the media—were. Reporters waited impatiently for the next press release she issued. They were always happy to see her because they knew she delivered the dirt.

"They're all in Trev's office," Miguel told her as he jerked a thumb in that direction.

So apparently, the partners of Street Legal were waiting impatiently for her, as well. Because the summons had been last-minute, she'd had to move some other appointments around, and Edward, her assistant, had been no help with that. He'd claimed he had a migraine and disappeared into the men's room, leaving her to make all the calls herself.

She really needed a new assistant. Maybe she should ask Miguel if he had a friend who might be interested in the position. She could use someone less welcoming than Edward. He tended to talk too much to clients and to the press.

She nodded in acknowledgment and headed down the hall that led to Trevor Sinclair's office. Excitement quickened her pulse with each click of her heels against the hardwood. She wasn't excited to see him, though. She was just excited because he must have finally taken on a new case.

And of all the partners, his cases were the easiest for which to advocate. Unfortunately, he was not the easiest of the partners for her to be around; he was the one who made her constantly remind herself that she did not like and could not trust lawyers.

When she arrived at the open door to his office, she found them all looking at her the same way, as if they did not like and could not trust her. She shivered at the coldness in their gazes.

Miguel must have alerted Trevor to her arrival. He was the one standing at the door, holding it open for her. He was also the first to shield that initial cold glance and replace it with a grin.

The grin unsettled her more than the coldness and not just because it made him, with his dark auburn hair and deep green eyes, look even more handsome. It unsettled her because her mother had always delivered her most vicious insults with a smile.

Maybe the partners hadn't called her here to take on a new assignment. Maybe they'd called her here to inform her there would be no new assignments for her at Street Legal.

For the past few months they'd been using her firm less and less even though they'd probably needed her services more. They'd had some bad press after one of them had been reported to the bar association. Word had also gotten out that they had been representing lying clients.

She could have turned that bad press around for them. But they'd been reluctant to involve her and hadn't even really explained what had happened.

What was going on at Street Legal?

And why did she feel as if it was going to affect her as well now?

"Come in," Trevor Sinclair urged her.

She hadn't even realized she'd hesitated in the hallway. But if she stepped inside that room, the odds were not in her favor. There were four of them and only one of her. Maybe she should have let Edward come along as he'd begged at the last moment. But she'd reminded him of his "migraine" and told him to take it easy the rest of the morning. Not that Edward would have been any help to her in this situation.

These four alpha dogs would have eaten him alive had he tried to come to her defense. Not that Allison needed defending from anyone.

She'd learned young to be able to take care of herself. And if they fired her, she would be fine. She had other clients.

But she felt a curious pang in her heart over the thought of losing them. Maybe it was just pride. But then she stepped closer to Trevor Sinclair, and her breath stuck in her lungs at his size and his handsomeness.

And she knew that it wasn't just pride that caused that pang.

Allison McCann stepped forward as if she was facing a firing squad. Her willowy body was tense, her delicate shoulders pulled back and stiff. As she neared him, Trev caught a flicker of something pass

through her pale blue eyes. The guys claimed she had
no emotions, but he'd seen something.

Fear?

Regret?

Guilt?

Guilt would have made the most sense—if she
had a conscience. But if she had no emotions, she
certainly had no conscience, either.

Then she stepped closer to him as she passed
through the door he'd been holding open for her.
And her hair brushed across his throat. The scent of
it—like cool rain—filled his senses while the silky
touch of it had his skin tingling. He dragged in a
deep breath, and she filled his head.

She was so damn beautiful with her eerily pale
blue eyes and deep red hair. She had to be at least
half-Irish—like he was—with that hair. It was too
rich a color to be dyed, richer even than his, which
was more brown than red. Like her eyes, her skin
was pale, too, and flawless like porcelain. She didn't
even seem real. She looked like one of those dolls
people didn't dare touch.

His mother had had a doll like that, one she'd
never taken out of the box because she hadn't wanted
to devalue it. It was the only thing she'd taken with
her when she'd left New York City for the brighter
lights of Hollywood. That doll had had red hair and
porcelain skin just like Allison's.

He expelled the breath he hadn't even realized
he'd still been holding. That breath stirred her hair,

and she shivered. As cold as she seemed, he would've thought she was immune to it. But then his breath would have been hot—not cold.

Trev was hot-blooded and hotheaded. So maybe it was good that he'd had the weekend to cool off, or he wouldn't have been able to hide his anger from her.

She glanced up at him, those pale eyes narrowed with suspicion. So maybe he wasn't doing as good a job hiding his emotions—or his attraction to her— as he'd thought. But then she passed him and approached the conference table near the windows of his office.

His partners stood and not particularly out of manners because a lady had entered the room. Stone and Ronan probably didn't trust themselves to be anywhere near her after what Trev had told them.

The only one of them who truly possessed manners was their managing partner. They were so ingrained in Simon, like his charm, that he held out a chair for her. As she sat down, he said, "We'll leave you two to your meeting now."

And Allison's brow furrowed slightly.

Ronan didn't even look at her as he passed around the other side of the conference table. He was not good at hiding his emotions. His body fairly vibrated with anger. As he passed Trev on his way out the door, he murmured, "I hope you know what the hell you're doing."

He wasn't certain that he did. But he forced himself to grin like he had it all under control.

Stone slapped his shoulder as he passed him. Trev wasn't sure if the slap was encouragement or recrimination, but he nodded at him.

Simon was the one who paused the longest in the doorway and stared up at Trev. He emitted a heavy sigh and murmured, "I don't know how I didn't see it."

And it was killing him that he hadn't, especially now that it was so obvious.

She had to be the mole.

Knowing it wasn't enough—they needed to be able to prove it. And Trev had taken it upon himself to do that using whatever means necessary.

"Good luck," Simon said as he stepped out the door and closed it for Trev.

Allison rose from the chair in which Simon had seated her and pivoted on one high heel, her navy blue dress billowing out around her long, slender legs as she turned toward him. She must not have liked having her back to him.

Trev could relate. As a kid living on the streets, he'd known to always keep his back to the wall, so nobody could sneak up on him.

Somehow Allison McCann had managed to sneak up on all of them. How had they never suspected her?

Was it because she was so gorgeous? Hell, she wasn't just beautiful. She was damn near perfect. Like a ballerina, her body looked delicate but strong, her muscles defined. She was probably a runner.

But no matter how fast she was, she wasn't going to outrun him.

Trev was going to catch her. He had the mole, and she was not going to get away from him. She was not going to get away with what she'd done.

CHAPTER TWO

Trevor Sinclair's office was huge, but when the door was closed, shutting her inside and alone with him, it felt small. And Allison felt trapped.

It wasn't just his physical size that overwhelmed her. She was tall, too. He was even taller, well over six feet. And he was muscular with shoulders so broad that he probably had to turn sideways to get through doorways. The only thing bigger than his size was his personality. He had a deep, booming voice that resonated inside a courtroom and outside it. He also had an energy about him, a restlessness that made Allison restless, too.

She hated that restless feeling even as much as it, and he, fascinated her. Or maybe that was why she hated it—because she didn't want to be fascinated. And she certainly didn't want to be attracted to him.

"I thought this meeting was with all of the partners," she said, glancing at the closed door, willing the others to return. Sure, she had been outnumbered with the four of them, but she'd liked her odds better with all of them than with being alone with Trevor Sinclair.

Admittedly, it wasn't just him she didn't trust. She didn't trust herself.

He shook his head, and his hair brushed across the collar of his black shirt. His hair was too long. Her fingers itched to run them through the dark auburn strands. He looked more like a rock star than a lawyer.

But then as a lawyer, he was a rock star. The minute he stepped into a courtroom, he commanded all the attention. He played it just like a rock star played the stage.

"My meeting was with all the partners," he said. "Your meeting is with just me."

Just me...

Nobody would ever refer to him as *just him*. He was so much more, and she had no doubt that he knew it, that he was fully aware of how damn handsome he was. Like a rock star, he had fans of his work as a lawyer and his prowess in the bedroom. She'd heard stories about him as well as his partners. They were legendary lovers.

Her skin heated at the thought of Trevor Sinclair touching her, of him stroking his big hands over her body. Of his lips moving over hers.

He didn't have the thin lips so many other men possessed. Trevor's lips were full and wide and moved easily into big, wicked grins. How would they feel against hers? Or on other parts of her body?

She suppressed a shiver, just like she'd tried when she'd felt his breath touch her hair moments ago. His breath had been hot and scented with coffee and something sweet, probably from the tray of goodies sitting in the middle of the conference table.

He must have noticed her glance at it because he gestured at that tray as he moved toward her. His legs were heavily muscled, too, his thighs straining against his dress pants as he walked. His body looked strong, powerful.

"Are you hungry?" he asked.

She was—but apparently not for food. Maybe she'd denied herself too long. She couldn't remember the last time she'd had sex and not just because it must have been a while ago but because it must not have been very memorable.

She suspected that it would be memorable with Trevor Sinclair. With his body, his mouth, his big hands, she had no doubt sex with him would be *very* memorable.

She shook her head. "No, I'm not hungry," she lied, willing herself to deny her hunger for him. She would not mix business with pleasure.

But for a few moments, when all the partners had been staring at her, she'd wondered if her business with Street Legal was about to end. Even if it did, she still wouldn't risk a sexual relationship with one of them.

Least of all Trevor Sinclair...

How would she feel if she were in bed with him?

Even more overwhelmed…

And vulnerable.

Allison hated feeling vulnerable. She wouldn't date someone who might affect her too much, who might make her want too much. She knew that only led to disappointment and heartbreak.

"Good," he said.

She blinked, trying to focus on what he was saying. It was hard to focus with him standing so close. He had moved quickly from the door to the table and she hadn't had a chance to step back. Not that she would have. Allison never backed down. "What?"

"I'm glad you're not hungry," he said, "because now we can get right to it."

She blinked again because it didn't make sense. Get right to what? Sex?

No. She didn't want that. Not with him.

All she wanted was another assignment, and that had to be the reason he'd requested this meeting. That had to be the reason the other partners had left.

"You took on a new case?" she asked, and excitement surged through her again.

It was much safer for Allison to focus on business. And she actually enjoyed business with Trevor Sinclair. His cases involved taking down big companies, making them pay for any harm they might have done the public or the environment. Helping him made up for the other Street Legal cases, like Ronan Hall's messy divorce ones or Stone Michaelsen's criminal ones.

But he shook his head. "Nope. I'm not taking on any new cases right now."

She felt a pang of disappointment, which was followed quickly with curiosity. "Then why did you want to meet with me?" she asked.

Alone?

He stared down at her for a long moment, his deep green eyes intense. She could feel the heat of his muscular body. An answering wave of heat rushed through her as her pulse quickened. Maybe she should have stayed in the chair Simon Kramer had pulled out for her because then Trevor might have sat down, as well. Then he wouldn't be so close.

"I wanted you to come here," he said, and his deep voice sounded even deeper than usual, "because I have a proposition for you."

A proposition? That had nothing to do with a case?

If it wasn't business, didn't it have to be pleasure?

She sucked in a shaky breath.

And he flashed one of those wide, wicked grins of his, and his green eyes sparkled with amusement and something else.

Desire?

No.

Maybe she was still sleeping. Maybe she was dreaming—that Trevor Sinclair was propositioning her...

Her mouth fell open, her lips—which were nearly as red as her hair—parted on a gasp. Her pale skin finally flushed with color while her pale eyes also darkened as her pupils dilated.

He had her. He'd caught the notorious ice queen off guard with his remark. She wasn't so cool now. He had flustered the usually unflappable publicist. He laughed. "Not *that* kind of proposition, Allison."

She shook her head, tumbling the red waves of her hair around her slender shoulders. "I—I don't know what you mean."

Trev was standing close to her, so close that he knew everybody who had called her the ice queen, himself included, was wrong. He felt the heat of her body even though he hadn't touched her. He *really* wanted to touch her. Hell, he really wanted her.

So he turned and slid onto the table right next to where she stood, and his knee bumped against her thigh. She stepped back, though.

She obviously did not want him touching her.

He chuckled again at her reaction. "You thought I was propositioning you for sex."

"Of course I didn't think that," she haughtily replied, her pointy little chin lifting in disdain.

"What if I was?" he wondered.

All restless energy, he stood up again, and he was close enough that his suddenly very tense body brushed against hers. How could he want her even knowing that she was the mole? How the hell could he feel any desire for her let alone so much that it had tension winding tightly inside him?

Of course, even though she was the mole, she was stunning. Maybe trying to seduce the truth out of her wasn't the bad idea he'd thought it was when Simon had tried it with Bette, and Ronan with Muriel.

"Would you be interested?" he asked.

She blinked as if trying to clear her vision before staring up at him. "Would I be interested?" she repeated. "In sex with you?"

And he almost thought she was considering it—until she laughed. That laugh—clear and sharp—cut his pride like a knife.

"Why is that so damn funny?" he asked.

"Because you're joking," she said purposefully.

Trev was suddenly very serious—so serious that he leaned a little closer to her. Their bodies brushed again. Her breasts touched his torso, just below his chest. He felt the mad pounding of her heart and the heat of her body again. She definitely was not an ice queen. He wasn't getting frostbite at all. He was getting hot.

Damn hot for the unscrupulous little publicist.

So hot that he couldn't resist his impulse to reach out. He slid his arm around her slim waist, and she moved her body more fully against his, clearly wanting him back. Then he lowered his head and covered her mouth with his.

Her lips were like silk, so smooth and soft. He nipped and nibbled at them, devouring her as that desire consumed him. He wanted her lips to part, so he could deepen the kiss, so he could slide his tongue inside her mouth.

But he wanted more than that inside her. He

wanted to bury his throbbing cock inside her, too. He'd never been so turned on before by just a kiss.

But she wasn't just kissing him…

His scalp tingled as he felt her hands in his hair, sliding through it, clutching his head to hers. Then, finally, she parted her lips, deepening the kiss.

And he knew her image was just that: Allison McCann was no ice queen. She was all fire and passion.

He tasted so damn good, just like she'd thought he would, like coffee and sugar. His tongue slid between her lips, stroking over hers. She would probably taste like the mint she'd swallowed when he'd jerked her into his arms. While one of his arms was wound around her waist, the other was around her back, as his hand cupped the back of her head, holding it against his as he kissed her.

And her fingers were in his hair, tangled in the thick strands of it. She wanted to slide her fingers down his face, over his muscular chest to the buckle of his belt.

She wanted to undress him. Wanted him to undress her…

She wanted more than a kiss. She wanted him to release the tension he'd built inside her. She wanted his tongue other places than her mouth.

She couldn't believe that she would want that, that she would want him. And it seemed mutual. She felt his erection straining against the fly of his jeans as he pressed his long, muscular body against hers—as he kissed her.

Trevor Sinclair was kissing her. And she was kissing him back.

That wasn't just unprofessional—it was career and emotional suicide. Just the kiss.

If they did any more, if they crossed the line any further...

She stepped back, jerking herself out of his arms.

"No," she said, her voice surprisingly steady despite how hard she was shaking with desire.

Breathing hard, he stared at her blankly, his brow furrowed beneath the fall of the hair she'd tousled with her fingers. "What?"

"If your proposition is for sex, my answer is no," she clarified. And she fought to still her trembling. She couldn't afford to let him see how badly he'd affected her, how badly she wanted him, because then he might call her bluff. He might pull her back into his arms and prove that she wanted him just as badly as he'd seemed to want her.

But she must have fooled him because he nodded. "That's right. I forgot that you said you hate lawyers."

She flinched with regret that she'd let that slip out once in a meeting with him and Stone Michaelsen. That had been nearly as unprofessional as letting Trevor kiss her. And kissing him back.

That had just been stupid, and Allison was rarely stupid. But she'd wondered for a long time what it would feel like to have that wide mouth of his against hers. It had been even better than she'd thought. What would it be like if they'd gone further?

She nearly shivered as sensations raced through her. And now she regretted pulling away as soon as she had. Maybe she should have let the kiss go on... to more.

"So I guess it's a good thing I might not be a lawyer much longer," he said.

She sucked in a breath. She hated lawyers but she knew they were necessary, especially good ones like Trevor Sinclair. "Why not? Did you get turned in to the bar association like your partner?"

His brow furrowed.

Maybe he hadn't known she'd been aware of that. But she had sources everywhere and she couldn't afford any surprises in her work.

He shook his head. "I didn't do anything to get reported to the bar," he said. "And neither did Ronan. That complaint was bogus."

She wasn't so certain about that. But she nodded as if she agreed with him. "Then I don't understand."

"Somebody forged those documents they claimed were from Ronan's case files—"

"No," she interrupted him. She didn't want to talk about his partners. "If you're not losing your license, why won't you be a lawyer much longer?"

He chuckled. "I'm not losing my license," he assured her. "I've decided to give up law in order to run for public office."

Now it made sense the comments she'd overheard

his partners making to him as they'd exited the office, all some version of wishing him luck. For a second she'd thought those comments might have been in regard to her. But until he'd kissed her, she hadn't been able to imagine why he might have needed luck with her.

Unless he'd planned to seduce her.

He hadn't. He had probably only kissed her because she'd stung his pride. She shouldn't have goaded him. But there was something about Trevor Sinclair, something that caused her usual guard to slip.

She fought now to put her guard back up as he studied her face. She wasn't certain if he was looking for her reaction to his kiss or to his news. She hid them both under a mask of mild curiosity as she asked, "What does your running for public office have to do with me?"

"I want you to help me," he said. "I want you to run my campaign."

That proposition was nearly as ridiculous as his wanting to have sex with her. Hell, she would have preferred that proposition to this one. She laughed again.

"I'm serious," he told her.

And as was the case with him, her professionalism slipped again and she admitted, "There's one thing I hate more than lawyers," she said. "Politicians."

"I don't need you to love me," he said. "I just need you to help me win."

She laughed again. She wasn't certain what was funnier. The thought of her falling in love with him or the thought of her helping him win an election. But her laughter sounded a bit hollow as it echoed inside his big office. And she forced herself to stop before it passed from hollow to hysterical.

She shook her head. "I'm a publicist," she reminded him. "I'm not a campaign manager."

"I know what you are, Allison," he said. And for a second something cold and determined passed through his deep green eyes.

She shivered.

Then he blinked and replaced the look with a twinkle of amusement. "And you're all I need right now," he said. "You're who I want."

She wanted him, too, but not like this, not as a client. She shook her head. "I'm sorry, Mr. Sinclair. I can't help you."

"You don't think I could actually win an election?" he asked.

She sighed. "No, I think you could." And that was the problem.

But he obviously couldn't see it. His brow furrowed again as he said, "Then what's the problem?"

"I don't play politics," she said. Not anymore.

"You're a publicist," he said, throwing her words back at her. "That's all you do is play politics."

No. She didn't have to play politics. Not ever again.

"I'm not interested in this assignment," she said.

And she stepped back, heading toward the door. "I'm sure you can find someone else."

"I don't want someone else," he said. "I want you."

If only he'd really meant that personally and hadn't kissed her just out of wounded pride.

She laughed again—at herself—because her pride was wounded. And once again her guard slipped and she found herself admitting, "You would have had a better shot at me agreeing to a proposition for sex than playing politics."

CHAPTER THREE

"ALLISON MCCANN DOES not exist."

Trev snorted over Simon's pronouncement. If she didn't exist, who the hell had he just been kissing in his office?

"You can't make her disappear just because I figured out she's the mole," he said.

It must have been killing Simon to know that Trev had figured it out before he had. It was probably killing him even more that he had been the one who'd hired her, which was probably why he'd had Miguel send Trev to his office the minute she'd left. Miguel must have told the managing partner when she'd headed to the elevator.

She'd done that quickly—right after turning down his assignment. But had she left the door open to something else? To something more personal than politics?

Or had she only been joking? He'd been so stunned that she might have accepted his sexual proposition that he hadn't moved fast enough to stop her from leaving his office. And by the time his dick had settled down enough for him to move, he'd rushed into the hall to find her already gone.

Then Miguel had redirected him here—to Simon's office where Ronan and Stone waited for him along with the managing partner. They must have all come here after they'd left his meeting.

Simon's office was very similar to Trev's with the tall windows, exposed brick and long conference table. Simon also had a leather couch along one of the interior walls.

Trev didn't have any comfy furniture in his. He was usually too restless when he was working to sit down and relax. Simon wasn't the type to relax, either. But according to office gossip, he didn't use that couch for taking naps.

Maybe Trev needed a couch like that. He could have taken Allison there. Hell, he could have taken Allison on the conference table. Or standing up.

But Trev always took no for an answer.

While Ronan and Stone sat around that conference table, drinking from the mugs of coffee they'd brought from his office, Simon sat at his desk. He studied his computer monitor through narrowed eyes as if he was trying to find something. Or someone…

"*I* didn't make her disappear," Simon said. "Allison McCann never appeared in the first place, at least not until she started her PR firm seven years ago. No birth certificate. No social security number. No nothing."

She'd certainly felt real in his office—in his arms...

Trev paced in front of the windows that looked out onto Midtown. He glanced down at the street, but he was too high to see any people clearly. Still, if she was down there, he would have noticed her. With her bright red hair and pale skin, she would have been recognizable from any distance.

"So what do you think?" Ronan asked Simon. "Did she create herself when she created her company?"

Simon leaned back in his chair and sighed. "Maybe she's not an ice princess at all," he mused. "Maybe she's a robot."

She was definitely flesh and blood—all very hot flesh and blood. But Trev wasn't ready to admit to his partners that he'd kissed the mole.

Trev shook his head. "She's not a robot."

Simon sighed. "Then I have no idea what she is or where she came from."

Trev had no doubt that she was real. "What are you thinking?" he asked Ronan, who'd brought up that she'd created herself. Why would she have done that? "Do you think it's just a PR stunt?"

Ronan shrugged. "A person who's all about image might have set out to create one for herself."

"I hope that's all it is and not the ultimate con," Simon said. The former con artist was probably beating himself up thinking he had missed a con. "I should have checked her out better." His face was tight with self-recrimination.

"You checked out her firm," Trev reminded him. "Hers was the best." Or Simon wouldn't have hired her.

"But who the hell is she?" Simon said. "And why would she suddenly turn on us like she has?"

Trev wondered that, too. "It doesn't make sense."

"You're not having doubts now, are you?" Simon asked. "She didn't already get to you, did she?"

She'd gotten to him—physically. Trev wanted her like he couldn't remember wanting anyone else in a hell of a long time. "No doubts that she's the mole," Trev said. He was even more certain now that he was right. "What doesn't make sense is why she agreed to work for us in the first place with how she feels about lawyers."

He focused on Stone, who'd been curiously silent this whole time. He was the one who'd been with Trev when she'd made that comment. And now she'd made one about her dislike of another profession.

Simon asked, "What about your plan? Did she take the bait?"

Trev shook his head. "No, she hates politicians more than she hates lawyers."

Simon expelled a ragged breath. "What the hell is her deal?"

"I don't know." But Trev was more determined than ever to find out.

Stone cleared his throat. "Bellows isn't Hillary's real last name," he said.

Trev and the other partners turned to him in surprise. He'd never mentioned that before. Hillary was an ambitious assistant district attorney. They'd never even suspected her of being the mole. What reason could she have had for changing her name? "Really?"

Stone nodded then he glanced at Simon. "You wouldn't be able to find any birth certificate for Hillary Bellows. She took her mother's maiden name."

"Why?" Trev asked. "Is her father a criminal and, as a DA, she didn't want to be associated with him?"

Stone shook his head. "Just the opposite. He's someone very rich and very important and she didn't want special treatment because of her real last name."

Ronan snorted. "I doubt that would be the case for a publicist. If her father's famous, she would undoubtedly use that to her advantage."

But Trev wondered.

While Allison McCann didn't have any problem delivering their press releases, she was careful so that she was never any part of the story herself.

Simon tapped the keys on his computer. "So if Allison took her mother's maiden name…"

"How are you going to find her real name?" Stone asked him. "I had no idea who Hillary really was until she told me."

Simon cursed.

"I'll find out," Trev assured them.

"How?" Simon asked. "You said she didn't take the bait."

Not that bait. But she'd given him another opening—when she'd kissed him back.

"I'm not giving up after just one shot," Trev said. Or one kiss.

"We don't just need to know who she is, though. We need to get evidence against her in order to bring her down like she tried bringing down Street Legal," Simon said.

The others nodded in agreement.

Trev might have found another way in—literally. But he wasn't about to share that with any of his friends yet. "I'm not giving up," he repeated. "I'm going to get her."

Simon shook his head. "I'm not sure I want you risking yourself like this," he said. "We don't really know anything about her. She could be dangerous."

"She is." She'd affected him like no other woman ever had. "But she doesn't scare me."

"That's the problem," Simon said. "You should be scared and you're not."

His friend's words chilled Trev for a moment, finally cooling off the heat of the desire he felt for Allison. He didn't want to wind up like his friends had. He didn't want to be in a relationship the way all of them were.

But he didn't have to worry about that happening to him. Allison was the mole, so there was no way he would ever fall for her. Hell, he was safer than his friends were, which was good because after that kiss, he was damn well going to get Allison McCann or whoever the hell she really was.

* * *

Allison had lost her damn mind. She couldn't believe she'd said what she had to Trevor Sinclair. Fortunately, he hadn't taken her up on the offer any more than she'd taken him up on his offer to help him run for office.

What the hell had she been thinking?

She hadn't. After that kiss she hadn't been able to think at all. That was her only excuse for her slip in judgment. Two slips...

Her first slip had been slipping her tongue into his damn mouth. Kissing him had been so stupid. And then to suggest that she might have agreed to have sex with him.

The sad thing was that she hadn't been kidding. She was tempted. But apparently, she hadn't been enough of a temptation for him. Maybe he couldn't believe she'd turned down his job offer, though.

And that had probably been her third mistake. Like she'd said, he had a damn good shot at winning whatever election he ran for. If she was the one who helped him cross from lawyer to politician, she could bring her business to the next level. But politics wasn't where she wanted it or her to go.

She wasn't sure it was the right place for Trevor Sinclair, either. He was a much better lawyer than he would be a politician. But he was so eloquent and so damn good-looking that there was no way he could lose...whatever he wanted.

For a moment, with the passionate way he'd kissed

her, she'd thought he'd wanted her. But he only wanted her to help him win.

She sighed. She probably should have taken the assignment. But politics and campaigns…

She shuddered as bad memories washed over her. Memories were all they were, and she was too strong, too resilient, to let them ever get to her again. She wouldn't let Trevor Sinclair get to her, either.

And just in case he'd tried to track her down later that day, she'd made certain to stay so busy that now, at the end of the workday, she was exhausted. She dropped her dress on her closet floor and grabbed her nightgown. Moments later she opened a bottle of wine and poured herself a glass as she glanced down at her view of the park.

She should have been out there, running. That was her fastest way to relieve stress. But she didn't think this was the kind of stress that could be relieved with exercise. She needed sex.

Sex with Trevor Sinclair. While she had other men she could have called, *he* was the one she wanted, which was stupid. She worked with him. At least she used to work with him. Mixing business with pleasure…

Was stupid.

But where else was Allison to find pleasure when all she did was work? She pressed her glass to her lips and took a long sip. The alcohol shot straight from her empty stomach to her head. Maybe she should have waited to open the wine until after she'd eaten. But she wasn't interested in food.

She just wanted Trevor Sinclair here. For more of his kisses.

For more of him.

She should have undressed him, should have seen if his muscular body looked as good without clothes as it did with them. But he hadn't really wanted sex with her. He'd wanted her to run a damn campaign for him. Anger coursed through her, replacing the desire she'd felt for him. That was better.

She'd rather be angry with him than attracted to him. But she doubted any amount of anger—or wine—could negate the amount of desire she felt for him.

She sighed but she took another sip anyway. She could handle her alcohol. Her mother had adopted the European attitude toward drinking, serving it to Allison well before she'd been of legal drinking age. So she'd built up a tolerance to it, which was unfortunate because she couldn't use being drunk as an excuse to call Trevor Sinclair and proposition him for sex.

Not that she would have. She knew better than to get involved with a man like him. It was bad enough that he was a lawyer; now he wanted to be a politician.

She groaned with disappointment and murmured, "What a waste."

The ding of her doorbell drew her attention away

from the windows, and she glanced toward the door. Her pulse quickened with excitement.

Could it be…?

Had *he* found her?

Had he found her?

After that unsettling second meeting with his partners, Trev had spent the rest of the day doing something he'd never done before: chasing after a woman. And Allison McCann was one busy woman. He never tracked her down at her office or throughout her day of outside appointments.

But as he stood outside the door of the penthouse apartment in a building on Central Park West, he truly hoped he had found her now. He pressed the bell for the second time and finally, the door opened. Allison McCann leaned wearily against the jamb as if she'd spent the day running from him.

Had she known he'd been trying to track her down? Had she been purposely eluding him? He wouldn't have put it past her, especially if she had any inclination that he suspected she was the mole.

She didn't look scared, though. She looked…

Incredibly sexy. So sexy that she struck Trev dumb once again. He couldn't talk. He could only stare at her.

She'd looked beautiful earlier that day in a navy blue dress. But then she'd also looked uptight and professional. Now she appeared soft and approachable. Her hair had begun to curl around her face, softening her sharp cheekbones and pointy chin. And while she wore another dress, this one was short, revealing her long, bare legs. Was it a dress or a nightgown? The silky white material was thin, nearly transparent, and clung to her every curve. And she had more curves than he'd originally thought. As he stared, her nipples tightened into points that pushed against that thin material.

A groan slipped out of his lips as desire coursed through him, heating his blood and hardening his body. She was incredibly sexy.

But even though she didn't look like the ice goddess anymore, she sounded like it when she asked, "What the hell do you want?" and her voice reached new icy levels of coldness.

If not for that kiss, Trev might have bought the ice queen act she played so well. But he couldn't forget the heat and passion of that kiss.

So he grinned and replied, "You."

"Fuck you," she replied.

He laughed and stepped forward, crowding her in the doorway. "That's why I'm here."

Her pale eyes narrowed in a frosty glare. And he wouldn't have put it past her to slap him. But instead, she laughed and stepped back, letting him inside the penthouse. A wineglass dangled from her fingertips, a deep red sloshing around inside the glass as she walked barefoot down the hall to the living room with its big windows looking out onto Central Park.

"I really need to fire Edward," she murmured as

she dropped onto the sectional couch in front of those windows.

Trev's mind had gone blank again as he stared at her long legs. She'd curled them beneath her on the cushions, like a cat curling up in the sun. "Edward?"

"My assistant," she said. "The one who must have told you where I live."

That was all Edward had told him for the moment. But Trev had a feeling he could eventually get even more information from her assistant, so he shook his head. "It was easy enough to track down your address through a deed search."

Despite how elegant she usually looked, she could swear like a sailor. She could even snort, which she did now. "That's bullshit."

She obviously wasn't buying his explanation. Edward wasn't getting easily off the hook with her. But that was his problem.

Not Trev's. *She* was Trev's problem.

"Don't lie to me," she warned him. "I don't appreciate being lied to."

"How do you know I'm lying?" he asked. Even the guys who'd known him since his teens couldn't tell when he was lying. He was that good.

"Because the deed for the penthouse isn't in my name," she told him.

Busted. He hadn't handled that well. But now he had even more questions, especially since Edward had made it clear it was her place. She wasn't leasing it. "Is it in your husband's name?" he asked.

And he wasn't entirely joking now. Edward had also made it clear that Trev had no shot with her. He'd had to convince her assistant that all he'd wanted from Allison was her professional services. Fortunately, Edward hadn't been able to tell that he'd been lying.

She snorted again. "I'm never getting married."

"Again?" Maybe she'd been before and that was why her name was different.

She shook her head. "Never been. Never will."

"What turned you off marriage?" he asked.

"Maybe I've worked too many cases with your partner, Ronan Hall."

Ronan was the divorce lawyer. "Ronan became a divorce lawyer because of his parents' lousy marriage."

Her face was like a beautiful mask, hiding all her emotions and reactions but for a slight flinch. He must have hit a nerve. Usually when he did that, he pushed even more to break whomever he had on the stand.

But Allison wasn't on the stand. She was on the couch. And she was so damn sexy. He didn't want her to get mad and toss him out of her place before he'd had a chance to kiss her again. To touch her.

He pointed at the open bottle on the glass coffee table. "Are you willing to share?" he asked.

She glanced at it, as if assessing if there was enough left. "Glasses are in the kitchen," she said, gesturing toward the breakfast bar at the other end of the living room.

But he dropped onto the couch next to her and reached for her glass. She wouldn't release the stem, so he just slid his fingers over hers. Her skin was so silky and warm beneath his. His mouth suddenly very dry, he directed the glass to his lips and took a sip from the rim.

It wasn't the dry red he would have expected her to drink. This one was full of nuances: berries, chocolate, coffee. It was bold like she'd proven to be. He flicked his tongue across his lower lip, where a drop had fallen, to savor the rich flavor. And her pale eyes darkened, her pupils dilating.

"Why are you here?" she asked. Her voice wasn't quite as icy now as it had been when she'd opened the door.

"I told you," he said. "I want you."

"To manage your campaign," she said and snorted again.

He shook his head. "That wasn't what I was proposing," he said. "I wanted you to revamp my image, so that I can run for office." Not that he actually wanted to but he needed a reason to spend time with her—a lot of time.

"Wanted?" she asked. "Did you change your mind?"

"Nope," he said. "But after that kiss today, that's not all I want from you."

He reached out again but not for the glass. Instead, he skimmed his fingertips over those long, bare legs of hers. Her skin was so damn silky, her legs so toned. She must have been a runner. He wanted those legs wrapped around his waist or arched over his shoulders or…

"You said you weren't propositioning me for sex," she reminded him.

"That was stupid," he admitted. "I should have been."

"Too late now."

"You said I had a chance of convincing you to accept that proposition." A better chance than getting her to work with him on a political campaign. Now he had some idea why.

If only he'd done a little more research on her before coming up with his plan…

But after that kiss and the comment she'd made before leaving his office, he'd changed his plan. He was much more excited about this new one than he'd been about pretending to run in an election.

He trailed his fingers from her calf to her thigh and toyed with the edge of her silk gown. Or was it just a long, loose pajama shirt? Did she wear anything underneath it?

He wanted to find out, so he moved his fingers up a little higher. And he held his breath, waiting for her to stop him. She could—with just a look. Her icy ones were capable of freezing anyone.

Except maybe him…

CHAPTER FOUR

TREVOR SINCLAIR WAS so damn hot with his thick, unruly hair, with his chiseled features, with his Olympian's body. If he wasn't this gorgeous, he wouldn't affect her like he did.

Allison would be able to retain her professionalism. But she'd lost that this morning in his office. Hell, she'd lost it a month or so ago when she'd confessed to her hatred of lawyers.

She was surprised they hadn't fired her firm then. But he'd offered her a new assignment. One she probably should have taken.

She hadn't lied when she'd said she'd rather accept his proposition for sex. Especially now.

With his fingertips sliding up her bare thigh.

Her skin tingled, and a delicious little shiver quivered inside her, making her nipples tighten even more than they had when she'd caught him staring at them. At her...

"So will you?" he asked as he moved his hand

even higher until he touched the curve of her hip beneath her nightgown.

She'd changed into something comfortable because she hadn't been expecting company.

Liar...

The little voice inside her head always called her on her bullshit. She'd known, or maybe she'd just hoped, that Trevor Sinclair would seek her out after the comment she'd made. That he would accept the challenge to change her mind.

From the powerful corporations he'd taken on in the past, he clearly knew no fear. Which was a thrill for her since most men were too frightened of her and her ice queen reputation to even approach her.

While she had purposely created that persona, sometimes it served its purpose too well. Sure, she didn't want any messy personal entanglements, but she wouldn't mind mixing a little pleasure into her business-only life. If his reputation was real and not just like hers, Trevor Sinclair might be able to give her that pleasure she'd been denied too long.

"Will I what?" she asked, and she moved, uncurling her legs to stretch them out behind where he sat on the edge of the couch.

"Accept my proposition."

She shook her head. "I'm not going to play politics with you, Trevor."

But despite her reservations, she was intrigued at the thought of making him into a viable candidate. It would be relatively easy.

"How about just playing with me?" he asked. "How about accepting my proposition for sex?"

She leaned back and studied him through her lowered lashes. Knowing he enjoyed a challenge, she challenged him with, "Convince me."

His wide mouth curved instantly into that wicked grin of his. How could a man with a grin that naughty ever inspire confidence in voters?

That wasn't her problem, though. She wasn't going to help him. She wasn't mixing business with pleasure. She just wanted pleasure from him.

It had been too long for her. That was probably why that kiss had affected her so. Once she had Trevor Sinclair, once she experienced his legendary sexual prowess, she hoped she'd be so satiated that she wouldn't want him anymore.

"What will it take to convince you?" he asked.

"Not an argument," she warned him. "I don't need words." She heard enough of them, used enough of them herself. "I need action."

She needed him. Her body was already beginning to pulse and throb in all the most intimate places.

His already-wide grin widened more, and he chuckled. But he heeded her warning and didn't talk. Instead, he touched.

He skimmed his fingers up the curve of her hip to her waist and then over her rib cage. She sucked in a breath as he neared one of her breasts. But he stopped beneath it. He leaned forward until their mouths nearly met. But he stopped again before their lips touched.

She smiled at his teasing. To show him she was unconvinced, she yawned.

And he laughed. She felt his breath against her lips and could almost taste the wine he'd drunk from her glass. Then his mouth covered hers, and she could definitely taste the wine. But it wasn't as rich as the flavor that was distinctly his alone.

He nibbled on her lips, parting them, and he deepened the kiss. His tongue slid in and out of her mouth—like she wanted it sliding in and out of her.

She shifted against the soft cushions of the couch. And his hand moved. He slid it up and finally cupped her breast in his palm. There were calluses on his hand, probably from weight lifting. All the Street Legal partners looked like they spent a lot of time at the gym but most especially Trevor and Stone.

Those calluses felt amazing against her nipple. Pleasure streaked from it down to her core where her pulse had begun to pound frantically.

A moan slipped through her lips and into his mouth. The kiss went on and on—open mouth to open mouth, tongues mating. It was the hottest kiss she'd ever had. But she needed more than kisses.

Trevor's hand moved on her breast, sliding over and over it until his thumb brushed across her nipple. He stroked it and then his other hand moved, sliding under her nightgown, as well. But this one stayed below her waist. First, his fingers stroked her thigh, caressing the smooth skin on the inner side before moving up. He eased his fingers beneath her silk panties and stroked over her core.

She gasped at the sensations streaking through her. Then she moved, parting her legs for him. He eased one finger inside her while his thumb rubbed her clit.

She moaned and dropped back against the couch cushions, away from his kiss. So he moved his mouth lower, over her throat. His tongue flicked across her pounding pulse. Then he pushed up her nightgown and closed his mouth over the nipple he'd teased to tautness. He pulled at it with his lips while he moved another finger inside her.

She panted for breath as the pressure built to an almost unbearable level inside her. She needed a release. She needed him. Desire overwhelmed her.

But before she could reach for him, he was moving lower again. And his mouth touched her core. His tongue flicked across her clit—back and forth—teasing her as he stroked his fingers in and out of her. Then he moved his tongue inside her, too.

And she arched up—against his wide, wicked mouth. Finally, the pressure broke as an orgasm shuddered through her. She screamed with pleasure and dropped back against the couch again, her body shaking from the force of the orgasm and the power of the desire that burned between them.

But despite that orgasm, the desire hadn't burned out. It still burned inside her. She wanted more.

* * *

Trevor's heart pounded hard in his chest, and his entire body ached with tension—sexual tension. He licked the taste of her pleasure from his lips and asked, his voice gruff, "Was that enough convincing?"

He was so damn tense he felt like he might shatter into a million pieces if he didn't get a release like the one he'd just given her. He couldn't remember ever wanting anyone the way he wanted her.

"You may have overplayed your hand," she said as she panted for breath.

He chuckled. "Oh, no. I have a lot left to show you," he promised. A lot he needed to show her. Now. "So do you accept my proposition?"

She narrowed her eyes and studied his face, as if debating. If she sent him away now, he'd know that she really was an ice queen, if she could be that cruel. It wasn't just a persona or an act. She was really cold and heartless.

Her lips curved into a slight smile.

And his heart beat even harder because he had no idea what she was going to do. He couldn't argue with her and not just because she'd told him he couldn't. No meant no to Trev.

But was she saying no?

That slight smile curving her lips was just a little too sexy for him to believe that she could turn him away now, knowing that he was as desperate for release as she had been moments ago.

Before he'd given it to her…

He wanted to give it to her again. "What do you say, Allison?"

Finally, she nodded.

And he reached for her.

But she grabbed his arms, holding him back. "But it's just sex," she said.

He nodded. "I know. No politics."

Her smile widened. "Yes, no politics but no emotions, either."

He furrowed his brow in confusion. Emotions? They'd said nothing about emotions. Trev had taught himself years ago to never feel those again. To never get attached to anyone.

It only led to disappointment and pain.

She laughed. "Good. You look as appalled as I am at the thought of getting emotionally involved."

He shuddered and it wasn't entirely feigned. "Usually I'm not on the receiving end of that warning, though," he admitted. That was what had taken him aback.

"You give it," she said.

"And now I want to give it to you," he said. And he reached for her again.

She didn't hold him back this time, not even when he scooped her up in his arms and stood up. She just giggled. "What are you doing?"

"Where's your bedroom?" he asked.

She gestured toward the windows. "Nobody can see us…if that's what you're worried about."

He knew that since the penthouse was on the top floor of a very tall building. "I'm not worried about being seen," he assured her. "I'm worried about having enough room. I hope you have a very big bed."

"Just a single," she said. But he heard the humor in her voice; she was teasing.

He would have laughed, had he not been so desperate for a release. "Do you have carpet on the floor?" he asked.

"Marble," she said. "Hard and cold."

Now he laughed despite himself, despite the desire he felt for her. "Come on, Allison, stop torturing me."

She had slung her arm around his shoulders. Now she moved her hand to his nape, running her fingers up into his hair. "Torture?" she asked. "Now, that's intriguing."

"You are one damn scary woman," he remarked. But he didn't care. He wanted her too badly.

Finally, she relented and pointed toward the end of the living room. He carried her across it to a short hall, onto which there were three doors. "Which one?"

She arched a red brow. "Should I make you choose? And if you choose incorrectly, you have to go home?"

He groaned. "I knew I should have stopped sooner." Because now she didn't need him as intensely as he still needed her.

Unless.

He moved the hand he held beneath her legs, sliding his fingers up.

And she shivered. "Okay, that door."

He pushed open the one she indicated. But he wasn't sure if she'd told the truth. The room was so dark, he could see nothing inside it. "Is this a torture chamber?" he wondered.

Maybe she was into S&M. He could easily picture her in dominatrix leather with a whip. But he wasn't about to be her or anyone else's submissive.

She reached out and hit the wall, and lights came on, but it was just a faint yellowish glow from the chandelier over a king-sized platform bed. Thick, dark gray drapes covered the entire wall that must have had the same tall windows of the living room.

But he was focused on that bed. That very big bed...

"Thought it was a single," he said.

"Must be the wrong room," she replied.

But through the open door to the walk-in closet he could see her navy blue dress lying on the thick gray carpet. It was a deep gray, like the walls, so dark it was nearly black.

"No cold marble, either," he pointed out.

"I must have been remembering another room..."

In another apartment. Apparently, this one wasn't really hers. She'd claimed her name wasn't on the deed. But then Trev didn't even know her real name.

Should he be doing this? Having sex with a woman he didn't even know?

He wasn't the indiscriminate lover his reputation made him out to be; he was much more careful when he chose lovers. Like her, he didn't want anyone getting emotional over him. He didn't want any messy entanglements.

But because she didn't want emotions involved, he was safe with her. Well, he would have been had she not been the mole. Maybe that made her even safer, though, because he wasn't about to fall for the mole.

As if he'd ever fall for anyone…

He snorted. "Maybe I should leave, then." He dropped his arm from beneath her knees so that she slid down his body. The nightgown bunched up between them, leaving her lower body bare but for the silk panties he'd pushed aside once already. He moved his hands to her hips as if to push her away. But before he did, he slid his palms down over her ass.

She laughed and said, "Well, you know where the door is."

Yes. He didn't have to worry about her acting like some women had in his past and in his partners' pasts. She wasn't going to get clingy.

While she didn't cling to him, she leaned against him, arching her hips against his erection.

He groaned as desire overwhelmed him. She was so damn sexy. There was no way in hell he would be able to walk away from her. He lifted her again, but just enough for her core to rub over his erection.

She moaned now. Sinking her teeth into her bottom lip, she murmured, "I thought you were leaving."

With one hand, he clutched her butt, holding her against him. With the other, he pulled her nightgown over her head. Her red hair tumbled around her bare shoulders, and she shook it back. And as she did, she arched her body. He lowered his head to her breasts, teasing one taut nipple with his tongue.

And she moaned again.

"Do you want me to leave?"

She didn't answer. So he nipped lightly on that nipple with his teeth. She cried out, but it was a cry of pleasure. Her fingers clutched his hair, holding his head to her breast.

But his legs began to shake. Not from her weight. Despite her height, she didn't weigh much, at least not to him. He and Stone regularly met at the gym and tried to outdo each other lifting.

She was light compared to what he usually lifted.

She was hot, too, so hot that he could feel the heat of her core through his fly. He needed to be buried inside her. Now.

So he carried her to that bed and lowered her down to it. The duvet was something soft, but like the walls and carpet it was nearly black.

There was nothing girly about Allison McCann's bedroom. He liked that; he didn't feel like a bull in a china shop like he had in some other women's bedrooms. There was nothing breakable in here.

Not even Allison...

And if he was ever going to prove she was the mole, he needed to break her. Maybe he could torture the truth from her.

He followed her down onto the bed and covered her mouth with his. He kissed her deeply before moving his lips down her throat.

Her pulse pounded wildly again. She was as excited as he was.

And she was needy again. Her fingers fumbled with the button of his jeans before tugging it loose. Then she lowered his zipper. She pushed aside his underwear and freed him from his boxers.

And he groaned.

She was torturing him with her touch as she slid her hand up and down the length of his pulsating cock.

"Allison…" he said, her name a growl coming deep from his throat.

She laughed.

But he was stronger than she was. He managed to pull back and free himself from her grasp. Then he lowered his mouth from her throat to her breasts. And he teased them with his kisses, with the flick of his tongue.

She arched up from the mattress and murmured his name. And he knew he'd built that pressure inside her again, the same pressure that threatened to shatter him if he didn't release it soon.

His blood pounded in his ears, rushing through him from his madly beating heart. He couldn't remember ever wanting anyone the way he wanted her. Was it because she was the mole? Because he knew he was safe having sex with her? Neither of them could get emotionally invested.

And that freed him to just enjoy it.

To enjoy her.

He moved his hand between her legs, beneath her panties. When he stroked his fingers over her core, he found her wet again—ready for him.

So ready...

His cock throbbed with the desire to feel that wet heat of her core. He needed to bury himself inside her. So he stood up.

And she cried out in protest.

Maybe he could have tortured information from her then. She wanted him as desperately as he wanted her. But because that desperation gripped him, he could think of nothing but taking her.

Hard.

And fast.

He pulled off his shirt and kicked his jeans and underwear down his legs, stepping out of his shoes as he did. But then he had to grab his jeans up from the floor and search the pocket for a condom.

"Are you always prepared?" she asked. "Or were you confident you'd convince me to change my mind?"

"Both," he answered honestly.

And she laughed. Then she pulled the condom from his hand. And for a second he felt a flash of panic. Maybe she'd changed her mind about having sex with him.

Before he could try to convince her again, she tore open the packet. Then she rolled the latex over his cock. And she lay back on the bed and told him, "Fuck me…"

She was nothing like he'd thought she was, nothing like the ice queen image she showed the rest of the world. She surprised him in the hottest possible way.

He dropped back onto the bed, kneeling between her long legs, which she'd spread wide for him. He couldn't resist lowering his head and tasting her again.

She growled now and arched up. But just as her body began to convulse, he pulled back.

"Trevor!" she cried out in protest, and she reached for him, her nails digging into his shoulders. Then she raked them down his back until she grasped his butt, and she tugged him toward her.

He eased his cock inside her. She was so ready for him, her inner muscles clutching and pulling him deeper. He moved inside her, in and out, driving deeper with each thrust.

She wrapped her legs around his waist, riding him—meeting his thrusts.

He lowered his head and kissed her, deeply, his tongue thrusting into her mouth like he thrust his cock into her core. Her body shuddered as she came, and she screamed his name.

He couldn't remember the last time he'd been with a woman as passionate as she was. Maybe never.

He didn't let her relax from her orgasm. He reached between them, rubbing her nipples into tight peaks again. And he moved his hand lower and rubbed his thumb over her clit.

She shifted beneath him and moaned. "Damn you…"

He chuckled. But it was tense and hollow-sounding. He was so close to losing control. To losing his damn mind.

And she must have sensed that he teetered on the brink because she tried to push him over the edge. She raked her nails over his butt as she kissed him back—passionately. She nipped his bottom lip and then his tongue. And she rubbed her breasts against his chest. He felt the tightness of her nipples even through his hair, against his skin.

And he groaned, the pressure threatening to overwhelm him. Her inner muscles clutched him again, convulsing as she came. She cried out.

But her voice sounded muffled as his blood rushed through him. His body tensed even more before finally the tension shattered. And he came and came…

The orgasm was so powerful, so long…

He felt as if it might never end. And hers felt the same as her muscles continued to pulsate around his cock. Then finally she sank limply back onto the mattress.

He pulled away and summoned the strength to

stand despite the shaking in his legs. There was another door next to the open closet one. He stumbled toward it and pushed it open. Fortunately, it was the bathroom. He stepped inside and closed the door.

He needed a minute. To clean up and to regroup…

He wasn't sure what the hell had just happened. Simon had warned him that she could be dangerous.

He'd had no idea just how dangerous she was.

CHAPTER FIVE

ALLISON STARED AT the closed bathroom door. And for a moment she wished it had a lock on the outside, so she could keep him in there. Not forever...

Just long enough for her to recover. What the hell had just happened?

She wouldn't have been surprised if security showed up at her door. She'd been screaming like a banshee. She couldn't remember ever enjoying sex as much as she had with Trevor Sinclair.

The door opened. Unfortunately, it hadn't taken him very long to clean up. He strode, in all his naked glory, back to the bedroom. And as he stared down at her naked body, lying limply on the tangled sheets, he groaned.

"Damn, woman."

"Damn you," she said. "Obviously, everything I've heard about your prowess was true."

He snorted. "Prowess?"

"You have to have heard all the talk about the legendary lovers you and your partners are."

"That's legendary lawyers," he said with a grin of pride.

"That, too," she agreed. "But that's not all you're known for…"

He lay down next to her on the bed. Wrapping his arm around her shoulders, he rolled her up against his side.

She tensed. "What the hell do you think you're doing?" she asked. "Snuggling?"

He chuckled. "You sound so appalled."

"I am. I told you—no emotions." There was no way in hell she was ever going to fall for a lawyer, especially one who wanted to cross over into politics.

"You're the one who sounds emotional," he said. "I'm just tired."

"Then go home."

"Why?" he asked. "When there's a perfectly good bed right here." He closed his eyes as if he intended to go to sleep.

And panic shot through her.

"It's my bed," she said.

"So this really is your room?" he asked.

"Yes."

He lifted a lid and peered around the room. "Looks like it could belong to a vampire. Why so dark?"

"So I can sleep."

"You have trouble with that?"

"Usually." She suspected she would have no

trouble tonight, not after all those orgasms. But she couldn't drift off to sleep—not with him in her bed.

"Guilt?" he asked.

"What?" She was tired, too, so tired that she had no idea what the hell he was talking about.

"Do you feel guilty over some of the stuff you've done?" he asked.

"What stuff?"

"Some of those PR releases?" he asked. "You can be pretty brutal."

"I'm doing my job," she reminded him. "Usually for you or one of your partners." Fortunately, they were not the only clients she had, though, since they'd started giving her so much less work.

He had offered her another assignment, though. One she had no desire to accept. Her only desire was for him. And despite all those orgasms, she wanted him again.

He was so damn handsome lying in the faint glow of the chandelier. His features looked sculpted from some rare wood; his hair was so thick and soft...on his head and on his chest...

His muscular chest. Every part of him was muscular, his thighs, his...

He was so big, even without an erection. But as she stared at it, it began to swell again. She jerked her gaze away and focused on his handsome face. He was staring at her, studying her with an intensity that had a strange sensation rushing through her.

This one wasn't desire. It was fear.

"Why do you work for us?" he asked.

"Because Simon Kramer hired my firm," she replied.

"But you admitted you don't like lawyers," he reminded her. "Why would you work for a law firm?"

"Because I have bills to pay," she replied.

His brow was furrowed as if he didn't believe what she was saying. "What bills?" he asked. "You don't own this penthouse."

"I own it," she said. "It's just not my name on the deed."

"Do you go by another name?" he asked, and his stare intensified even more as if he knew.

Damn Edward.

What had he told Trevor besides her address?

"Do you have a long list of aliases?" he persisted.

He could actually do a deed search using the address and find out the truth, so she had no reason not to tell him. "It's in my grandfather's name," she said. "In his trust…which I inherited."

"If you sold this place, you wouldn't have to worry about being able to pay any bills."

She shook her head. This place had been her sanctuary for too many years. She would never give it up. "I want my business to make it on its own."

That was important to her. So important that she would take work even from lawyers. Maybe she would have to take that other assignment he'd offered her, as well.

"I can understand that," he said. "That's the way

my partners and I feel about the practice. We'd do anything to protect Street Legal."

There was the strange note in his voice again, like he was aware of something she wasn't. She narrowed her eyes and studied his face. "I didn't know it was in danger."

He'd just won a huge case. Of course, his partners had run into some trouble lately but not enough to do them any real harm—if they would have let her address it.

But they'd curiously kept her out of it.

Why?

He shook his head. "It's not. There's no threat we can't handle."

"But there is a threat?"

He continued to stare at her for a long moment before he blinked and chuckled. "Of course not."

"What's going on?" she asked. And it wasn't the first time she'd wondered.

He had one hand on her hip, from the arm wrapped around her shoulders. Now he moved the other hand over her breasts, stroking one nipple until it peaked. "I want you again."

She wanted to deny him, wanted to send him away because she didn't feel safe anymore. She didn't think he would hurt her physically. But there was something he knew—something he wasn't sharing with her—and she worried that that could hurt her. Secrets had always done more damage in her life than the truth ever had.

That was why she felt no guilt over the press releases she'd given the media. Every time she'd thought she'd been telling the truth. It was only lately that she'd learned at least one of those times she'd been spreading other people's lies.

"It's late," she said. But with the drapes drawn, she really had no idea what time it was. "You should go."

"Why?" he asked. "You have trouble sleeping anyway."

She would have thought that she wouldn't anymore, at least not tonight. But he'd unnerved her.

As he continued to rub her nipple between his thumb and forefinger, he unnerved her even more. His touch affected her as she'd never been affected before.

Desire coursed through her body, heating her flesh, making her pulse quicken. He rolled onto his side, so that he stared down at her. Then he lowered his head and kissed her.

There was such intimacy in his kiss. He kissed her like he knew her. And no one really knew Allison.

She'd made certain of that.

But he kissed and touched her as if he was inside her head, as if he knew exactly what she wanted. Him.

She wanted him with an intensity she'd never felt before. That scared her, too.

That fear also excited her, making her pulse pound faster.

When he lifted his head from hers, she panted for breath, her lungs burning. He lowered his head to her chest. And he kissed his way across a breast before closing his lips around the nipple.

She arched up from the mattress as pleasure jolted her. Her body was so sensitive now to his. And he took advantage of that, stoking the desire inside her, so that there was no way she could have sent him away, not until he released the tension he'd built within her.

He did know her well—too well. How she hated feeling so vulnerable. But he made her feel other things she'd never felt before: desire and pleasure beyond her wildest dreams. He moved down her body, his hair tickling her stomach and then her mound. And he skimmed his lips across her clit.

She cried out at another jolt of pleasure.

"You are so sensitive…" he murmured as if surprised.

Maybe he'd bought her ice queen image. Unlike his legendary lover reputation, though, hers was not deserved. At least not with him.

If she'd been ice, she would have melted away from the heat of his touch, of his body sliding over hers. He moved his tongue over now, licking, teasing…

She came. She couldn't help it. She was so sensitized to his lovemaking. But she didn't want to be the only vulnerable one. She pushed hard to get him onto his back. Then she moved her mouth over his body, tasting and licking every inch of flesh and muscle.

He panted for breath now and squirmed against the mattress. And when she closed her mouth over his cock, he arched up as if helpless to resist her. But he was bigger than she was. So he easily lifted her away from him.

Then the sound of plastic tearing joined their pants and the pounding of their hearts. His hand shaking, he sheathed himself. Then he lifted her, guiding her to slide down on top of him.

She took him inside, deeper even than she had before. He was so big. He filled her in a way she'd never been filled before. Then his hands clutched her hips, and he began to move her.

Allison caught the rhythm and moved with him, driving them both out of their minds. He was so big, so deep, that she came easily, again and again. Her body convulsed around him.

And finally, he came, too, shouting her name.

She collapsed onto his chest and thought about letting him stay that way—in her bed, inside her...

But he moved, lifting her off so that he could return to the bathroom. That brief distance brought her to her senses. She couldn't let him stay. She couldn't risk doing that again. Not now.

Not when she was feeling so unsettled and vulnerable. She grabbed up his clothes. And when he stepped out of the bathroom, she thrust them into his hands. "Get dressed and get out."

"Brrr…" He mock-shivered. "And here I was beginning to believe your reputation was not deserved."

She'd wondered what he'd thought about that. Now she did not care. "I want you to leave."

And she trusted that he was too much of a gentleman to argue with her. He was.

He dressed, albeit slowly, almost as if he was doing a strip tease in reverse. She bit her lip to hold in a laugh and a sigh of desire.

She wanted him again. And that shouldn't have been possible after all the orgasms he'd given her.

She stepped into her closet and found a robe.

He uttered a sigh of regret when she sashed it around her waist. "This proposition wasn't just for tonight," he told her. "I want more."

She did, too. But she wasn't about to admit that or he might stay.

"Will I need to convince you again?" And he leaned toward her as if he was going to kiss her again.

She pressed her palm against his chest, holding him back. His heart beat hard and fast beneath her hand. "Not tonight."

If she was smart, she wouldn't risk it again with Trevor Sinclair. Or she might be the one developing emotions for him.

That, she definitely could not risk.

Tuesday was the day the partners usually met to discuss practice business. But since Trev had called the meeting the day before, he'd figured he could skip this one. No business was more important than finding the mole.

And now that he'd determined who it was, he needed to find the evidence to prove it. How the hell had he lost his focus so much the night before?

He closed his eyes and an image flashed through his mind of Allison McCann with her hair curling around her shoulders, clad only in that thin silk gown. Then he stripped off that gown to see all that silky pale skin beneath...

He groaned.

"Hungover?" a deep voice asked.

He opened his eyes to Miguel's concerned face and shook his head. "No."

"I have my hangover cure, if you need it," the receptionist offered.

Trev smiled. He'd only had the one sip of wine, but he did feel hungover, probably because he'd gotten drunk on Allison. She'd certainly been more intoxicating than alcohol had ever been to him.

"No, I'm fine," he assured the former gang member. "Why are you here?" he asked. His pulse quickening with excitement, he asked, "Is someone here to see me?"

Allison.

Maybe she'd missed him as much as he'd missed her the past few hours. She should have let him stay in bed with her, should have let him make love to her until they were both completely satiated.

Because he wasn't.

He wanted her again.

Still.

Always…

No. That thought sobered him. He'd never wanted anyone always. And he never would. He wasn't the besotted fool that his partners had become.

He wasn't ever going to fall in love because he knew that no one—not even someone you loved—could be counted on to stick around when you needed them. So he needed to make sure he never needed anyone.

"Simon sent me to get you for the meeting," Miguel said. "He tried calling but you must have put your phone on do not disturb."

He glanced down at his cell. He had put it on do not disturb because he'd wanted to focus on Allison. Not just on what they'd done the night before but on what he'd learned. He knew the deed to the penthouse was in her grandfather's trust. So he'd been able to find out who her grandfather was. Patrick McCann.

But Allison's last name wasn't really McCann, so he couldn't be her paternal grandfather. Like Hillary Bellows, she must have taken her mother's maiden name.

Why?

He needed to find out more about her. So he didn't have time for the business meeting and he told Miguel that.

The younger man arched a brow in an exact imitation of the way that Simon always did. "But this is the usual meeting."

Meaning that the meeting Trev had called yesterday was unusual. And it had been.

Miguel stood there, obviously waiting for an explanation. Usually Trev wouldn't have hesitated to bring in the receptionist on what was going on, but this whole mole problem had made him even less trusting than he normally was. Not that he suspected Miguel of any wrongdoing. He'd known the kid since he had been a wrongdoer. Then Trev and the others had helped him turn his life around; he wouldn't have turned on them.

Still, Trev hesitated.

Miguel wouldn't betray them, but he was a man, so Trev suspected a pretty face might be able to manipulate information out of him. And Trev hadn't seen another face as pretty as Allison's...

And her body...

It was perfect. She was perfect.

That made her dangerous as hell—not just to Trev but to any other breathing male.

"I don't have anything to say," Trev said. And he meant about yesterday's meeting.

Miguel understood because hurt flashed in his dark eyes. Then he nodded. "I'll tell Simon that..."

"Tell him I have no new information," he directed the receptionist.

Miguel nodded. If he suspected Trev was lying, he

didn't call him on his bullshit like Allison McCann had the night before. He just turned and walked out of the office.

Trev had some new information. But it wasn't enough. It didn't provide him with any clues as to why Allison had changed her name or her reason for hating lawyers so much that she would have betrayed their practice like she had.

Why was she the mole? What had she hoped to gain by ruining their reputation?

More work?

Job security?

What the hell was she after?

He wished it was him, but she'd had no problem throwing him out last night. She'd warned him that there would be no emotions involved. She hadn't lied about that.

Why had she lied about who she was?

Allison studied her assistant as he flitted nervously around her office. Edward darted forward to place a cup of coffee on the corner of her desk. Usually she needed it after a sleepless night. But last night she had slept—eventually—only to awaken abruptly when she'd dreamed of Trevor Sinclair, of being in his arms.

She'd awakened to find him gone. Herself alone. She'd wanted to believe that what had happened between them had just been a dream. But she'd been able to smell him on her sheets, on her pillow.

She'd wanted to stay in that bed, with her face buried in that pillow. Somehow, she'd forced herself to get up and shower. She'd had to come into work because she had to do something that was long overdue.

"What the hell were you thinking?" she asked Edward.

He jumped and sloshed coffee over the rim of the cup he still held. It pooled on the corner of her desk. He hastily wiped it up. "Didn't you want coffee?"

"I'm not talking about coffee," she said. "I'm talking about your telling Trevor Sinclair where I live."

"I never told him," Edward said.

Trevor had claimed the same thing, but Allison had been certain he was lying.

"Then how the hell did he find my address?" she asked. Just as Trevor hadn't easily fooled her, neither would Edward. "If you hadn't talked to him?"

"He was here," her assistant acknowledged. "He was snooping around, asking all kinds of questions about you. Of course I refused to answer anything, but before I could throw him out…"

She would have loved to see him try. She doubted Trevor would have hurt him, but there was no way Edward would have even budged the much larger man.

Edward continued, "A reporter came in trying to get a statement about another client. Sinclair said he had to use the bathroom. But when the reporter left,

I found him in here, going through your things. He must have found your address on something in here."

She glanced around and noticed a stack of household bills on the corner of her desk. They were all addressed to the service address: her penthouse. Heat rushed to her face with embarrassment over the conclusion to which she'd jumped.

"I'm sorry, Edward. I shouldn't have assumed you told him." She felt a flash of disappointment that he hadn't. It would have given her the perfect excuse to fire him, which was what she'd dragged herself out of bed to do.

Edward waved off her apology. "I don't blame you," he said. "That man is sneaky. I'm sure he made it sound like I'd told him."

But that was the thing: he hadn't.

Now she wondered again who was telling the truth. Then she remembered what else Edward had claimed. "You said he was asking other things about me."

Edward nodded. His blond hair was thinning. While he was younger than she was, he was no doubt going to be bald soon. "Yes, personal things."

"Like what?" Who she was seeing?

"If you've ever been married," Edward said. "If you've changed your name, if you date lawyers…" He sniffed as if the thought smelled. "As if you'd ever date him."

Date him. No. She knew better than that.

But fuck him…

LISA CHILDS 75

That had been incredible—so incredible that she really wanted to do it again. Soon.

Her body already ached for his. "Call him," she told Edward. "Summon him here."

She wished it was for sex. But this meeting wasn't about pleasure. It was going to be all business.

CHAPTER SIX

EXCITEMENT COURSED THROUGH Trev that he was about to see Allison again. He was so anxious that he nearly pushed aside her skinny assistant instead of following the guy down the hall to her office. Less than a day had passed since he'd been in her apartment, since he'd been inside her…

But he'd missed her.

"It's better for you to come to the office," her assistant said, "rather than trying to see her at home."

Edward. That was his name, wasn't it?

The young man continued, "She probably didn't even let you in last night, did she?" He glanced back at Trev as if waiting for a reply.

As he had with his own receptionist, Trev stonewalled this one, too. It was none of this guy's damn business if she'd let him inside her place or not. Inside her or not.

Trev had never been the kind of guy who bragged about his conquests. Not that he'd conquered Allison McCann. In fact, it might have been the other way around since he was no closer to getting evidence that she was the mole.

Maybe he needed to pump old Edward for more information. But they'd stopped outside her door. So he couldn't do it now, where she might overhear them talking.

"Would she have called me here if she had?" Trev asked, turning the question around on Edward. Obviously, Allison hadn't bragged, either, about her conquest. Edward had no idea they'd been together the night before.

And when Trev walked through the door Edward opened for him, he had no idea, either—when he looked at the cool expression on Allison's beautiful face. Her pale blue eyes stared right through him.

He stared back, hungry for the sight of her. Hungry for her.

While he couldn't see through her at all, he could see through her glass desk. She didn't wear a dress today. She wore gray slacks and a jacket over a pink blouse that was buttoned to her chin as if she didn't want to expose an inch of her body.

But he'd seen it already. And all he had to do was close his eyes to see it again. As he did, his body hardened with desire.

Damn, he wanted her. But it didn't appear that the desire was reciprocated today.

Why had she called him here?

He had a bad feeling that she was going to renege

on the agreement she'd made last night and that she didn't want to have sex with him again.

Hadn't it been as amazing for her as it had been for him?

Maybe he should have taken more time, made certain she had so many orgasms that she wouldn't be able to freeze up again, like she was now. Her stare was even colder when she turned it on her assistant.

"Please close the door on your way out, Edward," she informed him.

He hesitated, though, and glanced at Trevor. "I didn't ask Mr. Sinclair if he would like coffee or water—"

"I'm fine," Trev assured him. Edward couldn't bring him what he wanted. Only Allison could give him that, like she had the night before.

A powerful release...

He needed it again—needed her again—as the tension wound tightly inside him. It had begun to build from the minute he'd left her the night before. And when he'd been called to her office, he'd hoped that she'd felt the same way—and that she needed him again.

Edward hesitated yet inside the open door, tempting Trev to shove him out and slam the door shut. "Would you like anything?" he asked his boss.

"No," she said. But she was looking at Trev now. "I don't want anything."

"Ouch," Trev muttered.

Edward glanced at him before finally stepping

through the door and pulling it closed. Allison stared at the door, her eyes narrowed as if she was trying to see through it. Probably to see if her assistant was listening outside it.

Trev wouldn't put it past the skinny little guy. He seemed abnormally preoccupied with his boss. But then given how beautiful she was, it was no wonder the guy might have become obsessed with her.

Finally, she turned her attention to Trev and arched a red brow over one of those icy-blue eyes. "Are you hurt?" she asked. She must have been referring to his muttered ouch.

"I'm not going to lie," he said with a grin. "I am a little sore."

She sighed. "That's too bad. I guess we will have to give you a chance to recover."

"I'm fully recovered," he assured her as his erection pushed against his fly. He stepped away from the door, moving toward her desk. "Is that why you called me here?"

She shook her head. "No. This is business only."

He stopped within a few feet of her desk, not trusting himself to get any closer. If he did, he wouldn't be able to control his desire for her.

Hell, it was already out of control. Last night he'd totally forgotten his purpose for wanting to work more closely with Allison McCann. He needed to get proof that she was the mole.

"Business only?" he queried. "I thought you wanted nothing to do with playing politics."

"I was thinking about what you said last night."

She hadn't allowed him to say much, not wanting an argument. Instead, she'd challenged him to action. Heat flashed through him as he thought of all the actions they'd done.

"What in particular?" he asked. "How hot you are?"

Even though her face flushed, she narrowed her eyes. "Business, Mr. Sinclair."

He feigned a shiver. "Oh, Ms. McCann, it's so very cold in here."

It actually was. With its white walls and furniture, the office was very sterile—very cold. Trev wasn't really cold, not when he was anywhere near her because then all he felt was the heat of desire.

The office was the exact opposite of her bedroom decor—all dark and soft and warm. Just as she was the exact opposite of what she'd been last night.

Was she mad at him? Or was this how she would always act outside her apartment, outside her bedroom?

"I thought it was your public persona you wanted reworked," she said, "not mine."

That was all the ice queen image was: her public persona. After last night he knew she was very different in private. In private, she was the fire queen.

"You reconsidered?" he asked with surprise. She'd been so adamant that she'd wanted nothing to do with politics. "You're going to help me?"

"Just with your image," she said. "Not your campaign."

"Why not?" he asked. "What do you have against lawyers and politicians?"

She leaned back now in her white leather chair, and she studied him through narrowed eyes. The frigidness was back. "Why are you so curious about me?" she asked, and she glanced at the door.

Edward had given him up. The little weasel. But then Trev wasn't surprised she'd broken the man. With the way she was staring at him, he was starting to sweat, a trickle of perspiration running down between his shoulder blades.

"You're an intriguing woman," he said with a grin. "Of course I'm curious about you."

"Bullshit," she said. "Why'd you ask about my name? If I changed it?"

Damn Edward…

"Did you?" he asked.

She glared at him. "Apparently, you already know that. How do you?"

"Don't you Google everyone you meet?" he asked. "Of course, it wasn't possible to find out anything about you before you started McCann Public Relations."

She shrugged her slender shoulders. "That's because there's nothing to know."

"I doubt that," he said. There was a lot more to Allison McCann than he had ever realized. And he'd always been intrigued by her beauty, by her cool professionalism.

Of course, he'd seen that slip a couple of times. She held tightly to it now, using it like a shield against him.

"Why did you change your name?" he asked. "You on the run from the law or something?"

She smiled.

"A jealous lover?" That, he could believe. Just the thought of her previous lovers had jealousy coursing through him. And he hated that. He wasn't the jealous type. Competitive—hell, yes. He always had to win. But that was the only thing he wanted. The win. Not the woman.

Never the woman.

Until now. He wanted Allison McCann or whoever the hell she was. But that was just because he hadn't had enough of her yet. Once he was with her again...

Eventually, he would grow bored with her as he had every other lover before her. But a little voice inside his head whispered that no other lover had ever been as exciting as Allison was.

"You don't need to worry about me," she said. "I'm not going to run for office with you. It doesn't matter who or what I am."

"What are you?" he asked.

The mole?

She had to be. Nobody else had had the access she'd had to their case files. It had to be her.

But why?

"I'm a publicist," she said. "A damn good one. I can help you revamp your image."

"Maybe I like my image the way it is."

She shrugged. "Then you don't need me," she said, and she crossed her arms over her chest as if she needed to protect herself from him. And maybe she did. He was after her—in more ways than she knew. Or had she grown suspicious? He heard some suspicion in her voice when she asked, "Why did you try to hire me, then?"

He nearly shivered for real at her coldness. She was catching on, and he couldn't have that. He dropped into one of the chairs in front of her desk and sighed. "Okay, I do need you."

More than she knew.

His body ached for hers, tension gripping him.

"Then you need to be straight with me," she said.

His stomach flipped. How the hell had she gained the upper hand again? She was a more formidable opponent than he'd ever faced in court. And since he'd gone up against billion-dollar corporations, he'd faced some really high-priced attorneys. After his victories over them, he was now higher priced. He'd beaten them. He could beat her.

"You first," he said. "Why'd you change your name?"

She chuckled. "I'm not running for anything."

But she was running from something if she was

the mole, if she had any idea he was onto her. And he was damn well onto her.

"It doesn't matter who I am," she said. "But I need to know who you are."

He snorted. "You know me." After last night she knew him better than most people did. He wriggled his brows suggestively. "You know me very well."

Her lips curved into a slight smile before she pulled them back down as if fighting it. As if she was fighting him.

Why had she agreed to help him?

She shook her head. "I think you have a lot of surprises in you yet."

He wriggled his brows again. "Let's go back to your place and see how much I can surprise you." He lowered his voice to a gruff whisper. "And please you."

Color rushed to her face, and she released a shaky breath. He was getting to her. Pride suffused him that he could melt the ice queen.

But she sucked in a breath and regained her composure. "Voters don't like surprises," she said. "I need to know everything about you."

He narrowed his eyes now. What was she up to? Edward had obviously admitted that Trev had pumped him for information. Was she returning the favor? Getting payback?

He had no idea what she was up to. But then he'd never known or she wouldn't have gotten away with being the mole for as long as she had.

He shrugged, but that trickle of sweat streaked down his back again. He felt like he was on the witness stand, getting interrogated. "I think you know everything there is to know about me."

She was the one who'd decided to use his and his partners' pasts as teen runaways living on the streets in order to promote Street Legal. Not just as a rags-to-riches story but to show how resourceful and resilient they were.

"I know you're a runaway," she said. "But I don't know why. What were you escaping? Druggie parents?"

That had been Stone.

"Con-artist father?"

That was Simon.

"Fighting parents?"

That was Ronan.

"You know all our stories," he said. And he was chilled now. She knew them too well.

But she shook her head. "I don't know yours."

There was a reason for that. "I'm not a runaway," he admitted.

She sighed. "You lied?"

"I never said that I was."

"But you claimed you lived on the street with your partners," she said as if she was about to call bullshit on him again.

He nodded. "I did. But *I* didn't run away."

She froze and stared at him, her blue eyes wide

now with shock and her pale skin paled even more. "Your parents abandoned you?"

"Just my mom," he said with a nonchalant shrug as if it didn't matter. Hell, it had all happened so long ago that it really didn't. "I don't know who my dad is. I don't know if she actually knows. I don't even know where she was from. She moved to New York City to make it as an actress."

"How old were you when you moved here?" Allison asked.

He searched his memory and sighed. "Young. I don't remember ever living anywhere else."

"What happened to *her*?" Allison asked. "Where did she go?"

"Hollywood," he said. "She'd figured she'd have a better chance of getting acting jobs there. Maybe on a soap or something."

"How old were you then?" she asked.

He shrugged again even though he remembered exactly how old he'd been. "Thirteen…"

And she gasped. "Only thirteen? Is that when you started living on the streets?"

He shook his head. "I stayed with the guy I worked for, refinishing floors. He let me live with him as long as I kept going to school." Wally had only allowed Trev to help him after his homework was done. Wally Washington had also emphasized the importance of education, probably because he hadn't had much himself.

Like Trev, he'd had to start working too young to help support his family.

She gasped again. "You were only thirteen. You shouldn't have been working at all."

"I had to," he said. Despite all the auditions she'd gone on, his mother hadn't landed very many acting jobs. He'd had to work or they would have starved. "I had no choice."

Allison studied him quietly for a long moment, which made him uneasy. He couldn't tell what she was thinking now. Then she asked, "How did you wind up on the streets?"

For the first time since walking down memory lane, he felt a real twinge of pain over the past. He flinched. "Wally died," he said. "All the chemicals he'd been using on those floors had destroyed his lungs."

That was the first big corporation he'd taken on, the one that had killed his old friend.

"I'm sorry," she said. She hadn't apologized about his mother abandoning him as if she'd known that hadn't really bothered him. It had been easier in some ways to not have to worry about her; she'd never been a practical woman. But Wally...

Losing him had hurt. Trev was the only one who'd felt the pain. Wally's kids hadn't had anything to do with him for years. They hadn't even come to see him when he'd gotten sick. But they had certainly showed up to see what they'd inherited once he'd died.

None of them had wanted the gangly fourteen-year-old kid. Instead of letting any of them turn him over to foster care, he'd taken off. Fortunately, he'd found his friends or he probably wouldn't have survived.

"So that's how I wound up living on the streets," he said, and he jumped up from the chair. Restless, he paced near the tall windows of her office. "Will you be able to spin that the way you need to?"

"No spin required," she said. "It's a good story. The public will love it."

What about her? Did she *love* it?

"But it's not enough," she said. "You're going to have to make some changes."

"To my past?" he asked. Despite how hard it had been, there wasn't a thing he would have changed. He wouldn't have wound up where he was if anything had been different.

"To your present," she said.

"What do you want me to change?" he asked, and he neared her desk again. "My single status? Do I need a first lady?"

She gasped, and her face got even paler than it had been. She shook her head.

If he needed one, she obviously didn't want the position.

"No," she said. "You need to distance yourself from Street Legal. You need to leave the practice."

"What!" Just the thought struck him like a bullet in the heart. "What the hell are you talking about?"

"There's no way you're going to win anything with them as your partners or even as your friends."

The wound in his heart got bigger, leaving a gaping hole at just the thought of no longer being involved in Street Legal. "You want me to stop being friends with them?"

"That's the only way you're going to convince voters you're trustworthy," she said. "Your partners have had too much bad press the past few months."

"I wonder why…" he muttered. That was her fault; the damn mole was tearing down Street Legal. Was that why she wanted him to leave, to destroy the practice all together?

He wouldn't let her get away with it. But at the moment he was so angry he didn't trust himself. It was almost as if she'd set out to deliberately infuriate him, to push him into losing control.

But before that happened, he strode toward the door and pulled it open.

"You wanted me to help you," she called after him.

"I don't need your kind of help," he shot back at her before slamming the door behind him. Edward stood in the hall, just a short distance from her office.

He must have been listening, just as she had apparently suspected. The assistant smirked as Trev passed him. "Goodbye, Mr. Sinclair," he called after him as if he thought he'd never see Trev again.

But Trev wasn't giving up. His perseverance was

one of the reasons he'd survived growing up as he had. Friendship was the other.

Wally's and his partners'.

He wasn't giving up on Street Legal. And he was damn well not giving up on proving Allison was the mole and punishing her for all the trouble she'd caused.

But now when he thought of punishing her, it wasn't with criminal prosecution. It was with his hand slapping her sweet ass. And that was why he'd had to leave, because no matter how badly she infuriated him, he still wanted her.

Too much…

CHAPTER SEVEN

IT WAS OVER.

That was what Edward thought. He'd been gleeful over how angry Trevor Sinclair had been when he'd stormed out of her office earlier that day. He'd told her that she would never have to deal with Street Legal as a client again.

He'd said it like it was a good thing.

Allison should have fired him then. The guy had no idea that without clients, there was no McCann Public Relations and no position for him.

What had she been thinking to purposely infuriate Trevor like she had? She'd been angry that he'd been prying into her life. But more than angry, she'd been scared.

She didn't like anyone getting too close but especially a lover. That was undoubtedly over.

Trevor was too angry to want sex with her. While he'd been passionate, it had been about his friends and his practice—not about her. He wouldn't want her again.

But that was good. Then she wouldn't have to worry about him getting any closer to her. While he'd been inside her body, she didn't want him inside her head—or worse yet, her heart.

No. She'd been smart to push him like she had. But as the elevator carried her and her takeout to the top floor, she felt a flash of disappointment at the thought of spending the evening alone.

Which was crazy…

She loved being alone. Going for a run, enjoying a glass of wine, a book, the takeout that filled the elevator with the citrusy scent of the chicken in orange sauce.

Now that Grandpa was gone, she preferred her own company to anyone else's. He would have liked Trevor Sinclair. He'd had a lot in common with him since Grandpa had had to start working young in order to support himself and his big immigrant family.

Glad she was alone in the elevator, she expelled a shaky breath. She'd started prying into Trevor's past just as payback for his prying into hers. She hadn't really intended to help revamp his image to run for political office.

But she'd learned more than she'd bargained on learning. He was definitely a very credible candidate for whatever office he wanted. He was also an incredible man. Maybe as incredible a man as he was a lover.

Not that she would ever experience sex with him

again. Even if she hadn't infuriated him today, she probably wouldn't have. Like his partners, he was known for preferring one-night stands to relationships.

And that was fine with her.

She didn't want a relationship. At least not a personal one.

And maybe it was good that their business one ended, as well, and if Edward was right, it had probably ended. Trevor had been furious that she'd told him to leave the practice and his friends. And she couldn't blame him.

Good friends were hard to find. She had a few from her boarding-school days. She even had a few of Grandpa's friends she visited: the women her widowed grandfather had called his "lady" friends. She smiled as she thought of them, of how they all treated her as if she was their granddaughter.

Those were the only familial relationships she really had now. The elevator dinged, pulling her away from the pool of self-pity she'd been about to dip her toes into. She never did that—never felt sorry for herself.

And she probably wouldn't have if she hadn't been thinking about Trevor Sinclair and never being with him again as she'd been the night before. But as she started off the elevator, she noticed a dark shadow near her door at the end of the hall. Her pulse quickened with excitement.

Could it be?

She hurried toward it, toward him. He glanced up from the cell he held in his palm. He wasn't on a call, though. He must have just been looking up stuff.

"Find anything interesting on Google?" she asked, her heart beating fast.

His wide grin flashed, but she wasn't fooled. She could see the tension in his body. He was still angry with her. "Your grandfather, Patrick McCann, had one daughter. Patricia. Your mother?"

She felt sick. He was hitting back at her just as she had him. Exchanging prying for prying. "Is that why you're here?" she asked. "To learn all my secrets?"

He tensed even more. And she realized that it was. Her pulse quickened now, but it wasn't with excitement. It was with fear. But then she reminded herself that she had no deep, dark secrets. The only thing she really feared was Trevor getting too close—even closer than he'd been the night before.

"I am curious about you," he said.

"Why?"

"Because you're beautiful," he said. And he stepped away from the door so that only inches separated their bodies. "And smart and intriguing."

She stared up at him. "You were very angry with me earlier today," she reminded him.

"And infuriating," he added, and this time when he flashed his grin, it reached his eyes, warming the green.

"You wanted my help revamping your image,"

she said. "Is that why you're here? Because you've realized I'm right?"

He shook his head. "I'm here because I want you. Not your help."

So maybe she had been fired. But she didn't care when he lowered his head and covered her mouth with his.

"Mmmm…" he murmured against her lips. "You taste good."

She'd snuck a bite of the chicken from the container. And now Trevor snuck a bite of her lip, nipping the lower one between his teeth.

She moaned now. He tasted good, too, that rich flavor that was his alone. She slid her tongue into his mouth to savor him, to savor the kiss.

But he pulled back, lifting his head away from hers.

She blinked and stared up at him. Why had he stopped? Was he just messing with her?

But now his eyes were dark, the pupils dilated with desire. The same desire that burned inside her.

"Where are your keys?" he asked between pants for breath.

The kiss had affected him just as much as it had her. She fumbled in the front pocket of her purse and pulled out the keys. But her hand shook so much that she struggled to get the key in the lock.

Trevor wrapped his hand around hers. But instead of steadying it, it unsettled her more. Her skin tingled. Her pulse raced. She wanted him so badly.

His hand over hers, he turned the key and pushed open the door. Then he gently pushed her inside and slammed the door shut with his foot. Fortunately, she had a table in the foyer because she quickly dropped her purse, the takeout and keys onto it to free her hands.

Then she reached for him, her shaky fingers fumbling with the buttons on his shirt like they had the keys in the lock. She only undid a few before he stepped back and jerked it over his head, dropping it to the floor.

He undressed her, stripping away her jacket and her blouse before reaching for the clasp of her slacks. "You're wearing too damn many clothes," he said.

"Yes," she agreed. But then the slacks dropped to her ankles and she stepped out of them, left only in her heels and her silk underwear.

He groaned. "Maybe it was a good thing you were wearing all that when I saw you earlier or Edward might have heard something else through your office door."

"What—" But before she could ask any questions, he covered her mouth and kissed her again, deeply. And as he kissed her, he touched her. He unclasped her bra and pushed it from her shoulders. Then he cupped her breasts in his palms, teasing the nipples into tight buds with his thumbs.

She moaned into his mouth. Then he moved his hand lower, between her thighs.

He groaned. "You're so wet."

"For you," she said. He made her so damn hot. Her clit pulsed with the need for release. Then his thumb brushed over that, and she cried out.

"And hot," he murmured.

She needed him—so badly...

She reached for the button of his jeans, freeing it before jerking down his zipper. His cock sprang free, pushing against the knit material of his boxers. She pushed those down and closed her hand around his shaft. He was so big, so long.

She needed him inside her, filling her.

But he jerked back.

And for a moment she feared that he'd just been messing with her, getting payback for how she'd treated him. But then he ripped open a condom and sheathed himself.

And she expelled a shaky breath of relief—one he swallowed with his mouth. Then he lifted her right out of her heels. And he wrapped her legs around his hips as he guided his shaft inside her.

She shifted in his arms, clutching his shoulders and his back, trying to take him deeper. The muscles rippled in his arms and his chest as he held her up. Then he began to move inside her, thrusting.

And she moved, too, riding him in a frenzy. Desire overwhelmed her. She needed a release from the madness to which he'd driven her with just his touch, his kiss...

He continued to kiss her, their tongues mating like their bodies. He slid in and out. And she rode up and down. Her nails nipped into his shoulders as she struggled to move faster. She was so close.

Suddenly, she shattered, her body convulsing in a powerful orgasm that went on and on.

He drew it out of her as he drove inside her—over and over again.

She screamed his name. Then he tensed and a low groan ripped from his throat as he found his release. His body shuddered, his legs shaking slightly.

"If Edward is listening outside this door, he won't like what he just heard," Trevor murmured.

"If anyone was listening outside this door, they probably just called security," she remarked.

He lifted her off him, but when he set her on her feet, she found her legs were wobbly, so wobbly that she would have fallen had he not caught her.

"Are you okay?" he asked as he clutched her arms in his big hands.

She nodded and stepped away from him. But she wasn't okay. She wasn't sure what the hell had just happened. "I thought you were mad at me."

He nodded. "I am," he said. "I'm furious with you."

Trev was still very angry with Allison. But as angry as he was, he hadn't been able to stay away from her. And not just because he needed to find proof that she was the mole. He'd needed her physically. He had needed that powerful release she'd given him a short while ago.

He'd cleaned up, and she'd changed into yoga

pants and a tank top. And now they sat at her breakfast bar eating the takeout she'd brought home. It was all very comfortable, so comfortable that it felt right, very right.

Which struck Trev as very wrong. This wasn't his scene—sharing a meal with a lover. Hell, it wasn't his scene to spend much time with anyone but his friends.

Was this the existence to which his friends had succumbed? Was this why they had fallen in love, what they considered domestic bliss?

He snorted.

"What's wrong?" she asked.

Everything.

She was the mole. She had to be.

But why?

And why did it bother him so much that she was? It wasn't as if he wanted a future with her, like he wanted to sleep with her every night and eat meals with her and...

No. He did not want that kind of life. He was not the lovesick fool every one of his friends had become. The only thing he felt for Allison was desire.

And suspicion.

He shook his head and lied to her, "Nothing's wrong."

"You're still mad at me," she said.

He chuckled. "After what we just did, you think so?"

"You can have sex with someone when you're mad at them. Sometimes it makes it even hotter."

"Is that why you pissed me off today?" he asked. It had felt as if she'd done it deliberately, like she'd purposely made him talk about his past, like she'd deliberately exposed his vulnerabilities.

She was every bit as dangerous as Simon had warned him she was.

"I'm sorry," she said.

"So you did do it on purpose?"

She was quiet for a while, long enough that he took it for an admission.

"Why?"

"You're getting too close."

To what? To the truth? Or to her?

He gestured toward the foyer. "You didn't mind when I was inside you." His cock hardened at the memory of how it had felt, buried deep within her. "Can't get much closer than that."

"Yes, you can," she said. "That's why you got upset with me—because I pried."

"I got upset because you want me to ditch my practice and my friends."

She tilted her head, and her eyes narrowed as she studied his face. "But if you win an election, you're going to have to leave the practice—maybe even the city. I thought that was what you wanted."

Damn it!

He had roused her suspicions again. He could see them in her blue eyes. "I want you," he said and he reached across the counter for her hand.

But she curled it into a fist. "What do you want

me for?" she asked. "Sex or to help you become a viable candidate for office?"

"Both," he replied instinctively. He really just wanted the sex.

And proof. That was what he wanted more than anything. Proof that she was the mole. But the thought had his stomach flipping with dread. Now he didn't want it to be her. But there was no other viable candidate.

He smiled. "You really think I could win an election?"

She nodded. "Yes. Your backstory. The work you've done. Unlike your partners, you've taken cases where you represent the clear victim. You're David taking on Goliath."

He snorted. "Really?"

She looked at him, her gaze running over his body. He'd pulled on his shirt, but he hadn't done up the buttons. Her gaze felt like a caress of his chest. And she murmured, "Maybe more like Goliath taking on Goliath."

"And you think that'll make people vote for me?"

She nodded.

He held in a laugh. The politics thing had just been a ploy to get closer to her. But to think that he actually had a chance...

It was ridiculous to him. But he didn't want her to see that he had no intention of running for anything but her. He had no problem running for her.

But he wasn't sure if he should run toward her or

away from her. "How is it that you know so much about politics, Allison?" he asked. "Especially given how you hate politicians."

She sighed, and her shoulders slumped in resignation. Was he finally going to get the truth out of her?

His pulse quickened with excitement—with anticipation. He'd been close to her physically. But getting to know her secrets…

That was even more intimate than sex.

"I shouldn't have said that," she replied.

"So you don't hate politicians?" he asked. "What about lawyers?"

She glared at him. "You're not going to let any of that go, are you?"

Not when it could be her motive for turning against them. He shook his head.

She reached for the glass of wine he'd poured her while she'd changed. But her hand trembled slightly, and the wine sloshed around in her glass. After taking a deep sip, she said, "You're right. I did change my name."

"You took your mother's name," he said.

She shook her head. "I took my grandfather's name."

And he heard the fierce loyalty in her voice. "I take it he wasn't a lawyer or politician?"

She shook her head. "Just a hard worker who eventually started his own business and provided manufacturing jobs to other hard workers."

"What did he manufacture?"

"What didn't he," she murmured with a proud smile.

Her grandfather must have been an incredible man. But what about her father?

"What was wrong with the name you were born with?" he asked.

She sighed. "It changed too many times."

"What? Have you been married?" And he felt that annoying surge of jealousy again at the thought of her loving a man enough to become his wife.

"Not me," she said with a shudder as if she found the very thought of marriage repulsive. "My mother has had many husbands and she would convince every one of them to adopt me and give me their name."

His stomach lurched again but it was with sympathy for the life she must have lived. "What about your real father? He was okay with that?"

She shrugged. "Must have been. He never fought it. Guess he was just glad to be rid of her."

But he hadn't just been rid of his wife; he'd been rid of his daughter, too. Trev felt a sudden affinity with Allison. She had also been abandoned. And not just by one parent, it seemed.

"Was your father a lawyer?" he asked.

She nodded.

"And a politician?"

She shook her head. "That was my first stepfather. My mother married him because my father wasn't able to cross over into politics. He represents the

Goliath companies you've taken on—the ones with special interests voters don't trust. They didn't trust my father."

And apparently, neither did she.

"And your stepfather?"

She sighed. "He might have won if not for my mother."

He was even more intrigued now. "Why's that?"

"You would have to meet my mother to truly understand why," she said. "But it was a good thing he and her other husbands never made her the first lady like she wanted to be. She probably would have been beheaded for something bitchy she said."

"Marie-Antoinette?"

She nodded. "That's my mother. Grandpa always regretted spoiling her like he had. That was why he cut her out of his will." She took a long swallow of her wine. "Which is why she no longer speaks to me."

Because Allison had inherited and she hadn't.

"I'm sorry," Trevor said.

"For what?" she asked. "For prying?"

He wasn't sorry about that; he needed to learn everything he could about her so he could find out why she was the mole and prove it. "I'm sorry I upset you."

She shook her head. "I'm not upset."

But she was. And she looked scared, as well.

"Bullshit." He called her on the lie as she had called him on his.

She slid off the stool at the counter and pointed

toward the door. He didn't think it was because she wanted to repeat what they'd done there, which she confirmed when she told him, "Leave."

He flinched. He hadn't just upset her; he'd pissed her off. Maybe he'd pushed too hard, had made her say too much.

"Allison—"

"Get out!" she yelled.

He felt that sick feeling all over again. He didn't want to leave her—not like this. But that wasn't the only problem. He was beginning to realize that he didn't want to leave her at all—even though she was the mole.

CHAPTER EIGHT

PANIC RUSHED OVER ALLISON, leaving her trembling and clammy. She had never been as afraid as she was now. She wasn't worried that Trevor would physically hurt her.

But she was worried about emotionally.

She'd broken her own rule. She was starting to feel.

And she hated it.

"Get out!" she shouted at him again.

He flinched as if she'd struck him. She was tempted. She'd balled her hand into a fist when he'd tried to hold it earlier. She nearly swung it at him now.

But she already felt too out of control. She should have refused to tell him anything. It wasn't as if she'd been called to testify and had had to answer any of his questions—truthfully or otherwise.

"I'm sorry," Trev said again, his deep voice calming as if he was trying to soothe a child. "I'm sorry I brought up a sore subject."

She shook her head. "That's not it."

And it wasn't. The past couldn't hurt her anymore. But the present and the future could. She was worried about that, about letting him get too close.

"You're not upset that your mother no longer speaks to you?" he asked.

She laughed. "You obviously don't know my mother. It's much better when she doesn't speak to you than when she does." That was probably why her grandfather had done what he had—to protect Allison.

She studied his face. "What about you? Have you ever heard from your mother since she left?"

"She called a few times," he said, "when Wally was still alive. But she felt so guilty about leaving me that I assured her I would be fine and she didn't need to keep calling."

That fear gripped Allison again. She could not fall for Trevor Sinclair. Sure, maybe he wasn't like her father had been. Maybe he didn't lie and make promises he had no intention of keeping.

But she couldn't be certain of that. She'd already caught him in a couple of lies—about snooping into her past. Why was that so important to him?

"What are you really up to?" she asked.

His green eyes widened in innocence. Feigned innocence? "What do you mean?" he asked.

"You love Street Legal and your friends."

He nodded. "That's true."

"Then why would you consider leaving them?" she asked.

He shrugged. "I may not have to if I win something here in the city. And who's to say I would even win…"

"I do," she said. "I know you would." He was that viable a candidate. Voters would love him. Just voters.

Not her. She could not fall for a man like him, one her mother would have loved.

He snorted. "Why are you so sure?"

"If you did everything I told you to," she said, "if you distanced yourself from Street Legal's bad press now, you would definitely win."

But that was clearly something he wasn't willing to do.

"I'll think about it," he murmured. "But we've talked enough about business. Let's get back to pleasure."

She shook her head. "No. It's late. You need to leave."

He had to go now—because she was too vulnerable, her emotions too close to the surface.

But he shook his head. "I'm not leaving, Allison."

"Why?" she asked. "What do you want with me?" Because he wanted something. Her every instinct was shouting at her to protect herself—that he was going to hurt her. And she had no idea why.

Trev winced as he saw the suspicion enter Allison's eyes, turning the pale blue to ice. He couldn't risk her figuring out what he was up to—that he was onto her. He stepped closer and lowered his head to hers.

But she planted her fisted hand against his chest, holding him back and asked again, "What are you up to?"

"Nothing," he replied—probably too quickly—because her eyes narrowed even more.

And she asked again, "What do you want with me?"

"I want you," he said. And it was no lie. His body ached with desire for hers, to be with her again. "I want to be with you…"

Her breath escaped in a shaky sigh. "Trevor…"

She was torn. He could tell. She wanted him, too, but he'd scared her. He'd pushed too hard for information about her. But he hadn't learned enough yet. He hadn't learned why she would be the mole.

To get back at her father? Or her stepfathers?

He and his partners sounded nothing like those men. Except for him…since he'd claimed he wanted to run for office. He was the one most like the men from her past—the men who'd hurt her.

And by bringing all that up, he had probably hurt her now. "I'm sorry," he said again. "I shouldn't have pried."

"It was none of your business," she said.

But he shook his head. "No. You are my business, Allison." And not just because she was probably the mole. There had always been something about her that had intrigued him. He'd thought then it had been the challenge she'd represented with her ice queen persona.

But now that he knew that was just a facade, he was even more intrigued.

"Business," she repeated. "That's what we should have stuck to."

"Hell, no!" he protested. He'd much rather give up their business relationship than their personal one.

But she shook her head. "It was stupid mixing business with pleasure."

"Why?" he asked. Was she starting to have feelings for him?

"Because now you won't take me seriously," she said. "You won't listen to what I have to say about revamping your image."

"You think that's because we had sex?" he asked. She nodded.

"It has nothing to do with that." It was because he had no damn intention of running for anything. But he couldn't tell her that so he made another confession, of sorts. "I'm just struggling with letting someone else have the wheel, you know? With doing what you say."

Especially when there was no way in hell that he was ever going to leave the practice and his friends.

Her brow furrowed slightly as if she wasn't buying it.

"I think I need to ease into this," he said. "Why don't we start with my having to do whatever you tell me in our first arrangement?"

She tilted her head and narrowed her eyes. "What

are you saying? That you will do whatever I tell you to do?"

He swallowed hard. Maybe this wasn't such a good idea after all. But he nodded. "In sex. Just sex."

But it wasn't exactly just sex with them anymore—at least not for Trev.

Finally, her brow smoothed, and her lips curved into a smile that was nearly as sadistic as it was sexy.

He was definitely in trouble.

"Okay," she said. "But you have to do whatever I tell you to do…"

And he felt that sick feeling in the pit of his stomach again. He had a feeling he'd just made another mistake with her. Allison McCann was a very dangerous woman but now she was a very dangerous woman in control.

She was in control. So if she told him to leave again, he would have to do what she said. But now she wasn't so certain she wanted him to leave.

She'd never had power like this and never over a man as powerful as Trevor Sinclair. Of course, she didn't expect him to keep his promise.

But it would be fun to watch him try.

"So can I stay?" he asked.

She nodded. "But only if you do everything I tell you."

He hesitated a long moment before nodding. And she heard him mutter, "Why do I think I'm going to regret this?"

She was worried that she would, too. Every time she had sex with Trevor Sinclair she felt closer to him than she had ever felt to anyone else.

It was more than sex, though. They connected on another level.

Maybe it was just because some parts of their pasts were surprisingly similar. She hadn't had to work when she was as young as he'd been. And she'd never lived on the streets. But she knew that sense of abandonment he must have felt when his mother left for Hollywood.

That was all in the past. They weren't kids anymore. They didn't need anyone.

Allison's stomach tightened and her core ached with need…for him.

"What do you want me to do?" he asked.

"I'd tell you to clean up the kitchen," she said. "But that has nothing to do with sex."

"It does if you want me to take you on the counter," he said.

She smiled. "Oh, you're not going to be taking me," she warned him. "I'm going to be taking you."

Trevor closed his eyes and groaned. "What the hell did I get myself into?"

She laughed. "You have no idea."

Yet. But she intended to give him plenty of ideas on how to please her. He started by cleaning up the kitchen.

"When you're done here," she told him, "meet me in the bedroom."

She knew he'd be quick, so she didn't have much time to get ready for him. She changed quickly into an outfit she'd bought weeks ago.

It had been an impulse buy. Or maybe a guilt buy since the woman modeling this line of lingerie was one about whom Allison had unknowingly spread lies. She would have never issued the statements she had if she'd known the truth.

But maybe she'd so readily accepted those lies herself because of her past, because of her mother.

Damn Trevor for bringing up all those memories. She felt raw now. Exposed. And it had nothing to do with the scanty lingerie she wore and everything to do with what she'd told him: everything.

He knew everything about her now.

A knock sounded at the door, jolting her. "Can I come in?" a deep voice asked.

He was already in...in a way no one else had ever been. Allison thought about sending him away then—about telling him to leave. But she hadn't locked the door and the knob began to turn.

"I didn't say yes," she pointed out.

But it was too late. He'd opened the door. And once he saw her, all the breath left his lungs in a low groan. And the look in his eyes...

They burned with desire.

For her.

No. She was not going to send him away.

He drew in a deep, shaky-sounding breath. "What would you like me to do next?"

Me. But she only thought it. She didn't say it. She wanted to tease him a little.

Or maybe a lot.

"Undress," she told him.

He hadn't buttoned his shirt, so he just jerked it off his shoulders and dropped it onto the carpet.

"With maybe a little more finesse than that," she admonished him.

"What? Do you want me to do a striptease?" he asked, and he sounded appalled.

She held in the laughter that burned the back of her throat. "You said you'd do whatever I said."

He gestured at the room. "You don't have a pole," he said. Then he studied the room more intently. "Although it would be easy enough to install one."

She didn't want to ask how he knew so much about installing stripper poles. So she shook her head. "You don't have to do a striptease," she assured him. "You just have to strip."

He did as she'd told him, quickly shucking off his jeans and boxers until he stood in all his naked glory before her. And he was glorious with his dick strutting out from a soft bed of auburn curls.

Because she'd always hated being a redhead, she'd never been attracted to one before. But then Trevor's hair was more brown than red. And it was rich and thick.

Her fingers twitched to run through the overly long tresses. But she curled them into her palms to resist temptation. She would touch him.

Later…

"What do you want me to do now?" he asked, his voice gruff with desire.

"Just watch," she told him. Since he'd stepped through the door, he'd been staring at her, at the lingerie she wore.

Guilt had compelled her to buy it. But she could have chosen several other items besides this. The leather bustier pushed her breasts up and out. Maybe it was because she'd always felt they were too small that she'd bought it. Leather panties with bows on each hip matched the bustier. She'd even bought the leather choker that completed the outfit. It, of course, was bound with a bow since the entire ensemble was part of Bette's Beguiling Bows collection.

"The first time I saw this room, I figured you'd have an outfit like this," he said, and his voice sounded even gruffer now.

She nearly laughed since she'd just recently purchased it.

"Where's the whip?" he asked.

"You might find out," she said. "If you don't do what you're told."

"I am," he protested. "You told me to watch, and I haven't taken my eyes off you."

But she had yet to do anything.

Maybe this hadn't been the best idea. She'd wanted to tease him. But she felt self-conscious at first as she reached up and touched a breast.

But his eyes widened, and his breath escaped in a

hiss between his clenched teeth. And when she lowered her gaze, she found his erection pulsating as if reaching out toward her.

Confidence replaced the self-consciousness. And she raised her other hand until she held both breasts. As she held the weight of them in her palms, she rubbed her nipples. Then a moan slipped through her lips.

And his groan echoed it. "You're killing me, Allison. I want to touch."

She shook her head and continued to tease him as she touched herself. But she was making herself ache even more for him.

He fisted his hands at his sides as his big, muscular body started to shake. "Allison…"

Her breath escaped in a gasp as the pressure wound so tightly inside her. She needed him. Needed the release he could give her. "Okay," she relented. "You can touch me now."

He hesitated a long moment before he uncurled his hand and held it to her. "Where do you want me to touch you?"

She liked this, liked putting his hands where she wanted them. She had never felt as powerful as she did now. She replaced her hands with his, cupping her breasts in his palms. He squeezed gently.

"Kiss me," she told him.

And he lowered his head.

As much as she loved being in control, she wanted

to be out of control. So she whispered in his ear, "Fuck me."

He growled. Then he pushed her back onto the bed and followed her down. He kissed her as he always did—deeply, passionately.

Their lips clung together, nibbling and nipping at each other. Then his tongue slid inside her mouth, like she needed him inside her body. She wriggled beneath him, arching her hips, rubbing against his erection.

He groaned, and she realized she was rubbing the leather of her panties against his sensitive skin because she felt it, too—hot and smooth between her legs.

And she moaned.

She didn't even have to tell him, and he reached for those bows, tugging them loose from her hips so that the panties fell away.

Then he touched her there—at her core.

Another moan—almost a whimper—slipped through her lips. His fingers stroked over her and over her.

She arched against his hand, needing more. And since she was still in charge, she told him what she needed. "Go down on me."

He grinned. "You don't have to tell me twice."

He moved down the mattress until his head was between her legs. And he made love to her with his mouth, nipping gently on her clit before flicking his tongue across it.

She arched up again—against his mouth—and she nearly came. But he drew back—teasing her.

And she realized who was really in control, who had been in control the entire time. "No…" she protested, albeit weakly.

"No, what?" he asked. "No, stop? No, don't stop?"

"Don't stop," she said. "Don't stop." He had her teetering on the edge of madness.

Then he flicked his tongue over her clit again as he eased two fingers inside her. And she came, screaming his name.

He reached out for his jeans, probably to find a condom. But she pulled him back onto the bed and rolled him onto his back.

"Allison, we need protection."

"Not yet," she said. "I will tell you when."

"What do you want me to do?" he asked, his voice very gruff again.

"Just lie there," she told him. Then she lowered her head. She closed her mouth around his penis, then sucked it deep in her throat.

His hips lifted from the mattress, and he growled her name. "Allison, I'm not going to last."

She hoped not. She wanted him to go as crazy as he'd made her, as out of control. She moved her mouth up and down his cock as far as she could take him in her throat. Then she closed her hand around the base of his shaft and stroked.

He growled again, and cords of muscle stood out

in his neck and his arms as if he was struggling to hang on.

She moved faster and twirled her tongue around him. Then his hands clutched her hair, holding her down and he shouted her name as he came, filling her mouth.

She licked him from her lips and smiled up at him.

"You are dangerous," he said. "Very, very dangerous…"

She didn't think he was talking just about how she'd made him lose control. How else did he consider her dangerous?

CHAPTER NINE

A WEEK HAD passed since Trev had skipped the regular Tuesday business meeting. He knew better than to try that again—especially after all the calls he'd missed from his partners.

Well, he hadn't really missed them. He'd declined to take them because he'd been busy—with Allison.

Unfortunately, he hadn't gotten any closer to finding proof that she was the mole. But he'd gotten a hell of a lot closer to her in every position imaginable. His body ached a little from all the ways they'd had sex. And it ached because he wanted to do it again.

And again…

But he'd forced himself to leave her that morning, knowing that he had to make it to the office. Or else he'd continue to be a hypocrite. He'd been furious when she'd suggested he give up the practice and his friends but then he'd spent the past week avoiding them.

Some friend he was.

She'd distracted him with her beauty, with her body…

With her heart. He was beginning to know that, as well. She fiercely hid it behind that wall of ice she showed the world. But he knew she did that to protect herself because she'd already been hurt so badly.

He could understand not wanting to be hurt again. If she knew what he was really up to, that he had lied to her about running for office…

Then he would hurt her.

But if she was the mole, didn't she deserve it? She'd hurt him, and she had hurt the practice, as well.

His friends…

Guilt clenched his stomach as he walked into Simon's office where all the partners already waited for him. He felt as if he'd betrayed them. And he hated that feeling.

"He is alive," Ronan said to Simon. "You didn't need to worry."

And he felt another pang of guilt. He could see that Simon had been worried. There were dark circles beneath his blue eyes. Trev might have thought Bette was just keeping him awake showing him new lingerie designs. Simon's former assistant and current lover was the Bette of Bette's Beguiling Bows. But there were also lines of tension in Simon's face. So it hadn't been sex—at least not just sex—keeping him awake. He was definitely under stress.

"You shouldn't have worried," Trev admonished him. "You all know I can take care of myself."

Not only had he survived living on the streets, but he'd also survived all the threats against him when he'd taken on those billion-dollar corporations. A few of those companies had tried really hard to get him to drop the class-action lawsuit—so hard that he'd been jumped a couple of times. He'd handled those beatdowns better than he had Allison jumping him, though.

Every time she kissed him, touched him…he lost all control. All perspective.

"Allison McCann is more dangerous than anyone you've faced before," Simon insisted.

"We don't even know who she really is," Ronan added.

"I know," Trev said. And now he felt like he was betraying her—her confidence, her secrets—when he shared her past with them.

"So that's why she does it?" Ronan asked with a snort of derision. "She's tried to take down Street Legal because she has daddy issues."

Trev shook his head. "I think it's more mommy issues," he said. "And isn't that why you do what you do?"

Ronan's face flushed. "I haven't tried to take anyone down."

"Muriel might not agree with you."

Ronan's face flushed a deeper shade of red over the mistake he'd made with that divorce case, with the one involving the woman he was now dating. "I didn't know her sleazeball ex was lying."

"But you and Allison were both willing to believe him over her because of those mommy issues you both have."

"Fuck you!" Ronan cursed him.

He preferred it when Allison told him that. Hell, he preferred when Allison fucked him.

But he understood why Ronan was mad.

"So if she has mommy issues, why mess with us?" Simon asked.

Trev didn't know. There was nothing feminine about any one of them. Not even their receptionist. He shrugged. "It doesn't make sense."

So was she really the mole? But if not, then who else? She was the one who'd had access to every affected case. She was the one. She had to be.

How he wished like hell that she wasn't.

Stone groaned and shook his head in disgust. "I knew you were attracted to her. I knew she was going to get to you."

Heat rushed to Trev's face as he thought of her, of the ways she'd brought him more pleasure than he'd ever known. But she wasn't getting to him. That was just sex. He shook his head. "Not at all!"

"You're not attracted to her?" Stone asked. He was the criminal lawyer with killer cross-examination skills.

Even though he wasn't on the stand, Trev had no doubt that Stone could break him. So he just confessed, "Hell, yes, I'm attracted to her. Have you seen her?"

"You're sleeping with her," Ronan said, and now he sounded disgusted.

Hadn't any of them noticed how stunningly beautiful and sexy Allison was? What? Were all his partners blind?

"That wasn't part of your plan," Simon said. "You were supposed to get close *working* with her." Simon had once thought Bette was the mole and had tried seducing the truth out of her. But she'd seduced him instead.

Having seen some of her lingerie firsthand on Allison, Trev wasn't surprised Simon had gotten so distracted. He knew that he was, too—that he'd let her get to him.

"Yeah, how is the *campaign* coming?" Stone asked, amusement twinkling in his gray eyes. They all knew that there was no way he would actually run for office—any office.

He enjoyed what he did too much. He enjoyed taking down the big corporations who cared nothing about who they hurt, like they'd hurt Wally.

"It's stalled out," Trev admitted.

"Why?" Simon asked. "Because you're sleeping with her instead?"

"Because she wants me to leave the practice and ditch you losers," Trev said.

Simon gasped.

Ronan cursed. Her. In a particularly vulgar term that had Trev's hands clenching into fists. And Stone stood up, so he was between them.

"Settle down," Stone told them all. "It's not like he's actually going to do what she says."

"But why would she say that?" Ronan asked.

"Because Street Legal hasn't exactly had good press lately," Trev pointed out.

"And whose fault is that?" Ronan asked. "She's the one making us look bad."

"I don't have any proof of that, though," Trev reminded them. And until they did, they couldn't accuse her of anything.

"I don't care," Simon said. "We can't risk having her around the practice anymore. We need to terminate the business relationship with her and ban her from the building."

"And you need to terminate your personal relationship," Stone told him. "For your own sake."

Trev shook his head. "I've got it all under control."

"But you don't have the evidence we need to press charges against her," Ronan said. He was still furious.

And Trev couldn't blame him. If the documents submitted to the bar hadn't been proven to be forgeries, he could have lost his law license.

They'd all worked too hard to get where they were, to launch the practice, to risk losing it. He understood why they wanted to get rid of Allison now.

But he wasn't ready yet to let her go. "I will get the evidence," Trev assured them. He only hoped that the evidence he found proved she was *not* the mole.

"How?" Ronan persisted skeptically. "You going to try Simon's method of seducing it out of her?"

Stone snorted. "I think he's already tried that."

Trev couldn't deny that he had. But while he'd gotten some information out of Allison, he was unlikely to get her to just admit that she was the mole—even if she was.

But he was beginning to suspect that he was wrong about her. That it was someone else. Or maybe that was all just wishful thinking on his part.

"So what are you going to try next?" Simon asked him.

"I'll come up with something," he assured them—and himself. Now his goal was more to prove that she wasn't the mole than that she was.

"Yes," a female voice suddenly chimed in with all the male ones in Simon's office. "What are you going to try next?"

Trev tensed and whirled toward the door. They'd been arguing so loudly that none of them had heard it open. He certainly hadn't.

But as always, now that he saw her, his body reacted—tensing with desire. Allison looked so beautiful in a long purple dress that buttoned all the way down the front. It was professional-looking but also sexy as hell as he could imagine undoing every damn one of those buttons.

But desire wasn't all he felt. His heart pounded slow and heavy with dread.

What had she heard?

* * *

Allison glanced down to see if she was floating—because she felt as if the floor had dropped out from beneath her. And her stomach had dropped, as well. She had never felt as disoriented as she did now, not even when she had sex with Trevor.

"How the hell did you get in here?" Simon Kramer asked the question as if she'd barged into the meeting.

She turned back toward the hall, but Miguel was gone. "Your receptionist showed me back." And opened the door despite the raised voices.

Simon arched a brow as if he doubted her explanation. She didn't care what the hell he believed. Anger coursed through her now, replacing the shock she'd felt when she'd overheard what they were arguing about: her.

"Why are you even here?" Trevor asked her.

She couldn't tell him now, couldn't show him the breakfast she'd brought him. Fortunately, she'd handed the bag of pastries and cups of coffee to Miguel before he'd taken off. Or she would have dropped them and burned herself. And she certainly couldn't show Trevor what else she'd brought him: another outfit from Bette's Beguiling Bows.

"It doesn't matter why I'm really here," she said. And it didn't anymore. "Apparently, you all think I have an ulterior motive."

"How much did you hear?" Trevor asked.

Her stomach pitched. She hated being lied to,

hated secrets, and it was clear that Trevor still wanted to keep some from her.

The thing was she had no idea how long she'd been standing there. She'd been so stunned that it was as if she had gone into shock. She'd barely heard their voices over the sound of her blood rushing in her ears as her heart had pounded frantically. "I heard enough to know that you all suspect me of something, and I want to know what it is."

She'd noticed the suspicion on their faces when she'd seen them all the week before. And they had barely utilized her services the past few months.

Something was going on…

And they blamed her for whatever it was.

All four men exchanged glances with each other as if silently communicating. Maybe, after living on the streets together, they could communicate silently. They probably wished they'd been doing that before she'd overheard their conversation.

"I have the right to know what I'm being accused of," she pointed out.

Or how else was she going to defend herself?

But she wasn't so certain that she wanted to. If they could think the worst of her.

If Trevor could.

Did she want anything to do with any of them anymore?

She sucked in a breath as she felt a sudden twinge of panic in her chest and a hollowness in her core. It had only been a week since she and Trev had started sleeping together. She should not be so attached to him yet.

Or at all.

She knew better than to let her emotions get involved. And this was why.

Ultimately, people let her down. They lied. They broke promises.

"What is it?" she persisted. And she stared at the other three partners now. She couldn't look at Trevor anymore, not without that hollowness hurting inside her. "What do you think I did?"

"Sabotage," Simon replied. "We think you've been sabotaging Street Legal."

She laughed at the ridiculous accusation. "I'm the reason the practice has as high a profile as it does," she reminded them. She was the one who'd composed the press releases to spin their pasts into something glamourous—into something that had everyone talking about them.

"I'm also the reason you've won as many cases as you have." She'd helped them try their cases before they ever made it to court. She tried them where it counted—in the public.

Ronan Hall snorted. "Yeah, right. We're the ones who've won. You're not in court with us."

"Yes, I am," she reminded him. She'd attended court so that she could talk to the press after every session. She had spent more time with Street Legal than she had any other client she had.

For them to think she would purposely sabotage them...

For Trevor to think that...

She glanced at him now, but he was looking away as if he couldn't face her, either. She couldn't believe that he would think that.

"You do have access to all our cases," Simon said as if that was significant.

She shrugged. "You gave me access."

Now he flinched. "That was apparently a mistake."

"Why?" she asked, her voice getting sharp as her impatience grew. "Just what the hell do you all think I've done? How have I sabotaged anything?"

"You've brought up the bad press," Trevor began.

But she wasn't ready to hear from him yet. "That had nothing to do with me. You all won't even let me help mitigate that bad press."

And then she realized why. "You think I'm behind it? Why?"

"That's what we'd like to know," Simon said. "Why would you do that?"

"Is it because you hate lawyers?" Stone asked.

And she hated herself for letting that slip.

"If you guys look bad, I look bad," she pointed out. "Sabotaging your practice is like sabotaging my own firm. Why the hell would I do that?"

She had worked so hard to start it, to make it a success. She'd spent the past several years focused mostly on business. Until this past week with Trevor, she'd had very little pleasure.

Maybe that should have told her something, though. Maybe her business wasn't making her happy. It damn well didn't seem to be satisfying her client.

She'd heard them talk about firing her, about banning her from the building. Losing them as a client would hurt her business. Losing Trev...

But apparently, she had never really had him. Trevor had only been trying to get information out of her, evidence of her doing something wrong.

The only thing she'd done wrong was getting personally involved with him.

"Maybe you were looking for job security," Ronan suggested. "You create a problem and then you fix it."

"What problems do you think I created?" she asked.

"It started with Trev," Simon said. "His last big class-action lawsuit."

"He won it," she reminded them. What the hell were they talking about?

"That's just because he's that good," Simon said. "But information got leaked to opposing counsel."

"And you think I did that?" She looked at Trevor now and his eyes were narrowed, suspicion in the green depths. And she shivered.

"You said your father defends corporations like that," Trevor reminded her. "Was he defending that one?"

She shook her head. "But it wouldn't have mattered if he was," she said. "I wouldn't have helped him."

"Daddy issues," Ronan murmured.

And she glared at him.

"Is that why you went after me?" the divorce lawyer asked. "You sent Muriel those forged documents she turned in to the bar association."

"What?" She knew he'd been reported to the bar, but she'd tried to undo the damage. "I didn't forge any documents."

"What about the information that was given to the assistant district attorney in my last trial?" Stone Michaelsen asked. "She knew information, supposedly from my case files, before I even knew it."

Each of their accusations struck Allison like a blow. They all really believed that she'd betrayed them. Even Trevor.

"And how do you think I got that information?" Allison asked.

"You have access to all our files, to our computers," Simon said.

"So? I'm not the only one who does. It could have been anyone on your staff."

Simon shook his head. "I've checked all of them out. It's not."

"Well, it's not me," she said. But she was sick of defending herself, especially with them all looking at her like they were, like she was a criminal. "But please, block my access to your computers. Ban me from the building. I have no intention of ever coming back here." She turned on her heel then and stalked out of the room.

"Allison!" It was Trevor's deep voice that called out to her.

She didn't even look back, though. She just said over her shoulder, "Go to hell!"

She had no intention of ever seeing him again, either.

CHAPTER TEN

TREV HAD A sick feeling that he'd made a terrible, terrible mistake. As he'd told his partners, everything she'd said had made sense. Why would she sabotage them when it would also reflect poorly on her firm?

Sure, maybe he'd come up against her father on a case before. He couldn't know for certain when she didn't use her last name. But he had a feeling that if he had, she would have worked doubly hard to help Trev win just so her father would lose.

And if she'd had any real daddy issues, she probably wouldn't have taken on Street Legal as a client in the first place.

His partners were not as convinced of her innocence as he was, but he'd left them mulling it over to chase after her. Of course, she'd already left the building before he'd been able to break away from that business meeting.

But he'd rushed right over to her office the minute he'd been free. Of course, Edward stood guard in the reception area, staring resentfully at Trevor over his desk.

"What are you doing here?" her assistant asked. "I thought you all fired her."

Trev shook his head. "She told us to go to hell." Or had it just been him?

Edward smirked. "Can you blame her?"

Had the little weasel been with her at the office? Trev couldn't imagine her telling her assistant everything that had transpired. His suspicion must have showed because Edward added, "I've never seen her as upset as she was when she came back from Street Legal. She was just about ranting and raving about your accusations."

Trev flinched. While the others had piled on their suspicions, they had all been his accusations. He was the one who'd accused her first—to them. Maybe he should have waited more than that weekend before sharing his suspicions. Maybe he should have waited until he'd actually found evidence against her.

Because now he had a feeling that evidence didn't exist…

She wasn't the mole.

"I need to talk to her," Trev said.

Edward snorted. "Are you crazy? She will kill us both if I let you back there."

Trev didn't doubt what the man said. She had been furious when she'd left Street Legal.

"I'll calm her down," he assured her anxious assistant.

Edward snorted again. "I don't think that's possible."

"Neither is you keeping me from seeing her," Trev pointed out as his patience wore thin. He'd already wasted time talking to his partners when he should have stopped her from leaving before he'd talked to her.

Before he'd apologized...

No wonder she was so furious.

And if she tried to kill him, he wouldn't blame her. It was a chance he was willing to take—for her. He walked past Edward's desk and headed down the hall that led to her office. Edward jumped up and called after him, loudly, "Don't go back there! I'll call security. I'll call the police!"

But Trevor didn't have to look back to know that he wasn't picking up the phone. He wouldn't want to miss a minute of Trevor's confrontation with his boss.

Trevor reached the end of the hall and the door to her office. He hesitated for a long moment before turning the handle. Then he drew in a deep breath and opened the door, releasing the breath with relief when he found it unlocked. Not that a lock would have stopped him.

He would have kicked it down to talk to her— after he'd seen that look on her face. Her ice queen mask had slipped. She'd looked devastated and outraged. She had not looked guilty. Even his partners had remarked on that. Of course, none of them were trusting enough to believe that proved her innocence.

Until Trev found the real mole, they would all still suspect it was her. And they wanted the practice and him to have nothing to do with her.

But just as he hadn't wanted her telling him with whom he could be friends, he hadn't wanted them to do the same. Not that he was friends with Allison.

Hell, he wasn't sure what they were.

Lovers.

Enemies?

She looked up as he entered, and he saw the anger and resentment in her beautiful pale blue eyes. "Get out!" she shouted, but her voice cracked with the command.

She'd yelled at him before to get out—of her apartment.

He'd ignored her those times, just like he intended to ignore her now. But he didn't think he'd be able to change her mind as easily as he'd told Edward he would. Instead of stepping back through the door, he closed it behind him.

Allison jumped up from her desk and stalked toward him. Her finger pressing into his chest, she said again, "Get out! Get the hell out of my office!"

He caught her hand in his and held it against his chest. His hand encircled her wrist where he could feel her pulse pounding madly. "Please let me explain," he implored her.

"You did," she said. "You and your partners said everything you needed to back at Street Legal. I don't have to hear any more."

"I don't think it's you," he said.

She snorted and struggled to free her hand from his grasp. But he pulled her closer, so her long, willowy body pressed against his. He felt the tension in her but he also felt the heat.

She was so damn hot...

How had any of them ever considered her an ice queen?

"I did think it was you," he admitted.

"That's why you wanted to get close to me," she said. "To get evidence against me. I heard it all. I heard everything!"

He moved one hand to her hip and pressed her against his erection. "That's why I wanted to get close to you," he said. "Because I want you!"

As furious as she was with him, he wanted her. He could see the desire in her eyes, too. Her breath escaped in a soft gasp. But she shook her head as if trying to deny the desire. Then she murmured, "No..." She narrowed her eyes as she stared up at him. "You started this whole seduction as a way to get information out of me."

Seducing her had never been his plan until that kiss. But at the moment he didn't dare tell her that his political aspirations were a lie. She was already furious with him for not telling her the truth about the mole.

"I had sex with you because you're beautiful and exciting and sexy as hell," he said. And he pushed his erection against her again. His cock ached to be inside her. He ached for her. "Did I want information, too? Yes. Wouldn't you if someone had been sabotaging your firm?"

"My firm was sabotaged, too," she pointed out. "When a client is made to look bad, I do, too."

"I get that," he said. And he shook his head with self-disgust. "I should have never suspected you."

"Why did you?"

"Access," he said. "You were the only one with access to every case that was involved in the sabotage."

Her brow furrowed. "The only one?"

"We checked out everyone else," he insisted.

"Like you've been checking me out?" she asked.

And he smiled as he heard a trace of jealousy in her voice. "Not me," he said. "Simon checked out Bette. And Ronan, Muriel."

And Hillary Bellows had never been a suspect. But that hadn't stopped Stone from checking her out.

"It's not me," she said, and she lifted her chin with pride. Then she blinked hard as if fighting back tears. "I am not the mole."

"I know," he assured her. "I know it's not you." And to comfort her, he lowered his head and brushed a gentle kiss across her lips.

At least he'd intended for it to be gentle. But then she parted her lips, and he deepened the kiss. And passion ignited even faster and hotter than it usually did between them. As he'd imagined doing earlier, he reached for that long row of buttons on the front of her dress.

Then he'd thought it would be fun to undo them all, that it would draw out the anticipation of seeing her naked. But now he was too impatient. He undid only a few, his fingers fumbling, before he lifted the dress from the bottom and pulled it over her head.

And then he saw what she wore beneath. The underwear was purple, too, like the dress. And it had those damn beguiling bows on it. One held the underwear together at the front. And another held the bra together between the cups.

His fingers twitched, anxious to pull those bows loose. But Allison stepped back—out of his reach. Had she only let him undress her to tease him? To let him see what he would be missing?

Trev had a bad feeling that for the first time in his life he might be compelled to beg. He reached out to her, his hand shaking slightly, and implored her, "Please…"

His plea struck Allison harder than any of his accusations had. He wasn't just using sex as a way to manipulate her or get information out of her. It was clear from the desire on his face, and the tension in his muscular body, that he wanted her every bit as much as she wanted him.

And she did want him.

Too much to deny herself or him the sexual satisfaction they always found together. She reached up and tugged loose that bow between the cups of her bra until it fell away from her breasts. Then she lowered her hand to the bow on her panties.

And Trevor groaned.

His face was flushed, his nostrils flaring. He was as overcome with passion as she was. And they had barely touched.

She touched now, sliding her fingers beneath her panties instead of undoing that bow. She gasped as she felt the wetness of her curls. She was already nearly coming, just from the way he looked at her.

He stared at her so hotly. "Allison…"

She needed him. Needed to feel him inside her, filling that hollowness that had hurt so much earlier. She attacked his buttons now, undoing his shirt before pushing it from his broad shoulders. Then she reached for the snap of his jeans. But his hands were already there, pushing his pants and boxers aside to free his cock.

He must have already torn open the condom because he rolled one on before he tugged loose that bow on her panties. Then he lifted her, guiding her down onto his sheathed shaft.

She arched and stretched, taking him deep. Then she moved—frantically—wanting to release the unbearable tension inside her.

He lowered his head, kissing her lips, then her throat. Then he arched his back and moved his head lower, to her breasts. She leaned back to give him better access. As he tugged at one nipple with his lips, she came. Instead of crying out, as she always did, she bit his shoulder.

He wasn't quite as quiet as he released a low groan, thrusting deeper as he came. His body shuddered, his legs staggering a bit beneath their combined weights, before he released her.

She staggered a little, too, her muscles lax from the powerful release.

"I'm sorry," he murmured.

And she had no idea for what he was apologizing…until he added, "That was too fast."

She shook her head. She'd been ready for him. She was always ready for him. Was that desire she felt for him clouding her judgment, though?

Should she forgive him for not being completely honest with her? He slipped away into the bathroom off her office, and while he was gone, she hurriedly dressed.

She wasn't certain if they'd locked the door, and if they hadn't, Edward might be so bold as to just walk right in. She really needed to fire him. He was even nosier than Trevor had been about her life, about her past.

Now she knew why Trevor had been so interested, though.

"Don't," he said as if he'd read her mind. He had come out of the bathroom without her even noticing. He pressed his fingers to the furrow on her brow. "Don't even think about it. I have no doubts anymore about you. And I shouldn't have had any. You're right. Making us look bad makes you look bad."

She nodded. "Do you have any other suspects?" she asked.

"Besides you?"

She glared at him now. But she knew he was only teasing. She felt as if he really did believe her. Her sabotaging them made no sense. She'd worked too hard to make them as well-regarded as they were.

He shook his head. "I don't know."

"It's been going on for months," she said—since it had started with his last class-action case. "And you don't have any ideas?"

"Bette, Muriel…" He shrugged. "It doesn't make sense."

"There's nobody from your past or the partners' that might come after the practice?"

He shook his head again. "Not anyone with access to our case files."

Only her…

She could understand now how she had looked guilty. But their staff was large. "What about a worker?"

"Bette—"

"Bette was obviously proven to have nothing to do with it." She'd seen the managing partner out and about with his former assistant. They were very involved.

But then so were she and Trevor, and he'd suspected her of being the saboteur.

"What about Miguel?" she asked. And she shivered even as she suggested it.

Trevor laughed as if the thought was ridiculous.

"I came there today to see you," she said. She touched her bra through her dress. "To show you my new outfit. Miguel brought me back to Simon's office. He opened the door."

As if he'd wanted her to overhear their discussion about her...

Had he been trying to help her? Or hurt her? She couldn't read the receptionist any better than people claimed they were able to read her.

Trevor's brow furrowed now. "That is weird." Then he shook his head. "But Miguel has always been so loyal. He appreciated us giving him the job too much to risk it."

She shrugged. "I don't know. Maybe he's jealous that you all started out in the same place but you and the partners made a lot more money."

His brow furrowed again.

"And you said the opposing counsel for that pharmaceutical company got something from your case notes," she remembered. "I'm sure they paid dearly for it. Maybe this person—"

"Mole," Trevor said.

"Maybe this mole is just about making some extra money."

He shook his head. "No. Muriel didn't pay for those forged documents that she turned over to the bar association. And Hillary Bellows certainly didn't pay for anything from Stone's case files."

"So it's about a grudge, then." Miguel made sense to her since he probably went back with them as far as the partners did with each other. She would have suggested that it could have been one of them, but she remembered how furious Trevor had gotten when she'd told him to distance himself from his friends. If she accused one of them of having betrayed him, she had no doubt that they would be over.

They should be over—whatever it was that they had.

After knowing he'd been keeping secrets from her, she wouldn't entirely ever be able to trust him again. Not that she'd really trusted him.

She'd learned a long time ago never to trust anyone. But her grandfather...

Unfortunately, she'd begun to think Trevor was more like her grandfather than her father. She'd been wrong.

He was staring at her again as if he was trying to read her mind. And she wondered if he truly believed she wasn't the mole or if he was still trying to play her.

He'd told his partners that he would come up with something new to try to get the truth out of her. Was this it? Pretend to believe in her innocence?

She shook her head. "I don't know."

"It's not your problem," Trevor told her.

And for a moment she was confused—then she

realized that he thought she was just saying that she didn't know who the mole was.

"We'll figure it out," he said. "And I'll let you get back to work."

Fortunately, she did have other clients because no matter if his partners and he believed her or not, she was no longer going to work for Street Legal.

"I'll see you later?" He said it as a question. He must have sensed her withdrawal.

She wasn't certain if he would or not. She wasn't certain she trusted him or herself enough to be with him again. Maybe it was better to end the personal relationship along with the business one.

She just offered him a short nod as she walked back behind her desk. She wanted it between them. But he rounded it, too, and leaned down to press his mouth to hers.

"I will see you later," he said determinedly.

The penthouse wasn't the only property her grandfather had owned in the city. She could go someplace else, someplace he wouldn't find her. And she just might, to protect herself.

At the thought of not being with him, that hollow feeling spread in her body—in her heart. She nodded again.

He must have been satisfied with the response because he headed toward the door. It had only been closed behind him for a few moments before it opened again.

She glanced up from her desk, hoping it was him,

hoping that he could somehow convince her to trust him again. But it was Edward.

"You didn't knock," she pointed out. And she was glad he hadn't just walked in earlier—when she and Trevor had been having sex.

But that was all it had been.

They didn't make love. They weren't in love...

But then what was that ache in her chest?

"Turn on the TV," Edward directed her. But he didn't wait for her to find the remote on her desk. He found it himself and turned on the flat screen that was on the wall across from her desk.

"It's no secret," a local television reporter said, "that the Street Legal law practice has been having some difficulties lately. What has been strange is that the PR firm that has helped make Street Legal a household name has not been issuing any statements to address those difficulties. Now we have learned why. A source close to both the law practice and the PR firm has informed me that McCann Public Relations has actually been sabotaging the practice."

The reporter was a young woman with whom Allison had often had drinks. While the ambitious reporter always pumped her for information, she also spoke candidly with Allison about her own life—her love interests, her goals. She'd thought they were friends. How could she have reported this without talking to her first?

It was just another reason Allison had to trust no one, especially not Trevor. Had he been here, distracting her while his partners had been feeding these lies to the reporter?

The young woman continued, "We don't know yet her motivation for trying to take down the practice she helped build up, but given the reputations of the four partners, it could be the case of a woman scorned."

It hadn't been. But Allison felt scorned now.

Trevor had to have known about the report. And still he'd had sex with her.

She had been such a fool.

"Are you okay?" Edward asked with concern.

Allison stood up and for the first time since she'd overheard that meeting at Street Legal, she felt as if she'd found her footing again. She wasn't okay. She was furious.

And no matter how the hell sexy Trevor Sinclair was, he wasn't going to seduce her out of doing what she was about to do.

As she stormed from the office, Edward called after her, trying to stop her. But there was no stopping her now.

CHAPTER ELEVEN

TREV COULDN'T SHAKE the bad feeling he'd had since leaving Allison's office. She'd grown so quiet after they'd made love, as if she'd regretted it.

And she'd been so distant when he'd left.

He couldn't help but feel that he might not see her again. Fingers snapped in his face, drawing his attention back to the meeting he'd called in his office.

"Where were you?" Simon asked.

"Like you can't figure that out," Stone said with a snort. "I can smell her on his clothes."

Allison did have a distinctive scent: a combination of a crisp-smelling cologne and rain. She smelled like an ice queen might. But Allison was all passion and fire and heat. Or she had been until he'd hurt her. He knew that he had with his suspicions.

"Did you learn anything new?" Ronan asked.

Trev nodded. "That it's not her."

Stone snorted again. "Is that your head or your dick talking?"

Trev glared at him. "C'mon, you all heard what

she said. It makes no sense for her to sabotage us. If we look bad, she looks bad."

Simon sighed. "That's true. But if not her, who?"

They'd been racking their brains for months trying to figure it out. While no one had really wanted it to be her, it would have almost been a relief if it had been so that they would finally know. So that they could finally stop the sabotage.

Trev glanced at the closed door of his office. Was their receptionist like hers? Did Miguel listen outside their door?

Edward hadn't been at the door this time when Trev had left her office, which was good considering what he would have overheard. He'd been busy at his desk—on the phone and computer. He'd barely glanced up as Trev had passed him.

Miguel hadn't looked at him at all either time Trev had passed him since their receptionist had let Allison into that meeting. Did he feel guilty? Regretful?

Trev lowered his voice, just in case there was an eavesdropper outside the door, then he said, "Allison suggested that it could be Miguel."

Simon uttered a sharp laugh.

And Stone snorted yet again.

"He let her into that meeting," Trev reminded them.

"You know Miguel," Ronan said. "He has that weird sense of chivalry. Maybe he thought she deserved to know that we suspected her."

"And she repays that by casting the suspicion on him," Simon said.

"How did he know we suspected her?" Trev asked. And a chill chased down his spine. "Did any of you tell him that?" Because Miguel hadn't known when he'd tried pumping Trev for information about the meeting he'd called the week before.

Simon tensed, his blue eyes widening. Then he shook his head. "No. It's not possible. There's no way in hell Miguel would ever betray us."

Stone had represented him when he'd been brought up on gang-related charges. He'd gotten him off on probation, which Miguel had served at an after-school program he still worked at despite having completed his hours many years ago.

Trev didn't want to believe it, either. It didn't make sense. He uttered a ragged sigh. "I don't know who the hell it is."

"You know," Stone said, "you just don't want to face the fact that you're falling for the mole."

Trev tensed now. "No," he hotly denied. He wasn't falling for anyone. Ever…

"It has to be her," Stone continued, almost gently. "She probably took your notes to help out her father—"

"No." He shook his head.

"You don't even know who it is," Stone said. "She could have."

"But then why go after the rest of you?" Trev asked.

"Cast suspicion elsewhere," Ronan offered.

Trev knew she regretted helping smear Muriel. He suspected that was why she'd started buying Bette's Beguiling Bows. The lingerie didn't seem her style—although she looked hotter than hell in it. But since she felt bad about hurting Muriel, she certainly would not have tried to frame her for office espionage.

A knock sounded at the door.

Since it was his office, he called out, "Come in."

Miguel opened the door.

"Thanks for not walking right in this time," Trev said.

And Miguel's face flushed. "I shouldn't have brought her to Simon's office," he admitted.

"Why did you?" Trev asked.

"Because I don't believe she's the mole," he said. And now he met Trev's gaze, and his eyes were dark with reproach. "And she deserved to know that you suspected her."

He wasn't the only one who'd seen through Allison's ice queen facade to the vulnerable woman she really was.

"How did you know?" Trev asked.

"I wouldn't have survived the streets if I wasn't aware of what was going on around me," Miguel said. Then he looked at all of them. "And neither would any of you."

It was true. But Trev still felt uneasy.

"Why do you think it's not her?" Stone asked.

He seemed the most determined to think it was her now.

Miguel reached for the remote sitting on Trev's desk. A TV rose from the middle of the conference table. Miguel clicked it on and reversed footage to a breaking news report from a local station.

His stomach lurched. And he turned toward the others. "Which one of you called her?"

Each partner shook his head. They all looked as shocked as he was.

He turned to Miguel.

"Not me," the receptionist said. "But doesn't this prove to you that it's not her?"

Trev had already believed her. But now he worried that he wouldn't be able to convince her of that, not after she saw this report. He hoped like hell she didn't, or he had no doubt that he would never see her again.

But the thought had no more entered his head than the sound of heels striking hardwood echoed from the hall. The door opened this time without a knock. It opened so hard that it struck the wall behind it.

Allison stood in the doorway, shaking with fury. There was no doubt she had seen the report that played yet across the television screen. "Gloating?" she asked.

Trev tensed. "What?" He had never bragged about being with her. The others had just assumed.

She gestured at the television. "Which one of you talked to that reporter? Fed her those lies?"

They all stared at her, dumbfounded.

Miguel must have realized he'd left the front desk unmanned, or the burly former gang member was scared of her, because he rushed out of the room.

"It doesn't matter which one of you did it," she said, but she glanced at him as she said that. And he knew that it did matter—if it was him.

But he'd been with her. Surely, she had to realize that he'd had no time to talk to anyone let alone a reporter. Hell, none of them ever talked to reporters without her present.

"I'm going to sue you all for slander," she threatened them. "How dare you drag my company down with yours!"

"We had nothing to do with that report," Simon told her.

"What?" she asked. Her voice had gone so shrill she sounded nearly hysterical. "Are you going to blame me for that, too? What the hell do you think I'm doing—committing career suicide?"

They were all silent. Like Trev, they had to be realizing how off base they'd been about her. She was definitely not an ice queen or a fool. There was no way she would have risked damaging her own reputation to damage theirs.

"I've got this, guys," he told the others and walked toward his door to gesture them all out.

"You've got this!" she shouted. "Hell, no, you don't *got* this! I'm not going to be sweet-talked or seduced out of suing Street Legal! I'm going to bring your damn precious practice down for real!"

Stone and Ronan hurried out with not even a glance at him. They were letting him take this one for the team. And he understood why. He'd been the one who'd suspected her in the first place.

But he knew now if she had been the mole, there would have been a lot more damage done to the practice than had already been done. She wouldn't have just hurt them. She would have destroyed them just as she was threatening to do now.

Simon, as the managing partner, paused in the doorway. "I should handle this," he told Trev.

But he shook his head. He knew her better than the others. Now was not the time to argue with her, not when she was as angry as she was.

Her face was flushed, her body tensed. She bristled with fury. No. Simon would not be able to charm or threaten her out of a lawsuit.

Hell, Trev wasn't sure what he'd be able to do, except wait for her to calm down.

Simon glanced at her. She stood right in front of the television, watching the report again. And he shook his head. "You shouldn't be alone with her…"

Just how dangerous did he think she was?

Of course, Edward had warned him that she'd try to kill him. She hadn't at her office. He wasn't so sure that she wouldn't try now.

"I'll be fine," he lied to his partner. He had no idea if he'd survive another passionate encounter with Allison McCann. But he closed the door behind Simon and locked it, locking them inside together.

"Allison…"

She'd gone curiously quiet after all the threats she'd shouted. But now she turned back toward him, and he saw the tears running down her face.

Panic clutched his heart. He'd never done well with tears. Even knowing how his mom had been able to turn them on and off, he'd still let them manipulate him into agreeing to things, like working when he was too young, like letting her leave him to pursue her career…like telling her not to worry about him when she should have worried.

But Allison was more prone to act like nothing bothered her than to cry. No. Her tears were real. Just more hurt than angry.

"Allison…" he murmured again, and he started toward her with his arms outstretched.

But before he could pull her into an embrace, she stepped back and began to laugh and laugh and laugh as if she was unable to stop.

Allison's chest hurt from her laughter. Or maybe that was from the tears. She had no idea. And clearly neither did Trevor. He stared at her in horror as if he'd thought she'd lost her mind.

And maybe she had when she'd barged into his office with all her threats. But she was getting a grip now. She drew in a deep breath to stop the laughter, to stop the tears.

She hated crying—especially now when she had no right to her tears.

"Are you okay?" Trevor asked her. He held his arms out, but his hands just touched her shoulders, turning her fully toward him.

She shrugged. She had no idea if she was or what she would do now. "So this is karma…" she murmured.

"What?"

"I did that to so many other people," she said and she gestured back at the television screen. "I was the source for reports like that. Now I know what it feels like."

And she didn't like it.

"You issued statements about our cases," he said. "You helped me show what those corporations were covering up."

"Your cases were easy," she said. She'd never had a crisis of conscience over them. "But Ronan's… What we did to Muriel Sanz…"

"Made her a household name," Trev said. "Her career is bigger than it ever was. Hell, she was just voted the world's most beautiful woman."

But the magazine that had given her the title was only looking at her outside. Thanks to McCann Public Relations, everyone had thought the supermodel was ugly inside—that she was a liar and a cheat.

But that had been Ronan's client, Muriel's ex-husband.

"Stop beating yourself up about that," Trevor told her.

How had he known that it bothered her? Most other people thought she truly was an ice queen who had no feelings and no conscience—just like her mother.

She shivered. But Trevor had gotten to know her, so well that it scared her even more than someone trying to take down her firm. But since Trevor knew her so well, he would know exactly how to hurt her, take away what mattered most to her. Her company...

"Was it your idea?" she asked, and she gestured at the television again. It had stopped at the end of the report.

His eyes widened in shock or maybe innocence. Was it real or feigned, though? She couldn't trust anything about him—anything he said or did.

He shook his head. "I was with you right after I left here."

"You could have called her on the way to my office," she said. "Or you could have had one of your partners or Miguel do your dirty work."

Just like they had always had her do it.

Karma really had bit her in the ass. She deserved this, whatever this was.

"It was the mole," Trevor said.

"What mole?"

"Our mole."

But was it their mole? What if it had never been their mole?

"You said the cases that were sabotaged were ones I had worked on," she said.

He nodded. "Yes."

"Every one of them I had touched?"

"Yes, that's the only reason I thought it could have been you. You were the only thing every one of them had in common."

She released a shaky sigh as she realized what that meant. "Oh, my God," she murmured, "It was me…"

CHAPTER TWELVE

TREV FELT AS if she'd punched him in the throat. He couldn't breathe for a moment. His heart stopped beating. Had she just confessed?

"What?" he asked. "You are the mole?"

She shook her head, so violently that her hair tangled around her face. She reached up with a trembling hand to push it away. "No. The mole was never after Street Legal," she said. "The mole was after me!"

Trev felt as if he'd been hit again for a moment. What if she was right? But then he considered what she'd said, and as a lawyer his first instinct was to argue with her.

"It wasn't you who could have lost his license when those forged documents got to Muriel," he said. "That was Ronan."

"The mole couldn't have known for certain that Muriel would bring those documents to the bar association, though," she pointed out. "Maybe he thought she would only go to the press with them."

Trev drew in a shaky breath. She was right. "But helping out the district attorney…"

"Blew my media defense of the accused out of the water," Allison pointed out. "Hillary didn't just make Stone look like a fool. She made me look like one, too."

"And me…?" he asked. "Why go after me?"

"For the same reason as the others," she said. "I was promoting your case in the press. If you lose, I lose, too."

He shook his head. "I think you're taking this too personally."

She gestured toward that television screen. "How can I not? I thought she was my friend," Allison said, and her voice cracked with emotion. "That story wasn't really about any of you. It was about me. And it made me look horrible."

He couldn't argue with her about that. It had made her look horrible while it had cleared up Street Legal's reputation. All their bad press had been made to look like her fault.

One of his partners wouldn't have gone to the press, would they? Since the practice had been Simon's idea—one he'd come up with when they were living on the streets—he would do anything to protect it. And he was very well acquainted with all the local reporters.

"My business is ruined," she said. "Who would ever trust me again after that report?"

Trev flinched.

"Karma is a bitch," she murmured, and her pale eyes were bright, glistening with what Trev suspected were tears. She blinked them away, though, before meeting his gaze. "I'm sorry," she said. "Tell your partners I'm not going to sue."

Trev wouldn't blame her if she did. And if one of them had given the reporter that story, he would represent her himself. Pro bono...

But at least she had her grandfather's trust. If the business failed, she wouldn't be homeless like he'd been after Wally had died. She would be fine.

But she didn't look fine. She looked sick and pale and shaky.

"Are you okay?" he asked.

She nodded. "Yeah." But her voice cracked again and one of the tears she hadn't blinked away overflowed a beautiful eye and trailed down her cheek.

He reached out to wipe it away, sliding his thumb across the silky skin of her cheek. "We'll figure this out," he said. "We'll find the mole."

She smiled at him but the smile didn't reach her eyes. "How many months have you and your partners been trying to figure it out?"

"Too many."

"I wish you would have told me," she said.

"I'm sorry." They should have. He realized that now.

"But I understand," she said. "I get that none of you would trust me."

He wanted to assure her that he trusted her now.

But that little voice in his head, the one that had helped him survive the streets, whispered some doubts.

Sure, the report made her look bad. But it also made her look innocent of being the mole. And she'd admitted that reporter was her friend.

It was possible that she was the source for that story as she'd been for so many others. Maybe she'd figured it was safer to sacrifice her business than risk her freedom and a lawsuit from them.

Ronan had been talking about criminal charges and Simon had been talking about monetary restitution once they had their evidence.

Her eyes widened as she stared at him. Then she expelled a shaky sigh. "Oh, you don't trust me."

"It's not that—"

But she stepped around him and headed toward the door. He rushed after her and slammed his palm against it, stopping her from opening it no matter that she was turning the knob.

"You can't go," he told her.

"Why not?" she asked. "Did you call the police? Did you all issue a restraining order when you banned me from the building?"

"Obviously, we didn't ban you from the building," he said. Or she wouldn't have been able to storm into his office like she had.

But he wouldn't put it past Simon to have done it now. Just as he had his doubts, his partners would, too. They had all grown up the same way, in the same place, and they wouldn't have survived had any of them been too trusting.

"Then why won't you let me leave?" she asked him.

Because a horrible thought had occurred to him.

"If you really are the one who the mole is after," he said, "you might be in danger." And there was no way he was going to allow anyone to hurt her.

Anyone else.

He knew that he already had earlier when he'd suspected she was the mole and now when he hadn't been able to tell her that he trusted her.

But he wouldn't let her get hurt again, even if he had to put himself in danger to protect her.

Allison felt like the ice queen now—cold straight through her. Despite Trevor standing beside her in the small elevator, she shivered. Even the heat of his big, muscular body couldn't permeate hers now.

He cursed. "I'm sorry I didn't have an umbrella."

The minute they'd stepped out of the cab, the sky had opened up and downpoured on them. But that wasn't why Allison was so cold. Her chill came from within rather than her wet clothes, hair and skin.

He rubbed his big hand over her shoulder and down her arm. "You're so wet."

Hearing that, and remembering all the times he'd said that before, had a little ember of warmth flickering back to life inside Allison.

He chuckled, as he must have realized what he'd

said, too. And his arm tightened around her. He glanced at the control panel and murmured, "I've heard sex in an elevator can be exciting."

She chuckled now. "You heard that... Mmm-hmm..."

"Seriously," he said. "That's the only way I know about it."

"No firsthand knowledge?"

He shook his head. "Not yet." But then he reached for the top button of her dress.

She giggled and stepped back just as the elevator dinged. The doors slid open on her floor. But it wasn't empty.

Thankfully, no reporters waited for her. They hadn't been in the lobby, either, so Edward must not have told them where she lived like he'd told Trevor. He had texted her a warning that the media had camped out at the office, waiting for her to return.

It was early afternoon, and she usually worked late. At least she had before she'd started seeing Trevor last week. But she wasn't going back now.

There wasn't much to go back to except those reporters. She should give them a statement. Say something to exonerate herself and the firm.

But what?

She, who never ran out of things to say, could think of nothing. No spin to save this.

To save herself.

Trevor guided her out of the elevator and around

her neighbors who didn't even look at her. They must have seen the report, and the elderly couple was embarrassed for her.

She was embarrassed, too, which made her feel like a hypocrite again when she thought of all the people she'd embarrassed with her previous press releases. And maybe that was why she was in no hurry to issue any statements to exonerate herself.

She felt like she deserved this.

But Trevor didn't.

While some of his partners seemed to have questionable ethics, he didn't. He took on the big corporations for the little guy like his friend Wally.

She paused at the door to her penthouse and stared up at him.

"Can't find your keys?" he asked.

She pulled the key ring out of her purse, but she held tightly to the keys when he reached for the ring. "You saw me home," she said. "You don't have to come inside."

"I have to make sure you're safe," he said. And he took the keys from her hand and unlocked the door.

"You can see," she said, "nobody's here."

But he walked through the foyer and checked out every room. "Are you a bodyguard or a lawyer?" she asked when he joined her in the kitchen.

"I will gladly guard your body," he told her with that wicked grin of his. But instead of touching her body, he touched her hair. "You should take a shower, warm up."

She did feel frozen to the bone like the ice queen she'd tried so long to convince everyone else she was. Maybe she'd been too convincing.

"You can go," she told him again. "I'm safe."

He shook his head. "You're not safe at all."

But she suspected he wasn't talking about her being in danger but about her being the danger. She was a danger to him. Someone had already gone after him and his partners in order to get to her.

"Trevor—"

He pressed his fingers over her lips as if he knew he wasn't going to like what she was about to say. "It's your turn to do what I say," he said. "And I'm telling you to get into the shower. Now, before you turn blue."

Her skin was so pale that it did tend to turn bluish when she got cold enough that her veins stood out. She shivered as the chill permeated even deeper into her bones.

She would argue with him later, once she was warm. Then she would make him see that his partners were right. It was best she had nothing to do with Street Legal or with him.

But once she was standing in the master bath, on the cold marble floor, she struggled with the buttons on her wet dress. Her fingers were so cold that they were nearly numb. Then a shadow fell across her, and she glanced up to find that Trevor had joined her.

"What?" she asked him. "Did you forget to check the shower for the bogeyman?"

He shook his head. "No. I realized I'm wet and cold, too." He'd already unbuttoned his damp shirt. He pushed it from his shoulders and dropped it onto the floor. Then he reached for the buttons of her dress, but like in her office, he only undid a few of them before giving up and lifting it over her head. It dropped to the floor with his shirt. Then his jeans and underwear joined the pile.

And her purple lingerie slipped off next, the bows untied. She shivered despite the heat of his gaze, the desire in his green eyes.

He cursed, probably still over not having an umbrella. Then he turned on the shower. It heated quickly, so he tugged her into the big, open spa-like shower with him. The warm spray sprinkled down on her.

Then Trevor stepped into the shower with her, and she warmed even more, the heat of desire filling her as she watched the water streak down all his sculpted muscles.

The man was masculine perfection, his muscles rippling as he moved. While she stood there, too entranced to move, he washed her hair and her body, his hands sliding a soapy loofa over her every curve.

She moaned as he focused on her breasts. Then he moved the loofah lower, between her legs. She moaned louder and arched her head back; water splashed her face and ran down her throat.

And Trevor groaned. "You are so damn beautiful..."

He kissed her neck and traced her collarbone with

his tongue as if licking the water off her. Then his mouth was on one breast, teasing the nipple into a tight point.

She moaned again.

And he moved the loofa, teasing her with it. Her legs began to shake. So he lifted her from her feet. But the shower floor was slick, and he nearly slipped.

With a chuckle, he moved to the bench. He sat down on it and lifted her so that she straddled his lap. She hadn't seen him do it, but he must have brought in a condom packet with him. Because he tore it open and rolled it over his shaft, then he eased her over it.

She cried out at the sensation of him filling her, of him filling that hollowness that had ached inside her earlier—when she'd heard they'd suspected her of being the mole. That he was supposed to get evidence to prove that she was...

Was that what he was doing now? Or did he believe her?

She didn't care at the moment. All she cared about was the way he made her feel. The tension that had been wound so tightly inside her all day broke as her body convulsed in an orgasm.

It wasn't enough, though.

At least for him because he kept moving until she had another and another.

The cords in his neck and the muscles in his arms stood out as he struggled for control. He was holding back his own release to give her pleasure.

She'd never had as selfless a lover as Trevor Sin-

clair. She'd never known as selfless a man except
for her grandfather.

Trevor wasn't done giving her pleasure. He
touched her breasts and lowered his head to hers,
kissing her deeply. Then he reached between them,
rubbing his thumb over her clit, and she came again,
screaming his name.

Finally, his big body tensed before shuddering
with his own release. He groaned and leaned his
forhead against hers, staring deeply into her eyes.

What was he looking for? The truth? She'd already given it to him. She wasn't the mole.

But there was something she needed to tell him.
She slid off his lap, finished showering and dried
off. Instead of heading toward the bed, she found
a long, thick robe and wrapped it around herself.
Then she headed back to the living room and stared
down at the park.

"Are you hungry?" he asked as he joined her. He'd
dressed again in his damp clothes. Water streaked
from his hair, over his face and neck.

He hadn't dried off well. He must have been in a
hurry to be with her again. To watch over her.

She shook her head.

"You're not?" he asked. "Did you eat anything
today?"

She shook her head again.

"I'll make something."

"I don't have any food in the house," she warned

him. She hadn't shopped for groceries the past week. She'd shopped for lingerie.

"I'll order takeout," he said. "What would you like?"

"I want you to leave," she said.

"Allison—"

"I'm not in any danger," she said. She suspected the mole had gotten what he'd wanted anyway: public embarrassment for her. "Nobody's here. Nobody's physically trying to hurt me."

"But you don't know—"

"I know that you're in more danger," she said. "I know that you need to stay away from me."

He tensed. "What?"

"My professional reputation is ruined." Her personal one, too, but she wasn't worried about that. "I don't want yours ruined, not when you're getting ready to run for office."

"What?" he asked again.

And she had a sick feeling. "You were telling the truth about that, right? It wasn't just a ploy to get evidence against me like your seduction?"

He ran his hand over his face, to brush away the water. "Allison…"

She shook her head. "I can't handle any more lies."

"Don't worry about me," he said. "It's not like I'm trying to run for an election right now."

"No," she said. "You need to revamp your image first. I thought you needed to step away from your friends to do that. But now I know that I'm the trouble. I'm the one you need to stay away from."

Trevor looked at her, and for the first time since she'd known him, the big man looked helpless. He had no argument for her. She smiled sadly and pushed him toward the door. "You need to leave and never come back."

Or she was going to fall even harder for him than she suspected she already had.

Maybe that was why she was pushing him away. She didn't want to get hurt anymore.

And it was clear that Trevor hadn't been completely honest with her yet. He wasn't like her grandfather at all who would have never hurt her.

She knew that Trevor could hurt her more than anyone else in her life ever had…because she'd started to care the most about him.

He stopped at the door and turned back to her. But he must have had nothing to say because he just lowered his head and brushed his mouth across hers. Then, lips still clinging, he pulled away and headed out the door.

Out of her life.

It was for the best. If he stayed, Allison was only going to get hurt. She wasn't in any more danger from the mole. Trevor Sinclair was the danger—to her heart.

CHAPTER THIRTEEN

TREV FELT LIKE HELL. He'd lied to her. And he hated himself for it. No. He hadn't lied. He just hadn't told the truth. He should have been honest with her when he'd had the chance. Told her that he had never had any intention of playing politics.

She would know that he'd lied to her. Wouldn't she understand, though, that he'd been after the mole? But she was already hurting over his suspecting her of being the mole.

And that news report had devastated her, so much so that he couldn't stay away from her. He wasn't worried about his image or whatever she'd been concerned about when she'd thrown him out the night before.

He was concerned about her.

So, even knowing that she would be upset, he headed to her office. Reporters had the lobby staked out, and the minute he appeared, microphones got shoved in his face.

"Are you the one who scorned her?" a male reporter asked, his eyes bright with interest. He clearly wanted details. "Are you the one who thawed the ice princess?"

Trev glared at the man.

"If not, why are you here?" another reporter asked.

"It's business," Trev replied. Then he singled out the female reporter who'd given the special report. "That report was bullshit. The reporter who gave it has no business being a journalist or a friend."

The woman flinched.

"And as all you reporters should know," he said, and now he looked at them all, "reporting false, unsubstantiated claims leads to defamation and slander lawsuits."

"Is that why you're here?" another female reporter asked. "You're representing Ms. McCann in a lawsuit?"

He just smiled, letting them all believe what they would, then he headed toward the elevators. Why hadn't Allison done that? Why hadn't she given a statement to defend herself and clear up her reputation?

She was a publicist. She knew better than anyone how to spin bad press into good. Why hadn't she done that yet?

He stormed off the elevator onto her floor with such purpose that Edward jumped and spilled the coffee he was pouring.

"Where is she?" he demanded to know. But he didn't wait for an answer. He headed toward her office. When he pushed open the door, he found it empty.

"Where is she?" he asked again as Edward had followed him down the hall.

"I don't think she's coming in," her assistant replied. But it was clear he didn't know, especially as the elevator dinged and Allison stepped off it.

Her face was flushed. She must have had a run-in with the reporters in the lobby, as well. Perhaps after his threats, they had been a little more respectful, though.

"Did you straighten them out?" he asked her.

She walked past him and headed toward her desk, dropping into her chair as if her legs weren't quite steady enough to hold her.

"Looks like you're the one I need to straighten out," she said. "I told you to stay away."

"Do you want me to call security?" Edward eagerly asked. "The police?"

She shook her head. "I will handle this. You can close the door on your way out, Edward."

He hesitated a long moment, though, before he followed her order. So long that Trev considered shoving him out and slamming the door in his face. "Why do you keep that guy around?" He asked the question he'd been wondering for a while.

"He's a computer genius," she said. "Can find anything online..."

"A hacker?"

She shrugged. "I don't know how he does it."

"So he doesn't get all his information from listening at doors?" The door in question rattled as if Edward had fallen against it.

They both laughed.

"There, that's better," he said. And the tightness in his chest eased with the smile on her beautiful face.

She still looked pale, though, but for the dark circles beneath her eyes. She obviously was back to not sleeping well. He stepped closer and leaned over her desk. Then he ran his fingertip along her jaw. "You should have let me stay last night."

She shook her head. "I had a reason for making you leave. But you blew that by coming here today and talking to those reporters."

"Someone has to," he said. "But it should be you. You can clear all this up. If anyone can repair a bad reputation or spin it, it's you." Now he came around her desk and twirled her chair. "Spin it!"

She laughed but when her chair stopped and she faced him again, the humor didn't reach her eyes. She still looked sad. Defeated. And the tightness returned to his chest.

He hadn't come here just to fire her up again. He'd come here to tell her the truth. But now the words stuck in his throat. He didn't want to make her angry with him.

But maybe it was better that she get angry than seem so defeated. He opened his mouth to speak but Allison reached out and pressed her fingers across his lips.

"You've already said enough," she told him. "For both of us. You scared Monica."

"Monica?"

"The reporter," she said. "She thinks I'm going to sue her."

"You should," he said. "Or you should at least get her to tell you her source."

"It was a man," she said, and she stared hard at him now as if she wondered if he was that man.

"It wasn't me," he assured her. But it could have been one of his partners. He needed to talk to them again and make sure nobody had done anything stupid.

Like he had.

He never should have suspected her of being the mole.

"Does she know who?" he asked.

Allison shook her head.

"We'll find out," he assured her.

She shook her head again.

"This mole can't hide forever," Trev insisted. "We will figure out who it is."

"No," she said. "I will. You will focus on your practice and on running for office."

"Allison—" He needed to tell her.

But she pressed her fingers over his lips again. "This is my problem," she said. "Not yours."

He stepped back and studied her face. "Do you know who it is?"

Doubts creeped back into his head. Was she the

mole? Was all of this just a ruse to fool him? He only had her word that the reporter claimed a man was her source. Her source could have been Allison herself.

She was more likely to give press releases than anyone else.

"Do you know?" he asked again when she had been silent for far too long.

Allison shivered from the suspicion on his handsome face. He still didn't entirely trust her. But then she didn't trust him, either.

Maybe it was just because of the way they had both been raised—by mothers who didn't care—that they struggled to trust anyone.

"I don't know who it is," she said. There were so many people it could have been.

Muriel Sanz. Her friend Bette.

But Trevor had said they'd already ruled them out because his partners had slept with them. That was obviously how they conducted their investigation.

She wasn't going to run hers the same way. She was going to investigate. She wanted to know. And she had one suspicion. But she wasn't about to share that with Trevor. She didn't want him to do anything that might require him hiring Stone as his criminal defense lawyer.

"You act like you don't care," Trevor said as if that was an accusation, as well.

She sighed. "I care."

"Then why won't you do something about it? Why

aren't you threatening to sue that reporter and setting the record straight?"

Like he had. She'd been standing behind him in the lobby and had heard his every word. Nobody had noticed her because they'd been so focused on him. He commanded attention and respect.

He really would make a great politician. If her mother had married him, she might have had her shot at being first lady one day.

But Allison didn't even know where her mother was. Given her history, she was undoubtedly married again. She'd never been able to go without a man and his money.

Since she hadn't inherited her father's, she would have had to find another rich husband to support her expensive habits.

"Maybe the record is straight," she said.

And he narrowed his eyes. "You said you're not the mole."

"I'm not."

"But then how would the record be straight?"

"Karma," she said. "I deserve some bad press for all I've given out. I deserve this because I have become my mother's daughter."

She'd started training her from such a young age to be a bitch like her, to take people down with backhanded compliments and mean smiles. She shivered as she relived the coldness with which she'd been raised. "My mother is not a nice woman."

"Do you think she could be behind this?" Trevor asked. "Do you think she could be the mole?"

And Allison's heart clenched before she laughed. "She would not waste her time with me." She very rarely had.

"But you inherited from your grandfather and she didn't," Trev pointed out. "Don't you think she might want revenge?"

Her mother always wanted revenge for every imagined slight against her. But Allison was still her daughter, although at her grandfather's funeral, her mother had denounced her.

"But how?" Allison asked. "How could she be the mole? I haven't talked to her in years."

Trev glanced at the door. "I guess I should let you handle this," he said. "Especially since she's your mother."

"Yes," she said. But instead of feeling the relief she'd expected since he was backing down, she felt that achy hollowness inside again. "Thank you."

"Like you said," he continued, "I need to focus on revamping my image for politics."

"And being involved with me is only going to hurt you," she said.

He nodded in agreement.

And she felt a twinge in her heart. He was willing to step back. Running for office must have meant more to him than she'd realized.

"It's good that nobody knows that I was even considering it," he said.

"Your partners know."

"They didn't want that getting out," Trevor said. "Didn't want it affecting Street Legal."

She sighed. "And it would. It would look like you're abandoning a sinking ship."

His lips curved into a slight grin. "That's what you wanted me to do," he reminded her.

"To save yourself," she said. "To save your career. That's why you need to stay away from me now." Because she was exactly like her mother now, poison for any man's political career.

But instead of stepping away from her, he stepped closer. She knew what he needed—the same thing she needed. One last time…

One last powerful orgasm…

She was still sitting and he was standing, so she reached for his zipper. He groaned as she pulled down the tab and freed his cock. First, she glided her fingers over it, then she closed her lips around it.

It was so smooth and long. She sucked him as deep as she could in her throat. But he pulled back.

And when she looked up, he was shaking his head. Maybe he didn't want what she wanted.

But then he reached down and pulled her up from the chair. He lifted her onto the edge of her desk and slid his hands up under her dress. She wore a long one, but he pushed up the hem until he found her panties. Then he pushed them aside and stroked his fingers over her core.

And as he did, he lowered his head to hers and

kissed her. The kiss was passionate, as their kisses always were, but there was something else on his lips.

Regret?

Goodbye?

It had a twinge of pain striking her heart. But then his fingers eased inside her, and she felt nothing but desire and pleasure. She shifted against the desk, against his hand, and his thumb found her clit, rubbing it until she came.

She moaned into his mouth.

And he groaned. Then he fumbled in his pocket and pulled out a condom. After sheathing himself, he eased between her legs—sliding easily inside her.

She was so wet. So ready for him.

He moved his hands beneath her dress, over her abdomen to her breasts. He pushed down the cups of her bra and found her nipples, rubbing them with his thumbs until they ached with sensitivity.

Desire streaked from her nipples to her core, which throbbed for him. He moved his hips, thrusting in and out of her. He felt so good—so right—inside her, filling her the way that only he could.

He kissed her, his tongue sliding inside her mouth, mating with hers. She held on to his tongue with her lips, stroking it, and he groaned again.

"Come," he told her, his voice gruff. And she knew that he was barely hanging on, just waiting for her to come first.

Because that was the way he was. He wanted to make sure she found pleasure first. And thinking of that, thinking of how he had been every time they'd had sex, she realized something.

They weren't just having sex. They were making love.

At least she was.

She loved him.

Her body tensed with the realization, with fear. But then he slid his hand down and stroked it over her as he continued to move his cock inside her. And her muscles convulsed as the orgasm shattered her nearly as much as her revelation had.

Then he came, his body shuddering as he found his release. He leaned his forehead, which was damp with perspiration, against hers and stared deeply into her eyes.

What was he looking for?

Did he see it?

Did he know she'd fallen for him? She'd broken her own rule about emotions, and hers were more involved than they had ever been. They twisted and turned inside her, squeezing her heart, squeezing her stomach.

But because she loved him, she knew she had to let him go. She couldn't do what her mother had to all her exes. She couldn't let her bad reputation ruin his life. She loved him too much.

CHAPTER FOURTEEN

IT DIDN'T TAKE long for Trev's plan to work. He barely made it back to the office before he heard the breaking report on the news.

Monica again.

She obviously hadn't heeded his warning since she was so willing to report another unsubstantiated story. Maybe it had sounded believable to her. But it was unbelievable to him.

He was never running for office like Monica reported from the television in the middle of his conference table.

"Is it true?" a deep voice asked.

And he turned to find Miguel standing in the doorway. The receptionist looked shocked. And growing up as they had, on the streets, nothing tended to shock them anymore.

He hadn't known. He wasn't like Edward; he didn't listen at doors.

He shook his head.

"Maybe it should be," Miguel said. "You'd do this city a lot of good."

He shrugged.

"He's not leaving us," Simon said as he joined them in the office.

Miguel pointed toward the television. "That's not what she's saying."

Simon shook his head. "That's not true." He turned toward Trev. "Why'd you leak this story? We agreed that this would never go public."

That was why they'd been so careful to limit who'd learned about it. The other guys hadn't even told the women in their lives. So Trev shouldn't have felt bad that he hadn't told Allison.

But he did.

He'd had a few opportunities to come clean with her since she'd learned that he'd suspected her of being the mole. She might have understood if he'd told her right away. But he'd continued to keep the secret.

"Secret's out now," Ronan said as he joined them. "Did she put this out there to detract from what's going on with her?"

Trev shook his head. "No." He'd made certain to say—loudly—that the story could not come out now. There was no way she'd spoken to that reporter.

Miguel rubbed his head. "I don't understand what's going on. Are you running for an election or not?"

"Not," Simon answered before Trev could. "This was just a ploy for him to get closer to Allison Mc-Cann and find out if she's the mole."

"This proves she is," Ronan said as he pointed at the TV. "She's the only one besides the four of us who knew about your bogus run for office."

Trev shook his head. "No. This proves she's innocent."

"Are you so sure?" a female voice asked from behind the big body of the receptionist.

Miguel's face flushed that once again he'd left the front desk unprotected. He hurried off, leaving Allison standing alone in the doorway.

And Simon and Ronan exchanged a look.

"Are you confessing?" Simon asked her.

She nodded. "I confess to being a fool. I thought you were serious."

Trev was serious. About her...

But he doubted she was going to believe that or anything else he said at the moment.

"I tried telling you," he said.

"Not very damn hard."

That was true, and he flinched at the direct hit. Sure, she'd stopped him the night before and in her office. But he could have told her had he not been so afraid of losing her.

"I came here to apologize," she said. She gestured at the television. "I knew you didn't want anyone to know that you were going to run. Now I know why."

"So you are the source for this story?" Ronan asked, his eyes narrowed with suspicion.

Trev ignored his friend. And she did, too. "You know who it is," he said.

She nodded. "Edward."

He was the only one who could have overheard what they'd discussed in her office. "That's why I said that," he explained. "I knew it would make him run right to the press."

"Edward?" Simon asked. "Your assistant?"

She nodded again.

"But why?"

Trev glared now at his partners. They were so concerned about the damn mole that they didn't realize what was really going on, that Trev was losing the one thing he hadn't even realized he'd wanted.

Love.

In fact, he'd thought he'd wanted nothing to do with it. He'd never intended to risk his heart. But it didn't matter that they'd agreed on no emotions. He was emotionally involved. Hell, he was in love.

Maybe Ronan, who was usually oblivious, realized that because he tugged Simon out of the office. Once in the hall, he closed the door behind them, shutting Trev and Allison inside together.

Alone.

He'd faced some tough juries and judges in his career as a lawyer. But he'd never had any doubts that he could sway them to his side, that he could convince them to trust him and accept what he told them.

Until now.

Now, when it mattered most, he wasn't sure he

would be able to win Allison over again. Or had he ever really had her?

He'd thought so when she'd been so insistent that he distance himself from her. He'd thought she'd cared more about him than herself.

And that was when he should have told her the truth. But he'd been afraid that this would happen, that he would lose her.

"I'm sorry," he said.

"About what?" she asked, and she arched a red brow over one of her pale eyes. "About Edward?"

"About us," he said.

"Yeah, I'm sorry, too," she said. And she turned and reached for the doorknob. "I'm sorry it ever happened."

But he held the door shut, like he had before. He wasn't going to let her leave. He couldn't lose her. Just the thought of it had his chest aching with a hollow feeling he hadn't felt since his mother had left him.

Allison couldn't leave him, too. "Damn you," Trev murmured. But he wasn't sure if he was cursing her, his mother or himself. Probably himself.

He was the one who'd screwed this all up. He could only hope that she would give him the chance to fix it—to fix them. "Don't go," he implored her.

She was wrong. She'd been so wrong about every man currently in her life. Maybe she'd even been wrong about her grandfather. Maybe he hadn't been as sweet and honest as she remembered.

Trev certainly wasn't. He held the door shut. She couldn't budge it. She couldn't escape him. So she turned and put her back against the door and stared up at him.

"Which is it?" she asked. "You're telling me not to go even as you're damning me."

"I'm damning me," he said. "I should have been honest with you from the get-go."

"It's too late now," she told him. And it was. She wouldn't be able to trust him again, not that she ever actually had. But that was a good thing, wasn't it?

Or she would have fallen harder, would have been hurt more?

But how much more could she hurt? Her heart ached so badly now. Her body did, too, as if it had been run over by a bus. "I came over here right after I fired Edward—"

"You fired Edward?"

It was something she should have done long ago. She'd considered it so many times, but she wasn't the ice queen she'd wanted to be. She wasn't her mother.

She nodded. "Your plan worked to flush out the mole."

"Why was he doing it?" he asked. "What was his motivation?"

He'd stopped his friend from asking the question, so she wondered why he was. Was he just stalling? Trying to get her to stay…

That ache in her chest intensified, but it wasn't about him this time. Maybe that was why she'd rushed over here. She'd told herself that it was to apologize for the story leaking to the media.

But it had been because she'd needed him. She'd needed his comfort. His protection.

But she should have known it was better to need no one. People always let you down. Never more so than now.

"Is he in love with you?" Trevor asked, his voice gruff and his eyes dark with anger as if he was jealous that another man could love her.

He couldn't.

If he did, he wouldn't have suspected her of being the mole. He wouldn't have continued to lie to her.

"The only thing Edward loves is money," Allison said. "And my mother was paying him quite a bit to sabotage me."

"Why didn't she want your firm to succeed?" Trevor asked, his brow furrowed in confusion.

She shook her head. "She doesn't care about the success of the firm. Street Legal was the only client she paid Edward to sabotage."

"I don't get it."

She hadn't at first, either. But Edward had explained it to her. He'd actually felt a little guilty for betraying her, so he'd told her everything. Well, he'd told her everything after she'd threatened to call the police.

Unlike his empty threats, he must have known she would go through with it.

She probably should have. But she'd realized he'd just been a puppet doing someone else's dirty work.

"Why would your mother go after us?" Trevor persisted.

"You're all young, rich, successful lawyers."

"Isn't that her type?" Trevor asked.

Allison's face heated. "Yes, it is, and that's why she did it. She didn't want me getting involved with any of you—didn't want me to have the life she'd wanted."

Trevor's brow was furrowed yet with confusion. "I don't…"

Of course, he wasn't the marrying type—like her mother—so he didn't understand.

"Your plan worked," she said. "When she heard from Edward that you and I were spending time together—" her face heated again. Edward had always suspected she'd had a thing for Trevor Sinclair "—and then that you were running for office, she lost it."

Trevor finally nodded. "She didn't want you to marry a politician and become first lady like she wanted."

Allison's face burned with embarrassment. "She has no idea that there were no emotions involved with us, so she had Edward contact the reporter. She wanted to end our relationship. She didn't know there was no relationship to end."

"Allison, that's not true—"

"No," she interrupted him. "Nothing you told me was true." And no matter how much she loved him, she would never be able to trust him.

"I was trying to catch the damn mole," he said. "I didn't feel for you the way that I do now."

"Don't!" she shouted. "Don't lie to me anymore."

He shook his head. "I'm trying to tell you the truth. I was trying to last night and this morning. But you don't want to hear it."

"What I don't want to hear is a bunch of lies, a bunch of empty promises." Like her father had always given her. *We'll still spend time together. I'll come see you. I love you...*

Trevor was more like him than she'd realized. And because of that, she couldn't love him. Whatever she'd thought she'd felt for him, it hadn't been that.

"I won't lie to you anymore," he said.

She shook her head now. "That's just another empty promise."

"Allison!"

"It doesn't matter," she said. "What we had was just sex. No emotions, remember?"

"You didn't start to care about me?" he asked.

She drew in a deep breath before she replied, "No. It was just sex."

"Who's the liar now, Allison?" he asked.

She knew she'd been lying. But she didn't know if it was now or when she'd actually thought she'd fallen for him. She was her mother's daughter, and her mother had never cared about anyone but herself.

How could Allison?

It was better that she focus on business now and forget all about pleasure. She had to revive the firm. She wouldn't let it fail because of what her mother and Edward had done. But from now on, she would be a little more careful about the clients she took on.

No more lawyers.

No more liars.

"Let me go," she told Trevor.

But he'd already taken his hand away from the door. He wasn't physically keeping her, and he pointed that out when he said, "I never really had you…"

But he had. And even as she opened the door and walked away, she suspected a part of her would always be with him.

Her heart…

CHAPTER FIFTEEN

OUT OF NECESSITY, Trev had become a fighter. He'd fought his entire life. For himself. For his mother. For Wally. For all the other people who'd been hurt.

But now that he was hurt, he found he had no fight left. Maybe it was because of all those years he'd spent fighting. He'd just worn himself out.

And Allison McCann wasn't like any other opposition he'd ever met. She was stubborn and determined to stay away from him. He'd tried calling her. She declined them. And when he'd texted her, she'd blocked his number.

She wanted nothing to do with him, and he could understand why. He wished he'd been honest with her from the beginning. But he hadn't known her then.

He hadn't known that she wasn't the mole, that she wasn't the ice queen. He hadn't known how much he would come to love her.

God, he missed her. He ached for missing her.

"You need a case," Simon told him.

As the managing partner, Simon handled their money, too. He liked the cases Trev took on because he brought in the most money. Usually, Trev liked the cases he took on, but he couldn't get excited about one now. He couldn't get excited about anything now.

Not without Allison…

"You need to stop moping around," Stone said. "You're depressing the hell out of everyone."

So this week's business meeting was apparently all about him instead of the business.

"Fuck you," he told Stone.

"Fuck somebody," Ronan crudely told him. "Maybe you'll stop being so tense and stressed."

There was only one person he wanted to fuck. No. He wanted to make love to her, but Allison wanted nothing to do with him now.

"Muriel has a new friend," Ronan said. "Maybe she can set you up with her."

He glared at his partner. Maybe Ronan meant well, but it was as if he'd plunged a knife in Trev's heart and turned it. No. Allison had done that when she'd walked away from him the last time.

Ronan held up his hands, palms out. "Hey, don't look at me like that. I'm just trying to help. According to Mur, this woman's been through a tough time lately. Maybe you can cheer each other up."

"Stop trying to fix me up," Trev said.

"We're just trying to fix you," Ronan said.

And Stone added, "You seem broken."

He felt that way himself, like his heart was broken. But he knew there was only one person who could fix him.

"I didn't want to lose you," Simon said. "But maybe she was right. Maybe you need to quit the practice and run for office."

Great. Now even his friends didn't want him. He needed to stop moping around—just as they'd said.

"I am no politician," he said.

"Not yet," Simon agreed. "But if you hired someone to help you with your image…" He arched a blond brow.

And Trev groaned. "It's not going to work," he said as he realized what his friend was up to: matchmaking. "Allison will never take me on as a client."

Simon nodded in agreement. "She refused to work with any of us again," he admitted. "I've tried to hire her back a few times."

So his, apparently, weren't the only calls she was refusing to take. That didn't make Trev feel any better, though.

"Is she still furious with us for thinking she was the mole?" he asked, eager for any news of her.

Simon shook his head.

"You've talked to her?"

"No," Simon said. "I watched the news. Haven't you?"

She'd cleared Street Legal of all of the bad publicity. She'd spoken with a red-faced Monica Waters about the perils of spreading unsubstantiated stories and how she regretted that she had done it herself in the past. She promised that she would do better in the future with her clients and the media.

And Trev knew that was no empty promise.

"She's right," Ronan said with a ragged sigh. "We all need to be more careful."

Less ruthless.

More considerate.

Trev nodded in agreement but then absolved his friend of the guilt he must have still been feeling over how he'd believed his client over the truth. "Muriel's career is doing great," he reminded her lover.

Ronan nodded. "Even better now that she's hired a publicist. Maybe she can hook you up."

"Bette's using the same agency," Simon said.

Trev snorted. "I don't need a publicist. I'm not running for office."

"Trust us," Ronan said. "You're going to want to meet with this publicist."

And then he knew. Simon wasn't the only one matchmaking. The notoriously antiYrelationship Ronan Hall was also matchmaking. But then Ronan had fallen in love. They all had, so they knew why Trev was so miserable.

They knew that he was in love, as well. But unlike them, that love was not reciprocated. That was why he was miserable and they were all so damn happy.

He shook his head. "She's not going to agree to meet with me."

"Let Muriel and Bette worry about that," Simon said.

"And if she does, I'm not going to be able to convince her to give me another chance."

"So you're giving up?" Stone asked with disgust. "You, who has always been able to argue your way in or out of every situation, is going to give up without a fight?"

He didn't want to fight with Allison, though. He wanted to love her. But he wouldn't be able to do that if he didn't fight *for* her.

Allison could not believe what had happened, that her business hadn't only survived Edward and her mother's sabotage, but that it was also thriving.

She had quite a few new clients and was about to meet with a referral for possibly another one. She stared across her desk at two of those new clients. Bette Monroe's brown hair was bound in a tight bun while Muriel Sanz's curled wildly around her face. It had just about every color of hair in it, even some of Allison's red.

But these women weren't just clients. They had become her friends, as well.

Their friendship was far more important to Allison than their business. They were amazing women. It was amazing that they had forgiven her for what she'd done in the past.

She'd once offered representation to Muriel Sanz, but Muriel had pretty understandably told her to go to hell. And Bette, as her best friend, had no doubt supported that decision. But now they were supporting Allison.

"Why?" she asked.

"Why'd we bring lunch?" Muriel asked. "It's because you haven't been eating enough." She used chopsticks to pick a piece of chicken from Allison's nearly untouched plate. Hers was empty.

Bette bumped Muriel's arm. But she already had the chicken in her mouth. "Stop eating her food."

"She's not eating it," Muriel pointed out.

Allison really liked these two women. They were more down-to-earth than anyone she'd ever met.

"Eat," Bette urged her as she gestured at Allison's nearly full plate. "You're too skinny."

"What are you? Her mother?" Muriel teased her friend.

Allison wished. Of course, it wasn't possible since Bette was younger than she was. And nicer...

So much nicer than Allison's mother had ever been. "I wasn't asking why you brought lunch," she told them. "I was asking why you're here. Why you both brought me your business? Why you care?"

"We're your friends," Muriel said as if that answered everything.

"But why?" Allison persisted. "I haven't done anything to earn your friendship. Hell, I've done just the opposite."

"You were just doing your job." Muriel reminded Allison of what she'd told her when the supermodel had confronted her months ago.

"I was a bitch," Allison said.

Muriel bumped her shoulder against Bette's. "Some of my best friends are bitches."

"Hey!" Bette protested.

"Honest, loyal bitches," Muriel said with a smile as if she was delivering high praise. And it actually was. "That's how you've handled yourself with this whole mess. You didn't make it but you cleaned it up with class and integrity."

Allison expelled a shaky breath. She hadn't been certain that she had. She'd tried. But until now she hadn't had confirmation of her success. Now she knew—and these new friends were the proof—that she was becoming the person she wanted to be.

Nothing like her mother…

"Thank you," she said, and her voice cracked with emotion. Ordinarily, that would have bothered her, that she'd betrayed any emotion. But she wasn't pretending to be the ice queen anymore. She didn't want anyone to think she was cold and unapproachable anymore.

Not even Trevor.

But apparently, she had convinced him too well. She'd been so emotionally raw from Edward's betrayal, from her mother's and from what she had considered Trevor's betrayal that she had refused to take his calls and had blocked his every attempt to contact her.

But then he'd stopped trying.

And instead of being relieved that he was leaving her alone, she'd been devastated. If he'd really cared about her, he wouldn't have let her go so easily.

But he had…

So it was good that they were over; they'd never had anything real but sex.

How she missed the sex…

She pushed her plate toward Muriel. "You finish it."

"I've tried that," Bette said. "Giving her my food to fatten her up. But it doesn't matter what she eats. She never gets any bigger."

Muriel laughed and cursed her best friend. But she shoved the food into her mouth.

"You should be eating that," Bette said with concern. "I worry about you."

Allison's heart shifted and warmed in her chest. Nobody had ever worried about her.

But Trevor had that night he'd been so upset that she'd gotten rained on. He'd also been so concerned that someone was trying to hurt her.

But he'd hurt her far more than her mother and Edward had. But she was strong. She was resilient. And thanks to these women, she was feeling better.

"Thank you," she told them.

"It's just lunch," Muriel said.

"That *you* ate," Bette added.

"No, thanks for the referral." She glanced at her watch. "He should be here soon."

The two women exchanged a furtive glance and Allison's pulse quickened. "What? What did you do?"

"We might have tricked you a little," Bette sheepishly admitted.

"But we didn't lie to you," Muriel said. "He is our friend."

"And he does need a publicist," Bette added.

"But most of all he needs you," Muriel said.

And Allison groaned.

"He's been miserable without you," Bette said. "His friends can't stand to see him like this."

"And I can't stand to see him at all," Allison said. Or she would lose it—lose her heart completely. No. It was already too late for that. He'd kept her heart.

"Guess you'll have to sit, then," a deep, masculine voice murmured.

And Allison glanced up to find Trevor standing in the doorway.

Bette and Muriel jumped up from their seats. "We'll get out of your way," Muriel said as she headed toward the door.

"She didn't leave any food for you," Bette warned him as she passed him on her way out.

"Thank you," he told the women. Then as soon as they stepped into the hall, he closed the door behind them, shutting himself inside with her. Alone.

Allison's heart pounded furiously. "Do I need to fire my new assistant?" she asked.

"Why?" Trevor asked. "He's not listening at the door."

"Because he let you in."

"I know him," Trevor said. "He's a friend of Miguel's."

That was why she'd hired him. Miguel had recommended him. Like the women, Miguel had become a friend. For some reason he seemed to care about Allison.

Had she fooled anyone with her ice queen routine? Had she fooled Trevor? It had been a few weeks since she'd seen him last, that day in his office.

He stared at her as if he was eating her up with just his gaze. His green eyes had gone dark, nearly as dark as the circles beneath his eyes. And his hair was longer even than it usually was, hanging well past his collar.

He obviously hadn't been sleeping any better than she was.

"Why are you here?" she asked. "Do you really need a publicist?"

He shook his head. "No. I need you." He walked forward then. "I know you're mad at me and that you might never fully trust me. But I trust you so much that I'm giving you my heart, Allison."

He came around the desk and instead of pulling her from her chair, he dropped to his knees in front of it—in front of her. "I've never given anyone my heart before. I've never trusted anyone enough to not abandon or hurt me…but I trust you. I love you."

Tears blurred her vision, so she had to blink to be able to see him clearly. And for the first time she did see him clearly. He was so brave, so damn brave.

He inspired her to be brave, too.

"I love you, too," she said.

He reached up and cupped her face in his hands. And his fingers trembled slightly against her skin. "Then why haven't you wanted to see me?"

"Because I love you," she said. "I never felt like this before. So I got scared."

If he wasn't too proud to get on his knees in front of her, she wasn't too proud to tell him the truth.

He leaned forward and covered her mouth with his, kissing her deeply, hungrily.

She'd missed his mouth so much. His lips, his tongue, his unique rich flavor.

She deepened the kiss and tunneled her fingers in his overly long hair, holding his head to hers.

He stumbled back and pulled her out of the chair so that she fell on top of him, her body sprawled across his. She laughed against his mouth, her breasts pushing against his muscular chest.

His heart beat heavily beneath hers. "I've missed you so much, so damn much."

She nodded. "Me, too. I've missed us." That hollow ache had filled her—until now. Now warmth and happiness filled her. And soon he did, too.

They pulled at each other's clothes, undoing buttons and lowering zippers until they rolled around the floor, naked. Skin slid over skin. Lips over lips...

Then he moved his head, kissing his way down her body. He made love to her with his mouth, making her cry out with pleasure. Then before she could reach for him, before she could slide her hand and her mouth over him, he was moving inside her. He'd rolled on a condom and now he rolled onto his back, so he was the one on the floor.

And she was astride him. His hands moved from her hips to her breasts. He teased the nipples, building up the tension he'd just released. She squirmed against him, rocking her hips, riding up and down his shaft.

His hands moved from her breasts to her hips. He grasped them and helped her match the frantic rhythm of his thrusting. She lowered her head and covered his mouth with hers—kissing him deeply as he filled her.

Then her body tensed and shuddered, a powerful orgasm moving through her. She kept going and going...until Trevor's hands gripped her hips more tightly. He held her still as he came, too, joining her in ecstasy.

And it was ecstasy, being with him again. Back in his arms, she dropped onto his chest, and he held her tightly against him. "I've missed you," he murmured. "I missed you so much that it hurt."

She felt a twinge of regret. She hadn't meant to hurt him. She'd only been trying to protect herself from pain. Maybe she was her mother's daughter—concerned more about herself than anyone else.

"I'm sorry," she said. "I'm so sorry…" Tears pooled in her eyes, blinding her to him again.

He kissed her. "It's not your fault," he said. "I lied to you. I know why that would make it hard for you to trust me. But I promise—and this is no empty promise—I will never lie to you again."

"You'll tell me if I look fat in my jeans?"

"You'll never look fat, but I will tell you if you do," he promised.

And she believed him. She believed that he would always be honest with her. And so she had to always be honest with him. "I love you, but I'm not sure I'm the right person for you. If you want to run for office someday—"

"I know you hate politics," he said. "So I would never ask you to run with me."

"I would," she said, "if I didn't think I'd hurt your chances of winning."

"You won't," he said. "With you by my side, I know I can accomplish anything, even what I never had the guts to try before."

"Politics?" she asked. She would step back if her reputation was going to hurt his campaign. She would let him go—no matter how much it would kill her to do so. No. She was not her mother's daughter. She was herself—worthy of love and friendship.

He shook his head. "A relationship."

She smiled. She'd never really had one, either,

because the thought of getting that involved, of getting her emotions involved, had always scared her. Until now.

Trevor was right. Together they could handle anything. Moles. Sabotage. Sex.

And love.

And maybe someday, down the road, even a campaign for office. Whatever they wanted, they would be able to achieve together.

But right now all Allison wanted—all she needed—was Trevor Sinclair. And she knew he needed her just as much because he was already beginning to harden again inside her.

And then he began to move...

She smiled, and he kissed her smile.

"I love you," he said.

"And I love you..."

* * * * *

COMING SOON!

We really hope you enjoyed reading this book. If you're looking for more romance, be sure to head to the shops when new books are available on

Thursday 29th November

To see which titles are coming soon, please visit
millsandboon.co.uk